What People Are Saying
about the Left Behind Series

"This is the most successful Christian-fiction series ever."
 —**Publishers Weekly**

"Tim LaHaye and Jerry B. Jenkins . . . are doing for Christian fiction what John Grisham did for courtroom thrillers."
 —**TIME**

"The authors' style continues to be thoroughly captivating and keeps the reader glued to the book, wondering what will happen next. And it leaves the reader hungry for more."
 —**Christian Retailing**

"Combines Tom Clancy–like suspense with touches of romance, high-tech flash and Biblical references."
 —**The New York Times**

"It's not your mama's Christian fiction anymore."
 —**The Dallas Morning News**

"Wildly popular—and highly controversial."
 —**USA Today**

"Christian thriller. Prophecy-based fiction. Juiced-up morality tale. Call it what you like, the Left Behind series . . . now has a label its creators could never have predicted: blockbuster success."
 —**Entertainment Weekly**

Tyndale House products by
Tim LaHaye and Jerry B. Jenkins

The Left Behind® book series
Left Behind®
Tribulation Force
Nicolae
Soul Harvest
Apollyon
Assassins
The Indwelling
The Mark
Desecration
The Remnant
Armageddon
Glorious Appearing
The Rising
The Regime
The Rapture
Kingdom Come

Other Left Behind® products
Left Behind®: The Kids
Abridged audio products
Dramatic audio products
and more . . .

Other Tyndale House books by
Tim LaHaye and Jerry B. Jenkins
Perhaps Today
Are We Living in the End Times?
The Authorized Left Behind® Handbook
Embracing Eternity

For more information, visit www.leftbehind.com

Tyndale House books by
Tim LaHaye
How to Be Happy Though Married
Spirit-Controlled Temperament
Why You Act the Way You Do

Tyndale House books by
Jerry B. Jenkins
Soon
Silenced
Shadowed
Riven
Midnight Clear (with Dallas Jenkins)

LEFT BEHIND:
APOCALYPSE

APOCALYPSE
UNLEASHED

BASED ON THE BEST-SELLING
LEFT BEHIND® SERIES

BEST-SELLING AUTHOR
MEL ODOM

TYNDALE HOUSE PUBLISHERS, INC.
CAROL STREAM, ILLINOIS

Visit Tyndale's exciting Web site at www.tyndale.com

TYNDALE and Tyndale's quill logo are registered trademarks of Tyndale House Publishers, Inc.

Apocalypse Unleashed

Designed by Mark A. Lane II

Published in association with Tekno Books, P.O. Box 8296, Green Bay, WI 65308, 920-437-6711.

Scripture taken from the New King James Version®. Copyright © 1982 by Thomas Nelson, Inc. Used by permission. All rights reserved.

Library of Congress Cataloging-in-Publication Data

Odom, Mel.
   Apocalypse unleashed / Mel Odom.
     p. cm.
   ISBN-13: 978-1-4143-1636-9 (pbk. : alk. paper)
   ISBN-10: 1-4143-1636-4 (pbk. : alk. paper)
   1. Rapture (Christian eschatology)—Fiction. 2. End of the world—Fiction. I. Title.
PS3565.D53A865 2008
813'.54—dc22   2008028662

Printed in the United States of America

14   13   12   11   10   09   08
 7   6   5   4   3   2   1

Village—Designation South 14, U.S. Army Rangers
Seven Klicks North-Northeast of Harran
Sanliurfa Province, Turkey
Local Time 2104 Hours

Goose drove his boot through the frail wooden door of the burning house. The door ripped free of its hinges with a loud screech that nearly drowned out the noise of the flames greedily consuming the structure. With an arm wrapped around his face to protect it from the questing, twisting flames, he dashed through the doorway.

Inside the small room, he looked for the people he was certain he'd seen through the window during his approach. Smoke blurred his vision and stung his eyes.

He pulled his assault rifle to his shoulder immediately and assumed a profile position that streamlined his body to make a smaller target. He'd been carrying the weapon for so many years the M-4A1 felt like a part of him.

"I'm First Sergeant Gander of the United States Army Rangers," he said in his command voice, stern and direct. "I'm here to get you out."

Two teenagers hunkered down beside a patchwork chair that was probably a castoff from a hotel in Sanliurfa. They stared at Goose. The older one, a girl of maybe sixteen, held a hand over her mouth and nose and the other hand over her younger sister's.

Goose lowered his weapon. "It's all right." Smoke burned his sinus passages and made his throat raw. "You need to get out of here. Do you speak English?"

The girls just looked at him with fear-filled eyes.

A pool of flame suddenly rushed across the ceiling like an incoming tide. The surface burned black in seconds and chunks fell. The fire breathed in cracks and whooshes as it claimed new territory.

Goose stepped toward the girls.

The older one wrapped the younger one protectively and pulled her back. They coughed and hacked as the smoke threatened to overcome them.

Holding a hand out, Goose said, "Please come with me." He wished he had the words to make them understand. Since he'd been stationed as part of a United Nations peacekeeping effort along the Turkish-Syrian border, he hadn't learned more than a few words of Turkish. Making matters more problematic, the area also contained several Arabic and Kurdish languages and dialects. The villages and towns were often melting pots for several cultures. He had no idea what language the girls spoke.

At the other end of the room, a timber sagged with a loud crack. A large section of the roof pulled free and dropped to the floor.

The girls screamed and held each other.

"Please," Goose said as he continued to hold out his hand. "Please." The heat boiled all around him and the air thickened with smoke. He coughed.

The younger girl looked at the older one and spoke rapidly. She pointed meaningfully at Goose.

Goose knew he wasn't at his best. He was dressed in sweat- and dirt-stained khaki BDUs, and he was armed with the assault rifle and a Beretta M9 pistol. A bandolier of extra rifle magazines crossed his Kevlar jacket. He hadn't shaved or rested well in days. He knew that, at the moment, he didn't look like the kind of guy anyone should trust.

"United States Army," Goose said. "United Nations. Good guy." Those words had served him in tours of duty in several foreign countries. A lot of people who didn't understand English at least understood those words.

"Good guy," the younger girl said hopefully and turned to the older one. "Good guy."

The older girl shook her head vehemently. She spoke rapidly, but the smoke choked her out. When the younger girl tried to get up, the older girl wrapped her arms around her and pulled her back.

"Please," Goose said again, "you've got to come with me."

The younger girl fought off the older one and struggled to get up. A coughing jag took her strength away and almost knocked her off her feet.

Goose put a hand on the girl's shoulder and steadied her. When he glanced back at the door, he saw that flames had spanned the opening. Embers spiraled up into the night sky. He could faintly see other soldiers from his squad running from house to house, getting people out.

Goose squatted down to her level so he wouldn't seem so threatening. "I'm going to get you out of here. Okay?" He nodded, wanting to establish some kind of communication bedrock.

The girl nodded back. Tears coursed down her cheeks.

Goose slung the M-4A1 across his back and reached for the older girl with his other hand. "C'mon. You've got to get out of here. Good guy. Good guy."

Another section of ceiling, closer this time, crashed to the floor. The older girl became a believer then. Whether she believed in the soldier in front of her or the fact that she was going to die if she stayed in the house, Goose didn't know. In the end, it didn't matter. He took her hand in his and pulled her to her feet.

He glanced around and found a blanket on a small pallet in the corner of the room. He let go of the girls long enough to retrieve the blanket, then shook it out and wrapped it around them.

Flames spat and cracked like live things. The smoke was now so thick that simply looking from one side of the room to the other was almost impossible.

"Hold on to the blanket." Goose held the cloth over their faces and tried to get them to understand. "Hold on."

Neither of the girls moved.

Feeling panicked by the increasing heat in the room and his own vision starting to go in and out of focus, Goose took one of the younger girl's hands and put it on the edge of the blanket.

"Hold on," he repeated.

She grasped his meaning and wrapped her fingers in the blanket's edge.

"Good," Goose said and started coughing. Tears blurred his vision. He started the girls back toward the wall of flame that filled the door.

They froze at once. Goose knew they'd figured out what they were going to have to do and weren't happy with it. He pulled the blanket down over their faces.

"Hold on," he said. "Just hold on." *God, if You're listening today, please help me get these girls out of here.* He prayed, but it seemed like his faith hadn't been as strong as it should have been lately. He pulled the girls toward the door.

At that moment, the ceiling gave way and the roof of the house collapsed. Everything rushed down to fill the room, and a heavy weight crashed against Goose's shoulders.

❋   ❋   ❋

Local Time 2106 Hours

"Which house did Goose go into?" Danielle Vinchenzo swung from the passenger seat of the Land Rover before it came to a full stop. The tires crushed the baked earth of the dirt roadway that cut through the heart of the village.

"That one." The driver pointed. "The one on fire."

Danielle raked the houses and tried to figure out which one was "that one." It was hard. The houses were all on fire. She turned to her cameraman, a young man in a concert T-shirt and shorts who was scrambling from the Land Rover's rear deck with a camera over one shoulder.

"Are you ready?" Danielle smoothed her blouse and combed fingers through her short dark hair.

"Shouldn't we be helping evacuate the people?" the cameraman asked.

"Believe me, Gary," she said, "we'd only be in the way. Goose and his men know what they're doing, and they're much better at it than we would be. We're going to do the guys here more good by letting the world know what they're facing and that they need help. Now get that camera on me."

"Get out from in front of the fire." The cameraman settled the camera on his shoulder. "You're going to be nothing but a shadow with that directly in the background."

Danielle shifted to the side, took a deep breath, and exhaled the fear and anxiety of the last few minutes.

"Ready?" Gary asked.

"Ready." She held up a hand and counted down. "Three, two, one." Her hand fell to her side. "This is Danielle Vinchenzo of OneWorld NewsNet. As you can see behind me, we're at ground zero of a recent attack in Sanliurfa Province in Turkey. The United States Army's 75th Regiment out of Fort Benning, Georgia, is presently engaged in trying to keep back the encroaching Syrian military forces threatening to invade Turkey."

Something in one of the houses blew up. Flaming debris lit the sky like a Fourth of July fireworks display. Men yelled, and someone screamed in terror.

"First Sergeant Samuel Gander, whom you've gotten to know through my previous broadcasts, is commanding a resupply convoy to Harran. The United States Army entrenched here has established observation points throughout southern Turkey for field spotters. Since U.S. forces have been in Sanliurfa, they've been under constant attack from Syria."

One of the army Hummers rocketed by and closed on the exploded house. Rock and loose dirt sprayed from under the locked tires.

"I got wounded!" someone cried. "I got wounded! I need a medic for these people!"

Focus on your job, Danielle told herself. *A reporter helps most by revealing where help is needed.*

"Only moments ago," Danielle went on, "Sergeant Gander's scouts spotted this village blazing." She turned dramatically to gesture at the houses. "Although the origin at this point remains unconfirmed, this appears to be an attack made by one of the local warlords. The warlords have torn through towns and villages in an effort to provision themselves. Water and food are in short supply."

A Ranger corporal Danielle had gotten to know over the last few days barked orders at soldiers. They quickly formed a line and kept the villagers back from the worst of the burning houses.

"Since the mysterious event that caused nearly a third of the earth's population to disappear weeks ago," Danielle said, "the world has been in turmoil. I know that you—wherever you are—have gone through the same kind of turmoil these men now face. But I doubt many of you have the enemy beating on your front door."

Below the camera's view frame, Danielle pointed toward the line of burning houses. The cameraman swung instantly in that direction. She continued with the voice-over.

"In addition to the peacekeeping efforts they've been providing here," Danielle said, "the 75th Rangers have also set up triages and camps to take care of the wounded and survivors of the Syrian SCUD attacks. But the army troops are hard-pressed and spread thin. Eighteen- and twenty-hour days are taking their toll."

"Please," a man called in heavily accented English as he staggered into the street. "My daughter. You must help me find my daughter."

The cameraman picked up the man as he stumbled out of the shadows. He was covered in ashes and disheveled. Blood leaked from a cut over his eye.

Two of the Rangers approached the man. One of them held his assault rifle centered on the man's chest. Frightened, the man raised his hands high above his head. The other Ranger quickly threw the man to the ground on his stomach and locked his arms behind his back.

"Please," the man begged. "My daughter was in the house when we were bombed."

Danielle spoke quickly. At home, the scene could easily be misinterpreted. "Due to the constant threat of Syrian militia, terrorists that have targeted the Turkish government for their pro-America stance, and the warlords, the Rangers aren't able to let their guards down. Everyone outside their tightly knit unit is suspect."

"How old's your daughter?" The Ranger frisked the man quickly, then looked up at his teammate and shook his head. The other Ranger lowered his weapon.

"Seventeen," the man wailed. "She's only seventeen."

"All right. Stay calm. We're gonna help you find her." The Ranger helped the man to his feet. "Which house?"

The man pointed to a house that had flames shooting twenty feet and more above it. More flames gushed from the windows and chewed into the house's exterior.

"There," the man said. "That one."

"Ain't nothing alive in that house," one of the Rangers said.

Danielle silently agreed, but she knew she was racking up dead air on the newscast. "Even responding as quickly as the Rangers did, there isn't much they've been able to do here."

Suddenly a young woman sprinted across the open space, screaming. Both Rangers brought up their weapons. A cold knot of fear formed in Danielle's stomach as she grew afraid she was about to witness the young girl's death. She couldn't fault the soldiers; they were in a land of hostiles.

"It's all right," the man shouted. "It's my daughter!" He rushed forward and threw his arms around the girl, lifting her from her feet in his joy.

"What happened here?" one of the Rangers asked.

The man put his daughter down and turned to the soldiers. "It was the bandits. They came and they bombed the town."

"They didn't take anything?" the Ranger asked.

"No. Nothing. They just started attacking the village. Most people were already in bed. We had no chance to fight back."

Danielle's mind churned that new information into a working hypothesis. She didn't like where her instincts were leading her.

Evidently the Ranger's thoughts were following the same track as Danielle's. He turned from the father-daughter reunion and put a hand to the ear-throat communications device he wore.

"Where's Sergeant Gander?" he asked. He waited a moment; then his head swiveled in the direction of one of the hardest-hit homes. "Are you sure he went inside?"

Danielle stared at the whirling inferno that the house had become. No one could have walked through that fire, and if they had, she feared they weren't coming back.

The corporal and his friend ran toward the building. Two young girls covered in a flaming blanket burst through the doorway. As one, the nearby soldiers grabbed the two girls and stripped the flaming blanket from them. Other soldiers beat embers and flames from their clothing.

"Where's the soldier that went in after you?" one of the Rangers asked.

The girl shook her head.

"She don't speak English," another Ranger said.

The corporal grabbed his Kevlar vest, yanked on it, then pointed back to the burning house. The younger girl nodded, obviously getting the context.

"Good guy," the girl said.

The corporal smiled. "That's right. That's our designation. Good guy."

The young woman kept pointing toward the house.

Looking at the flames, Danielle knew there was no way anyone could live through that. If First Sergeant "Goose" Gander was inside that house, she felt certain that he wasn't coming back out.

At that moment, the house's roof collapsed. Flames and smoke belched out of the windows and the open door. Rangers started to run toward the house.

"Sergeant Gander's inside the house," one of them said hoarsely, and that brought them all. "We gotta get him out."

"Back up," a grizzled veteran squalled.

"But First Sergeant Gander is in there!" someone shouted.

"And it's already too late. Stay back. We don't want to lose anyone else."

Village—Designation South 14, U.S. Army Rangers
Seven Klicks North-Northeast of Harran
Sanliurfa Province, Turkey
Local Time 2109 Hours

Goose's senses swam. He knew he was supposed to get up, but movement was hard. Then fire bit into his left shoulder and galvanized his resolve. When he opened his eyes, the smoke was almost too thick for him to see through. Coals danced and gleamed along exposed wooden surfaces.

A flaming timber lay across his back. He wedged the M-4A1 under the timber with the buttstock braced squarely against the floor. He curled his body and shoved, forcing the beam from his shoulders. When he finished, there was no breath left in him. He tried to get to his feet and failed. He was going to die there.

Suddenly, that didn't seem so bad. His youngest son—Chris, only five years old—had disappeared with all the rest of the children in the world. If Megan was right, God had taken Goose's son. And there wasn't anything he could do about that.

None of it made sense.

"Sergeant."

Goose coughed and wheezed, unable to find any air in the room. His lungs felt like they were already on fire. But he recognized the voice.

"Sergeant, you've got to get up," Corporal Joseph Baker said.

You're dead, Goose wanted to say. *I buried you weeks ago.* The image of Baker's torn body, mangled by a fragmentation grenade, had haunted Goose's sleep nearly every night.

"Get up, Sergeant. It's not your time to die."

It wasn't yours either, Corporal.

"How do you think Megan will feel to learn you just lay down and died?"

Goose knew the answer to that. Somehow, in spite of everything that had happened, she'd found the strength to keep going and to believe in God more fiercely than she ever had before. He'd heard it in her voice. Even if God forgave him for quitting, Goose knew Megan never would. He'd promised her on the day he married her that he would never give her less than what she deserved.

"Then get up," Baker's voice said.

Goose stopped thinking about dying. He stopped wondering how he was hearing from a dead man. He did what the United States Army had taught him to do every day for the last seventeen years.

He got up.

And he had his assault rifle in his hand when he did. But the smoke was so thick and his eyes tearing so much that he didn't know which way was out through the flames.

"Here."

Goose moved at once. He ran through the flames because he knew he wasn't going to get a second chance. Arm across his face, he felt the heat of the flames surround him for two strides . . . then three . . .

. . . and then he was out, racing into the night in front of the house. Overcome by smoke and exhaustion, he dropped to his knees and tried to breathe. His lungs remained frozen for a moment, then kick-started to life. Without warning, he threw up and felt a little better. His lungs opened up.

"Sarge!" someone yelled. "You're on fire!"

Looking down at his pant legs, Goose saw flames clinging to the material. He raked up a handful of dirt and smothered the flames. Then he stood on shaking legs. His left knee, damaged so long ago and never quite right since, ached and felt infirm. He looked around at the villagers and the Rangers gathered there in the firelight. When he spotted the two girls he'd gone in to rescue, he felt better.

"Thought we'd lost you, Sarge," Private First Class Billy Hendricks said. He was in his early twenties, new to the army and to the area.

"Not yet," Goose said. "We're going to be all right."

"I knew that when I saw you come out of that burning house."

Goose spotted Corporal Jamal Donner, his second on the transport assignment. Donner was an African-American in his early thirties, only a couple of years younger than Goose. He kept his head shaved clean, even managing to do so in the confusion of these past few weeks.

"Where do we stand?" Goose asked.

"We're all present and accounted for," Donner said. His voice was soft and smooth with the Southern accent he'd acquired while growing up in Atlanta, Georgia. "We got lucky."

Goose looked at the handful of bodies lying on the ground. Some of the other villagers sat beside the corpses and wept without restraint.

Thank God there are no children, Goose thought. They would have been among the casualties for certain. Then he realized that God was exactly the reason why no children were there. That only brought up thoughts of Chris again, and he tried not to go there.

"Not everybody got lucky," Donner said.

"Does anyone know what happened?"

"Got a man over here who says he saw the whole thing. Ain't had time to talk to him."

❈   ❈   ❈

Local Time 2112 Hours

The man's name was Achmed. Sixtyish and frail, he spoke English well.

"They came out of nowhere," Achmed told Goose. The village continued to burn. There was nothing anyone could do to save it.

"Who?" Goose asked.

"Niyazi."

Goose reached into his BDU pouch and took out his PalmPilot. He brought up the file they'd assembled on the local warlords and showed the image they had of Niyazi to Achmed. "This man?" Goose asked.

Achmed nodded. "This man. Very bad man. He likes to kill."

The files Goose had read on Niyazi agreed with that. Although the Turkish military hadn't liked sharing all their information with the United States Army, they'd done so once it became apparent that sharing was necessary.

"Why did he attack the village?" Goose asked as he put the PalmPilot away.

Achmed shook his head. "I don't know. Normally he is not in this place."

"Not in what place? Here?"

"Not here," Achmed agreed. "Niyazi stays to the north. Many kilometers away."

"Something brought him down here," Donner said.

"I don't know what that might be," Achmed replied. "We are a very poor village. It is known. Everyone knows how poor we are."

Goose looked around the village and silently agreed. Except for a few goats and little patches of vegetable gardens, there wasn't much to the village. Over the past weeks, he'd traveled with a convoy by the village at least a dozen times. They'd never bothered to stop.

"You ask me," Donner said, "and I don't mean to be rude about it, but this place ain't worth the powder it would take to blow it up."

A bad feeling twisted through Goose's gut. He turned to Donner. "Gather the men. We need to get rolling. If Niyazi didn't hit this village out of spite or to get something, he was just using it as a diversion."

Understanding filled Donner's liquid eyes. "The convoy."

"Yeah," Goose agreed. "And we ran off and left it unguarded." He turned toward the nearest Hummer, ignoring his aches, bruises, and burns.

※ ※ ※

United States 75th Army Rangers Temporary Post
Sanliurfa, Turkey
Local Time 2114 Hours

"Captain Remington."

Tired and frustrated, Cal Remington looked up from the computer screen he'd been studying. The army captain was six feet four inches tall with broad shoulders and short-clipped dark hair.

"What is it, Private?" Remington snapped.

"Got a problem with the convoy, sir." The private was young and baby-faced, one of the geek army that had moved up quickly as the military had become increasingly reliant on technology.

"Which convoy?" There were currently three out. Remington checked the time on the bottom of the computer screen. *Two*, he amended. One of them should have reached its destination by now.

"Harran, sir."

Goose's convoy. The thought that something had gone wrong there irritated Remington. Then again, he didn't know if it was the thought that something had gone wrong or the thought of Goose that irritated him most.

"What's wrong with the convoy?" Remington asked.

"It's under attack, sir."

"By whom?" Remington stood and walked out of his office. The private led the way through the computer workstations that had been set up and now ran off noisy generators.

"We don't know, sir." The private gestured to one of the large LCD computer monitors.

Remington studied the screen and saw satellite imagery of the convoy racing across the rugged terrain toward Harran. Only the four supply trucks and two support Hummers remained together. Six units were MIA.

"Where is the rest of my convoy?" Remington demanded.

"Sergeant Gander pulled most of the support vehicles off the convoy, sir," the private said.

"Why?"

"There was a village on fire, sir. Sergeant Gander wanted to see if they could help." The private gestured to another monitor.

Remington made out the burning houses and the six Hummers parked in front of them. His irritation with Goose turned into full-fledged anger.

"Who authorized this?" Remington demanded.

"No one, sir. Sergeant Gander radioed us, said he'd take a quick look-see and be back to the convoy."

"Did those people ask for help?"

"Not that I know of, sir."

"How did Sergeant Gander know they needed help?"

"Sergeant Gander saw the burning buildings from the route they were traveling."

Remington cursed. "And he didn't think that maybe they were being set up?"

"I don't know, sir."

"Are we in radio communication with Sergeant Gander?"

"Yes, sir."

"Good. Hand me that headset."

The private passed the headset over, and Remington put it on and pulled the chin mic into place. "What's his call sign?"

"Drifter Leader."

Remington pushed a button on the mic and opened the radio channel. "Drifter Leader, this is Base. Do you copy?"

"Sir," the computer tech next to him said, "I've got bogeys vectoring in on the supply convoy."

Remington flicked his gaze back to the computer screen and watched as seven . . . eight . . . *nine* speeding vehicles closed in on the convoy. He cursed and queued the mic again. "Drifter Leader, this is Base. Do you copy?"

Private First Class Jimmy Robinson sat in the back of the cargo truck and sipped metallic-tasting water from his canteen. He rode on an ammo box and swayed with the motion of the truck lumbering across the uneven terrain. Through the parted canvas partially covering the rear of the truck, he constantly watched the terrain.

"Man," Butch Strahan complained from the other side of the truck. "You couldn't ask for a bumpier ride."

"You could," Robinson said, "but I'd shoot you on account of you being too sadistic to live."

Strahan laughed. "I'm just glad it isn't so bumpy that some of this ammo goes off."

"Wouldn't do that. This stuff's packed all right. I helped get it done."

"I guess if you're wrong, we'll never live to know about it." Strahan shifted, obviously trying to find a more comfortable position. "I heard you got to talk to your girl."

Robinson nodded and tried to keep the smile from his face. The other men teased about such things. "Got Pablo's Xbox 360 up and running. Hooked it into the Internet coming out of command. Captain Remington finally okayed that."

"Good thing you guys didn't get caught using it before he allowed it."

"Tell me about it. But that Xbox just sips bandwidth. Even when you're talking back and forth over the gamer network."

"So what did your girl say?"

Robinson's happy thoughts fled. "Her parents are missing."

Strahan looked suddenly solemn. "Well, if Joe Baker was right in what he was saying, that God came and took all the Christians home to begin the Tribulation, that's a good thing."

"Maybe. But right now Nikki's alone." Robinson hesitated, wondering if he should say anything about what was really on his mind. "And she's still here."

"Oh," Strahan said, suddenly understanding.

"I've known her since I was fourteen," Robinson said. "Used to sit behind her in algebra. Her parents were always involved with the church. So was she."

"You're wondering why she's still here while her parents are gone?"

"She says it was because she didn't believe as much as her parents did. She thinks she was just going through the moves."

"I think a lot of us were like that," Strahan said. "I have to admit, I ain't always played things on the straight and narrow, and maybe I've been too interested in other things than God's Word, but I didn't think I'd be left behind like this."

"I never gave it any thought," Robinson admitted. "I treated everybody fairly, tried to get along, but I didn't make much time in my day for thinking about where I might end up when it was all over."

"That's because it's not normal to sit around thinking about everything being all over."

"Nikki's parents did. Every Sunday and Wednesday at church. And I'm sure they didn't forget about it during the rest of the week either."

"But it's not over. Not if what Joe Baker was saying was right. About how we can redeem ourselves in God's eyes now."

"I know. I'm hoping."

Strahan shook his head. "You gotta do more than hope. You gotta *believe.*" He paused. "I don't know about you, but before I hit my rack every night, I hit my knees and give thanks for getting through one more day."

"I know. Me too. Nikki and me, we even prayed together on that Xbox hookup the other night. I mean, she doesn't even have an Xbox. She was over at a friend's house. They were logging on and staying on whenever they could because Nikki knows I like to play. She said that she knew if I was still alive, sooner or later I'd log on."

"Then that conversation you two had was meant to be."

"God wanted us to talk." Robinson sipped his water again. "Nikki and I both believe that."

Strahan abruptly sat up a little straighter and peered out the back of the truck. "Did you see that?"

Robinson put his canteen away and picked up his M-4A1. "See what?"

"Thought I saw movement out there in the brush." Strahan pushed the canvas aside and swiveled his head. Then he jerked back.

Robinson stared at the other man, wondering what had happened, when the sound of the gunshots caught up with the cargo truck. He ducked immediately and scrambled over to Strahan as the truck's driver floored the accelerator and started evasive maneuvers.

Blood welled from an ugly wound in the side of Strahan's neck. For a moment Robinson thought the man was dead. Then Strahan reached up and caught his arm.

"Help . . . me," Strahan wheezed. "Please. Help . . . me."

Praying out loud, Robinson grabbed for a field dressing from his kit and slapped it against Strahan's neck to stop the bleeding. From the amount of blood, he knew he had only minutes to stop the flow before his friend bled out.

More bullets ripped through the canvas over the truck's cargo deck. Robinson wanted to scream at the men doing the shooting and ask them if they knew the trucks were loaded with munitions. Instead, he kept his head low and kept pressure on the field dressing.

❊ ❊ ❊

Local Time 2118 Hours

"Drifter Leader, this is Base. Do you copy?"

Goose heard Remington's voice in his ear over the headset's crackling connection. Even though they had access to geosynchronous communications satellites, the connections weren't always solid.

"Drifter Leader," Remington said again, "this is Base. I repeat, do you copy?"

Goose didn't want to take the call; he knew how it was going to go, but he didn't have a choice. He couldn't blame Remington. He sat in the passenger seat of the Hummer and held his assault rifle canted forward. The seat-belt harness cut into his hips and chest, but it was the only thing keeping him from flying out of the seat. At times in its mad dash across the uneven terrain, the Hummer was airborne.

"Base, this is Drifter Leader."

"Goose, that convoy is under attack. Where are you?"

The news hit Goose like a sledgehammer. He'd guessed that the convoy might get attacked, but he'd hoped the radio silence had been because everything was okay. They'd tried to reach the convoy, but the hills had interfered with the signal.

"On our way back now," Goose said.

"You shouldn't have left them."

"No, sir," Goose agreed. "I shouldn't have."

"What were you thinking when you—"

"Begging pardon, Base, but unless you have pertinent information I need right now, I suggest we shelve that particular topic."

"That's fine," Remington said. "We'll make time for it when you get back."

"Yes, sir. Can you tell me how many hostiles we're looking at?"

"We read nine vehicles." Remington's voice calmed as he focused on the mission.

"Manpower?"

"That's unknown at this point. The nine vehicles are all light and fast. No heavy rolling stock."

"Copy that." Tanks wouldn't have been able to keep up with the convoy, but Niyazi and his people could have been waiting in ambush with heavy weaponry. Goose glanced at his watch automatically. Running gun battles generally didn't last more than a few minutes.

And they were behind.

When he glanced over his shoulder, Goose saw the jeep carrying Danielle Vinchenzo trailing by only a few feet. The reporter's face was a pallid oval in the passenger seat as she clung to the seat belt and roll bar.

"Harlan," Goose called over the headset.

"Yeah, Sarge."

"You were a state police officer in Tennessee, weren't you?"

"You bet. Got called up in the reserves for the Iraq situation and decided I'd stay on."

"Do you know how to get that vehicle out of our hair without hurting anyone?"

"Yeah." The grin was apparent in Harlan's voice. "It's called a PIT. Pursuit Immobilization Technique."

"I'd rather the civilians didn't arrive with us. I want them out of harm's way."

In the jeep, Danielle turned around in her seat and pointed at one of the Hummers coming up on the left. She shouted at the driver. Her actions let Goose know she was monitoring his ops frequencies.

Harlan was a better driver than the man handling Danielle's vehicle. He crept up on the left side and gently nudged the left rear quarter panel with the right front bumper of his Hummer. Danielle's vehicle launched into a spinout and came to a dead stop in a whirl of dust.

"Man," Cody Brenner said behind the steering wheel of the Hummer Goose occupied, "Harlan makes that look easy."

"My daddy taught me how to do that when I was twelve," Harlan replied. "Before I took up with the state police, I ran stock cars on circuit racing."

With Danielle out of the way—at least temporarily—Goose turned his attention to the coming battle. The Hummer roared over the next hill, went airborne for just a moment, then crashed back to the ground in a skidding, sliding advance.

At the bottom of the hill, the convoy was hurtling cross-country, the Rangers inside fighting for their lives. Muzzle flashes sparked white-hot holes in the night.

"Come up on the left side of the attack vehicles," Goose directed. "If we can take out the drivers, we take out the attack teams."

❋ ❋ ❋

Local Time 2120 Hours

"I can't believe Gander ordered them to do that." The driver keyed the ignition and tried to get the jeep started. The ignition engaged and the engine turned over, but the motor didn't start.

Danielle growled in rage as she watched the line of Ranger vehicles disappear over the ridge. "This is exactly something Goose would do."

"I thought he was your friend."

"He is. That's why he did it."

The driver tried the engine again. "We could have gotten killed."

"No, man," Gary the cameraman said from the back. "That was a classic move. And I know Harlan. Man's a master of anything with four wheels. He put us right where he intended to."

"Is this thing going to start?" Danielle asked. "There's a story breaking right over that hill, and I'm missing it."

"The way things are going," the driver said in disgust, "if you miss this one, there'll be another one tomorrow."

Danielle barely checked an angry reply in time. The driver was new to her.

"Dude," Gary said, "out here you don't just want another story. You want Goose's story. That guy's like a magnet in this whole thing. If there's trouble brewing somewhere, it'll find a way to try and get a piece of him."

Danielle silently agreed. She climbed out of the jeep. "Grab your camera, Gary. We're walking."

Frustration chafed at her. With everything she'd discovered since the Syrian attack, she believed she was at the eye of a vast conspiracy. One that seemed to involve her new boss, Nicolae Carpathia. Everything tracked back to him.

But every time Danielle thought she'd unearthed a new lead to the puzzle, someone or something got in her way. Her producer had shut down most of her lines of inquiry, freezing her out from the vast information archives within OneWorld NewsNet. She couldn't prove that, but she was certain it was true.

Only a couple of weeks before, she'd chatted up one of the new people in research and had been starting to make some headway in her internal investigation of Carpathia. But someone had discovered that. The research assistant was released, and Danielle had been assigned to cover Goose's convoy. If she hadn't been thinking about the cover-up, the convoy story would have made sense. It was a good one.

The downside was that she might very well get killed tonight.

If OneWorld NewsNet wasn't already out to kill her. She still wasn't certain of that, and the possibility, when she wasn't scrambling to stay alive, frightened her.

She shouldered her bag and started walking.

"Gimme a sec," the driver said. "All that whirling around we did in the dust probably choked out the carburetor intake. It'll clear." He tried the ignition again. This time the engine caught, blatted unevenly, and finally managed to run steadily.

Without a word, Danielle climbed back into the passenger seat. The driver engaged the transmission, and they got underway. Even over the roar of the engine, Danielle heard the sharp reports of automatic weapons fire from over the ridgeline.

**U.S. Rangers Convoy
One Klick North-Northeast of Harran
Sanliurfa Province, Turkey
Local Time 2121 Hours**

"Drifter Transport, this is Drifter Leader." Goose calmly braced his feet against the Hummer's floorboard and unlimbered his assault rifle. "Do you copy?"

"Transport reads you," Juan Martinez responded in a stressed voice. "We're gettin' all shot up, Sarge. Where are you?"

"We got your six, Transport. Drive it like you stole it."

"Copy that. I see you now. Bust 'em up."

"All right," Goose stated to his team calmly and confidently, like this was something they did every day, which was almost getting to be the truth. "We stay in single file, and we stay together as long as we can. Hold your fire until I give you the signal. So far they haven't seen us and I want to keep it that way."

"Won't stay that way for long." Brenner had a death grip on the steering wheel.

"Ease up," Goose said. "You're fighting the wheel."

Brenner pushed out his breath and loosened his hands a little. The ride became smoother. "You got it, Sarge."

"Just hold it steady till I tell you to break. Then check your left side and head that way as quickly as you can. We'll figure out the rest of it as we go along."

Brenner nodded.

"Now get us up there."

The bandit vehicles were running slower than the army Hummers because the cargo trucks' top speed wasn't as good as that of the smaller vehicles. Five bandit vehicles harried the convoy on the left side. Four were on the right. Getting all of them on the first pass-through was going to be impossible.

"Twenty feet outside their vehicles," Goose told Brenner. "Then hold it as long as you can. Or until I tell you to break formation."

"I will, Sarge."

The Hummer sped up beside a pickup truck that bounded across the hard-packed ground. The pickup's shocks were obviously gone, and the front end was a deathtrap in the making. Three men stood in the bed and fired into the rearmost truck.

"You ready, Crain?" Goose asked.

"Yes, Sergeant." Crain was manning the .50-cal machine gun mounted on the Hummer's rear deck.

"You've got the gunners."

"I do," Crain agreed grimly.

Goose lifted the M-4A1 to his shoulder and took aim at the driver of the pickup. The man was barely a silhouette in the rear window when the gunners shifted. Goose waved Brenner forward, then held the rifle again. When the driver came into view through the side window, Goose said, "Now." His finger tightened on the trigger.

The driver must have sensed something coming up on his side of the pickup. He turned and stared at Goose. The man's eyes widened, and Goose knew he was about to steer away from them. Before he could, Goose squeezed the trigger and rode out the rising recoil in four three-round bursts.

Most of the bullets caught the man in the face. Others tore through the side of the pickup or the windshield. The vehicle swerved out of control.

"Floor it!" Goose ordered as the pickup drifted over in front of them. At the same time, he was aware of the .50-cal machine gun chattering to sudden life behind him. The three men in the pickup bed fell in rapid succession.

The pickup kept coming.

Brenner started to steer away. Goose grabbed the wheel and held the Hummer steady, then rammed his foot down on top of Brenner's. The army vehicle surged forward again and locked up briefly with the pickup. Metal grated and shrilled; then the bandit vehicle gave way under the Hummer's greater weight.

Out of control, the pickup pulled back to the right, narrowly missed the last convoy truck, and slammed into the rear pursuit bandit vehicle on the right side. Both vehicles slid out of control and rolled, becoming a conflagration of shattered bodies. Pieces of metal flew in all directions as they came apart.

Goose released the steering wheel. "Good job," he said.

Brenner just looked at him and said, "Yes, Sergeant."

Evidently the bandits had some kind of communications system. The other four vehicles ahead of Goose suddenly split away from the convoy. They ran two by two; someone had obviously trained them.

"Up the middle," Goose directed. "Get them firing at each other."

"They're going to be firing at us too," Brenner protested.

"If you get through them fast enough, they'll have less time to react. Work on not getting hit." Goose emptied his rifle clip at a pair of the vehicles. Men inside ducked as others returned fire.

Bullets chopped through the Hummer's windows, and broken glass sailed. Goose swapped out the empty rifle cartridge for a full one. Gray steam poured back over them from the front of the Hummer. Thankfully the engine didn't lose power.

Brenner screamed in frustration as the Hummer zipped through the middle of the four bandit vehicles. Goose and his group drew fire immediately, but the move had caught their enemies off-stride. Panicked, the bandits opened fire, but they had a hard time catching up to the speeding Hummer. Instead, they caught themselves in a deadly cross fire.

Driven away by their own fire, the bandits circled wide. They still fired their weapons but became more careful about where those stray rounds went.

In the meantime, the rest of Goose's team slipped up beside the bandits. The Rangers opened fire at once.

More bullets slapped the Hummer's body with rapid metallic thumps. Goose turned in his seat, ignored the gunner, and aimed at the driver of the jeep just behind them. He squeezed the trigger and watched the driver jerk back suddenly. From the slack way he sat in the seat, Goose knew the man was mortally wounded.

Out of control, the jeep skidded and suddenly flipped sideways, gaining speed and coming right at the Hummer.

"Hold on!" Goose yelled as he braced for impact. "Hold that wheel steady!"

The jeep slammed into the Hummer's rear bumper, then fell away. Goose jerked with the impact and tried to keep his upper body loose so he wouldn't get whiplash. His battered knee screamed in agony as he braced his leg against the floorboard.

The machine gunner, Crain, hadn't been able to get himself strapped in before the impact. He struggled to hold on to the machine gun, but it whipsawed around on the gimbals. Goose reached up and caught the man in one hand, closed it into a fist in the BDUs, and yanked Crain down and forward between the seats.

Brenner fought the wheel.

"Hold it steady," Goose roared. "Don't fight it. Ride it out. Get your foot off that brake."

Brenner nodded and held the wheel steady as he lifted his foot from the brake pedal. The Hummer gradually straightened out and came under his control.

"Don't stop," Goose directed. "We've still got a convoy to protect."

"Yes, Sergeant." Brenner put his foot on the accelerator and downshifted the transmission. They sped back toward the fleeing convoy.

"Thanks, Sarge," Crain said weakly. "Thought I was a goner for sure."

"My pleasure." Goose helped the younger man back to his feet on the rear deck. Knives dug into Goose's knee, and he knew the joint was going to be difficult to deal with over the next few days.

He turned in the seat and surveyed the battleground. In addition to the bandit vehicle he'd caused to flip, another sat wreathed in flames and a third was overturned and upside-down. A lone survivor quickly scrambled from beneath the disabled vehicle, saw the Rangers bearing down on him, and dropped to his knees with his hands clasped atop his head.

"Base, this is Drifter Leader," Goose said.

"Go, Drifter Leader," Remington responded.

"I count four hostile vehicles down."

"Affirmative, Leader. Four down. Five left in the field."

Goose spotted one being pursued by two of the Ranger Hummers. That left four on the other side of the convoy. "Are they still in pursuit?"

"That's a big roger, Sarge," someone said. "Guys are climbing onto my truck. I can't get 'em off."

The second truck in line broke formation and started weaving back and forth.

"Hold on," Goose said. "We're on our way." He pointed at the truck.

Brenner gave a tight nod and accelerated again. He closed the distance to the truck.

"Stay on this side," Goose said. "I don't want the bandits to know we're coming." He reached down and unfastened his seat belt. "Crain, you're with me."

* * *

United States 75th Army Rangers Temporary Post
Sanliurfa, Turkey
Local Time 2123 Hours

"Do you see what Goose is doing?" one of the techs yelled out.

On the screen, Goose climbed from the Hummer onto the side of one of the cargo trucks. He fought his way up the side onto the top of the careening vehicle.

Remington stared at the computer monitor and watched with cold anger. He hadn't missed the fact that Goose was a favorite among the men. Everywhere Remington had served with Goose, even back when they were both noncoms before Remington had chosen to pursue a path through Officer Candidates School, Goose had had the same response from men. They genuinely liked him.

That was a quality of leadership, Remington knew. But men didn't have to like an officer to obey him. Fear was another good tool. The British navy under Lord Nelson had employed fear and brutality among the crew, and it had worked.

"Man," another tech said, "there's nothing the sarge can't do."

"He's got God looking out over him," someone else said. "Remember when the Syrians rolled those tanks into the streets? Sarge stood up to one of them and took it out single-handedly."

"Quiet!" Remington roared. "Do you think this is some kind of ice cream social? or a John Wayne movie? Those are my supplies. Dedicated to my outpost. I want my supplies to reach my outpost in one piece. Do you understand?"

"Yes sir," several of the techs responded. The good mood didn't exactly vanish, but it went underground. They focused on the screens.

"We wouldn't have to be rescuing my supplies if Sergeant Gander had followed orders," Remington said. He tried to keep the anger from his voice but knew he'd failed. He pushed his breath out and got control of himself. Something was going to have to be done about Sergeant Samuel Adams Gander.

Soon.

"Are you getting this?" Danielle demanded as she stared at the trail of destruction that littered the countryside. She held on to the seat belt tightly.

"I am; I am," Gary replied. "But even the Steadicam programming in this unit isn't going to keep the picture from jumping everywhere."

"Just keep shooting. Do you know where Goose is?" Danielle stared through the burning and overturned vehicles. Thank God none of them belonged to the Rangers.

"Not yet."

"Find him."

"I'm trying."

Danielle turned to the driver. "Can't this thing go any faster?"

The man refused to look at her, but he did put his foot down harder on the accelerator. "You're crazy, you know that?"

"If you want to pull over, I'll drive myself."

He shook his head. "Is any of this even real to you?"

"All of it is real," Danielle told him. When she got back to Sanliurfa, she was determined to find another driver. "This is the biggest story of my career. A third of the planet disappears. A lot of world leaders are talking—behind closed doors—that this is some kind of religious thing."

The driver swerved to miss a tree, and the cameraman yelped in surprise.

"We're in a nation that has the only city in the world that sits on two continents," Danielle continued. "Which city, by the way, has been a point of contention between Christianity and Islamic beliefs since they laid the first stone of the first building there." She paused. "It's real to me."

"I found Goose," Gary said.

"Where?"

"He's on top of the second truck back." Gary laughed like a madman. "You know, that guy is certifiable. I've filmed extreme sports athletes who wouldn't do what I've seen him do since this started. I love that guy."

Danielle clung to the honest emotion in Gary's voice. That was how Goose played before the young male audience. He was a man's man, a warrior in the truest sense of the word. And for the women, he was the hero, the guy they all hoped to fall in love with. Those were the demographics she'd pushed at her producer at OneWorld NewsNet to get permission to stay with his story.

But if he got killed . . .

She pushed that thought out of her mind. She couldn't imagine Goose getting killed. When the chips were down and everything was on the line, he was unstoppable. She'd never met a man like him before.

The jeep whipped by a burning vehicle. A group of Rangers held bandits at gunpoint and were slapping restraints on them. The heat from the flames rolled over Danielle just for a moment, but her eyes remained on the lone figure atop the cargo truck.

❋   ❋   ❋

Local Time 2125 Hours

Wind tore at Goose as he clung to the canvas covering the steel support ribs of the cargo truck's payload area. The metal banged against his body, though the Kevlar vest blunted some of the trauma. He held on to the M-4A1 with his right hand as he went forward.

Crain climbed behind Goose. The younger man didn't keep his body snugged into the canvas and was taking a beating that slowed his progress. He hadn't yet gotten on top of the truck.

"Sarge! Sarge!" the truck driver called. "Are you there?"

"I'm here, Jenson," Goose said. "You just hold her steady for one minute longer." He dug his elbows and knees into the canvas and straddled the supports. His knee burned with pain at every bump and lurch.

"He's almost at the door! I see him in the mirror!"

"I'm there," Goose said as he pulled himself to the side of the truck and thrust the assault rifle forward.

The bandit clung to the truck's side. The man's feet rested on the edge of the payload area through the canvas tarp, and he held on to the tarp with one hand. Balancing himself, pistol in one hand, the bandit swung forward and tried to shove his weapon through the broken window.

"Sarge!"

Goose squeezed the trigger and felt the M-4A1 thud briefly against his shoulder. A three-round burst shattered the bandit's head, and he fell from the truck's side.

One of the bandit vehicles racing beside the convoy on the right side immediately returned fire. Goose stayed low. The canvas didn't offer much protection, but he was grateful for what he got. Bullets sizzled through the air over his head. A round struck one of the supports and sent a vibration singing through it. And at least one punched into his Kevlar vest.

Goose plucked an M67 fragmentation grenade from his combat webbing, flicked the clip out with his thumb, and released the spoon and pin. Arching up for a moment, he threw the spherical grenade at the jeep as it roared to within thirty feet.

The bandits fired at him immediately, but between the rough ride offered by the jeep and the bouncing of the cargo truck, they missed him. Goose pulled his helmet low and crossed an arm in front of his face.

"Fire in the hole!" he roared.

Crain hunkered down atop the cargo truck.

A thunderclap exploded beside the cargo truck, and shrapnel from the grenade peppered the vehicle's body. Goose pulled the M-4A1 to his shoulder and peered over the side. The jeep was a smoking ruin carrying dead men. It rammed into the cargo truck's side, then got caught up under the wheels. The truck reared like a bucking bronco as it rolled over the bandit vehicle.

The three remaining bandit vehicles hesitated, then veered away from the convoy's side. Unable to see the Ranger Hummers on the other side of the trucks, or possibly mistaking them for their comrades, the drivers of the bandit vehicles closed in again and focused on the lead truck.

"Drifter Two," Goose called as he scrambled to the rear of the truck.

"Reading you five by," Donner radioed back.

"Swing around behind the convoy and let these boys know you're here."

"Affirmative."

Goose caught hold of the support bar across the opening and flipped across, stepping backward into the cargo area. He'd organized the way the payload was distributed before they'd left the post. He knew where everything was.

The dead bodies of the two Rangers who'd been assigned to the payload area rocked restlessly with the sway and jar of the cargo truck. For a moment, the sight of them held Goose in his tracks. Both of the men had been young. Losing soldiers under his command hurt, and lately he'd lost a lot of them.

Get your job done. You can grieve later.

He stepped over the dead men and used a penflash from the pocket of his BDUs to make certain of the crate he wanted. When he found the equipment crate he was looking for, he slung his rifle and opened the crate. He reached inside and took out an SMAW.

Using the Israeli B-300 Shoulder-launched Multipurpose Assault Weapon as a model, the United States Marine Corps had originally fielded the SMAW MK153 Mod 0 for use against tanks and heavily fortified installations. It had proven effective time and again. During Operation Desert Storm, the U.S. Army had used some of them. Impressed with the performance of the SMAW, the army had continued to borrow the marine weapons while in the Middle East, and the Rangers had a cache of them along the border for use against the Soviet-made tanks the Syrian army fielded.

Goose slammed an 83mm rocket home in the launcher, then swung around to the rear of the truck. Crain was hanging upside down over the opening.

"Thought maybe you needed a hand," Crain said.

"I got it." Goose stepped through the opening and put a foot on the truck's bumper. He slid to the side of the truck, swaying along with the vehicle's bumping, then shouldered the weapon and aimed it back toward the jeeps in front of the Hummer.

"Weapons upgrade?" Crain asked.

Goose took aim through the scope and centered the crosshairs on the lead vehicle.

"Just a little video game humor," Crain said.

"I'm not much into video games."

Crain's rifle barked again and again.

Donner led the Ranger vehicles in a close sweep behind the cargo trucks. Goose saw them edging into view. The bandits spotted them as well and pulled away from the trucks.

The rocket launcher was overkill in this situation, and Goose knew it. But he thought about the village Niyazi had attacked and all the dead victims and wounded that had been left behind, and his heart hardened.

You're not just taking out the bad guys, he told himself. *You're sending a message tonight. And that message is, you don't mess with United States Army Rangers.*

He squeezed the trigger, and the rocket leaped into flight. It shot across the hundred yards of distance and slammed into the rear of the lead jeep. In a blink, the jeep became a fireball that bounced erratically across the broken ground. The explosion sounded loud and definite. The flash was incredibly bright in the darkness, and Goose felt the heat wave a hundred yards away.

Crain cheered his approval from on top of the cargo truck. "Hit 'em dead center, Sarge! Yeah!"

Goose lowered the weapon and shoved it back inside the payload area. The two surviving jeeps veered off and headed away from the convoy.

"Looks like they've decided to cut their losses and run," Donner said.

"Let them," Goose said.

"We can still take them."

Goose thought of the two dead men lying in the back of the truck and knew there were probably more. Guilt over leaving the convoy weighed on him.

"Taking them out isn't going to bring our dead back," Goose said. "And chasing after them will only split our forces again." He fully expected Remington to chime in with a comment then and was surprised when the captain didn't. "We stay together and finish this run. Besides that, those men will know they were lucky to survive tonight. They'll tell their buddies, and maybe next time they'll think twice about trying to hit one of our convoys."

❈   ❈   ❈

United States 75th Army Rangers Outpost
Harran
Sanliurfa Province, Turkey
Local Time 2219 Hours

The outpost was a skeletal affair that wouldn't stand up against an armored cavalry attack. Then again, it wasn't meant to. If everything worked right, the outpost was only going to be backup eyes and ears for the observation satellites the 75th currently had access to. Given the nature of everything that had happened these past weeks, Goose knew Remington didn't want to depend on GEOINT while operations around Sanliurfa were pending. Geospatial intelligence gathered from satellite reconnaissance only worked as long as the satellite links were maintained.

Harran was a small village. All of the buildings were older and cheaply made, and none of them had any height to speak of. The Rangers had settled on the ruins of the Ulu Cami for their primary spotting base. Goose didn't know how long ago the congregational mosque had been constructed, but it looked weathered and ancient. It was the highest point in the village. Someone had told Goose that the mosque had been built by the Ayyubids. When he professed ignorance, he was told they'd been a Muslim culture that had ruled a large empire from Egypt to Iraq in the twelfth and thirteenth centuries. They'd been driven out of the area by the invasion of the Mongols.

As Goose swung down from the cargo truck, he reflected that wars had constantly been fought in these lands. What was going on now was nothing new. Blood had soaked this soil for thousands of years. Now it was getting a fresh supply donated by the United States Army Rangers.

The village's strangest feature was the collection of beehive houses two klicks outside the main population area. The houses looked like footballs someone had shoved end-first into the hard-packed earth. Constructed completely of adobe, the beehive houses lacked even a wooden frame.

When the Syrians had invaded, most of the ethnic Arabs that lived in the village had pulled up stakes and left. They'd headed back into the harsher country in hopes that they'd be left alone. Some of those that had stubbornly remained had fled when the Rangers had occupied the village. Only a scattered few continued to live there.

"Goose."

Turning, Goose saw Danielle Vinchenzo approaching him. Her cameraman was at her heels.

"I really don't have time to speak with you right now, Ms. Vinchenzo," Goose said. "I've got a lot to do here. If you want to talk about anything, we can discuss it later."

Danielle looked like she wanted to argue. Then Crain and Martinez brought the first body out of the payload area. The reporter's face softened, and she pushed the camera down.

"I understand," she said. "I'm sorry. If there's anything we can do to help, please let me know."

"Yes, ma'am," Goose said. "Some of these boys will be wanting something to eat. If you and your team could help out with seeing to the mess hall and give those folks there a hand, I'd be much obliged."

"Of course." Danielle turned and left.

Goose headed to the back of the truck to see how bad it was going to be. His headset beeped for attention. He knew it was the frequency he used to speak with Remington away from the public channel. He'd known the contact was coming.

"Goose," Remington said without preamble.

"Yes, sir," Goose responded. Although he and Remington had been friends for years, that friendship wasn't going to be acknowledged at the moment.

"Leaving the convoy in unfriendly territory was stupid."

"Yes, sir." Goose had no other answer. Excuses didn't cut it in the army.

"How many dead do you have?"

"Five. Nine wounded. Three of those are going to be out of commission for a while. I'll know more when the docs get through with them."

Remington cursed with skill. That was one thing Goose had to give the captain. When it came to a full-fledged dressing-down, nobody threw one with as much castigation as Remington. The captain had refined it to an art form.

"I'm running short of Rangers as it is, Sergeant," Remington said. "I sure don't have enough for you to squander needlessly."

"No, sir."

"I'm holding you accountable for those men."

"Yes, sir." Goose was already doing so. Remington's jumping on the bandwagon didn't add any real weight. But a formality did come with the captain's assist.

"I'm going to be reviewing your actions tonight, Sergeant."

"Yes, sir." Goose knew that if they were lucky enough to get out of their present situation alive—and he had his doubts about that— he'd never spend a day the rest of his life without thinking about a lot of the decisions he'd made.

"For the moment, I want you to remand yourself to house arrest."

"What?" Goose couldn't believe that. Despite how the night had turned out, Remington couldn't possibly mean what he'd just said.

"You heard me, Sergeant. Remand yourself to custody. I'm going to turn the convoy over to Corporal Donner. He can bring the men you didn't kill back home."

"Yes, sir." Goose felt himself go numb and hollow inside. In all the years of their association and friendship, he'd never thought it would come down to this. "But I'd appreciate it if you'd at least let me help square things away here before I do that. These boys, they could use the help. Taking two hands and a strong back out of the equation right now ain't an answer."

Silence sounded loudly on the headset connection.

For a moment Goose thought he'd dropped frequency. It sometimes happened. He knew there was a chance Remington would order men to take him into custody by force.

"Get it done, Sergeant," Remington barked coldly. "Then place yourself under house arrest. I'll have Lieutenant Swindoll set aside a place for you."

"Yes, sir. Thank you, sir."

"It shouldn't have come to this, Goose," Remington said. "You and I have been through a lot together."

Goose didn't say anything to that. It was the truth, but there was no accounting—at least in his book—for what was going on now.

"If anyone was going to stick by my side during a tough situation," Remington said, "I would have always said it would be you."

"I've always been there for you, sir."

"Then why aren't you now?"

Goose didn't know. He thought he was, but Remington didn't see it that way.

"Get that operation squared away, Sergeant," Remington growled. "Then we'll deal with what I'm going to do with you."

"Yes, sir," Goose said, but he didn't get the reply out before the frequency clicked dead in his ear.

United States of America
Fort Benning, Georgia
Local Time 0539 Hours

Seventeen-year-old Joey Holder couldn't sleep. The nightmares had been going on for weeks. He'd thought they would have weakened by now, but their hold on him seemed only to grow. Every time he went to sleep at night, he saw the old Asian man's face again.

"What you two boys doing in my store?" the old man had demanded. "You boys no good boys. You thieves."

He'd been old and frail and afraid. Joey knew that now. At the time, Joey had been so panicked himself that he couldn't see anything but the pistol the old man held. He and Derrick, one of the boys he'd started hanging with after he'd left his house, had stood there frozen.

Derrick had a pistol too. They'd found it in one of the empty houses they'd broken into to spend the night. With so many people gone, that hadn't seemed like such a big deal at the time. The world had been in chaos. Half the world thought the Russians or Chinese or even Islamic terrorists had perfected some kind of death rays shot from space. The other half was convinced aliens from another world had attacked the planet.

That's what Zero believed.

When he thought of Zero, the fear inside Joey intensified. Zero was the most dangerous guy Joey had ever met.

That night in the mall, Zero had stepped from the shadows, leveled the .357 Magnum he carried like some Old West gunfighter, and shot the man. Seated in front of the couch in his family home, Joey shivered as the thunderous roars filled his imagination again. He wrapped his arms around his knees and wished he didn't feel so cold and alone.

Even with his mom in the house, sleeping just down the hall, Joey felt incredibly vulnerable. He wished Goose were there. Whenever Goose was around, Joey always felt safe. Not that his mom hadn't tried to make him feel the same way, but there was something that had always been solid and dependable about Goose.

Until Chris was born.

Thinking of his younger brother, who had disappeared with all the other young kids in the world, Joey felt sad and more than a little guilty. When Chris came along—truthfully, even before then—Joey had gotten jealous. He'd even told his mom he wished Chris hadn't been born.

Now Chris was gone, and Joey was afraid that he'd never see him again.

After all, if his mom was right and Chris had been taken to heaven by God, Joey wouldn't see his little brother again. Only good people went to heaven, and Joey wasn't a good person. He'd helped get that old man killed in the mall. He'd been where he shouldn't have been, with guys he shouldn't have been with, and in God's eyes he was probably just as guilty as Zero.

The gunshots rang out in his memory again.

Joey put his head down on his knees and wept silently. He wished he could tell his mom what had happened that night, but he couldn't. He was afraid if he did, she'd have to tell the police, and he'd be locked up for murder. Then he wouldn't see his mom either. It was bad enough that Chris was gone and Goose was over in Turkey.

I'm sorry. I'm sorry. Joey thought his apology to God, but he didn't know if God was listening. The Bible was full of forgiveness and redemption; Joey remembered hearing about that. But he didn't know for sure how to go about getting it. He'd just figured he soaked it up by going to church. So these last few weeks he'd been going to church with his mom. He'd felt a little better, but nothing like what he'd hoped.

The kid sleeping on the couch shifted, and his hand thumped against the back of Joey's head.

Angry at himself, at the kids who had invaded his home, and at everything that had happened, Joey shoved the guy's arm back onto the couch harder than he needed to.

The kid woke up. He was thirteen or fourteen, a skater dressed in ragged pants and wearing a wild haircut.

"Sorry, dude," the kid mumbled. "My bad."

"It's okay," Joey said, though he didn't mean it. He resented all the kids now living in his house. Their presence had been one of the reasons he'd left weeks ago.

The fact that so many of the newly orphaned kids on base had found their way to his house wasn't surprising. His mom was a counselor. She already knew a lot of them. Military kids seemed to have lots of problems.

"I was having a nightmare," Joey said.

"It's cool. But if you're having nightmares, dude, maybe you oughta find something else to watch. Zombie flicks ain't exactly bedtime stories."

Joey glanced at the television. He'd been channel surfing with the sound muted. Dialogue scrolled across the bottom of the screen.

The television showed zombies closing in on a building. They were torn and ragged, in various stages of decomposition. Their arms were stretched out before them.

The scrolling subtitles proclaimed, *Brains! Brains! Eat brains!*

"Yeah, I guess not." Joey found the remote and changed channels.

"Hey, dude," the skater kid asked, "do you think your mom is gonna fix breakfast today? Or do you think she's gonna have us eat at the cafeteria?"

"How should I know?" Joey replied. He flicked through the channels and hoped the kid would stop talking to him. None of the brats in the house seemed to get the idea that he wasn't happy they were there.

"You're Mrs. Gander's kid. I thought maybe—"

"I'm seventeen," Joey interrupted. "I'm not a kid."

"Okay. Sorry. Anyway, since she's your mom, I thought maybe she would have told you."

"There's a schedule on the refrigerator."

"Oh."

Joey tried his best to ignore the guy. He didn't want to talk to any of the invaders. That wasn't his job. That was his mom's. She was so busy doing her job that she kept forgetting about him and his troubles.

"I like it when your mom makes breakfast," the kid said. "It's really cool."

"Hey," Joey said.

"Yeah?"

"Shut up, okay?"

"Dude, that's really harsh."

"I don't care."

"Whatever." The kid rolled back the other way and pulled his blanket back over him.

Joey felt a little guilty, and he resented the emotion. He shouldn't have to feel guilty in his own house. He tried to focus on the television and kept flipping through channels.

It was going to be dawn soon. When the sun was up, the nightmares seemed farther away. He couldn't wait.

A news story on OneWorld NewsNet caught his eye. He recognized the reporter's name: Danielle Vinchenzo. She was the one who was over in Turkey with Goose.

Fear tightened in Joey's belly again. Goose was in some of the worst fighting taking place over there. Syria's military hadn't been as depleted as the American, United Nations, and Turkish forces by the mysterious occurrence. The dictator in Syria had attacked even before the vanishings had started, and he was keeping up the offensive.

Joey unmuted the TV so he could hear what the reporter was saying.

"—was the scene of a running firefight earlier," Vinchenzo said.

Behind her, a ragged line of burning vehicles dotted the landscape. Black and gray smoke twisted up toward the purple sky. Camou-clad figures moved on foot through the burning vehicles. Joey didn't know if they were American forces or Syrian.

"Sergeant Samuel Adams Gander, known to many of you through these reports simply as Goose," Danielle said, "was leading a resupply convoy to one of the outposts overlooking the Turkish-Syrian border. Things have gotten desperate here, but the men of the United States Army's 75th Rangers are persevering."

The television cut to a close-up with a young soldier. Bruises and cuts showed on his face.

"I gotta tell you, ma'am," the soldier said, "things here are mighty bad. Syria isn't letting up, and they'd like to sweep on into this area and take over. There's generations of bad blood between most of the people here, and those soldiers aren't afraid of spilling any of it."

The camera's eye swept over a scene of the running gunfight. Joey stared at the images intently, trying to figure out which one was

Goose. They all looked the same to Joey. His inability to see Goose frustrated him, making him angry and scared all at the same time.

Would Goose understand what had happened at the mall that night? Joey wasn't sure. As much as he wanted Goose there, he was also terrified of telling his stepfather what he'd done.

"It was a close thing out here tonight," the soldier went on. A caption identified him as Private First Class Mike Dunney. "But Goose—Sergeant Gander, I mean—he pulled us through it all right. He's a good soldier. The best the army has to offer, if you ask me."

Pride flushed through Joey.

"That's your dad, isn't it?" the kid on the couch asked.

"Yeah." Joey was surprised at how choked his voice was. Goose had been more of a dad than Joey's biological father had ever been.

"Must be scary. Him being over there, I mean."

Joey wanted to be angry with the kid, but he couldn't. It felt good to talk about Goose. "It is. I think Mom's really scared."

"Yeah. I get that." The kid hesitated. "I don't know where my dad is. Don't know where my mom is either. I got up one morning; they were gone. I was all alone in the house."

"Scary," Joey commented.

"Yeah."

"That was here at the post?"

"Yeah."

"Your dad's army?"

"My mom. First lieutenant. Dad taught high school. Physics."

"Never cared much for physics," Joey said.

"Me neither. But Dad would talk about it all the time." The kid sat up on the couch and wrapped the blanket around him, though it wasn't really cold. Not like it would be in another month. "I kind of tuned him out when he'd talk about stuff. Wish I hadn't done that now."

"I know what you mean."

They were silent for a moment, watching as Danielle Vinchenzo ran another of the pieces on Goose.

"Seems like that reporter has a thing for your stepdad," the kid said.

"What do you mean?"

"She's always talking about him."

"I don't think it's that," Joey replied.

"Then what?"

Joey thought about it for a moment. "I think she sees Goose as

kind of every soldier over there. Goose is just . . . a soldier, you know.
Just the kind every guy over there is like."

"She talks about him like he's a hero."

"I guess he is." Joey thought it was strange that he hadn't thought
of Goose that way before. Goose had always been there for him.
Always been such a . . . dad. A lump formed in the back of Joey's
throat. *If I told you about this—about what happened at the mall—would
you understand, Goose?*

Thankfully, according to the news report, Goose was all right.
Joey let out a tense breath as the news program shifted to a speech
Nicolae Carpathia was going to deliver to the United Nations later
that day.

"Is anything else on besides the news?" the kid asked.

"Like what?"

"Cartoons. Something like that."

Giving in to the inevitable, knowing the kid wasn't going to shut
up, Joey tossed him the television remote control. "Knock yourself out."

"Thanks."

Joey stood.

"Leaving?" the kid asked.

"Yeah. Gotta go walk."

"Want company?" The kid reached for his shoes.

"No." Joey started for the door, not giving the kid the chance to
catch up to him.

❉ ❉ ❉

Local Time 0611 Hours

Joey took his old ten-speed from the garage out back. He'd helped
Goose build that garage, along with the fort that Chris had played
in. For a while after Chris was born, Joey had been small enough to
swing in the swings with his little brother. That had changed pretty
quickly.

He made himself stop thinking about Goose and Chris as he
swung aboard the ten-speed. He pedaled by memory, trying hard not
to give any thought to where he was going.

Fort Benning seemed deserted. According to the news, at least a
third of the people around the world had vanished. Numbers were
still coming in every day. Those numbers could change. Military bases

had been really hard hit, as had the police forces, fire departments, and emergency medical services.

Military jeeps with armed soldiers riding shotgun patrolled the camp housing. After the disappearances, a lot of soldiers and their families living outside the fort had moved back inside the perimeter. When it got dark, though, everyone went inside. The camp was still on alert, and the nocturnal hours were carefully watched.

Joey loved the feel of the breeze in his face. For a few moments, he could pretend that he was younger, that he was just a kid again. But as soon as the military jeep sped up behind him and switched on its lights, that feeling went away.

The alarm clock woke Megan Gander. She shot out a hand and silenced it before the second offensive bleat could sound. She lay quietly on the camp cot in her bedroom and listened to the snores of the girls sleeping in her bed.

It was the most peaceful sound in the world right now. At least in this corner of the world, people were safe and well cared for.

As always, her first thoughts and prayers were for Chris. Though she felt certain in light of everything she'd come to understand about events in the world that Chris was in a far better place, her son's absence remained difficult to deal with.

She missed Chris terribly. Some nights, when Goose was away in the field, as he was now, Megan would let Chris watch cartoons and share her bed. She'd done the same thing with Joey. Especially after the divorce from her first husband.

They'd both been lonely, and the apartment she was renting at that time had only a single bedroom. She hadn't wanted Joey sleeping on the couch all the time. As soon as she was able, she'd gotten a two-bedroom apartment.

Her cell phone vibrated in the pocket of the flannel pajama pants she wore. Reluctantly, she pulled it from her pocket, checked caller ID, and pushed herself from the cot.

The number came from the fort's hospital. That couldn't mean good news. Not this early.

"Megan," she answered in a whisper.

"Did I wake you?" Aisha Waller asked. She was the night supervisor at the hospital.

"No. The alarm did a few minutes before you called." Megan looked at the girls sleeping in her bedroom. All seven of them, three on the bed and four in sleeping bags on the floor, were between thirteen and sixteen. All of them had lost their parents and siblings in the rapture.

"I wanted to let you know that Lindsey Perlman got admitted a couple hours ago," Aisha said.

"What happened?"

"She tried to commit suicide. Took a straight razor to her wrists."

The announcement hurt and scared Megan. The Tribulation had already manifested all around the world. The next seven years would be the most trying and terrifying mankind had ever seen. People who failed to find Jesus during these times ran the risk of being lost forever.

"How is she?" Megan went to her closet and took out pearl gray slacks, a midnight blue blouse, and fresh underwear.

"The docs got her leveled off," Aisha answered, "but it was a near thing."

"You could have called me earlier."

"And let you miss out on sleep? Sure. But that wouldn't have helped the kids you've got to counsel today, would it?"

Megan made herself relax and breathe out. "No."

"All you could have done was the same thing I was already doing: pray for that girl. I promise, I was doing enough for both of us."

"I know."

"Even had a couple of MPs in here helping. Between us, we got it all done."

"You're right."

"Just because I called doesn't mean I'm in a hurry to see you in here. I know you usually get up about this time, and I didn't want you finding out about Lindsey from anyone else."

"Thank you for that."

"You're welcome. The docs say she's going to be sedated most of the day. They don't want to run the risk of her fighting to get out of bed and tearing open everything they had to do to save her. When you get rested, and when Lindsey gets rested, then we can see about you talking to her."

"All right."

"So my advice, girlfriend, is just do whatever you had planned to do today. Then come in for your regular schedule. It's going to be a long day."

✳ ✳ ✳

Local Time 0624 Hours

After a quick shower instead of the bath she craved—with a house full of teens, hot water would be at a premium—Megan dressed, prayed for Goose, and went into the kitchen. She'd planned to make breakfast at home this morning, and she didn't want to change that. With everything else that had gone awry in the world, she needed simple household chores as a touchstone.

"Hey, Mrs. G." Gangly Brian Wright sat at the kitchen table with a PSP in his hands. He was thirteen and obsessed with video games. A mop of brown hair hung in his eyes.

He was a recent addition to the Gander home, brought in from his parents' house only a few days ago. His dad was in eastern Europe at the moment, and his mom—one of the best women Megan had known—had disappeared in the rapture.

Brian had lived on his own for weeks. Megan had organized a search for children of military families who lived off-post. The provost marshal's office had put the search teams together. They had most of the families squared away now, but new ones still came in every now and again.

"Good morning, Brian," Megan said. "Did you get any sleep?"

"Some." Brian's fingers flew across the video game. He was ADHD, and Megan knew he often didn't sleep well.

"Want to help me with breakfast?" Megan went to the pantry and peered in. Thankfully the military was bankrolling all the homes at this point. Especially the ones that had taken in stray teens whose families had gone missing.

"Girls' work," Brian replied scornfully.

"I'll keep that in mind when it's time to wash dishes and take out the trash. Even boys can do manual labor like that."

Brian sighed theatrically. "Man, you're tough."

"Yep. Just be glad I don't make you salute or drop and give me fifty every time you don't 'ma'am' me."

Brian paused his game and gazed at her. "Are you kidding me?"

"About the salute, the fifty, and the 'ma'am-ing,' sure. About having a choice between helping make breakfast or cleaning up after it, no."

"The most I know about breakfast is pouring it out of a box and adding milk."

That, Megan lamented, seemed to be the case with most of the kids she'd come in contact with. She took a magnetic Post-it pad from the front of the refrigerator, wrote COOKING LESSONS on it, and put it back.

"'Cooking lessons'?" Brian asked. "For me?"

"For all of you. I'm quite sure the commissary could use the help, and you guys could definitely use lessons that will make you more autonomous."

"What's *autonomous*?"

"It means self-sufficient. Able to take care of your own needs." Megan took loaves of French bread from the pantry, cinnamon and powdered sugar from the spice rack, milk and eggs from the refrigerator, and sausage links from the freezer. "How do French toast and eggs sound this morning?"

"Great."

"Good. Let's try to keep the mess to a minimum."

❋   ❋   ❋

Local Time 0632 Hours

Preparing breakfast relaxed Megan as it always did. There was something about the simple task of making a meal for someone else to enjoy—although making breakfast for nearly thirty people was by no means simple—that grounded her. It was mindless labor, a series of movements that had been perfected over seventeen years of being a wife and mom.

God, thank You for this work right now. I don't know how I'd keep it together if I didn't have it.

As the kitchen filled with breakfast smells, teenagers started to pour from the bedrooms and game room like zombies in a horror film. Most of them weren't verbally social in the mornings, but they liked to be around each other.

A few of the girls stepped in to help with the cooking. As they came on board, Megan fired up extra burners as well as three electric hot plates. Within minutes, the extra laborers had been absorbed into the process, and French toast started to pile up. That also signaled the feeding frenzy. Syrup flowed and smothered plates of powdered French toast.

Megan poured whole packages of sausage links into quart-size Dutch ovens full of water, brought them to a boil, and fished the sausages out. That way there wasn't as much grease. Then she dumped the water and started all over.

"Everyone knows you have school today, right?" Megan asked.

A collective groan swelled up from the group.

"That's what I thought," Megan said. "Since this is Monday, a new chores list has gone up. Check it before you leave."

That drew forth another groan.

The negative response actually made Megan feel better. If the teens were feeling good enough to complain about school and chores, they were getting closer to normal. At least, as normal as the world would ever be again.

For seven short years, Megan reminded herself. She looked around the group, suddenly realizing that Joey wasn't among them. A wave of guilt washed over her. She was constantly overlooking him these days, it seemed, and she didn't know why that was.

"Is Joey still asleep?" Megan asked.

The five boys who currently sacked out in Joey's room shook their heads. "He wasn't there when I got up, Mrs. G.," one of them said.

"He was watching television this morning," Snake said. He was the skater boy who'd turned up a few days ago. He still hadn't told Megan what his real name was, and he didn't have any ID on him. She was going to have to do some kind of paperwork on him eventually.

"Watching television?" Megan repeated.

"Yeah." Snake shoved a triangle of syrup-covered French toast into his mouth, chewed briefly, and swallowed. Syrup ran down his chin, and he wiped it away on a sleeve.

"Ewww," one of the girls said. "Maybe you want to chew your food next time."

"What?" Snake asked in honest puzzlement.

"Joey," Megan reminded.

Snake focused on her and nodded. "Yeah. Joey. Television."

"What was he watching?"

"Surfing. Caught a little of the news. Saw a piece on there about your husband."

Megan's heart raced. She forced herself to be calm. "What about my husband?"

"He was in some kind of battle over there." Snake shrugged.

One of the girls smacked Snake on the back of the head.

"Hey," he protested.

"Maybe you could tell her what it *said* about her husband," the girl said icily.

"He's fine. He was running a supply route. Took some fire. They killed the bad guys. End of story."

Megan breathed a sigh of relief, but she added another nugget of information to her cache about Snake. He was relaxed with the military-speak. Either he was a gamer or he had a parent involved in the armed forces.

"Probably catch it later, too," Snake said. "That hot chick on OneWorld was covering the story."

"We don't refer to women as 'hot chicks' in my house," Megan said.

"Yeah, well, if you saw this one, you might change your mind." Snake colored. "I mean, if you were a guy."

And he embarrasses easily, Megan noted. *Maybe you're not as tough as you act like you are, Snake.*

"You are such a jerk," Kendal said. She smacked the skater in the back of the head again.

"Hey," Snake protested again and stepped to the side so he'd be out of reach. "Don't be such a—" He brought himself up short. He'd already been warned about language.

"Neanderthal," Kendal said, folding her arms and frowning with as much displeasure as a fifteen-year-old could muster. "Maybe you should find a cave to live in."

"Enough," Megan said, putting the teacher edge into her voice that she'd learned helped to keep order in her house.

The kids quieted. They kept passing food around.

"Joey was watching television," Megan said. "Then what?"

Snake shrugged. "He blazed. Got up. Walked out. Sayonara, baby."

"Did he say where he was going?" Megan didn't feel good about Joey's sudden departure. The last time he'd disappeared like that, he'd come back days later with his face a mass of bruises and afraid of his own shadow.

"I offered to go with him," Snake said. "He told me no."

"Did he say where he was going?" she repeated.

"No. He just left."

"Was he upset?"

"I don't know."

"He knew Goose was all right?"

"Yeah. We talked about it."

"What did he act like?"

"Like he wanted to go somewhere else. That's why he left."

Frustrated, Megan turned her attention back to the latest batch of French toast and barely managed to rescue it from burning. "Who has class with Joey?" she asked.

A few of the kids raised their hands. Most of the classes were a lot smaller these days. With none of the lower grades to teach, the teachers had divided up the rest of the students.

"If I haven't heard from him before I leave, please let him know he's supposed to call me. And make sure he does."

They said they would.

This isn't a problem, Megan told herself. *God didn't bring Joey back into your life just so you could worry about him all over again. God, please. My plate really isn't big enough to handle this again.*

But she kept thinking about the bruises on her son's face and the fear in his eyes the night he'd returned to her.

8

"Pull the bicycle over to the side and stand down," one of the men in the jeep ordered.

Joey's mouth went dry, and his first instinct was to flee. He just knew the soldiers were there because of what had happened at the mall. They were going to arrest him for murder. He didn't know how his mom was going to deal with that.

Dawn was starting to light the eastern sky, but the soldiers still needed light to see well. The one in the passenger seat got out. He shined his flashlight in Joey's eyes.

"You got ID, kid?" the soldier asked.

Joey calmed a little at that. If they didn't know who he was, that was a good thing.

"Yeah," he answered. He made sure to keep his hands where the soldiers could clearly see them. Goose had taught him that, saying that night patrols were often performed by young and inexperienced soldiers who could overreact. "My dog tags are under my shirt. I've got a driver's license in my wallet."

"Lemme see them."

Joey caught the chain around his neck with a thumb and lifted the dog tags free. He remembered how cool he thought they were when he'd gotten them. Then they'd become something he had to have with him.

The guard checked the dog tags and the driver's license.

"You know Sergeant Gander?" the guard asked.

"He's my stepdad," Joey said.

"He's a good soldier."

Joey didn't know what to say to that, so he kept quiet.

"What are you doing out here, Joey?"

"Thought I'd clear my head."

"We haven't had any problems in the camp, but it might not be safe on the streets."

"Don't see why it wouldn't be. You guys are out here." Joey gave the guy a smile.

For a moment, the soldier held his expression; then he grinned too. "Yeah, we are. What do you have on your mind?" He handed Joey back his license.

"My mom is one of the camp counselors. She's taken in a lot of kids." Joey shrugged, borrowing one of the teen habits he knew adults attributed to kids. It was camouflage for the moment. "Kind of crowded at my house right now."

"I bet. I heard your mom is doing really good things."

Joey nodded, but he wanted to scream. "Just wanted to catch a breath of fresh air. Maybe ride down to the main gates and look out at the city."

"There's not much to see," the soldier said. "Things there are still pretty confusing."

"I know. I've seen it on television."

"Just stay back from the gate. The guys there have jobs to do. The general has given orders that everyone's to stay on post. If you leave, it's going to be hard to get in again."

"No plans on leaving," Joey replied.

"Take care of yourself, Joey." The soldier climbed into the jeep.

Joey waved, then got back on his bike.

✵　✵　✵

Columbus, Georgia
St. Francis Hospital Chapel
Local Time 0641 Hours

"Miss McGrath?"

Jenny McGrath blinked her eyes awake. For just a second, panic filled her because she couldn't remember where she was. Bright lights reflected off white walls. She felt stiff and uncomfortable, and she was aware that the back of her thighs had gone numb.

"Jenny?"

Someone shook Jenny's shoulder. Instinctively, Jenny reached for the hand that held her, gripped two of the fingers, and prepared to pull the hand from her. She'd had to defend herself against unwanted attentions before. She was used to moving quickly.

She looked up into Ester Pryne's face. A diminutive woman in her forties, Ester wasn't at all a threatening figure. She was a nurse in the cardiac ward, where Jenny's father was currently awaiting a miracle.

That's what the doctor had finally come out and said a few days ago: that it would take a miracle for Jackson McGrath to recover from the car wreck he'd had a few weeks ago.

"Are you all right, child?" Ester wore granny glasses and kept her peroxide blonde hair short. Laugh lines—she refused to allow them to be called crow's feet—surrounded her eyes and marked the corners of her mouth.

"My father," Jenny said, because that was the first thought in her head every time someone woke her. Jackson McGrath hadn't regained consciousness since the accident.

"Your father is still with us," Ester said. "I'm worried about you, though."

"I'm fine," Jenny said. "Thank you." Conscious of the slack way she was sitting in the church pew in the hospital's chapel, she sat up straighter and felt for her backpack at her feet. Thankfully it was still there.

"I thought I might eat breakfast this morning after my shift. I'm off at seven. If you don't mind, I could use the company."

Ester's ploy was so thinly disguised that Jenny thought she would have had to still be asleep to be taken in by it. Still, she felt grateful for the attention. "Don't you think you've bought me enough breakfasts lately?" Jenny asked.

"No. I don't think you've gained an ounce. In fact, I'm worried that you might have lost weight."

Jenny knew that she had. Her jeans no longer fit her the way they had, and she'd needed to tighten her belt. Before the last few weeks, she'd always been in good shape. Working extra jobs to pick up the slack left by her father's drinking had kept her fit.

"Let me buy breakfast today," Jenny said. Three weeks ago, one of the hospital administrators had offered her a job in janitorial. With all the people who had gone missing, St. Francis was seriously understaffed. Jenny suspected the nurses had made the suggestion. Since then, she'd been working forty-hour weeks, and the hospital had turned a blind eye to the fact that she was sleeping in the waiting rooms and the chapel.

"Well, I appreciate the offer," Ester said. "Do you want to come by the nurses' station and get me?"

"Sure." Jenny glanced at the clock on the wall. "Do I have time for a shower? And I want to go by and check on Dad."

"You have plenty of time. I've got some paperwork I can noodle around with if you're running late." Ester held out a plastic bag. "I also brought you this."

Jenny hesitated. Growing up as Jackson McGrath's daughter had brought only two kinds of attention: scorn and pity. Over the years, she hadn't cared for either of them.

"What is it?" Jenny asked.

"A gift. Something a few of us got together and wanted to give you."

"Ester, I don't want charity. I just—"

"This isn't charity, child," Ester interrupted. "It's a gift. There's not a nurse on this floor who hasn't seen hard times. A lot of us learned not to believe in much outside our own skins, but we learned to accept small kindnesses that came our way. If we hadn't gotten them, we might not have made it through those dark times. One thing we know: you don't get through them alone." She pushed the bag forward.

Reluctantly, Jenny took the bag and peered inside. A pair of jeans, khakis, and a handful of blouses were neatly folded inside.

"We know you've had to struggle to keep your clothes clean," Ester said. "We've seen you washing your clothes in the bathroom and drying them outside."

Jenny's face burned with embarrassment. She'd been doing all she could do to keep herself clean. She hadn't wanted to get thrown out of the hospital, and being unclean would only have made her feel like everything she had to deal with was impossible.

"We had to guess at the sizes," Ester said, "but most of us are pretty good at that. You'll have to let us know how good we did."

"I don't know what to say," Jenny whispered.

"You say, 'Thank you.' That's all."

"Thank you," Jenny said. Surprising herself, she reached out and hugged the older woman.

"You're welcome, child. You're welcome." Ester patted Jenny on the back and hugged her. "Now you get your shower. Both of us need to eat."

❋ ❋ ❋

Fort Benning, Georgia
Local Time 0649 Hours

Guards held the checkpoint with the barriers in place. There were more of them present than Joey had ever seen. On other occasions, before the disappearances, the guards had often laughed and joked, though they'd always been professional. There was no laughing and joking now. In fact, two jeeps filled with armed men sat farther back. Their presence was obvious and powerful.

Other guards, these with sentry dogs, walked the perimeter. The dogs moved effortlessly and remained ever watchful.

As he watched them, Joey felt more safe than he had in days. The nightmares about the mall shooting, about Zero and the others, had left him wrecked. He knew that. Seeing the guards at work helped him relax. As long as he didn't leave the camp, he was safe.

Unless Zero or one of the others got picked up and busted for the murder of the old man. Then they could blame everything on Joey.

As soon as those thoughts crept into his mind, Joey felt sick with dread and fear all over again. His hands shook on the bike handles, and he thought he was going to be sick.

"Hey, kid."

Joey looked over at the K-9 soldier and the German shepherd at his side. "Yeah?"

"Do you feel okay?" The soldier was older, probably Goose's age, and he wore sergeant's chevrons on his sleeves.

"Yeah."

"You don't look so good."

"Just kind of creepy thinking about it, you know?"

The sergeant hesitated a minute, then nodded. "Yeah. Really creepy. I keep thinking I'm going to wake up and find out this was all a bad dream."

"But it's not."

"No, I guess not." The sergeant looked at Joey again. "But don't worry about it too much, kid. The brass will figure this out. They always do."

"I hope so," Joey said. "The sooner the better."

"I'm keeping my fingers crossed. In the meantime, stay back from the fence, okay? It makes the snipers tense."

Snipers? Joey looked around at the nearby buildings.

"They're there, kid. Always on watch."

"Okay." That made Joey feel even more safe. The camp was like one of those old medieval castles. The armed guards were the moat that cut it off from the rest of the world.

"I gotta get back to it," the sergeant said. "Got a lot of miles to cover before my shift's over."

"Have a good day," Joey said. After the sergeant and the dog had moved on, Joey sat astride the ten-speed and stared out where Columbus sat touched by the early dawn. He thought about the madness that was in the city.

Many metropolitan areas had tried to return to a semblance of order. That was what people did, he supposed. Just picked up the pieces and moved on. Like his mom had when his dad left them. And like what she'd done in the camp when so many kids needed somebody.

But that was just the surface. Looting and violence had broken out all over. People were scared and mad, and they were going to be that way until they knew for sure what had happened.

And that it wasn't going to happen again.

✣   ✣   ✣

St. Francis Hospital
Local Time 0656 Hours

Jenny luxuriated in the hot shower. The nurses had allowed her into their locker room weeks ago, once they'd discovered she was living at the hospital. Megan Gander had tried to get her to return to Fort Benning, but Jenny didn't want to leave her father. Her whole life, every time he'd gotten bad, wherever they'd been living, whether in jail or in a psych ward, she'd always managed to be there for him. She lived with the fear that if she wasn't there, something would happen to him.

Dark hair washed and dried with a community hair dryer, she quickly dressed in a pair of khaki cargo pants, a white blouse with three-quarter sleeves, and her tennis shoes. She used a separate plastic bag to put her dirty clothes in. She planned to wash them later.

Jenny looked in the mirror and noticed how hollow-eyed she was becoming. Red rimmed her green eyes. *No wonder the nurses are worried about you. They probably think you're going to be their next patient.* A little makeup would have helped, but she didn't have any.

Satisfied she'd done all she could do, she turned from the mirror.

Having possessions was turning out to be a problem. Over the last few weeks, Jenny had pared everything she owned down to one backpack. The new clothes didn't fit inside. She got frustrated thinking she was going to have to carry her bags around like a homeless person.

"Problem?" a voice asked.

Jenny turned to see a nurse putting on makeup two sinks down. "No."

"You look like you don't have enough arms." The nurse was in her early thirties. She wore a charm bracelet that had pictures of a small girl on it. The woman didn't look familiar, so Jenny assumed she was on loan from one of the other floors.

"Things were easier," Jenny admitted, "when everything fit into one bag."

The woman laughed. "I know that's true. But that's not really life, is it?"

Jenny silently thought that all the good things that had happened in her life could have fit into one bag with plenty of room left over. It was trouble that seemed to come in bushel baskets.

"No," Jenny said.

"Tell you what," the nurse said, "I've got an extra lock here somewhere." She rummaged through a big purse. "Bought one and never used it." She produced a Master Lock with two keys taped on one side. "You're welcome to use it."

"I can pay you back," Jenny said.

The nurse laughed. "Well, I appreciate that. Just promise me you'll help somebody in the future. With everything that's going on in the world, I'm starting to think that's the only thing that matters. So me helping you today? I'm already one good deed down the road."

The nurse's good humor and smile were infectious. Jenny couldn't help smiling back. She took the lock and the keys.

"Help yourself to a locker." The nurse pointed at the wall. "There appear to be quite a few of them these days."

Jenny stashed her stuff while the nurse dashed out.

❖   ❖   ❖

Local Time 0710 Hours

Jackson McGrath looked small and sickly lying in the hospital bed in the intensive care unit. He was at least twenty pounds under his best weight. Several days' growth of beard stubble, all black and gray, covered his face. His hair was too long and uneven from bad haircuts he'd given himself. Yellow tinged his skin.

Jenny knew her father was that color because his liver was trying to fail. Once it did, death was right around the corner.

The doctors had already examined Jackson McGrath's liver and said it was a miracle he'd lived as long as he had. Both legs and one arm were in casts from the single-car collision that had landed him here. He'd been drunk when he drove off the street and hit a tree. Bruises still showed on his pallid, too-thin chest where the seat belt had cut into him.

Seated in the chair beside her father's bed, Jenny stared at him, recalling numerous memories of him drunk and sober. None of it was pleasant. Jackson McGrath had never been a happy man. For a long time, he'd blamed his unhappiness on Jenny, telling her that raising a daughter by himself was too hard. At least, too hard to do sober.

Truthfully, though, Jenny had been forced to learn how to raise her father. And he'd fought her at every turn.

"How are you doing this morning, kiddo?" Katie Lang, one of the morning ICU nurses, filled out the chart at the foot of Jackson McGrath's bed. She was in her late thirties, a heavyset woman with a quick smile and an even quicker comeback. Patients learned early not to give any guff to Nurse Lang.

"Doing okay," Jenny said.

"You look pretty this morning."

"Thanks. Ester said the nurses got me the new outfits."

"You deserve them."

"I appreciate them, that's for sure."

"We were happy to get them for you."

"Has there been any change with my father?"

Katie took in a deep breath and let it out. Then she shook her head. "Not yet. I'm sorry."

Despair swallowed some of Jenny's good mood. "The longer he stays in a coma, the less chance there is of him recovering."

"Don't give up on him," Katie advised. "I've been a nurse for a long time, and I can tell you right now, I've seen some of the most audacious things happen that you wouldn't believe."

Jenny nodded, not because she believed what the woman was saying but because she knew it was expected. Everyone talked about miracles in the hospital like it was a requirement or something. But she knew that not many people believed.

"If you give up on him," Katie whispered, "he might give up on himself. Just because they don't respond to you doesn't mean they're not listening."

That was something else Jenny had heard a lot about. She made it a point to talk to her father every day. Sometimes she read stories she thought he might like from the newspaper. Other times she created a make-believe horse race and reimagined it for her father. She embellished the race and the names of the horses and jockeys. In addition to alcohol, gambling was also a problem for her father. She felt bad about feeding that addiction, but she didn't know what else to talk to him about that he would have found interesting.

"I know," she said to Nurse Lang, and she felt guilty at once. Before coming to the hospital, when she first heard that her father was in bad shape, she'd resented him all over again for disrupting her life. She'd been happy with Megan Gander at Fort Benning. While there, Jenny had found purpose in helping teens who had been left behind.

Now she was here in the hospital. Waiting for the worst like she'd been doing for years.

"As long as he's hanging in there," the nurse said, "you've got to do it too."

"I know."

The woman patted Jenny on the shoulder as she passed. For a few minutes, Jenny sat there and looked at her father. Then she spoke. "Dad, I don't know if you can hear me or not, but I hope you can. I'm here for you. I've been here for you every day. But I'm getting tired. And maybe I'm getting a little scared. You know how I hate being scared. This is the hardest thing I've ever done."

The machines kept beeping and chirping. The ventilator pumped up and down, filling Jackson McGrath's lungs with oxygen and emptying them again.

"What I need you to do," Jenny said in a voice so thick with emotion she could barely get it out, "is come back to me. Everything you've done, we can fix it. Somehow. All you've got to do is come back."

There was no response.

Gently, Jenny took her father's free hand in both of hers. His flesh was cold and felt slightly stiff, but that might have been her imagination. She kissed the back of his hand and felt hot tears fill her eyes. She blinked them away with effort.

God, I know a lot of people don't like my father, and I know he's given them plenty of reasons not to, but he doesn't deserve to die like this. And I don't want to watch it happen.

Jackson McGrath's thin chest rose and fell.

I'm not even sure what I'd say to him if he makes it back from this. We didn't have a whole lot to talk about before. But he's my father. I love him.

She massaged his hand, trying to put some warmth into it.

If Megan Gander is right—if these are the end times and we're all going to be facing hell itself in the next seven years—I want my father to have a chance to know Your mercy. That's what these times are about. Touch him, God. Heal him and make him whole. He's not going to be able to do it on his own.

For a moment, Jenny thought about praying for herself. That felt foolish and selfish, though. Praying for her father was one thing, but she didn't know how much she believed in God. God hadn't ever been a big part of her life, and she saw no real reason to change that now. But since she couldn't help her father herself, she knew she had to pray so she'd have at least something she felt she was contributing.

Silently, she lowered her head and prayed again for her father's swift recovery. Then she placed his hand back on the bed and went to join Ester for breakfast.

✳   ✳   ✳

Fort Benning, Georgia
Local Time 0731 Hours

"You mind having company, Joey?"

Seated at one of the long tables in the camp mess, Joey looked up and saw Heather Simpson standing across from him with a breakfast tray in her hands. She was sixteen, a year younger than he, with long brown hair and soft brown eyes. Freckles spattered her nose. She wore capris and a printed blouse.

Joey knew her from camp and from school. Her dad worked in the motor pool. He hadn't exactly been friends with Heather, but he'd known her well enough to talk to her in the halls and in passing.

"I don't mind," Joey replied.

Heather sat at the table and picked up one of the waffle squares on her plate. Her nose wrinkled in disgust. "Was breakfast this bad before all this weirdness?"

"Don't know. Mom always fixed breakfast."

"Isn't she fixing breakfast this morning?"

"Probably." A twinge of guilt sped through Joey when he answered. He knew his mom would be expecting him there.

"So you chose this misery over your mom's cooking?" Heather shook her head in disbelief.

"Kinda crowded at my house right now."

"I heard." Heather opened her carton of milk. "I thought about crashing breakfast some morning. People I talk to say your mom is great. That her breakfasts are great."

Joey ran a spoon through the runny powdered eggs on his plate. "Yeah. She is. It is."

"If you ask me, I'd have stood in line at your mom's house and got a good breakfast."

A spark of anger flared through Joey. "But nobody asked you, did they?"

"Nope. Somebody got up grouchy today, I see."

Joey ran a hand through his hair. "What is it about girls that they think they have to ask questions about everything?"

"We're girls. It's our job. We allow people to get in touch with their feelings."

"Maybe some of us don't want to be in touch with our feelings."

"Why is it boys never want to be in touch with their feelings?"

"I'm not a boy."

"You're not a man."

"Close enough."

"Okay. Men are even worse than boys." Heather cut her waffles.

"Why did you come over here?"

"Because no one else seemed willing to brave the rancorous waves you're giving off."

Self-consciously, Joey looked around the mess hall. He was surprised to see familiar faces scattered around the room. He hadn't noticed them till now. And no one had even bothered to make contact. Some of them were friends.

Joey swiveled his gaze back to Heather's. "You're sitting with me because you feel sorry for me?"

"Yep."

"You know, there can be too much honesty in the world."

"It helps combat denial."

"So now I'm in denial?"

"Joey," Heather said, "we're all in denial. Look around at these people. The mess hall is only half-full. On a regular day, it would be crammed. I know because I eat here a lot since my dad has to be at work so early, and I'll take powdered eggs over cooking for myself."

Joey forked a syrup-drenched waffle piece into his mouth and chewed.

"Everybody thinks everything is going to go back the way it was," Heather said. "They don't get the fact that the world is ending. At least, this world is ending."

"You don't know that."

"Have you been going to your mom's classes on the Bible? on the end times?"

"Yeah. But I don't buy into that." Actually, what his mom had been talking about had been too scary to think about much. Joey had tuned it out, and lately there had been so many kids going to the meetings that it had been easy to duck out on them. His mom talked about that stuff at home, too, but all he had to do there was nod and keep his mouth shut.

"Your mom does."

"My mom is looking for answers about why my little brother disappeared." Joey was so mad that he didn't realize how much that hurt to say until he'd already said it.

"Didn't you hear about Gerry Fletcher? How he disappeared?"

Joey had.

"Your mom was trying to save him when he fell off a rooftop. He *disappeared* before he hit the ground. Only his clothes landed. There's a tape and everything. The military put your mom on trial. Now the general has the tape locked away until the White House makes a decision about what to do with it."

"I've heard about the tape," Joey said. "I also know a lot of people are starting to say it was all faked."

"Have you asked your mom about it?"

"No."

"Maybe you should."

Joey stood and picked up his tray. Even the little appetite he'd come into the mess hall with had disappeared. "I've got enough going on right now. Have you ever thought about that?" He turned and walked away before she could say anything.

❋ ❋ ❋

Fort Benning, Georgia
Local Time 0749 Hours

Outside at the bike rack, anger still gripped Joey. He worked the combination to his bike lock and opened the chain. Before he could get to his feet, someone roughly shoved him to the ground.

Joey pushed himself back up, instinctively sliding away from the shadow that fell across him. When he saw who'd shoved him, his heart momentarily stopped.

"Hey," Bones said, grinning wildly. "We were wondering when we were going to run into you here."

Backing away, Joey looked around nervously. Bones was tall and gangly. He looked like one of those old puppets Joey had played with in elementary school. His ears stuck out from his head and were made even more pronounced by his mullet. He wore a black gaming T-shirt and holey jeans.

He was one of the guys who hung with Zero, the guy who'd shot the old Asian man in the mall. Joey couldn't believe Bones was there by himself.

"What are you doing here?" Joey asked.

Bones took out a stick of gum and shoved it into his mouth. "Looking for you. Zero has been wanting to let you know we were here, but you haven't left mommy's house."

"You don't belong here."

Bones smiled, exposing crooked, yellow teeth. "Your buddy Derrick got us in. He talked to the guards, told them our families were all gone and that we really needed help and a safe place to be."

Derrick's father was stationed over in Germany. Derrick's mom was one of those who had disappeared. When Joey had left the camp, he'd run into Derrick, and they'd hung out together until they joined up with Zero and his buddies at the video game arcade.

"Zero's really looking forward to seeing you," Bones said.

Joey almost threw up what little breakfast he'd managed to choke down. "We don't have anything to talk about," Joey said.

"Zero don't see it that way. He wants to make sure you understand things."

"The last time I saw Zero, he tried to kill me."

Bones shrugged. "Yeah, well, he's sorry about that."

Sorry that he didn't kill me? That was the only way Joey could see it. "There's nothing to understand," he said.

"Zero thinks there is. He wants to meet with you and explain how things are."

"How are they?" Joey demanded.

"He don't want you going to the police."

"I haven't."

"*Ever* going to the police."

"I can't," Joey said. "I'll be arrested and tried for murder too."

Bones grinned. "Smart thinking. You keep thinking like that, you're going to stay alive."

That didn't make Joey feel any more relaxed.

"Zero still wants to talk to you," Bones said.

"I don't want to talk to him."

"Too bad. We're gonna be outside the rec center here in camp at eight tonight."

"I'm not coming."

Bones frowned. "That would be stupid. If you don't show up, Zero's going to come looking for you. You don't want any of your friends hurt, do you? Or your mom?"

Joey felt panic swell in his chest. His heart pounded, and he felt dizzy. Even if he knew what to say, he wasn't sure he could speak. The nightmares he'd been having were coming true.

"Eight p.m." Bones held up four extra-long, extra-skinny fingers on each hand. "Be there. Don't make us come looking for you." He turned and walked away.

Weak and dizzy, Joey leaned against the bike rack and tried to think. He didn't know how everything had gotten so messed up. He closed his eyes and was once more in the trunk of the Cadillac Zero had stolen. They'd intended to take him back to one of the empty houses and kill him because they didn't trust him. Joey had managed to escape, and they'd shot at him several times before he vanished into the night.

Now they were here, and he didn't doubt they'd try to kill him again.

"Sergeant Gander?"

Goose came awake instantly. He'd been dozing, not really sleeping. The army had taught him to do that. Soldiers rested when they could and slept when they were able. He'd woken at mess call and received a tray from the guards at his door.

"Yeah?" Goose swung his feet off the field cot and sat up. Lieutenant Swindoll hadn't been any too generous with the accommodations of the house arrest Remington had imposed. The local warlords attacked on a regular basis, hoping to drive the entrenched American soldiers from the city so they could loot it at will. As a result, clean housing was at a premium. Goose occupied a cellar under a dilapidated house that looked ready to fall at any moment.

"Chaplain Miller. We've met."

"Yes, sir." Goose got to his feet. Miller was a captain.

"Might I have a word with you?"

"Of course, sir."

Miller came down the steep stairs with a bright electric lantern fisted before him. The light hurt Goose's eyes, and he looked away instinctively to preserve what night vision he could.

"Sorry." Miller turned the lantern down to a dim glow. "I didn't think about what that was going to do to you."

"It's all right, sir." Goose saluted and stood at attention.

"At ease, Goose. This is just a visit." Miller was in his fifties, a lifer in the Rangers who—scuttlebutt had it—just couldn't step away from the military. He was thin and leathery, with a seamed, plain face, a hooked nose that looked like it had been broken in the past, and shaggy gray eyebrows over deep-set eyes.

Goose automatically dropped into parade rest.

"Take a load off, Sergeant. This is totally informal."

"Yes, sir." Goose hesitated. "There's not much in the way of comfort, sir. I'm not exactly set up for guests here."

Miller surveyed the small room. It stank of damp earth and was roughly seven feet cubed. The field cot took up one whole wall. Shelves containing canned goods took up another. Sacks of rotting potatoes sat on the floor. Bags of onions hung suspended from the low ceiling.

"This is ridiculous. Until I got here, I had no idea your quarters were this bad."

"It's dry."

Miller shook his head. "I can't believe Captain Remington has decided this is in the best interests of these men." He breathed out heavily. "Scratch that. In the best interests of his command."

"The captain has his own view of things, sir." Goose felt strangely self-conscious of his surroundings, as if he were to blame for their meagerness and his inability to be more hospitable.

"He certainly does, and I must tell you, it's not a popular view." Miller hung the lantern from one of the hooks. The dim light chased most of the shadows from the room.

"What do you mean?"

"I mean several of the soldiers—men you came in with as well as soldiers on-site here—are starting to talk about liberating you."

Goose shook his head. "That's nonsense, sir. I'd appreciate if you'd give those men a message from me and let them know they need to stay out of this."

"I'll do that, but I don't think it'll do much good. I've already counseled against anything like that."

"Tell them I fight my own battles." Goose's voice hardened. "Tell them if they come in here without me being relieved by the captain himself, that they'll have to fight me too."

Miller smiled ruefully. "They know that. They've talked about that among themselves. Truthfully, I think that's the only thing keeping them out of here now."

Wearily Goose wiped at his face with a hand. His beard stubble crackled against his rough hand. "Me and the captain, we've been crossways before. We've always seen it through all right."

"Not to intrude into your personal business too much," Miller said, "but you've never been under house arrest before."

"No, sir, I reckon not." Goose's cheeks burned a little in embarrassment at that. During the seventeen years he'd been an army Ranger, he'd never once been called on the carpet like this.

"Why do you think Captain Remington acted the way he did?"

"I disobeyed a command. I was to stay with the convoy. I didn't. Men were lost—good men."

"You helped a village."

"I fell for bait in a trap."

"Have a seat." Miller waved Goose to the cot, then pulled over a barrel from the shelves.

Reluctantly, Goose sat.

"We need to talk about what you're going to do." The electric lantern light softened Miller's features and bleached them to almost the color of bone.

"I'm going to do whatever Captain Remington wants me to do."

"Even if it's wrong?"

Goose bristled a little at that. "Begging your pardon, sir, but I ain't seen nothing Captain Remington has done wrong. I'd defend everything he's done."

"I know. But these times we're in, Goose, these are perilous times. Men are going to be weighed and judged by the way they conduct themselves over these next few years."

"I'm a soldier, sir. I've been a soldier most of my life. If things work out right, I'm going to retire as a soldier."

"You have a young son, don't you?"

A ball of pain suddenly knotted up in Goose's throat. He tried to speak and couldn't. He settled for a nod.

"Where is he now?" Miller's gaze didn't waver.

Goose kept his gaze level, but he felt tears burning his eyes. He wanted to speak, but he could barely breathe.

"All those children disappeared like that." Miller's voice grew soft and husky. "A miraculous thing by all accounts."

Goose forced himself to sit with his forearms resting on his knees. His hands knotted before him, knuckles white.

"You talked to Joseph Baker about this, Goose. Before he was killed, he told me that the two of you had spoken."

"We did." Goose's voice was a hollow whisper in the dank quiet of the cellar.

"He told you he believed this was the time of Tribulation and that the children had been taken to heaven because they were innocents. Do you believe that?"

Hesitating, Goose stared at the chaplain. Finally he forced the words to come. "I want to. God help me, I truly want to."

"But you continue to doubt?"

"Yes, sir." Shame burned Goose's face.

Miller was silent for a moment. "Everyone I've talked to who knows you speaks of what a good man you are."

Goose didn't know what to say to that, so he said nothing.

"They respect you, and as men love fellow warriors, they love you too. But if you're a good man, Goose, why aren't you in heaven with your son?"

Anger stirred in Goose, dark and rich and almost unconquerable. His legs tightened and almost lifted him from the field cot, but a muscle spasm in his left knee blinded him with pain. By the time he had the pain pushed out of his mind, the anger had gone too.

"Your son is safe," Icarus, the rogue CIA agent, had told Goose. *"God came and took your son up as He took all the other children."*

"I don't know, sir," Goose stated quietly.

"Do you believe in God?"

"Yes, sir."

"Have you ever given yourself to Him?"

"I was baptized, sir. Back in Waycross. Momma saw to it all of us were."

"Your mother made that decision for you?" Interest gleamed in Miller's gray eyes.

Goose shrugged. "Momma was a powerful churchgoer when she was alive, sir. She talked Daddy into getting baptized before they were married. When the time came, she let me know she wanted me baptized too."

"So what did you do?"

"I got baptized."

"Did you talk to God about this?"

"No, sir. Didn't have to. Momma was enough."

"Have you ever asked God into your heart, to forgive your sins, to work His will through you?"

Goose immediately felt uncomfortable. "Momma and Daddy taught me wrong from right, sir. I wasn't ever no trouble to them. Everything I've done, I've been proud of."

"It's not enough to be a good man in this world, Goose. Unless you're perfect—and nobody is—then you've got to let God work through you, too."

"I figure He's had me do things from time to time. I've gone to church, and I've given time and money to help out."

"That's just lip service. God wants a personal relationship with you." Miller paused and licked his lips. "He may have chosen to put you through this, through these times, to build that personal relationship with you."

When he spoke, Goose's words had a hard, dangerous edge to them that he didn't expect. "Then God picked a bad way to try to get me on His good side. You don't take a man's son from him without an explanation. You don't strand a bunch of soldiers in harsh and unfriendly lands just so they can get chopped to pieces by an invading army or by warlords gathering around like carrion feeders. Meaning no disrespect to you, I don't approve of God's ways of doing things. And I ain't feeling any too friendly toward God about now."

Downtown Sanliurfa
Sanliurfa Province, Turkey
Local Time 0549 Hours

Driving his personal Hummer along the downtown street, Remington was cognizant of the suspicious and hostile stares he drew from the citizens who'd decided to press their luck by staying in the city. He disregarded them almost automatically. The way people felt about him was something to factor into his plans but nothing that could deflect or cripple his efforts.

And Remington knew that whatever fear and respect he commanded was nothing like the hold Goose seemed to have on so many of the soldiers in his unit.

They're my men, Remington thought angrily. *I'm the one that decided to go to OCS. I'm the one that took the risks and the abuse everyone handed me while I busted my butt to make something of myself. Goose didn't do that.*

Officer Candidates School hadn't been an easy choice for Remington. He and Goose had shared a blue-collar background, though they were from different parts of the country.

Goose had elected not to take his chances with the college boys and elite. Remington had risked his pride and ego by signing up; then he'd sacrificed a large part of his life pursuing the grades he'd needed to earn his second lieutenant's bars.

He'd progressed rapidly after that, always pushing his way up through the ranks. He hadn't earned any friends there, either. As it stood, he was an ill fit among the officers and the enlisted.

Until recently, though, he'd always had Goose. He cursed bitterly.

The problem was, he still had Goose. The sergeant didn't even have the decency to die when Remington had set him up.

Twice.

But Remington felt confident Goose wasn't going to come out of the box he was in now.

❊   ❊   ❊

United States 75th Army Rangers Outpost
Harran
Sanliurfa Province, Turkey
Local Time 0551 Hours

Miller was quiet for a moment. "I didn't always approve of God's ways either. I suspect that's why I'm here." He paused. "As a chaplain, I've been thirty years in the army. I've always told myself I was doing God's work. But I stopped being a big fan of it over twenty years ago."

The electric lantern flickered for a moment, then swung slightly from side to side. Goose watched it with interest.

"I've held dying soldiers in my arms." Miller's voice cracked. "Watched young men die scared and in pain. I've tended women who'd been raped and savaged by enemy soldiers—or even by men whose eternal salvation I was supposed to secure. I've buried children in Iraq, Kosovo, South Korea, and a handful of countries in Africa." He blew out a breath. "At some point I started asking myself if this was truly God's work."

"Momma always said the devil was loose in the world," Goose said. "She told me he was the reason bad things happen to folks."

Miller nodded. "Your mother was right, of course. But somewhere in that, I lost sight of it. But it's not just Satan. It's men. They have free will. They can choose to be close to God or distant from Him. I suspect a lot of them get out of the habit of making that choice or figure once they make it that they don't have to tend to the relationship."

Goose studied the pain he saw etched on the chaplain's face. Men who talked of war had such looks. Goose had seen it in his own face every now and again. "You could have gotten out of the military a long time ago," Goose pointed out.

Miller grinned wryly. "I could have. You could have too. Why didn't you?"

"Ain't in me to be anything other than what I am."

"The private security sector has grown a lot over the last few years.

You could have signed on with a firm, got a bigger paycheck, and been closer to home. Probably been home more often."

"Yes, sir. It's been pointed out to me. I've had offers. Men I've trained are there now."

"So why didn't you do that?"

Goose reflected on the reasons for a moment. He'd never thought about it too deeply because he'd never been interested in leaving the army. "Because, sir, I never quit on anything I've ever set my mind on. And at the end of the day, I serve a flag, a country, and a way of life. Not some corporate bottom line."

"Do you think life is that simple?"

"*My* life is. I keep it simple."

Miller smiled. "No wonder you're so well liked."

That embarrassed Goose. He shook his head. "My job isn't to be liked. I just do what I'm told to do."

"Except when you don't."

"Yes, sir. But I'll stand to take the fall for that."

Leaning back, Miller looked around the cellar. "Yet for all that, here you sit under house arrest."

Goose remained silent.

"Actually," Miller went on, "it's worse than that. If the armed men guarding the cellar entrance are any indication."

"The captain's just keeping me honest."

"Do you really think that's what those men are there for?"

"I wasn't trained to second-guess a commanding officer," Goose said.

"You may have to, Sergeant." Miller's voice came a little harder now. "The men out there ready to champion you aren't happy with how things are going. Most of them aren't sure that circumstances back home are safe for their families. In fact, most of them have lost family. Just like you lost your son."

Goose winced. He forced himself to breathe as an image of Chris momentarily filled his thoughts. Guilt hammered him when he told himself he had to quit thinking about his son at the moment. For that split second, he rebelled against being a soldier. Then he grew calm.

"You know," Miller said, "if you think about it, maybe this next seven years of unrest and horror we're about to face is God putting all of us under house arrest. We're here by choice, and we're going to have to work our way through it."

"If you want to believe that, you go on ahead."

"Can you think of another reason everything's happened as it has?"

Goose didn't say anything.

"This isn't a good time to be without answers," Miller went on.

"I know that, but I don't have any."

"The men—many of them—trust you, Goose. They believe you care about them and have their best interests at heart. They don't feel the same way about Captain Remington."

"Then they're making a mistake. He's a good man."

"I don't doubt that you believe that," Miller replied. "But with you sitting here in this cellar, maybe you can see how some of them would begin to doubt it."

Goose folded his arms across his chest and leaned back against the earthen wall. He *could* see how men would think that. Remington, for whatever reason, had made a critical mistake.

"What makes it worse," Miller said, "is that the man who killed Corporal Baker hasn't yet been found."

"The captain has a detail looking for the person or persons who did that."

"Why aren't you on that detail?"

"Captain Remington felt I'd serve the company better elsewhere."

Miller regarded Goose for a moment. "Then the captain has made another error in judgment. The men want *you* investigating Corporal Baker's murder."

"We don't know that it was a murder." Goose automatically repeated the line Remington had taken on the incident. "It could have been a tragic mistake."

"Strange that we haven't had a tragic mistake before or since. Don't you think?"

"This is a war zone, Chaplain. Things happen out here that don't happen during peacetimes."

Miller's gaze pierced Goose. "Do you think Corporal Baker's death was a tragic mistake, Sergeant?"

Goose tried to answer immediately that it was. But the words got stuck in his throat. By the time he got the way clear, it was too late.

"I don't think so either," Miller said. "Corporal Baker wasn't liked by Captain Remington. His efforts to tend to the men's religious needs were not appreciated." He took a breath. "It shames me that I wasn't one of those leading the men in prayer. Instead, I was drawn to Corporal Baker and looked to him for answers I should have known myself."

Hanging from the rafter, the electric lantern shimmied. Light wavered throughout the cellar. Uneasiness descended on Goose. He checked his watch.

"It's morning outside, right?" he asked.

"Yes."

"We got clear visibility?"

Miller nodded and looked slightly puzzled.

The lantern vibrated again. A puff of dust descended from the wooden crossbeams that shored up the earthen ceiling.

"What's wrong?" Miller asked.

Goose nodded at the lantern. "Vibration like that, coming steady, means we got armored cav moving around somewhere."

"We don't have many tanks or Bradleys here."

"I know. I'm crossing my fingers that it's just earth tremors."

"Wouldn't they be noticed by someone else in the camp?"

"Not necessarily."

"I thought the nearest Syrian armor was days from here."

"That was according to the last reports." Goose stood. The pain in his leg flared to renewed life, and he winced. "Captain Remington's kept the scouts pulled back, and we're not doing any air recon because our pilots have been sitting ducks for entrenched Syrian ack-ack guns."

The antiaircraft guns had knocked down five scout planes in the last two weeks. Air support was as hard to come by as armored cav, and Remington didn't want any of it squandered.

"We've been working blind south of the border," Goose went on. "Satellite recon has been iffy."

The lantern swung wider this time.

"Excuse me," Goose said. He limped up the stairs carved into the earth. At the top, he rapped on the door with a handful of knuckles.

"Who is it?" one of the guards demanded.

"Sergeant Gander."

The hole the men had drilled into the door darkened as someone stuck his eye to it. "Back away from the door."

Angrily Goose took two steps down the stairs.

"What do you want?" the guard asked.

"I need to talk to Lieutenant Swindoll."

"Can't let you out, Sarge. It'll be best if you go on back down and have a seat. Where's the chaplain?"

"He's fine."

"You need to let him see Lieutenant Swindoll," Miller said from behind Goose.

"No can do. I'm under Captain Remington's direct orders."

"Then get the lieutenant here." Goose used his command voice.

The guard banged against the door with the butt of his assault rifle. Goose identified the heavy thump immediately.

"You don't give any orders here, Sarge. Not anymore. Now you back away from the door. Chaplain, your visit's over. You're coming out of the hole."

Goose retreated down the steps. Miller had to go first because there wasn't room to step past. Back in the cellar, they traded places, and Miller went up.

"I'll get Lieutenant Swindoll," Miller promised Goose.

Goose nodded. The lantern swung as another puff of dust dropped to the floor.

"You'd better make it quick," Goose growled.

"I will." Miller hurried up the steps.

Bright sunlight stabbed into Goose's eyes when the door opened. Then Miller passed through, and the darkness returned.

Goose sat on the steps and watched the lantern as it danced again.

Downtown Sanliurfa
Sanliurfa Province, Turkey
Local Time 0605 Hours

SCUDs and missiles had destroyed many of the downtown buildings. Bombing runs by Syrian planes and the attack on the city only weeks before accounted for other damage. Remington had put Rangers on cleanup detail to make sure the streets were clear enough to navigate in case they had to. They'd been aided and abetted by the United Nations teams that had survived the attack along the border and had regrouped in Sanliurfa. Eventually citizens had joined in.

For the most part, the cleanup detail had amounted only to shoving debris to one side of the street or the other. They didn't have time to haul the remains of the broken buildings away, and there was no real place to dump everything that had been destroyed.

Earthmovers roared and snorted like mechanical beasts all around the city as they labored to continue clearing streets. With the Syrian army and air force mostly intact, Remington had had no choice except to figure out fallback positions within the city. If they were pursued from Sanliurfa, they were going to be targets while they raced to the next city.

A moment later, Remington reached the street he wanted. It took some scouting to find streets because he was having all the signage torn down as well. In case an invading Syrian ground effort reached them and had maps, directions would be harder to figure out without neatly labeled streets and thoroughfares.

He stopped at the intersection and spotted the restaurant he was looking for. It was open. Bright flags—Turkish, United States, British, Canadian, French, and Russian—flew above the open-air café.

The fact that the restaurant was open didn't surprise Remington. War zones brought capitalists swarming like flies to honey. Everywhere he'd served, there had always been a thriving black market and local entrepreneurs willing to risk their necks to make a profit.

He turned onto the street and took a space out front next to a station wagon loaded down with chicken crates. Evidently not everyone had finished leaving. There were still a few rats deserting the ship.

Felix Magureanu's midnight blue Mercedes sat nearby. Though a patina of dust covered the city, the luxury car looked freshly scrubbed. The personalized license plate on the back read, *DEALZ.*

❊   ❊   ❊

Local Time 0609 Hours

The restaurant's interior was clean and well lit. The power was out; electricity throughout Sanliurfa was generally absent, except in key locations like the hospital and the mess area, where food perishables were kept refrigerated. But there were plenty of candles. The burning wax filled the air with a sweet, heavy scent.

"Welcome," a young woman greeted. She wore black slacks and a white dress shirt. "Will you be dining with us today?"

"I'm looking for a friend."

"You are Captain Remington?"

"Let me guess," Remington said irritably. "The uniform gave it away."

"I am sorry, but I see many uniforms. They all look the same to me. It's hard to tell American soldiers from British and the others."

"I'm Remington."

The hostess smiled. "Good. Your friend was wondering how long he would be kept waiting. This way, please."

Remington followed the woman across the restaurant's floor space. Only a handful of patrons sat at the tables. A ragtag family that matched the station wagon sat near the front windows, obviously concerned about their chickens. A handful of soldiers, all of them wearing blue berets of the United Nations, occupied other tables.

A moment later, the hostess showed Remington to a private dining room in the back.

She knocked on the door.

"Come in," a booming voice called from within.

The hostess slid the door open and ushered Remington inside. The wood paneling and tables were old and dark, looking black as ink in the uncertain shadows created by the wavering candlelight. "Would you like anything to drink?" she asked.

"Coffee," Remington said.

"Of course." The hostess left.

"Good morning, Captain." Felix Magureanu sat in front of a superthin computer. He waved Remington to the chair on the other side of the square table. Candles stood at attention in an elegant centerpiece.

Remington removed his hat, set it on the table, and took a seat.

The long fingers of one of Felix's hands trailed through his red goatee. His head was shaved and pale as milk, matching the rest of his complexion. He looked like a man who'd never been out in the sun. As always, wraparound sunglasses with ruby lenses hid his eyes. His black suit was Italian and tailored to his lean, hard physique. A gold Rolex gleamed on one wrist. Rings adorned his fingers.

"You're late," Felix said.

Irritation gnawed at Remington. Although he'd learned to work with Felix, he hadn't learned to care for him. The man was too arrogant to be likeable. Remington kept his expression neutral. "You asked for this meeting, not me."

"True." Felix leaned forward and accessed the Internet on his laptop. A small satellite unit sat near the computer on the table. "I wanted to talk to you about Sergeant Gander."

Remington waited just a beat, making sure he had Felix's full attention. "Sergeant Gander isn't any of your concern."

Felix frowned like a disappointed child. "In that regard, Captain, I'm afraid we disagree. I feel that the sergeant is very much a threat to what we're trying to do here."

"Before we explore that possibility," Remington said, "maybe you'd like to clarify exactly what it is we're trying to do."

"What do you think you're trying to do?"

"Survive. I've got the Syrian army waiting to pounce across the border and encroach on Turkey. If they do, they intend to kill anyone who tries to stop them." Remington paused for effect. "That would be me."

"Good, good." Felix rubbed his hands together enthusiastically. "Deep resolve. A show of force. It's reassuring to see that you're taking this matter so personally. War, with all the technological advances, has become too dispassionate for my taste."

"What do you know about war?"

"A challenge, Captain?" Felix grinned mockingly. "Do you think I've never been in a war? never killed? never had blood on my hands that wasn't my own?"

The threat hung naked and ugly in the air. For just a moment, a primitive fear touched Remington, and he despised the weakness he felt within himself. He couldn't see anything in Felix to be wary of, but the fear was there all the same.

"Killing is easy," Remington said. "Fighting someone to the death, when they have just as good a chance of killing you as you do of killing them—that's different."

"Do you give all your enemies chances?" Felix looked delightfully appalled.

"They all have whatever chance they can make for themselves."

"If that's your attitude, I'm surprised you're still alive and walking around."

"I'm good at what I do."

"Why give them any chance?"

"I didn't say I gave them chances."

Felix shook his head in obvious disapproval. "You take a risk of dying. That's foolish."

Quick as a wink, Remington unleathered the Beretta M9 from his hip and took direct aim at Felix's right eye. The barrel never wavered. The captain's forefinger was on the trigger, ready to fire, not along the guard.

"I don't take kindly to being called foolish, especially by a fool," Remington said softly.

Felix didn't move. His grin never faltered. "I guess not."

"I don't like you." Remington stared hard at the other man. "I didn't like you the first time I laid eyes on you. It wouldn't be much of a decision for me to ventilate your head."

"Then do it." Felix's voice was low and throaty. His eyes gleamed excitedly. "Pull the trigger and let's see what happens."

Remington wanted to. The temptation within him was strong. Not just for himself but for Goose too. Felix represented an obvious threat to Goose.

"Why choose to threaten me like this?" Felix asked. "Aside from not liking me?"

Remington didn't answer.

"Is it because of the sergeant?"

"Leave him out of this."

Felix shook his head. "Your attachment to Sergeant Gander may well be your downfall, Captain."

"I can handle Goose."

"From where I'm sitting, it doesn't look like it." Moving slowly, Felix tapped a key on the notebook computer's keyboard.

Immediately the LCD screen changed. A segment of OneWorld NewsNet flashed on.

"Sergeant Gander is turning out to be something of a celebrity, isn't he?" Felix taunted.

Although he didn't want to, Remington's attention took in the computer screen. He kept his eyes locked on Felix, but he tracked the news story on the computer.

Footage of the attack on the convoy played. The icon of Goose that had become one of OneWorld NewsNet's most recognized symbols flashed on the screen: it was the silhouette of an American soldier.

"Isn't that precious?" Felix asked. "Goose has his own icon on the television network. Millions of people around the world are getting to know him. He's a hero, isn't he?"

In that moment, Remington hated Goose. He knew Goose hadn't sought out the celebrity status. The Vinchenzo woman had assigned it to him. Remington coveted that attention. He had been the one who had managed to save all those men and machines along the Turkish-Syrian border.

"That's television," Remington snarled. "He's just a man."

"You and I know that, Captain." Felix ran his fingers through his beard. "But there are other people out there who aren't so sure. A man like Sergeant Gander, at a time like this, can be dangerous."

"I can handle Goose," Remington said again. He put as much emphasis in his words as he could muster.

"By putting him under house arrest?"

Remington didn't say anything.

"Surprised I knew that?" Felix cocked an eyebrow that was just as fiery red as his beard. "You shouldn't be. It's on the news." He tapped another key.

On the notebook's screen, Danielle Vinchenzo appeared. Remington watched in silence and left the pistol aimed at Felix Magureanu.

"Things are tense here in Harran, Turkey," Danielle said, facing the camera. "These American soldiers have dug in to try to hold back the advancing Syrian army and help the Turkish military shore up their defenses."

The camera swept across the war-torn cityscape littered with damaged historical buildings. It focused on a lone tower in the distance.

"But there's more tension than just soldiers awaiting an attack or orders," Danielle went on. "The army Rangers stationed here in Harran are confused. Sergeant Goose Gander, whom many of you have gotten to know through these reports, has been placed under house arrest by Captain Cal Remington, the man who's—at least for the moment—in control of the 75th Rangers in Turkey."

Footage of Goose helping carry a hospital litter flashed on the screen. He looked worn and tired. Remington spotted the familiar limp that told him Goose had stressed his bad knee again.

"Wow," Felix said, then laughed. "Doesn't sound like you're going to be on her Christmas card list anytime soon."

The camera cut back to Danielle. "According to the stories being told by the men I've talked to, Captain Remington—"

"And she makes your name sound like something unpleasant."

"—placed Sergeant Gander under house arrest for disobeying orders. Sergeant Gander was assigned to provide security on a supply caravan from Sanliurfa when he stopped to help a village under attack from a local warlord."

"All she needs is a few orphans to really sell this story." Felix grinned hugely.

"Maybe she's the danger," Remington suggested.

Felix kept his attention on the screen. "No. You can't touch her, Captain. That woman's strictly off-limits."

"Says who?"

"Nicolae Carpathia." Felix eyed Remington directly. "He gave me strict orders regarding her part in this little drama."

"He didn't tell me."

"That's one of the reasons I'm here." Felix focused on the pistol for a moment, then back at Remington. "The hostess is on her way back here. Things are going to look strange if you're holding a gun on me when she comes through the door. There are still a few policemen in this town. At the very least, her screams may draw some of the United Nations soldiers in the next room."

Remington didn't say anything.

"Decide what you're going to do, Captain. You've got only a handful of seconds."

"Leave Goose out of this."

"Then you're going to have to find a way to get a handle on him."

"I will. But if you hurt him in any way, I'll kill you. That's a promise." Remington put his pistol away.

Felix grinned at him with a thoughtful expression. "You are a most curious man."

Remington glared at the man, gained no ground, and shifted his attention to the computer. In the next moment, the hostess returned to the private dining room with drinks.

"Is that all you wanted to tell me?" Remington picked up his coffee and sipped. Then he asked the hostess for a menu.

"The menu won't be necessary," Felix said. "I've already taken the liberty of ordering for both of us."

Remington didn't care for that either. It was too invasive, too controlling.

"Your food will be out momentarily," the hostess said when she left.

"No." Felix swirled his wine, peered at the color against the candlelight, then drank with obvious gusto. "I came here to tell you that Nicolae Carpathia is going to persuade the secretary-general and the White House to combine forces over here. As well as throughout the rest of the world."

"Combine forces how?"

"When Nicolae is through, there will be only one military throughout the world. And he will control it. Anyone who doesn't side with him is going to be viewed as an enemy."

"He's wasting his time. The DOD chiefs will never agree to anything like that."

"Nicolae can be quite . . . persuasive."

"I'll believe it when I see it."

Felix smiled again. "You'll be seeing it, and *believing* it, soon enough." He sipped his wine. "In the meantime, you need to find an effective way to deal with your sergeant."

"I'll handle it."

"Handle it. Soon. Before this thing gets any further out of hand. Nicolae would like to see you keep your command intact. He doesn't want the forces over here to become splintered."

"That's not going to happen."

"It was happening under Corporal Baker."

The comment stung Remington's ego. *How does he know so much?* The captain had no clue.

"You were fortunate when Baker was killed." Felix's eyes gleamed.

"Very fortunate. Even though Baker wasn't saying anything to subvert your command, it was happening. Two camps were starting up between the men."

Remington had known that was trouble when he'd seen it taking place.

"Sometimes, though," Felix said, "you can arrange for *fortune* to come calling." He turned his empty hands palms up.

"You're suggesting I kill Goose."

"If you're going to achieve the goals I have in mind for you, that Nicolae has in mind for you, then you're going to have to push yourself. Merely leaving him behind enemy lines and hoping they kill him isn't going to do it."

When the hostess returned, she brought with her two servers carrying a veritable feast. Despite his reluctance, Remington dug in. But only a few moments later, his walkie-talkie buzzed.

Felix had turned his attention back to the computer and was typing in commands.

Remington dug his ear-throat headset from a pocket and strapped it on. He jammed the cord into the device and listened to the beep that signaled activation. "Remington," the captain barked.

"Sir, I thought maybe you'd want to know that Harran is under attack by the Syrian military."

Anger and dread warred for supremacy inside Remington. He'd known the attack was coming, but he hadn't wanted to deal with it so early. The troops weren't ready, and he didn't have a fallback position set up.

"How do you know that?"

"We're fielding reports from there. Lieutenant Swindoll says it's a massive incursion."

"We missed a troop movement that large? Why didn't the satellite surveillance warn us about the troop movement?"

"The system has been on the blink all night, sir. We kept you updated."

The reports were on Remington's desk. The satellite system had been performing well. Nicolae Carpathia had granted Remington access to the satellites shortly after the disappearances, during the first wave of Syrian attacks.

"Do we have satellite surveillance over that area now?"

"No, sir. We believe our ground relays in the area are being jammed."

Remington's mind flew. It was possible that the Syrians had gotten troops into the city to jam the ground stations. It was just as possible the local and temporary systems were being tasked beyond their capabilities.

Felix focused on the computer. His long-fingered hands flew across the keyboard. "Harran?"

For an instant, Remington held back an answer. He didn't like spreading military intelligence around, nor did he care for anyone else usurping control. But in the end, he needed to see whatever intel was available. "Yes." The admission was grudging at best.

"I can get you access." Felix's confident tone further irritated the captain.

"How?"

Felix smiled. "Danielle Vinchenzo is part of OneWorld NewsNet. We're everywhere."

Remington was only slightly surprised that Felix acknowledged the ties to the international news agency. It was no secret that Nicolae Carpathia owned OneWorld Communications. The Romanian president owned or managed several international companies and corporations. But for a man like Felix, who talked of murder as a good thing, to be affiliated with the broadcasting corporation in any way seemed wrong.

The LCD screen cleared immediately. The focus was tight on Danielle Vinchenzo. The reporter was no longer calm, cool, and collected. Hunkered down behind a stone building, she tried valiantly to report the news.

"—repeat, Mark. The 75th Rangers here in Harran have just come under attack by what is believed to be Syrian forces." Danielle ducked as a nearby explosion threw debris over her.

The camera shot wavered and spun drunkenly. The camera operator cursed and the angle changed as he obviously dropped into what he believed was a better defensive posture.

"Sir?" The prompt came from the outpost officer. "Captain Remington?"

"I'm here." Remington tried to ease his grip on the walkie-talkie.

"Get Harrison and Macauley into my ready room. Tell them I'll be there in ten."

"Yes, sir."

"And keep me updated."

"Yes, sir."

Remington put the radio on standby.

"Your men have lost satellite feeds?" Felix took a sat-phone from inside his jacket. The device was so thin that it hadn't broken the line of the jacket in any way.

"My support staff believes the local relays are being jammed."

Felix smiled. "Well then, we'll have to cut out the local relays, won't we?" He spoke into the phone fluently in a language that wasn't English. It sounded guttural and dark, and Remington could only assume it was Romanian. A moment later, Felix folded the phone and put it away. "You'll have a work-around in place within minutes. It should provide you with anything you need."

Remington wasn't happy. Minutes cost soldiers their lives.

Looking unhappy himself, Felix shrugged. "It's the best I can do, Captain."

Remington stood and took his hat from the table. "I've got to go."

Felix nodded. "I understand. I'm sorry you didn't get to finish your breakfast." He took a roll and buttered it, showing no concern for the violent tableau taking place on his computer.

The camera panned over streets where Rangers took cover. A tank round slammed into a Hummer and threw it end over end till it crashed through a storefront window.

"Are you getting this?" Danielle asked.

"Yeah, yeah," the cameraman muttered angrily. "I'm filming."

"Stay with it."

"I am. *I am.*"

The camera swung around and focused on the Ulu Cami mosque. The Ranger fire team assigned there was trying to call in coordinates for army artillery units. In the next moment, a Syrian jet streaked out of the sky and opened fire. Cannon rounds chopped into the ancient structure, knocking stone and mortar away. A Ranger tumbled over the edge of the mosque's tower, but before he could strike the ground, the jet fired two rockets that exploded against the building. The mosque fell to pieces, tumbling into a pile of rubble.

Remington started for the door.

"Good luck, Captain." Felix waved, then switched his attention back to the computer.

❄   ❄   ❄

Local Time 0631 Hours

Remington clambered into his Hummer, started the engine, and backed out of the parking area. Then he stopped. Felix's midnight blue Mercedes was parked in front of him.

Uncertainty wove a tangled web inside the captain. He was jealous of Goose, and he recognized the potential for a split pull in the command because the first sergeant was so popular, but Goose was his to deal with. No one else had that right.

And no one else is going to tell me what to do or how to do it.

The fact that the satellites had been jammed without anyone's knowledge bothered him too. The feeds came through Carpathia's corporations. Remington didn't know how people there could miss the fact that they were being jammed. The fail-out and recovery had gone on all night, usually lasting for only minutes at a time.

Then Felix had called and demanded a meeting this morning. Another attempt to tell Remington how to do his business.

Snarling an oath, Remington turned the Hummer's wheel a little and released the clutch. The Hummer surged forward, and the reinforced bumper slid across the Mercedes's right rear quarter panel. The luxury car's fender caved instantly, and the security system alarm blared.

Remington experienced momentary satisfaction with the destruction when he imagined Felix's discomfiture, but that quickly faded. Several important resources were at risk in Harran. He had to find a way to save what he could.

With any luck, Goose would be buried in that cellar Lieutenant Swindoll had assigned him.

By the time Chaplain Miller hurried back down the basement stairs, Goose was almost ready to crawl out of his own skin. He'd been pacing for the last twenty minutes in an effort to burn off the excess energy that filled him. In the last seven minutes, the outpost had come alive. Screaming Klaxons and the sound of grinding equipment invaded the basement.

The lantern jumped all the time now.

Miller breathed rapidly and blood suffused his face. "The Syrians are coming."

"The lieutenant knows?"

"Yes. I was in his office trying to persuade him to come see you when we got the news."

"How bad is it?"

"They're throwing everything at us but the kitchen sink."

Fear swarmed Goose for a moment, but he wasn't thinking of himself. The 75th had some old-timers in the unit, like him, but there was a lot of young blood too. Iraq hadn't prepared them for what they'd seen these last few weeks. He knew because he'd buried them.

Goose shook his head in disbelief. "They're catching us flat-footed. How'd they get so close?"

"They jammed the communications relays to the satellites."

"We haven't had sat-recon?"

"Not for hours."

"Swindoll should have known this was coming. Captain Remington should have known."

"The systems out here haven't been reliable all the time."

"You never trust hardware 100 percent. Swindoll should have known that."

"He's today's army." Miller frowned.

"The army's got a lot of tech backing it these days. Good stuff. But too many of these kids rely on the toys too much." Goose blew out his breath in disgust. "It's not completely their fault. The brass puts too much stock in them too. But we're in a fix now."

Miller focused on Goose. "You knew they were coming."

"I thought they were."

"From the lantern."

Goose nodded. "Heavy armor can come quietly sometimes, but the vibrations still give them away."

"The lantern's movements could have been caused by vehicles moving around here."

"Could have been. But it turns out it wasn't." Goose headed up the stairs.

"Where are you going?" Miller hurried to catch up.

"Out. There's a lot of boys out there who are going to be in trouble."

"The lieutenant hasn't released you."

Goose ignored that. He banged on the door. The eye reappeared.

"Get back in your hole, Sarge," the guard snarled.

"The Syrian army's coming." Goose mustered his full voice. "I'm not going to be down here when those troops arrive."

"Until I get different orders, you're staying there."

"Goose," Miller said, "maybe—"

Goose slammed a shoulder into the door. The cheap lock fractured and fell apart. Propelled by his strength and weight, the door swung out and caught the guard flush, driving him from his feet. The harsh sunlight made Goose wince in pain as he stepped outside.

A second guard pointed his M-4A1 at Goose while the first guard tried to get to his feet. "Take another step and I'm going to shoot you."

"You or the Syrians," Goose said. "Either way, I'm not dying down there. Not today." He pointed at the nearby jeep. "I'm going to walk over there and get my gear. If you feel like you have to shoot, I'll understand. But just so we're clear here, I have to get that gear."

The familiar ratchet of assault rifles charging reached Goose's ears.

Several Rangers surrounded the basement. Goose knew he couldn't escape them all. But he couldn't stand idly by either.

"Nobody's going to shoot you, Goose," Sergeant Mack Theissen stated. He was in his early thirties and had been in the Rangers since high school. Lean and leather-faced, he'd seen action in Africa, Kosovo, and Afghanistan. "With what we got coming at us, the last place you need to be is out of the action. These boys are about to realize the error of their ways and stand down." He paused and looked at the soldier holding the rifle on Goose. "Ain't that right?"

With obvious reluctance, the soldier lowered his weapon. "Sure. Just following orders."

"I get that, Private," Theissen said. "Why don't you and your buddy go *follow orders* someplace else? The real soldiers here got a job to do."

The two guards beat a hasty retreat.

Goose crossed to the jeep and got his gear. He strapped on his Kevlar vest, helmet, and sidearm, then picked up the M-4A1 and settled it comfortably in his arms.

"I appreciate what you did, Mack," Goose said quietly, "but when Remington finds out about it, things might not go so easy on you."

Theissen grinned. "Yeah, I figured that out all by myself. But this whole invading Syrian force kinda put me off my feed anyway. The captain being mad at me? I can deal with it. I'll get someone to bring me a deck of cards in the brig and start working on my pension."

Goose couldn't help but grin a little. "Thanks."

"What we got coming at us, we need every able-bodied man."

"How bad is it?"

"Plenty bad. This is a major effort. They're hoping to claim some serious real estate today."

"We're not in a position to stop them."

"No. Best we can do is try to get everybody out safe."

Goose filled his BDUs with extra magazines for the rifle, then strapped on a bandolier. He checked to make certain the water bladder on his LCE was full as the morning heat baked into him.

Antiaircraft guns mounted behind sandbags screamed to life.

Goose glanced at the sky and spotted four fighter jets streaking toward Harran. Missiles jumped from the wings.

"Incoming!"

Men dove for cover wherever they could find it. Many of them faded into the alleys between the buildings.

"Stay away from the windows!" Goose roared as he ran toward a young private who had taken shelter near the closed electronics store next door to the house where he'd been kept captive. "Stay away from the glass!"

The private looked up as Goose closed on him. Goose grabbed the younger man by the sleeve of his BDUs and yanked him to his feet. They ran deeper into the alley.

Theissen picked up Goose's instruction.

The missiles slammed into the city. Goose hunkered down against a wall away from any loose debris and watched as a Ranger fell from the Ulu Cami mosque's tower an instant before one of the missiles took out the structure. The moment seemed surreal as the mosque fell in a heap of loose and broken stones before the sound reached him. The other missiles chewed into the city.

Buried in the thunder and noise of the attack, Goose waited and hoped that casualties would be light. But he knew they wouldn't be.

Cannonfire ripped into the nearby buildings as the jets whipped by overhead. The concussions of the detonations shattered the windows of buildings that weren't hit. Shards of flying glass turned into daggers and jagged spears ready to pierce the flesh of anyone taking shelter nearby.

Goose got to his feet and readied his rifle. He looked at the men around him. "C'mon. You guys didn't come all this way to sit this one out, did you?"

Most of the men had been blooded before the Syrian confrontation, but there were a handful who stood up on shaking knees and had ashen faces. Still, they stood, and that was what the Rangers had trained them to do.

The jets flew past the city and began a turning radius.

"Let's go. Single file and spread out." Goose jogged toward the city's edge where the front line was going to take shape. That was where he belonged.

❋   ❋   ❋

Local Time 0636 Hours

Danielle threw herself to the ground beside a small dentist's office. The Closed sign posted on the door had faded from exposure to the sun.

Gary took cover beside her. His arms wrapped the camera as he sat with his back to the wall. The chin strap on his Kevlar helmet hung loosely, but it reminded Danielle to clap her own back onto her head. She'd grabbed it from the ground when they'd broken for cover.

Machine-gun fire ripped into the buildings and the street. Pockmarks appeared on both. The noise reverberated between the buildings.

"Do we still have satellite feed?" Danielle asked.

Gary looked at her as though she were insane.

Danielle raised her voice. "Can you hear me?"

"I heard you." Gary glanced at the camera, then nodded. "We still have sat-link."

"Then let's get moving."

Gary pointed at a group of Rangers tucked into shelter across the street. "They're not going anywhere. I'm taking that as a sign that we probably shouldn't be going anywhere either."

"They're waiting for orders." Danielle stood and looked up in the sky. The jets had passed again, but they were turning. "We already have our orders. We've got to bring this story to the public."

"I'm thinking maybe the public would understand if we sat here quietly and just spent some time being afraid."

Danielle reached down and pulled Gary to his feet. "You have just as much chance of getting shot sitting there as you do trying to get somewhere else."

"It doesn't feel like it."

"Trust me."

"Man, you get me into more trouble. It's like you're jinxed."

"Thanks. But just keep reminding yourself that what we're doing here might just net you a Pulitzer." Danielle ran back toward the residential area where Goose was being held. She held on to her flak jacket. Perspiration trickled down her body from the heat.

They crammed in tight against a sundries shop as the jets passed overhead again. Cannonfire hammered the building across the street. One of the structures tumbled down in a loose heap of debris.

"I don't think we're going to make it out of this one." Gary breathed rapidly, on the edge of panic.

Danielle grabbed his shoulders and shook him. "You stay with me. Do you hear? Stay with me, and we're going to be fine."

Gary nodded, but he didn't look convinced.

"The army's got helicopters on the other side of the city. We can get out of here in one of those. Do you hear me?"

"Yeah. Yeah, I hear you."

"Good." Danielle took a shuddering breath and hoped what

she told him was the truth. She hoped he at least believed it more than she did, because her belief wasn't so strong. "We need to find Goose."

"Why?"

"Because he's our story." More than that, Danielle wanted to make sure he'd been let out of confinement. "We stick with our story."

United States 75th Army Rangers Outpost
Harran
Sanliurfa Province, Turkey
Local Time 0647 Hours

"Take cover!" Goose watched the fighter jets return for another sweep. He waved the soldiers following him into defensive positions against the supermarket they'd jogged to.

As the jets neared and opened up with their cannons again, the anti-aircraft gunners replied with bursts of fire. Rounds chewed into three of the jets. Goose's sharp eyes spotted the canopy cracking on the lead jet just before the aircraft dove for the ground. Another jet streamed black, oily smoke from one engine and no longer moved as easily in the air.

The lead jet spiraled into the city and headed for the supermarket where the Rangers had gone to cover. The scream of descent rattled through Goose's ears.

"Get down! Get down!" Goose put his right hand on top of his helmet and ducked his face into his left shoulder while he held onto the M-4A1. He thought of himself as the smallest target in the world and did the same for the other Rangers. The jet couldn't hit them. The payload on board wasn't going to—

The jet slammed into the building across the street. Even though he knew better than to look, Goose peered over his forearm anyway. The aircraft drove down into the three-story building like a great nail driven by a huge hammer. The building shattered and fell apart. Rock and mortar were strewn across the street. Several chunks thumped against the supermarket and shattered the plate glass windows filled with advertisements. Flames wreathed the ripped and broken fighter jet.

A moment later, just as Goose thought everything was going to be all right, the remaining ammunition in the jet cooked off. Several explosions tore through the building's corpse and threw more debris into the air and across the street. The next few seconds became a whirling nightmare of potential death.

Once the ammunition was expended, Goose peered at the torn body of the fighter jet. Black smoke curled into the sky. The pilot could not have survived the destruction. He just hoped no one had been inside the building.

"Anybody hit?" Goose asked.

The men quickly acknowledged that none of them was wounded. None of them believed it was possible either. With the storm of flying death that had taken shape around them, everyone was surprised to be alive.

"All right." Goose stood. "On your feet, Rangers. We got a job to do." He ran, giving the fallen jet and the gutted building a wide berth in case there were any more surprises. His bad knee ached with the strain but felt solid enough to push it as long as he didn't try any sudden turns.

❀   ❀   ❀

United States 75th Army Rangers Temporary Post
Sanliurfa, Turkey
Local Time 0651

Remington left the Hummer in front of the building he'd chosen as his command center. Sandbags reinforced the walls. Machine-gun teams surrounded the building. The soldiers standing guard immediately stood at attention and briskly saluted.

The captain performed a quick return salute and stepped through the doorway into the cooler atmosphere of the nerve center. The window-mounted air conditioners hummed in the background, echoed by the rapid-fire pop of the generators that powered them. The computers needed the cooler environment. Screens lit up blue-white in the background.

Lieutenant Archer stood in front of the tactical board in the center of the room. The tactical board was acrylic and unpowered. They worked on it with marker pencils in case the power went down.

The lieutenant was a rawboned man with a neat mustache and an impeccable manner. Captain Sanderson of the British army stood nearby. He was aloof and in his forties, and he served as the liaison for the United Nations forces that had been driven back to Sanliurfa as well. Normally a liaison job would fall to a junior officer; Remington suspected the UN command had chosen to assign Sanderson because he was a man with rank equal to Remington's.

Archer spotted Remington bearing down on them. The lieutenant turned quickly, dropped his clipboard under his left arm, and saluted crisply. "Sir."

"At ease, Lieutenant." Remington stopped at the nearest computer and gazed at the screen. "We have satellite recon again?"

"Yes, sir. The satellites just came back online."

Remington let out a sigh of relief. At least Felix's word was good.

On the screen, Remington stared at the advancing line of Syrian troops and cavalry. Tanks, armored personnel carriers, and artillery rumbled rapidly over the broken terrain headed into Harran. All of the tanks, APCs, and howitzers were Soviet made. The equipment was decades old but still serviceable and deadly.

"How far out are they?"

"Twenty, twenty-five minutes," Archer said.

"Have we got our birds in the air?" Remington walked behind the line of techs at their workstations.

"Yes, sir. I scrambled the helos as soon as you ordered them in."

On one of the screens, a line of fifteen helicopter gunships flew nap-of-the-earth across the scrublands toward Harran. Six wide-bodied UH-60 Black Hawk helicopters outfitted for medical transport and rescue trailed behind.

"What about the fuel convoy?" Remington stared at the computer screen a moment longer, then checked the marker board out of habit.

"En route as well."

"Have you got an ETA on the helos arriving in Harran?"

"Five minutes after the Syrians, sir."

Remington cursed.

"Pardon me, Captain." Sanderson stepped forward and imposed himself. "If I may speak."

"Quickly." Remington remained deliberately brusque. He and the United Nations troop commanders hadn't quite worked out their pecking order. The UN officers had a better knowledge of the Turkish army, but the UN forces were appreciably smaller than the Ranger troops.

"Forgive me if I'm out of line, but aren't you risking a lot by sending in those helos?"

"There's a lot at stake, Captain." Remington fixed the other man with a scathing glance. "In case you didn't know it, I have a lot of Rangers in Harran. The United States Army isn't in the habit of discarding men."

"No, sir. I understand that. But it seems to me you're risking a lot more by deploying those helos. We're not exactly in our fighting prime here. Those machines could be hard to replace."

"Maybe you'd feel differently if you were in Harran right now."

"Those men knew the risks when they went there."

Remington glared at the British captain. "*I* knew the risks when I sent them there. They're there because *I* put them there. And I'm going to do my best to get them out of there."

"Yes, sir, I understand that. But we're not at liberty to squander hardware resources—"

"Enough." Remington turned from the man. "If you want to go talk to your people about squandering resources, go ahead. I'm not going to squander Rangers that are the finest fighting men alive in this miserable corner of the world. If you can't contribute something that will help me get those men out of there, keep your mouth shut—"

"Sir—"

"—or I'll have you escorted out."

Sanderson's ruddy complexion deepened as he frowned in displeasure.

"Are we clear?"

"Positively crystal."

"Outstanding." Remington turned to Archer. "Keep this board updated."

"Yes, sir." Archer drew his marker and set to work.

Remington addressed the communications officer. "Get Swindoll for me."

On the screen, the Syrian army relentlessly moved forward.

✳   ✳   ✳

United States 75th Army Rangers Outpost
Harran
Sanliurfa Province, Turkey
Local Time 0708 Hours

"What are you doing out here?" Lieutenant Swindoll demanded.

Goose was suddenly conscious of the attention he drew from the soldiers around the lieutenant. All of them were familiar faces, but only some of them appeared friendly.

"I came to help, sir." Goose met the young lieutenant's gaze.

"You were supposed to remain under house arrest."

"That didn't seem to be something that would help in the current situation."

"Sergeant." Swindoll drew himself up and turned on Goose. The lieutenant dropped his hand on the pistol at his hip. "You were given orders to remain under house arrest. Men were assigned to keep you there."

"They tried."

"Begging the lieutenant's pardon, but Sergeant Gander didn't get here on his own." Theissen stepped forward. "He had help."

"You did this?"

"Sir, I—several of us—believe Sergeant Gander needs to be out here. With men that are prepared to fight and die in the next few minutes."

"I hadn't expected this from you, Sergeant Theissen."

Theissen grinned but little of the effort was humorous. "Truth to tell, I didn't expect it from me either. But I gotta admit, I'm a little proud of myself."

For a moment the tension held. Lieutenant Swindoll was loyal to Remington. That much was immediately obvious. Several other men were as well. All of them were afraid, and most of them were young and inexperienced and still believed that an officer was the only one who could get them out of a bad situation.

"You got the Syrian army headed this way, sir." Goose worked to sound respectful. "You're going to need every man you can muster. This . . . this is where I belong."

That simple truth hung on the hot, dry air.

"Goose." The voice coming through Goose's headset belonged to Remington. Goose knew the captain had been monitoring his com channel; hearing from him now was no surprise.

"Yes, sir."

"Go to our private frequency."

Goose did. As he flicked the headset, he watched surprise widen Swindoll's bloodshot eyes.

"I'm here, sir."

"Don't talk. Just listen. You know the kind of jam we're in. We can't hold Harran. We'd never planned on it. Of course, we'd never planned on getting caught with our pants down either."

Goose took his binoculars from his BDUs and slung the assault rifle. He stepped up onto the nearest Hummer and stood on the rear deck. Training the binoculars due south, he saw the line of dust in the distance that marked the advance of the Syrian army.

"I've got helos en route." Remington's voice remained calm. "The problem is that they're going to arrive there probably three to five minutes after the Syrian army does."

Perspiration trickled down Goose's stubbled face as he realized what Remington was about to ask the Rangers to do. Three to five minutes wasn't much of a commute, but it could be a lifetime on a battlefield when forces were engaged.

"You know what I'm going to order you to do, don't you?"

"Yes, sir."

"There's not another way around it."

Goose knew that a lot of the men with him were probably going to die. Maybe he'd die too. "I know that."

"If you try to retreat, they'll roll over you."

"Yes, sir."

"What I need you to do, Goose, is to hold that position. For three to five minutes."

A lifetime.

"Long enough for the helos to arrive." Remington spoke calmly, as if he were ordering a drink in a bar. "They're equipped with M139s. When the helos drop their payloads, that should buy you some time to retreat."

"Yes, sir. But after three to five minutes, there may not be a clear division between us and them."

"Understood. It's the best I have to offer. I don't want to lose those men."

"Neither do I." The dust line in the distance grew taller and nearer.

"Then let's do the best we can to bring them home."

"Yes, sir. You'll have to clear this with Lieutenant Swindoll." Goose was acutely conscious of the lieutenant's grim stare.

"I will. You just work your magic, Goose. Buy those helos time."

"Yes, sir."

Megan stared at the pile of papers on the desk before her. She felt overwhelmed. No matter how much she did, there still seemed to be an incredible amount yet to be done. She was beginning to believe that every time she took her eyes off of the papers they duplicated themselves.

God, help me, because I'm not going to be able to do this on my own.

She took a deep breath and reached for the top sheet on one of the stacks. The paperwork wasn't going to do itself.

Someone knocked on the door of her office. Feeling guilty about the relief she felt at the distraction, Megan looked up.

Sue Davis stood in the doorway. She was in her early thirties and married to one of the Rangers currently assigned to Germany. Thanks to the level of technology they both had access to, she was able to talk to him on a regular basis.

Megan waved her into the room and stood to greet her.

"You're working late. Did I catch you at a bad time?"

"No. Just up to my ears in paperwork. Have a seat." Megan waved toward one of the chairs in front of the metal desk.

Sue wrinkled her nose. "I guess the military doesn't really do much in the way of creature comforts. That desk doesn't exactly scream *success.*"

Megan sat and smiled. "I don't think it's supposed to."

Sue was a real estate agent in Columbus—a very successful real estate agent. She was also a super mom, somehow managing to handle three rambunctious kids while her husband was out of the country. In addition to the real estate job, she was a homeroom mom and soccer coach. She looked tired and her clothes were a bit rumpled after a long day and a late evening in the office, but her brunette hair was neatly cut, and her business suit looked fitted, though Megan was pretty sure Sue had done the alterations herself.

"When I saw you were still here, I thought I'd come by to check on you."

"I appreciate that, but there's no need. I'm handling everything."

Sue hesitated, started to say something, then stopped. She tried again a moment later. "I still get up every morning thinking about Micah." Her eyes welled up with tears. "I still . . . miss him . . . very much."

Seeing the woman's pain brought Megan's back to the surface as well. She was conscious of Chris's photograph sitting on the corner of her desk. He was smiling and happy, and he looked so much like Goose with his wheat-colored hair and blue eyes that her heart felt like it was breaking all over again.

"I know." The words came from Megan's throat like broken glass. Micah had been—*still is*, Megan corrected herself—Sue's youngest child. He was eight years old, and he'd vanished like Chris and every other child younger than thirteen.

Sue blinked away her tears without touching them so she wouldn't ruin her makeup. "I still catch myself setting out his plate for breakfast. Makes me feel crazy, you know."

"You're not. It just means you're thinking of him."

"You'd think I'd remember that he's not here anymore."

Megan hesitated. "This . . . isn't easy to get used to."

"Not even when you believe in God?"

Megan met the woman's eyes with her own. "Not even when you believe in God. I believe—no, *I know*—that Chris is in heaven right now. Just waiting on me to join him. And I will be there soon because I know God has touched me and washed me of my sins. But I still miss my son."

Sue nodded. "I can't . . ." Her voice broke and she tried again. "I can't . . . help but be mad at God."

"Being mad at God is all right. I was mad at Him too. After I figured out what had happened. Being mad is normal."

"It doesn't seem very smart to be mad at Him."

"Not on the face of it, no. But by being mad at God, you're acknowledging Him. It's like when you fight with Stan over whatever you fight with him about. You know he's there, and you know he loves you. But you're mad at him anyway."

"It just seems there could have been a better way to do this."

Megan was quiet for a moment, thinking about her words before she said them. No matter how she felt about them, they still needed to be said.

"Do you know what's coming, Sue? what the next seven years are going to entail?"

"I do." The other woman's voice was a hoarse whisper. "I have to tell you, I'm scared. I'm scared for me and I'm scared for Robby and Taylor."

Those were her older son and daughter.

"We're going to see horrible things." Sue's hands knotted in her lap. "I've started going to church here on base Sundays and Wednesdays. Not all of the churches are talking about the Tribulation. That really surprises me, you know?"

"I know."

"Not everybody believes. Not even now."

"Not yet, but they will." Megan was certain about that.

"I hope it's not too late."

"That's why we're trying to get the word out."

Sue nodded. "So many people out there are scared, but so many others don't seem like they care. With everything that's gone on, how could they choose to live in ignorance?"

"People have since the Bible was written. Since Moses came down Mount Sinai carrying the two stone tablets that contained the Ten Commandments."

"I should talk." Sue laughed bitterly. "Obviously my family has been missing some fundamentals that were covered in the Bible."

Megan didn't want the woman to feel like she was the only guilty one. "All of us were. We just didn't believe. Not the way we're supposed to."

"But I thought good people were believers."

"Goose had a friend named Bill who said most people were good people but not believers. In order to be a believer, you have to ask God to come into your heart and forgive your sins and give you eternal salvation. At the time, I didn't think much about what Bill was saying. I was a good person. Goose was a good person. We went to church. But I didn't stop and ask God to save me, to point me along the path and the work that He'd have me do."

"But now you have?"

Megan nodded.

"When?"

"Before the court case." Megan had been tried for improper conduct regarding a young patient. Videotape had revealed that Megan hadn't hidden Gerry from his abusive father but that he'd disappeared in midair after falling from her grip.

"I heard about that." Sue stared at Megan. "I was told that the boy vanished before he hit the ground."

For a moment, Megan was back on that rooftop. Then she pushed the memory away. "He did. But even after that I didn't ask God's forgiveness and for Him to save me. It was only when there was nowhere else for me to turn, when I couldn't deal with thinking Chris could possibly be anywhere else, that I turned to God."

Hesitantly Sue looked at Megan. "I've tried to pray to God. Honestly I have. But I can't quite find the right words."

"They don't have to be the right words. They just need to be your words."

"All right." Sue got quiet and stood. "I've taken enough of your time. I really just wanted to stop by and see how you were doing."

"I appreciate that." Megan looked into the other woman's eyes. "Would you like me to?"

"What?"

"Pray with you?"

"Yes." Sue's voice was a croak. "Yes, I would."

Megan took the other woman's hands. Together, they knelt on the floor and prayed. As Megan watched, she saw a smile spread across Sue's face. The sight reminded her of her own feeling of well-being when she'd asked God to come into her heart.

After a little while longer, Sue looked up at Megan. "I didn't know . . ."

Megan nodded. "It's wonderful."

"I've got to talk to Robby and Taylor."

"That's a great idea, but they have to come to God in their own way. You can't force it."

"I won't. I'll just talk to them and tell them what I found here today." She stood, and Megan rose as well. Without warning, Sue threw her arms around Megan and hugged her fiercely. "Thank you."

"You're welcome."

❋ ❋ ❋

Local Time 0026 Hours

Tired, Megan stood in front of the drink machine in the vending area. She stared at the buttons and felt like they'd been written in hieroglyphics.

"There isn't anything in that box that you haven't seen before. Make your selection and move along, girlfriend."

The raucous voice could belong to only one person. Megan turned and saw Evelyn Banks standing behind her. Evelyn was in her sixties, surely past retirement age, but she insisted she wasn't yet sixty-five, so personnel had kept her on the payroll. Skinny and feisty, Evelyn worked as a custodian in the building. She knew every person who worked there as well, and she knew all the news and gossip too. She wore a faded blue sweater over her khaki shorts and 82nd Airborne T-shirt. Granny glasses covered her keen gray eyes. She wore her silver hair up in a bun.

"Hey, Evelyn," Megan greeted.

"Hey, yourself. Have you picked a drink yet? If you haven't, you can have my dollar and my favorite flavor is grape."

Megan selected a water and pressed the button. "Sorry. I was lost in thought."

"I guess so." Evelyn fed her dollar into the machine. She punched a button and a grape soda tumbled into the dispensing slot. "Must have been some mighty heavy thinking." She twisted the top off the drink and took a healthy slug.

"Long days will do that to you." Megan opened her water and took a sip.

Evelyn glanced at her watch. "Not to mention long nights. I'd tell you that you probably need to get home, take a load off, get some sleep, but I know you've got all those teenagers waiting for you. I swear, you must be crazy to put yourself through all that."

"Maybe a little. But I enjoy the kids. And they need someone."

"What about you?" Evelyn took another healthy drink.

"What about me?" Megan was confused.

"Don't you need somebody?"

"You mean Goose?"

"Unless you got another man I don't know about, that's exactly who I'm talking about."

Megan's face warmed in embarrassment. "No."

"Too bad. I love to gossip. Probably my biggest sin." Evelyn shrugged helplessly. "Probably what's kept me here after everyone else has gone on to heaven."

"Then why do you do it?"

"What? Gossip?"

"Yes."

"Girlfriend, life wouldn't be worth living without those juicy little morsels every now and again. I live for gossip." Evelyn grinned. "And anyway, I'm just kidding about that. I had a long talk with my preacher. Him and God have got things sorted out, and I think he helped me sort them out as well. I know I'm feeling a whole lot better about life these days."

"That's wonderful."

"You know, that's exactly how it feels, too." Evelyn adjusted her glasses. "But I was serious about having somebody for yourself."

"Goose is over in Turkey."

"I know. And they ain't no telling when he's coming home." Evelyn shook her head. "It's just sad is all."

"What's sad?"

"That the two of you can't be together. Especially right now, when you need each other the most." Evelyn drank more of the grape soda, then bought a package of peanuts from another vending machine. She opened the peanuts and poured them into the bottle. Purple fizz bubbled up.

Megan watched, almost fearful the concoction might explode. It was something she knew would have delighted Chris.

Evelyn swirled the peanuts in the grape soda. "I probably shouldn't do this. Those peanuts play heck with my dentures." She took a swig, crunched peanuts, then hooked a finger in her mouth to adjust her teeth.

Despite the uninhibited display, Megan was paying only slight attention. Her mind had seized on the idea that the old woman had set forth.

What they needed—what they *all* needed—was a sense of family. That was why so many teens had crashed at Megan's house. They had nowhere else to go to get that sense of family. Otherwise they'd have gone there.

It was a sobering realization, and it made her miss Goose even more fiercely.

"Megan! Megan!" Dorthea Whitlow came around the corner and peered into the vending area. "I thought I saw you in here."

Panicked, Megan gave her full attention to Dorthea. The other woman was about her age, but she didn't have a husband or children.

"You've got to come." Dorthea waved one hand.

"What's wrong?"

"It's on television. The Syrians just crossed over the border. They're headed into Harran now."

Megan recognized the name. That was where Goose was. She hurried after Dorthea as they hustled back to the nurses' station.

Oh, God, please don't let anything happen to Goose.

United States 75th Army Rangers Outpost
Harran
Sanliurfa Province, Turkey
Local Time 0727 Hours

Heat shimmered across the drylands between Harran and the advancing line of Syrian armored. Fighter jets continued assaulting the city. Waves of cannonfire and rockets destroyed the beehive houses.

Goose lugged an FIM-92 Stinger missile launcher to one of the forward buildings. A young private named Fernando Sanchez followed him and humped spare rockets for the weapon. Goose carried one in the launcher and two more across his back.

The Harran outpost had ten launchers. Some of them were U.S. Army–issued. Others had been scavenged from the UN and Turkish equipment that was initially left behind at the border when everything had started weeks ago. Goose didn't feel bad about appropriating the weapons or anything else they'd managed to scavenge. The Rangers were primarily the ones standing against the Syrian offensive. They needed the hardware.

A Syrian jet flew overhead. The cannons opened fire and decimated a nearby machine-gun nest. Thankfully the Rangers manning it had time to break for cover before the missiles hit, but the .50-cal machine gun became a superheated, twisted chunk of scrap. The sandbags ruptured and created a miniature sandstorm.

"Falcon Leader." Goose spoke into the headset as he readied the Stinger launcher. Falcon Leader was Lieutenant Swindoll's call sign.

"I read you, Falcon Three."

"Pull the soldiers from the machine-gun nests."

"Why? We need them there."

"They're going to be casualties if you don't. The hostiles have marked most of their twenties. They're targeting them."

Another jet launched an attack. This time radio contact was immediate. "We're hit! We're hit! I need help! Somebody help me!"

Goose's heart went out to the injured soldier. Then he focused on his task. *Get your part done. That's all you can do. You do your part; everybody else's part will get done too.*

"Get me ready," Goose said as he pulled the launcher onto his shoulder.

Sanchez slapped the BCU into place in the Stinger's handguard. The battery coolant unit hissed as it shot argon gas and a chemical energy charge into the weapon. The Stinger's targeting and acquisition systems came online. Without the BCU, the system wouldn't work.

With the Stinger locked and loaded, Goose trailed the fighter jet. The weapons system beeped to let him know the target had been acquired. His finger slid into place, and he fired.

The Stinger missile was about five feet in length and weighed almost twenty-three pounds. When it left the launcher, powered by a small ejection motor, the recoil was noticeable. The load on Goose's shoulder was immediately less; only the twelve and a half pounds of launcher rested there now.

The missile headed skyward; then the solid-fuel, two-stage motor kicked to life and accelerated it up to over Mach 2. The fighter jet had slowed to initiate its attack on the Ranger ground forces. As a result, it was almost a sitting duck for the Stinger.

"Load me," Goose ordered as he watched the missile intercept the Syrian jet's left engine. Sanchez slapped another missile into place, using one of the four he carried instead of the two Goose had. If they became separated, Goose could still fire the launcher on his own, but not without ammunition.

The Stinger detonated and turned the fighter jet into a fireball that shed pieces of broken aircraft like a dog shaking off water.

"Ready." Sanchez slapped the top of Goose's helmet.

Goose searched the sky for another target. Another jet, farther out, swooped in for the kill. A brief glance at the readout showed Goose the target was twenty thousand feet out. It was well within the 12,500-foot ceiling of the Stinger, but it needed to be another four thousand–plus feet closer.

C'mon, Goose thought as he tracked the fighter jet and waited for the acquisition beep. He couldn't help thinking that Rangers were in the enemy pilot's sights and were about to die.

The Stinger beeped, and the system showed a solid, steady signal.

Goose fired. The missile streaked away and kicked in the solid-fuel afterburners.

"Load me."

In the sky, the Stinger closed on the fighter jet. Evidently the onboard systems warned the pilot he'd been targeted. He tried to take evasive action, breaking and rolling to the right. The missile passed through the space the jet had been; then the heat-seeking systems autocorrected the warhead's trajectory and sent it back after the fighter jet. Less than a second later, the missile sped into the aircraft's jet engine and detonated, tearing the wing off. The fuselage careened wildly out into the empty lands and exploded when it struck the ground.

Sanchez slapped Goose's helmet. "You're loaded, Sarge. Good shooting."

"Thanks." Goose didn't take any glory in the kills. Soldiers were separated by necessity, but they were usually cut from the same cloth. Those men had families they wouldn't be going home to tonight, but it was better that Goose's men went home to theirs when a choice had to be made.

He snugged the Stinger launcher into his shoulder and looked for another jet. When he spotted one, he started to sight in on it when he saw another Stinger missile lift from the ground in pursuit. The Syrian turned into a flaming midair mass and rained down over the other side of the city.

"Falcon Leader," someone called over the headset. "This is Falcon Two."

Goose listened intently. Falcon Two was Lieutenant Wolper. He was in charge of the front line.

"Go, Two," Swindoll replied.

"We've got hostiles at the door." Full-auto fire rattled around Wolper's words, interspersed by the reports of the main guns of the approaching Syrian tanks.

Fall back, Goose thought, urging Swindoll to make the call. *Sell them real estate, but do it an inch at a time. You can't hold it.*

"Pull back to the second line," Swindoll ordered.

Goose searched the sky for another fighter jet, but there didn't appear to be any. Evidently the Stinger response had persuaded the Syrians that the cost in hardware was too high to continue. On the other hand, the tanks and APCs were now close enough to do considerable damage.

"Falcon Three, this is Falcon Eleven." The soldier's voice sounded tense. Machine-gun fire chased his words.

Goose's mind spun. Falcon Eleven was Corporal Brett Rainier, also one of the Stinger crews. A map of the city unfurled in Goose's head. Rainier was a hundred yards or so to the southwest.

"Eleven, you've got Three."

"We're under attack by hostiles, Sarge." Panic clawed at Rainier's words. "They came outta nowhere. They've got us pinned down."

"Understood. I'm on my way." Goose turned and handed the Stinger to Sanchez. "Stay here. Kept this zone clear of jets. If you have to go, go. I'll find you."

Sanchez nodded. "Good luck, Sarge."

"You stay frosty, son. A cool head will see you through this." Goose slipped the two extra missiles from his back, took his M-4A1 into his hands, and ran for Rainier's position, praying he wasn't too late.

❋   ❋   ❋

Local Time 0731 Hours

A burst of machine-gun fire sent Danielle diving to the ground near one of the mud-brick houses. She'd been listening to the sound of the big guns and the gunfire from the jets overhead. Hearing the sound at ground level was unnerving.

Gary slid down beside her.

Danielle looked at him, seeing the fear in his eyes and knowing she wore it in hers too. "Where did that come from?"

Gary shook his head. "Don't know. Close."

More machine-gun fire ripped into life just ahead of her. Danielle pressed against the mud-brick house and tried to imagine she was no bigger than another layer of dust. This time bullets chopped through the house and punched out fist-size holes.

"Danielle, what's going on there?" The voice came over the earpiece she wore that connected her to OneWorld NewsNet. "We're getting a picture of the ground, but not much else."

Gary grimaced and lifted the camera to his shoulder.

The voice belonged to Vincent Terrell, the late night New York anchor at OneWorld NewsNet. Nicolae Carpathia's news program had been granted an emergency twenty-four-hour news channel in the United States market only weeks ago.

OneWorld no longer had to depend on other channels to carry

its feeds. It now owned a large share of the viewing market because it had reporters in the field in all the hotspots and because its communications satellites worked better than anyone else's. The fact that Terrell was able to talk to Danielle in real time was proof of that.

"I don't know. I think we're under attack." Danielle slid back up the wall and got her nerves under control.

"We've still got the advancing Syrian army in view. They're some distance from Harran."

Full-auto roars sounded again.

"Can you lock in on my position?" Danielle peered around the side of the house.

"Give us a minute." Terrell sounded incredibly calm.

Of course he is. He's not the one getting shot at. Danielle stared at the scars from bullets that tracked the house. It was scary how easily she identified the holes as ammunition damage. *Way too much familiarity.*

Danielle looked back at Gary. "Are you good?"

"Man, I don't know if I'm ever going to be good again."

"Can you keep that camera going?"

"Yes."

Focusing, Danielle eased out around the house and followed the sound of the weapons fire. Only a little farther ahead, she saw a man clad in Bedouin robes scale one of the flat-roofed houses and slip a rifle from his shoulder.

Looking down at the house, Danielle spotted a U.S. Army helmet through the window. She caught a glimpse of a blood-smeared, frightened face. The Bedouin man's intent was immediately interpretable.

Before she knew what she was doing, Danielle shouted, "Look out! There's someone on the roof!"

The Bedouin man turned and brought his rifle to his shoulder. Other Bedouins beside the building stepped into view and brought up their weapons as well. Staring down the muzzles of the weapons, Danielle was convinced she was only a heartbeat away from death.

Then someone hit her broadside and knocked her back and down. A shadow fell across her, blotting out the morning sun and creating an instant barrier between her and the Bedouins.

Even in profile, with the buttstock of the M-4A1 blocking part of his face, Danielle recognized the soldier.

Goose.

Standing over Danielle Vinchenzo, Goose leveled the M-4A1 and fired by instinct. Instead of using the assault rifle, he pulled the trigger on the M-203 grenade launcher mounted under the rifle barrel. The 40mm grenade thumped from the launcher and struck in the middle of the Bedouins.

Knowing he'd be fighting at close quarters around his own men, Goose had loaded a high-explosive round in the launcher's chamber instead of an antipersonnel grenade. The area of effect would be reduced, and the likelihood of hurting a fellow soldier—if he used the weapon judiciously—was reduced. He felt certain the thick mud-brick walls would protect the Rangers inside the house.

The HE round exploded and flung five Bedouins backward. The lead man who had taken the brunt of the detonation was dead, his chest and face almost obliterated.

The Bedouin on the rooftop tried to keep his weapon on target. Rounds chewed into the mud bricks beside Goose. At least one of them ricocheted off his Kevlar vest and drove some of the wind from his lungs.

Forcing himself to remain standing and alert, Goose pulled the M-4A1 toward the Bedouin and slid his finger over the carbine's trigger. He stitched a three-round burst from the Bedouin's right hip to his left shoulder. The man stood for just a moment, then toppled from the roof.

By that time the Bedouins on the ground had semirecovered. They fumbled for their weapons and brought them up as Goose fired the M-4A1. The bullets chopped two of the Bedouins down, but two others escaped.

"Falcon Eleven." Goose had to force the words from his mouth as his lungs labored for air. The run and then the ricochet had left him short of breath.

"I'm reading you, Sarge."

"You got two hostiles in your twenty. I'm right outside. How are you?"

"Got a man down, Sarge. He's leaking all over the place. I've been hit."

"Affirmative. You sit tight, and I'll come get you out of there." Goose looked back at Danielle.

The reporter lay sprawled in the dirt, just now getting her breath back. Dirt covered one side of her face. Blood trickled from the corner of her mouth.

"That was a brave thing you did, ma'am, but you need to stay back now. This is going to be bloody."

Danielle nodded.

Staying low, the carbine held across his body, Goose sprinted across the open space. His knee ached but held together. The sounds of the battle and the approach of the Syrian heavy armor echoed all around him. The sun beat down on him unmercifully.

Somewhere ahead of him, at least two hostiles were in motion, and the close-set houses were a rat's warren.

✵   ✵   ✵

United States of America
Fort Benning, Georgia
Local Time 0034 Hours

Aching inside, Megan watched the video footage of the battle in Harran. She hated how helpless she felt while Goose laid his life on the line.

The picture was tagged with a slug line at the bottom: *Live Feed from Special OneWorld NewsNet Correspondent Danielle Vinchenzo.*

On the television screen hanging from the ceiling in the break room, Goose went forward into the mass of bodies that had been scattered by his weapon. The camera followed his movement, and the swaying camera motion only added to the sick feeling churning Megan's stomach.

"You just hold on to yourself, girlfriend." Evelyn threw her arms around Megan and held her fiercely. "That man of yours is savvy. He knows what he's doing."

"I should be there." Megan's voice was hoarse. "I should be there. Not here. Those men over there, they don't have anybody. With the situation being what it is, they're not going to come home anytime soon. The Bible talks so much about the final battle being fought in the Middle East." She shook her head and fought her tears. "That's where they're going to serve until this thing is finished."

"You don't know that."

Goose kept moving forward till he disappeared around the house.

Danielle Vinchenzo, captured in the camera's eye, waited a moment. Then she grabbed the cameraman's sleeve and pulled him forward. From the erratic movement of the camera, it was easy to see that his compliance was anything but willing.

"I do know that." Megan tried to hold on to that last view of Goose. "Those men are going to be there. As long as they're able to fight. The Holy Land is going to be the eye of the storm."

"Megan's right," one of the other women gathered in the break room said. "When the Antichrist comes—and he will—events are going to unfold over there that are going to bring about the end of days. It's all in the Bible. All you have to do is read it."

"That doesn't mean *those* men are going to be the ones stuck over there." Evelyn remained stubborn.

"They will be," Megan said. "The Rangers are always put in the line of fire." And she couldn't imagine Goose stepping away from the duty he'd sworn to see through.

"We should be there," a young woman said. Tears ran down her cheeks as she watched the television.

Megan looked at the woman, whose words echoed her own thoughts. They *should* be there. Those of them that still had family members in Turkey should be with them.

Gunshots cracked through the television speakers. Megan jumped. Evelyn tightened her grip and offered soothing encouragement.

I should be there, Megan thought and felt guilty that she hadn't realized that before.

❂   ❂   ❂

United States 75th Army Rangers Temporary Post
Sanliurfa, Turkey
Local Time 0735 Hours

Cal Remington watched the action on the television feed that had opened on one of the computers. Danielle Vinchenzo's reports from ground zero couldn't be ignored. The fact that she was, again, so close to Goose—*like a bad penny*, Remington couldn't help thinking—displeased the captain. But the intel she was sending back about what was taking place in the city was valuable.

Remington was torn as he watched Goose move carefully through the ancient city's narrow streets. On one hand, it would have been easier if Goose were killed or medevaced out. The schism that was starting to pull the Rangers in two directions would heal. Or at least not be exacerbated.

The problem was that Goose was also the one man Remington knew he could count on to get the job done when the chips were down.

"Captain Remington," one of the security team said from behind the captain.

Remington answered without turning around. "Busy, soldier." He watched Goose sweep the alley with his assault rifle, then glance back at Danielle Vinchenzo and wave her away.

"Yes, sir," the guard said. "But CIA Special Agent Alexander Cody says it's urgent that he speak with you at this time."

The CIA section chief's name grabbed Remington's attention immediately. Cody was a dangerous man. He was also a direct conduit to Nicolae Carpathia.

Remington nodded. "Bring him forward."

"Yes, sir." The corporal spun and trotted back.

Remington kept his attention riveted on the television broadcast and computer monitors relaying the live video feeds from other news network and satellites. He glanced at the Syrian cavalry leaving a line of dust in the terrain. They'd fed up the main highway from Syria, then spread out into the foothills.

"Lieutenant Archer."

"Sir?" The lieutenant turned from the marker board where he was doing the latest update.

"What's the ETA on the Syrian forces?"

"Minute, minute and a half, sir."

CIA Section Chief Alexander Cody stepped into a position next to Remington. The agent looked tired and worn. Under the baseball cap, his short-clipped black hair seemed to have gone grayer at the temples. Wraparound sunglasses masked his eyes. He wore a light Windbreaker over khakis and a white golf shirt. Combat boots completed the ensemble.

"Captain." Cody's voice was a dark rumble.

"I take it you weren't looking forward to this meeting," Remington said.

Cody's answer was unflinching. "No."

Remington glanced at the wave of advancing Black Hawk helicopters on one of the computers and raised his voice. "Lieutenant?"

"Sir?"

"Where are my helos?"

"Four minutes out from Harran, sir. Making good time."

"Com."

"Yes, sir."

"Open a frequency to Black Angel."

"Roger, sir. You've got a frequency . . . now."

"Black Angel Leader," Remington greeted, "this is Base."

"Affirmative, Base. Black Angel Leader reads you."

"I appreciate the haste. Those men there at the site will appreciate it more."

"Affirmative, Base. Looking forward to spreading the love with those hostiles."

"The Rangers there have orders to pull out shortly before your arrival."

"Understood, Base."

"Those Rangers need your support to effect a successful exfiltration. Equally important, we need to damage as much Syrian hardware there as we can."

"We'll do our best."

"I'm counting on it. Good luck, Black Angels." Remington glanced at the television feed again and watched Goose for a moment. "Now, Section Chief Cody, what brings you back to my watch? The last I recall, we weren't exactly on speaking terms."

"Since your sergeant wrecked my communications site, I haven't had much cause to be exactly trusting of you."

"Right back at you." Remington didn't look at the man.

"If I hadn't been ordered to work with you, I wouldn't be here."

Remington smiled cruelly. "Just because you've been ordered to work with me doesn't mean I'm going to work with you."

"You will." Cody sounded far too sure of himself.

"Why?"

"Because we share the same mysterious benefactor."

Nicolae Carpathia. The name hung between Remington and the CIA man like a weeping sore.

As if on cue, Remington's sat-phone vibrated. He hauled it from his BDUs and checked caller ID. *Nicolae Carpathia* showed on the viewscreen. The number was in New York. Remington knew Carpathia had recently been appointed as leader of the United Nations.

Feeling a little nervous, Remington flipped the phone open. "Remington."

"Good morning, Captain Remington," Carpathia greeted in his warm, ebullient voice. He made it sound like he'd waited hours just to speak with Remington, as if the captain were the most important person he'd speak with all day.

"Good morning, sir." Remington resented the fact that he had to kowtow to the man, but there was no one else in the world who could give him what he needed to keep his efforts alive in Sanliurfa.

"I can see by the news that your people have their struggles cut out for them in Harran."

"Yes, sir. We're doing our best to work it out."

"Excellent. I have the utmost faith in you."

Just those few words suddenly lifted the weariness from Remington's shoulders. He felt better than he had in days. "Thank you, sir."

"I believe you are also aware of my appointment to United Nations secretary-general."

"Yes, sir. Congratulations." Remington still couldn't believe how quickly that change had taken place. Carpathia had only come to New York to talk about all the disappearances and urge the world to work together. The previous secretary-general had stepped down, and Carpathia had been voted into office.

"We have not had a chance to talk since a few days after the disappearances around the world took place."

"No, sir." Although Remington was conscious of the clock ticking

down as the helos neared Harran, and although normally he wouldn't
have allowed anything to distract him, he was strangely calm while
listening to Carpathia.

"I regret that," Carpathia said.

"So do I, sir."

"I will make certain that so much time is not allowed to pass in
the future."

"I'd appreciate that, sir."

"In the meantime," Carpathia said, "I would like to make a
request."

"Anything." The answer was out of Remington's mouth before he
knew he was going to say it.

"I know that you and Section Chief Cody do not exactly see eye-
to-eye on things there."

That's putting it lightly, Remington thought. He didn't like the CIA
section chief playing in his backyard without letting him know what
was going on.

"However, Section Chief Cody has a problem—one that involves
you—and I fear he has no one else to turn to in order to rectify it."

Remington nodded. "I'd be happy to help."

"Good," Carpathia enthused. "Is Felix taking care of you?"

"Yes."

"I am glad the two of you are getting along so well."

"Yes, sir."

The clock on the helos' ETA now read fifty-two seconds. Remington
watched the digital readout dropping numbers in heartbeats.

"I will be making some changes in the UN," Carpathia went on.
"Most of the changes will involve restructuring various military com-
ponents around the world in order to bring everyone together. I take
great pride in telling you that you and your men will be the benefi-
ciaries of that restructuring very soon now. You just need to stay alive
for a short time longer."

"That's our intention, sir."

"Let me know if I can be of any further assistance in the future,
Captain. I expect our partnership to encompass a long life and many
successes over the coming years."

"I'm glad you think that, sir." Remington was surprised to learn
how glad he actually was.

Carpathia said good-bye and hung up.

Remington folded the phone and dropped it back into his BDUs.

"Our benefactor?" Cody asked smugly.

"Yes." Remington squared his shoulders. "What do you need?"

"Icarus."

That was the code name of the mysterious agent the CIA had been trying to intercept since shortly before the Syrians' initial attack. Remington hadn't been able to learn much about the man. Icarus had infiltrated a terrorist organization called the Kurdistan Worker's Party. The PKK had been set up to liberate an independent Kurdish state within Turkey.

To draw further notice to their goals, they'd decided to assassinate Chaim Rosenzweig, an Israeli botanist who had invented the synthetic fertilizer that had turned Israel into fertile ground and made that country rich almost overnight. Icarus had managed to foil the assassination plot, but his cover had been blown. He'd been marked for death and captured. Goose had taken a team and managed to intercept the terrorists before they'd gotten away.

Since that time, Icarus had been on the run. For reasons known only to him, he'd chosen to strike up a relationship with Goose.

"Icarus is your problem," Remington said.

Cody pushed out an angry breath. "Icarus is a problem for all of us. Nicolae wants the man caught and disappeared."

The idea of killing the man didn't bother Remington. "Again, that's your problem. Not mine."

"I wish that were true." Cody sounded genuinely saddened by the turn of events. "From what we've been able to ascertain, Icarus is no longer here in Sanliurfa."

"Then I can't help you." Remington watched the screen. The Syrian tanks and APCs had reached the town's limits. He raised his voice. "Falcon Leader, this is Base."

"Go, Base. You have Falcon Leader." Swindoll sounded rattled.

"Begin your withdrawal. Quickly as you can. Evac the wounded by air. Get the rest of your people out of there by convoy. The Black Hawks will provide cover."

"Affirmative."

"You're going to have to help me," Cody stated quietly.

"You just said Icarus isn't here," Remington reminded.

"He isn't. He's in Harran."

Remington kept his face impassive with effort.

"We suspect that he's trying to seek out your first sergeant again."

"Why?"

"Because I had a team on First Sergeant Gander, in case of this eventuality. They spotted Icarus this morning and contacted me."

"Then why don't they bring him in?"

"After repeated efforts over the last forty minutes, I haven't been able to reach them." Cody pursed his lips and looked like he'd bitten into a lemon. "I'm fairly certain they're dead." He nodded at the screen. "Given that the Syrians are about to be in possession of Harran, I figure your people are likely the last chance I have of getting Icarus back."

Remington stared at the destruction overtaking the ancient city. Tanks and APCs plunged through houses and buildings. Infantry jogged behind the mechanical behemoths. Other computer monitors offered views of the Rangers retreating through the streets in vehicles and on foot. Survival had become a deadly footrace.

"Do you really expect me to find Icarus in that?" Remington asked.

"You're the best chance I have, Captain. That city is sinking. Icarus is going to be like any other rat. He'll try to find a way out to safety. Circulate his image. Let's see if he pops up."

❂   ❂   ❂

United States 75th Army Rangers Outpost
Harran
Sanliurfa Province, Turkey
Local Time 0736 Hours

Goose wished that Danielle and her cameraman had stayed back. Following him was dangerous. Then he realized that anywhere in Harran was dangerous for an American citizen. Even the people who lived in the town would be forfeit if the Syrians caught up to them.

"Falcon Three," Swindoll called.

Goose didn't respond. Two of the Bedouins still remained on the loose. He guessed that they would be listening for him.

When he reached the narrow alley ahead of him, he turned and looked down it. Nothing stirred, though the town seemed to vibrate with the rock and roll caused by the advancing Syrian cavalry. Then, from the corner of his eye, he caught movement in the house in front of him.

Goose whirled and hunkered down. His weak knee screamed in agony, but he somehow forced it to hold up under him. He brought the M-4A1 online and squeezed the trigger. Bullets ripped across the windowsill and through the thin curtains, where a rifle muzzle protruded. Rounds from the Bedouin weapon pocked the wall over Goose's head.

The Bedouin tumbled backward without a sound.

"Goose!" Danielle yelled. "The rooftop!"

Glancing up, Goose barely made out another Bedouin atop the roof. Goose threw himself to one side just before bullets whipped through the space where he'd been. He fired again, emptying the carbine's magazine in a final chatter of full-auto. The bullets stitched up the roof, easily piercing the thin cover, and tracked onto the Bedouin. The man lost his weapon and fell from the other side of the house.

Goose fed a new magazine into the M-4A1 and got up. It felt like a colony of fire ants had taken up residence in his knee.

"Falcon Three," Swindoll tried again. "Goose."

"Three reads you, Leader. I was sidetracked with a couple things." Goose limped forward and checked the two Bedouins. Both men were dead.

"We're exfiltrating," Swindoll said.

"Affirmative. I've got wounded here. I'll get there when I can." Goose turned back the way he'd come. "Falcon Eleven, are you still with me?"

"Yes. I need help."

"I'll be there." Goose walked past Danielle and the cameraman. "Ma'am, you two shouldn't be here."

Danielle didn't say anything.

"Do you know where the airport is?" Goose asked.

"Yes."

"Then get there. This town's about to get turned inside out, and you don't want to be here when it happens."

"You've got wounded men back there."

"Yes, ma'am. I'll take care of them."

"It'll be easier if *we* take care of them." Danielle fell into stride with him, easily catching up to him. His leg throbbed and felt unsteady.

"Ma'am—"

"The Rangers aren't the only ones who don't leave people behind, Goose. And if that's the best you're able to walk, you're not going to be able to help those men much."

Ruefully, Goose closed his mouth and nodded. "Yes, ma'am." He kept the assault rifle across his chest as they went back to the house where Corporal Brett Rainier had holed up.

At the house, Goose held Danielle and the cameraman back from the window.

"Corporal," Goose called.

"Sarge." Rainier sounded weaker.

"Yeah. It's me. Okay to come ahead?"

"Yes."

Goose stepped through the door but kept the M-4A1 at the ready in case some of the Bedouins had made their way inside the building and were holding the two men hostage.

United States 75th Army Rangers Outpost
Harran
Sanliurfa Province, Turkey
Local Time 0738 Hours

Darkness and heat filled the house even with the windows open. If the windows had been larger, more light might have come in. As it was, they barely allowed light or a breeze.

The people who live here don't stay inside much, Goose thought. They lived a lot like the backwoods people he'd grown up with in Waycross. There were a lot of houses back there that didn't have air-conditioning and got by on box fans.

Rainier and Johnson were hunkered down in one corner. Rickety, mismatched furniture occupied the small room, barely making a dent in the meager space. On the other side of the room, a small wood-burning stove had a hot surface that held cooking utensils.

The people who normally lived here were used to hard ways, Goose couldn't help thinking. There were no pictures on the walls and no electronics.

Rainier was in his early twenties and had been in the Rangers for a couple of years. He was compact and neat, but his face was scruffy with whiskers, and his left arm was covered in blood.

Johnson was in worse shape. Blood saturated his abdomen and soaked his BDUs. He was black and gangly, no more than eighteen or nineteen years old.

Goose listened to Johnson's raspy breathing. *God help that poor boy.*

"Hey, Sarge," Johnson whispered. Both of his fists tightly clenched his shirt over his stomach. "I got shot."

"You did, son," Goose said, "but you're going to be all right. We're going to get you out of here."

"I don't want to die over here, Sarge." A spasm racked Johnson. "I promised . . . my granny . . . that I wouldn't die over here."

"Promises to a granny are awfully important," Goose said. "My granny would cut a switch if I ever didn't do something I promised her I'd do."

Johnson smiled. He was in so much shock that Goose doubted the young man felt much pain. He was just scared. "Then you know I can't die over here," Johnson said.

"No, sir. We can't let you do that." Goose listened for the approach of footsteps or vehicles. With all the noise outside, discerning either was problematic. He knelt beside the wounded man. "Let me see what we're dealing with."

Johnson didn't let go of his shirt.

Goose laid his rifle to one side and pulled at the young man's hands. He paid no attention to the blood on his hands. On this battlefield, in this moment, the threat of HIV was so far removed that he refused to acknowledge it. He didn't know if any of them were even going to make it out of the town alive.

"You're going to have to let go," Goose said.

Johnson swallowed hard. "I'm scared to let go, Sarge. I'm afraid if I do, I'm gonna fall apart."

"If you do, soldier, then I'll put you back together."

"Okay." Johnson's hands shook as he released the stranglehold he had on his shirt.

Goose palmed his lock-back knife and slashed the straps holding the Kevlar vest in place. "You doing okay, Brett?"

"Yeah. Bullet hit me in the arm, but it's already almost stopped bleeding. Just numb."

"That's normal. Nothing to worry about. You alert enough to keep a lookout?"

"Yeah, Sarge."

"Then help me do that."

Rainier nodded and sidled over to the nearest window. "Hey, that reporter woman's gone."

Goose looked back to where he'd left Danielle and the cameraman. Danielle was nowhere to be seen. "Where'd she go?" Goose demanded.

"Said she'd be back," the cameraman responded with a shrug.

"You let her go?"

"Hey, one thing I know about her since I've been working with her: once she gets it in her head to do something, you can't stop her."

Goose forced himself to turn his attention back to the wounded man. Maybe problems didn't come one at a time, but that was how he had to deal with them.

At the moment, Robert Johnson was his problem. The man's stomach was a mess. An ugly tear showed where a bullet had ripped across his abdomen and came close to spilling his intestines outside his body. Thankfully the bullet hadn't nicked an artery. There was a lot of blood, but it was already starting to slow. He was still going to need blood or plasma to keep his heart beating.

Johnson shivered and watched Goose with frightened eyes. "How bad is it, Sarge?"

"Plenty bad," he admitted, "but I've seen men with worse pull through just fine. You ain't gonna look as good in a Speedo, though."

"Man," Johnson said, "I ain't never wore no Speedo."

"Well, then you won't miss anything." Goose looked around the room and found a threadbare blanket.

"Don't see how that bullet got through my vest," Johnson said.

"It didn't." Goose tore the blanket into strips. "You got kissed by a ricochet that slipped up under the vest."

"Lucky me."

"You'd have been a lot luckier if it had missed you altogether." Working quickly, Goose slipped the strips under the young man and bound them across his abdomen. "One thing you can't do is sit up."

"I can't. I already tried. I thought I'd been paralyzed. But I can still feel my feet."

"Your stomach muscles have been cut," Goose said. "Docs can fix 'em good as new, but you don't have them right now. So you just lay back and let us get you out of here."

"Yes, First Sergeant."

Goose nodded and picked up his weapon. He adjusted his helmet and stood. Carrying Johnson back to the airfield wasn't an option.

And he still didn't know where Danielle Vinchenzo had gone.

❋ ❋ ❋

United States of America
Fort Benning, Georgia
Local Time 0042 Hours

The Battle for Harran scrolled across the OneWorld NewsNet television channel.

Horrified, Megan stood in silence and watched Goose working on the wounded young man in front of him. The cameraman still had the video rolling, and the video link came through clearly.

"As you can see," anchorman Vincent Terrell stated calmly, "things in Harran are not good for the Rangers out of Fort Benning, Georgia. You're watching First Sergeant Samuel Adams Gander performing some kind of emergency procedure on a wounded soldier."

The television monitor split into two equal screens. The other screen showed a downward view of the battlefield as Syrian tanks and vehicles drove into the town. Megan couldn't believe the amount of devastation that filled their backtrail.

"At the same time that Goose, as most of this station's viewers have come to know the sergeant by, struggles to save his fellow soldier, the Syrian army has arrived and is plowing through the town of Harran," Terrell went on. "We're being told that the Rangers hope to reach the makeshift air base outside the town in time to evacuate before the Syrians shoot them down."

The view on the left screen tightened up and displayed the small, postage stamp–size airfield where a few cargo helicopters sat idling. Two of them lay spread across the terrain like a child's broken toys. The Syrian jets had proven disastrous before the Rangers managed to retaliate.

A wave of jeeps braked to a halt and off-loaded wounded in gurneys. As soon as the helicopters filled up with wounded, they took off.

Watching them go, counting down the number of vehicles available, Megan knew she was watching Goose's chances of escape and survival grow slimmer and slimmer. She took comfort in Evelyn's strong embrace.

"Mom?"

Recognizing Joey's voice, Megan turned toward the door. Joey stood there looking as frightened as she felt. Evelyn released her hold. Megan didn't ask Joey why he was out so late, didn't ask where he'd been; she just stepped toward her son with open arms.

"Is Goose . . . ?" Joey couldn't finish.

Megan held her son close. "No, honey. Goose is fine. He's just fine. Look there." She pointed at the screen, where Goose was working on the young Ranger.

"Isn't he supposed to be getting out of there?" Joey asked.

"He will. He will. Goose just can't leave anyone behind."

"We have temporarily lost video contact with Danielle Vinchenzo, our reporter there on the ground in the beleaguered town of Harran," Terrell continued, "but we'll bring you more news of Harran as it develops. Right now we're going to take you live to the United Nations building in New York, where Nicolae Carpathia, the newly elected secretary-general, wants to say a few words."

"No," Megan said.

Mercifully, the screens remained split, and the one depicting Goose stayed in place.

Carpathia looked unimpressively ordinary yet somehow natural on camera. He was thirty-three years old and broad-chested. His hair was neatly in place, as was his hesitant smile, and his dark suit looked fresh despite the late hour in the day.

"Good evening, Mr. Secretary-General," the news anchorman greeted. "Thank you for agreeing to speak to us concerning the continuing unrest in Turkey."

"Please," Carpathia said good-naturedly. "Address me as Nicolae. I am not comfortable standing on titles."

Despite her attention to Goose, Megan couldn't help watching the Romanian leader. There was something . . . not quite right about him. Something that bothered her. It was also something she hadn't noticed till recently. When the man had first started appearing on television, she'd been taken in by the warm generosity he exuded.

"For a person not comfortable standing on titles," Terrell said, "you've certainly acquired a number of them in short order."

"I have been very fortunate and very diligent about the opportunities that came my way. But everything I do, I do for the good of the world and the people who are in it. We should all pay more attention to each other. Especially these days when there is so much confusion in the world."

"I agree," Terrell said. Then he smiled. "And not just because OneWorld NewsNet is one of the corporations you have a big interest in."

Carpathia smiled as well. "I am glad to hear that. I came here to New York today to talk about the violence running rampant in the world. Before the disappearances, so much of the violence we have seen in recent days was barely kept in check. While I was living in Romania, I remained constantly aware of the tensions in Kosovo that threatened to spill over onto us, as well as the Russian-Chechen problems. Israel has always been a source of contention, and I fear that nation's newfound wealth has only made her a greater target for her enemies."

"He's right," someone said.

Megan looked around the room, amazed at how many people had gathered and were focused on Carpathia. There was something almost sinister about that.

United States of America
Fort Benning, Georgia
Local Time 0046 Hours

"These wars and all the infighting have to stop," Carpathia said from his half of the split television screen. "We must find a way to live in peace with each other if we are going to survive whatever has happened to this world. A third of the people who had lived on this planet are now among the missing."

Not missing, Megan thought. *They're with God.* Her eyes never left Goose as he labored to save the life of the young soldier.

"I am working now on a new plan that I think will benefit all the nations of the world," Carpathia said. "Many changes will come directly through the United Nations. President Fitzhugh and I have talked about what part he and the United States are going to play in this new world I am envisioning."

New world? Megan thought. *We don't need a new world. We need to figure out how to live in this one.* But she noticed that several of her fellow workers were nodding their heads in agreement. A chill crept up her spine at Carpathia's words.

"The United Nations has put military forces in many nations across the globe," Carpathia went on, "but these forces have seldom been allowed to act. I propose to change that. I am going to empower the men and women in those military forces to work more vigorously to make changes in the nations that have struggled to get along. I feel certain that a way can be made."

"That's certainly a lofty idea," the anchorman, Terrell, said.

Carpathia grinned like a little boy. "I know. It sounds very much like a dream, but it is a dream I have had since I was very small. My mother brought me up to love peace, and she helped bring peace and wellness to the house I grew up in. I can only hope that my own efforts will honor her in some small way."

"What do you visualize doing?"

Megan shook her head. Terrell's questions might as well have been scripted.

"I want to change the United Nations into another entity, one that I propose calling the Global Community. I think that name better communicates what we can expect of the world we live in these days. With the access we have to the Internet and wireless devices, and with news media scattered around the world—"

"Especially OneWorld NewsNet," Terrell interjected during Carpathia's pause. "We can't forget the tireless work that goes on behind the scenes here."

"No," Carpathia agreed. "We cannot. I am very proud of the work that the news agency does. I only wish I could claim credit for it, because you people have certainly racked up a lot of awards."

"Thank you." Terrell beamed. "Danielle Vinchenzo is surely going to be up for an award for her work in Turkey."

"If she is not," Carpathia said, "then there is no justice in the world." He paused just a moment, then went on. "I will be in touch with you more as my plans for the Global Community solidify. But for the moment, let me say that I am very proud of those men— United Nations soldiers as well as Fort Benning's own Rangers—who are assisting Turkish troops in trying to keep the peace in Turkey. From what I have seen today, that is a very hard thing to do."

On the screen in Harran, Goose retrieved his weapon and stood. He spoke, but his voice had been muted.

"One thing I would like to tell the families of those Rangers serving in Turkey," Carpathia continued, "is that I have taken steps that should see big changes occurring there. Turkey is an important linchpin between East and West, and that division needs to be maintained until I can deal with it."

"You sound very confident that you'll be able to handle everything over there," Terrell said.

"I am." Carpathia smiled a little. "I think, given the strangeness that has taken place recently, that most people are more ready to listen to reason than at any other time in history. Nothing on this grand of a scale has ever before occurred, and I doubt that it ever will again."

Some of the listeners vocally hoped that the disappearances wouldn't happen again.

They're not going to, Megan thought. *Those of you who didn't vanish the first time are going to be stuck here for the next seven years.*

But Carpathia's words had reawakened the fear of the unknown in the listeners. None of the people left behind wanted to face the unknown again.

"They are ready to listen," Carpathia said. "And in a little while, I will be ready to begin negotiations in those places. Like Turkey."

Terrell smiled. "Very good, Secretary-General Carpathia."

"Nicolae, please." Carpathia grinned affably.

On the television screen, Goose walked toward the camera, which turned and panned on him as he walked through the door.

Without warning, the wall suddenly caved in. A tank tread plunged through, sloughing debris. The cameraman dived for cover, and the camera angle slid around in all directions.

✳ ✳ ✳

United States 75th Army Rangers Outpost
Harran
Sanliurfa Province, Turkey
Local Time 0741 Hours

The roar and clank of heavy armor filled Danielle's ears as she ran down the street from the house where Goose worked on the wounded soldiers. She hadn't been able to stay there even though she knew her departure would drive Goose crazy. Her skills included first aid, and she was certain—even without looking underneath the Kevlar vest as Goose had—that the young Ranger was well past needing first aid.

He needed a doctor. Goose carrying the man through town on his back wasn't an option. If Goose had to try, Danielle had no doubt that he would do exactly that. But she'd noticed Goose limping as well. He wasn't exactly in tip-top condition either.

Give me a car, Danielle thought desperately. *A pickup. Please.* Something. *And quickly.* She kept running.

Not many cars sat idle in Harran. Given the town's poor economic conditions, very few people in the area owned vehicles.

But less than a block farther on, Danielle spotted a forty-year-old Russian delivery van with peeling black paint. The vehicle was definitely on its last legs. Arabic script covered the sides.

When she peered inside, Danielle saw that the ignition was empty. However, there were plenty of wires sticking out beneath the dash. She gripped the door and yanked it open. The old hinges screeched as the door moved. She climbed into the driver's seat and ran a hand under the seat to make certain the keys hadn't been tossed underneath.

Then she noticed that two of the wires near the steering wheel were stripped and hanging down. She grabbed them and touched them together. The truck's engine tried to catch, the vehicle surging forward and shuddering because the clutch was left out.

Encouraged, Danielle pulled herself inside the cab and gazed through the cracked windshield. A rumbling, grinding noise came closer, sounding like approaching thunder. For a moment, she sat paralyzed by the sound, dreading what it portended.

Farther up the street, a mechanical assault vehicle plunged through a small house with a tremendous crash. Pieces of the house clung to the APC as it surged out into the street. Instead of wheels, the vehicle had tank treads that clanked menacingly and chewed through the pavement. It was so low and so broad that Danielle at first thought it was a tank; then she saw that it had no main gun. The Syrian camouflage design, light green and dark green, stood out clearly on the vehicle's dust-covered hide.

Danielle cursed.

"Danielle," Terrell said over the headset she still wore that linked her to OneWorld NewsNet, "can you tell us what's going on? We're still monitoring you. The cameraman seems to be nowhere near you."

Gary wouldn't want to be here right now, Danielle thought as she tried to break out of the paralysis.

A forward hatch opened on the tracked vehicle, and a man popped up like a gopher out of a hole. For a moment the comparison was hilarious, but it didn't stay amusing for long. The Syrian soldier grabbed hold of a machine gun and spun it in her direction. He started firing too early, though, and the rounds chopped across the street in front of Danielle's borrowed vehicle and smashed against the building beside her.

Danielle held the two wires beneath the steering column together. Sparks leaped. Heat singed her fingertips, but she held on stubbornly as the engine struggled to catch. For one sickening moment, she thought that maybe the delivery van had been left behind because it was broken down. She pumped the accelerator.

Don't flood it, she told herself. *Flood it, and you're dead.*

The machine gunner spun his weapon toward her again. Bay doors opened behind the forward hatch and revealed nearly a dozen Syrian soldiers.

Then, with a less-than-inspiring rattle of metal, the engine found a life of its own. Danielle shoved the transmission into reverse, revved the engine, and prayed that it wouldn't stall.

"Danielle," Terrell tried again.

Ignoring the call, Danielle peered into the cracked side mirror to see where she was going. That was a lot easier than staring back at the Syrian APC. The roar of the machine gun filled the open cab of the van. Bullets tore through the passenger side of the windshield and pieces of glass fell across the seat.

Danielle yelped in fear and took evasive action. The van's rear bumper scraped a wooden cart that had been left in the street and reduced the cart to splintery pieces. The van bumped and jostled as it rolled over them. The transmission whined loudly.

Daring a forward glance, Danielle saw the line of machine-gun bullets tracking back toward the van. Desperately she spun the wheel and cut away just before the machine-gun fire vectored in on her. Pulling the wheel sharply, she tried to back into an alley. Unfortunately she wasn't as talented or lucky as she'd hoped. The rear bumper collided with the corner of the building and the van came to a sudden stop.

Hammered by the collision, Danielle ricocheted off the seat and the steering wheel with bruising force. She changed gears and tried to go forward, then realized the van's engine had died. Still unable to catch her breath, driven purely by survival instinct, she reached for the wires and held them together again.

Machine-gun rounds thudded against the van's side and passed through without slowing. The sound echoed deafeningly within the van.

Don't hit the tires, Danielle thought desperately. *Please, God, don't let them hit the tires. Or me.*

The engine caught again, easier this time. She shoved the gearshift into first, floored the accelerator, and let out the clutch. The van shot across the street just ahead of a hail of .50-caliber rounds that would have destroyed the vehicle and her.

Panic filled Danielle when she realized she didn't know where she was. In the confusion, she'd lost her orientation. All the houses and buildings along the street looked the same.

Think. You just came this way.

The side mirror showed that the Syrian military vehicle was trailing her. Machine-gun fire sounded behind her. A few bullets punctured the rear of the van and passed through the front windshield.

Danielle cut the wheel to plunge down an alley. The left side of the van scraped against the building. The impact ripped the side mirror off. Bolts bounced off the window. Fighting the wheel, she barely regained control before she crashed into the building on the other side.

The alley was a lot narrower than she'd thought it was. Only inches separated her from the sides as she rumbled toward the street at the other end. The Syrian vehicle was too wide to get through. She took hope in that.

In the next moment, the Syrian APC paused at the entrance of the alley.

Danielle hunkered lower in the seat, expecting the machine gun to open fire again. Instead, the gunner dropped back inside the vehicle. The rear bay doors closed as well. Then the APC surged forward. The tank treads chewed into the sides of the building like a harvester taking down wheat.

"No!" Danielle said in disbelief.

The Syrian war machine was actually gaining on her now. Behind it, buildings toppled into ruin. The APC suddenly transcended in Danielle's mind to a thing crafted by her worst nightmares. She wasn't going to be able to escape. The Syrians chasing her were unstoppable.

She reached the next street and cut hard left. The van skidded out of control, the bald tires struggling to find traction. She slewed sideways. A moment later, the Syrian vehicle powered through the final few feet of the alley and cut after her.

Just as she was preparing to abandon hope of getting away, much less of reaching Goose, Gary, and the wounded Rangers, Danielle spotted the house where she'd left them. Goose emerged from the door and looked in her direction.

Danielle knew he couldn't have been expecting the sight that greeted him, but Goose never flinched. Or hesitated. Smoothly, like he had all day, he reached into his BDUs. After he'd inserted something into his weapon, he pulled the rifle to his shoulder.

Realizing that the sergeant wasn't going to run, Danielle felt immediately guilty. Instead of helping the Rangers, she'd doomed them.

❋ ❋ ❋

Local Time 0747 Hours

Goose took careful aim at the Syrian vehicle's right tread. He recognized it as a Russian-made BTR-50. It was the only model that was tracked. All the other BTRs were wheeled. Tracks had been discontinued because they presented vulnerabilities similar to tanks, but the BTR-50s lacked the firepower tanks packed that kept soldiers back.

Danielle roared by in the van.

The forward hatch flipped open, and a Syrian soldier took hold of the machine gun. Fifty-caliber rounds filled the air around Goose like fat bumblebees. He heard them pass him only inches away.

Calmly, Goose slid his finger over the M-203's trigger and launched the HE round at the APC's right tread. The grenade flew thirty yards and impacted against the tread only inches above the street, almost exactly where he'd hoped it would hit. Trapped between the treads and the street, the HE round's blast was even more concentrated.

The right tread came apart and started slapping the APC's side in a deafening cacophony. Out of control, the left tread still digging into the street and powering the fourteen-ton vehicle forward, the APC came around in a tight circle. Then the tread lost traction, and the APC slid across the street.

By the time the tread grabbed hold again, the APC had come around 270 degrees and was now pointed at the house where the cameraman, Rainier, and Johnson lay. Goose watched helplessly as the APC surged forward a short distance and slammed into the house. The tracks ground through the side of the house, then started slipping on the debris.

Goose pulled the M-4A1 to his shoulder and took aim at the APC's gunner as the man tried to bring the machine gun to bear. Goose fired four quick three-round bursts, ensuring that the man was down, then reached into his kit for an incendiary grenade. He pulled the pin, popped the spoon, and heaved the grenade toward the back bay doors as they started to open.

The grenade bounced against one of the doors, and for a moment Goose felt certain he'd missed the bay. Then the grenade dropped into the transport area.

Grimly, Goose concentrated on feeding an antipersonnel grenade into the M-203's breech. He didn't like using the incendiary grenades against soldiers. They burned at four thousand degrees and guaranteed instant death for the lucky ones and debilitating burns for anyone who survived the initial blast.

But he thought about the Harran citizens who had undoubtedly lost their lives in the morning's attack. And he thought about Robert Johnson, who might not live to see noon. He turned off his compassion and closed the grenade launcher's breech.

The incendiary grenade exploded as Syrian soldiers lined the transport area and prepared to open fire on Goose. Sheets of white-hot flame enveloped them. The ones who weren't killed outright screamed in pain and terror. Two of them managed to clamber over the APC's side and drop to the ground. Flames wreathed their bodies.

Steeling himself, Goose took deliberate aim and shot them, putting them out of their misery. *God forgive me.* He watched as the APC burned until he was satisfied no one remained alive on board. The stench of cooked human flesh filled the air.

Danielle pulled the van to a stop behind the APC. She remained well away from the curling flames. Getting out, she started forward, then stopped at the burned bodies of the two men Goose had shot. Her eyes fell on Goose and were filled with stunned disbelief.

Goose didn't try to defend his actions. He was locked tightly into survival mode.

"You got the van, ma'am," he said.

After a brief hesitation, Danielle nodded.

"It's still running?"

"Y-yes."

"You done good, ma'am. That was an awfully brave thing to do."

"I brought these people down on top of you."

"No, ma'am." Goose walked back toward the house, peering through the ruined wall and seeing that Rainier, Johnson, and the cameraman hadn't been injured by the flying debris. "They come here all on their own. They're responsible for how they ended up."

"I could have gotten you killed."

"Ma'am, you brought a vehicle to transport *our* wounded." Goose deliberately used the plural pronoun to point out their shared responsibility for the injured Rangers. "Nobody else here had the time to look for something. You done good."

Inside the house, Goose finished tearing the door from its hinges. He laid it beside Johnson.

"You still with me, Private?"

"Yes, First Sergeant."

"Good man. We're going to take a little trip now. You ready for this?"

Johnson grimaced a little, then nodded as best he was able. "Yes, First Sergeant."

"Ma'am, I'm going to need your help."

Danielle came closer but was obviously uneasy about all the blood.

"Just hold on to his head. Keep him from getting banged around too much."

"All right." Danielle put her hands on either side of Johnson's head.

"Ma'am, like this." Goose interlaced his bloody hands, interlocking his fingers. "Make a cradle for his head. I'm going to be taking most of his weight, but I don't want him to get hurt any more while we're doing this."

Danielle made a cradle.

Irritated, Goose noticed that the cameraman was still shooting. "Son, you could put that camera down long enough to give us a hand."

"Gary," Danielle said, "keep shooting." She looked at Goose. "I can do this."

Goose knew he didn't have time to argue. He knelt down and slid his arms under Johnson's lanky form. The pain in his knee throbbed to renewed life, feeling as though a shark's jaws had closed on it and were grinding away. His breath caught at the back of his throat and for a moment he felt like he was going to black out.

You hold it together, Sergeant. You got to get these people out of here.

"Brett," Goose said to Rainier.

"Yes, First Sergeant."

"You're lookout, son. Keep your eyes peeled."

"Yes, First Sergeant."

"Goose." Remington's voice sounded in Goose's ear.

"Falcon Three reads you, Base." Goose lifted Johnson's body as carefully as he could, then maneuvered the wounded Ranger onto the door. He laid him gently on the wooden surface.

"You've got to get out of there," Remington said. "The helos have almost all lifted."

"Tell them to hold one," Goose said. "I got a seriously injured man with me. He needs a medic right now."

"I will, but I can't hold it for long."

"We'll be there. Just buy me some time."

Danielle stripped out of her Kevlar vest and outer shirt, leaving only a blue sleeveless shirt. She folded her blouse and put it under Johnson's head.

"Thank you, ma'am," Johnson croaked.

"You're welcome, soldier."

"Get that vest back on," Goose said.

Danielle nodded and pulled the body armor on again.

Taking a roll of ordnance tape from his kit, Goose lifted one end of the door and quickly ran lines of tape across Johnson's chest to hold him to the door. Then Goose did the same to the young Ranger's feet.

"I'm thirsty," Johnson whispered.

Danielle reached for the canteen at her hip. Goose was pleased to see that she'd made a habit of carrying water. She was learning quickly.

"No water," Goose said.

Danielle looked at him.

"Private," Goose said.

"Yeah, Sarge."

"With the injuries you've got, drinking water right now isn't a good idea. Let the medics have a look at you first."

Johnson nodded. "Yes, First Sergeant."

Instead of putting the canteen away, Danielle opened it and poured some of the water onto a gauze pad from the emergency medical kit she retrieved from the cameraman's bag. She pressed the saturated gauze pad against Johnson's mouth.

"It's not much," she apologized, "but it'll wet your lips."

Johnson nodded and sucked at the gauze. "Thank you."

"You're welcome."

Goose turned his attention to Gary, the cameraman. "You're going to have to put that camera down now. We need help."

Gary glanced at Danielle, and she nodded. With obvious reluctance, the young man put his camera into a case and zipped it shut. He slung the case, then joined Danielle at the foot end of the door. Goose managed the other end by himself. Rainier started to put his carbine away and help.

"No," Goose said. "You got point. Stay ready. Let's go."

"You can't leave Sergeant Gander there, Captain," Alexander Cody said.

Remington ignored the CIA section chief. The captain was already deeply aware that he couldn't leave Goose behind in Harran. OneWorld NewsNet was making him out to be a hero. Again.

The news channel's screen remained split, displaying the continuing attack on Harran as well as looping the footage that had been shot of Goose's own struggles to stay alive.

"If the sergeant dies," Cody said, "we've lost the only link we have to Icarus."

Remington was more conscious of Goose's public image. Goose had gotten a lot of international attention whether he'd wanted it or not. Abandoning him in Harran, especially when he was risking his life to bring home a wounded fellow Ranger, was out of the question.

"Lieutenant Archer," Remington barked.

"Sir." The junior officer wheeled about rapidly.

"Get me a twenty on First Sergeant Gander. I want a sat-eye and constant GPS on him."

"Right away, sir." Archer abandoned the marker board and hurried over to the computer techs.

"Black Angel Leader, this is Base."

"Go, Base."

Remington peered at the large computer monitor that displayed the overhead view of the city. He spotted the ten Black Hawk combat choppers winging over Harran from the north. Farther south, the Syrian forces had slowed only slightly, like waves crashing onto a rocky shore.

"I need a pickup performed inside the town," Remington said. "I want a pilot who can sit one of those birds on a dime and take off again in the heat of battle."

"Affirmative, sir. I have just the man."

"Get him up front first to off-load those mines, then have him double back. I want him on a private frequency to handle the pickup." Remington rattled off the channel they'd be using for the exfiltration.

"Base, this is Black Angel Eleven," a calm male voice said over the new frequency.

"Eleven, this is Base. First Sergeant Gander is loose in the streets with a wounded Ranger. He's not going to make it to the evac site. I need you to pick him up."

"Understood. Happy to do it, Base. The top has always been a good guy in our books."

Remington resented the implied familiarity with Goose. Even though the sergeant didn't make a conscious effort to get to know everyone, it always seemed like he did. Faces and names, as well as the circumstances where he'd encountered them, just came easily to Goose. Remington was convinced that Goose could walk up to a fence post and strike up a conversation.

Switching to the frequency Goose was monitoring, Remington called for him.

"I read you, Base," Goose answered. His voice sounded strained and distant.

"You're not going to make the evac, Goose," Remington said.

If Goose was upset at the news, he didn't let it show. "I'm sorry to hear that, sir. I'd counted on it for Johnson's sake."

"One of the Black Hawks is going to pick you up. We're negotiating an LZ right now."

"I appreciate it, Captain. We've lost enough good men out here today."

Remington glanced over at the television and discovered that Danielle Vinchenzo was back on the air. There was no picture, but the audio was coming through, and a transcription was being printed across the split screen under looped segments of the rescue of the Rangers in the house.

"Is that reporter always so close to Sergeant Gander?" Cody asked.

"No, but she is a lot of the time. Too many of the wrong times, as it turns out."

"Captain," one of the security teams called in Remington's ear.

"I want no interruptions," Remington said.

"Understood, sir. But you also left orders to let you know if a reporter from OneWorld NewsNet showed up. There's one here now, sir."

Remington glanced back at the door to the command post. A clean-cut young man with blond hair stood in the doorway. An older man carrying a camera case in one hand stood beside him.

"Show them in," Remington said.

The young man crossed the floor and extended a hand. He exuded confidence and competence. "I'm Josh Campbell, Captain Remington. It's an honor to meet you."

"Mr. Campbell." Remington took the young man's hand and released it.

"This is my associate, Ben Howard." Campbell nodded toward the cameraman.

Howard inclined his head but didn't say anything.

"What are you doing here, Mr. Campbell?" Remington asked.

"My news director, at the request of Nicolae Carpathia, sent me here to get your story."

"Why?"

Campbell smiled hugely, exposing keen white incisors that were made for the camera. "Because your efforts here in Sanliurfa are important, Captain Remington. Nicolae feels that the world should know about them."

Remington noticed how easily the younger man threw around Carpathia's name. It was like they were old friends. Strangely, the usage didn't hit the captain's lie radar.

"Nicolae has big plans for you, Captain," Campbell said.

"What plans?"

Campbell grinned again and shook his head. He mimed zipping his mouth shut. "Nope. You're not going to hear it from me. That's Nicolae's surprise to spring. I'm just here to make you look good and make sure the whole world knows who you are."

"Sir," Archer called.

Remington glanced at the lieutenant.

"We've located Goose." Archer touched one of the computer screens.

"Find me a location where a Black Hawk can sit down," Remington ordered. "Then get First Sergeant Gander there."

"Yes, sir." Archer turned to the task.

"I can see you're really busy at the moment," Campbell said. "Maybe you could point us to an out-of-the-way place."

"Corporal," Remington addressed the guard who had brought the newsmen over.

"Sir."

"Escort these men to a neutral area. Keep them in the loop, but sit on them."

The corporal saluted smartly and led his charges away.

"Having the media underfoot isn't a good thing." Cody scowled in irritation.

"Maybe not if you're living the life of a cockroach and can't stand the light," Remington said, feeling better about things already. "I'm not involved with anything that's going to send my career down in flames."

"You're involved with me. I'm involved with Icarus. If that man shows up at the wrong time, if what he knows falls into the wrong hands, everything over here could go wrong."

Remington gazed at the man coolly. "You're making me think I should reevaluate this working relationship we have."

"That's not what I meant."

"Then perhaps you should think more quietly," Remington suggested. Personally, he was looking forward to having his story told in the media. This was where he belonged: in the limelight. He turned his attention back to the events unfolding in Harran.

Jenny McGrath sat by her father's bed and ate her dinner. The day at the hospital had been hectic. Even weeks after the disappearances, everything hadn't returned to normal. People were more paranoid and vulnerable than ever. A lot of traffic accidents had come in today, and victims of gang- and drug-related violence had been steadily appearing through the evening.

She'd been cleaning the waiting rooms outside the ER when a young police officer was brought in. He'd been shot during a domestic squabble between a wife and a husband. They'd almost lost him twice before his father arrived at the ER. The father had already been upset about the unexplained disappearance of his wife. Now he had this to deal with.

Jenny had been tempted to tell him of Megan Gander's belief that God had called up all the children and those who believed in Him during the rapture. But her own lack of faith and her hesitancy to believe that what Megan said was true had held her tongue.

All those long, lonely years of growing up in Jackson McGrath's drunken shadow had taught her to believe in little outside her own skin. So instead of saying anything, she'd finished her job and walked away. She still didn't know what had happened to the young police officer.

Unexpectedly the television came on.

Surprised, Jenny glanced at her father, thinking that he might have regained consciousness and switched it on. No matter how drunk he'd gotten wherever they'd lived, he'd never been too inebriated to turn on the television. Or drive. Drunk driving had finally cost her father his license.

But Jackson McGrath still slept. His sallow cheeks had already started to darken from his beard growth. A piece of toilet paper was still stuck to his chin where she'd accidentally cut him that morning. Just looking at the slight wound made her feel guilty all over again. She'd learned to shave him when she was little so he wouldn't cut his face to pieces while shaking with the DTs. Delirium tremens had been another aspect of her home education that most of the kids her age had never had to deal with.

Jenny guessed that one of the remote controls in the other rooms had activated her father's television as well. Sometimes they did that and changed channels, which proved disturbing to some of the patients and their families.

She watched the television out of habit, not really paying attention. Then she saw First Sergeant Samuel Adams Gander in combat gear and firing a rifle.

The first time Jenny had seen Goose on TV, she hadn't recognized him, but it was hard to live in Megan Gander's house even for only a few days without seeing the sergeant's photograph. In those pictures, he was seldom alone, except in staged photos for the army. The other pictures were of Goose and Megan at their wedding and other special occasions and of Goose with Joey and Chris at various ages.

From the beginning, Jenny had seen something solid and generous in the sergeant. He wasn't the kind of man that she'd often met, and never while with her father.

Seeing the danger First Sergeant Gander was in—or had been in; Jenny wasn't sure from the news story—she bowed her head and prayed for him. Then, because she heard her father's breathing, she prayed for him as well.

Footsteps entered the room.

Startled, Jenny looked up and spotted Tony Murray, her father's midnight-to-six nurse, standing on the other side of the bed. Tony was in his early forties, a nice guy with a quiet disposition. He wore earrings in both ears and a thick, black goatee that matched his hair and bushy eyebrows behind his John Lennon glasses.

"Sorry," he said in a soft voice.

"It's okay."

Tony took her dad's vitals and made notations on the clipboard on the wall. "I see more people doing that these days."

"What?"

"Praying."

Jenny's cheeks warmed, and she turned her attention back to the bowl of macaroni and cheese she'd brought up from the hospital cafeteria. She suddenly felt really uncomfortable.

"Man, my bad," Tony said. "I didn't mean to embarrass you."

"I'm not embarrassed." Jenny lifted her gaze to meet Tony's, and he rolled his eyes.

"Anybody else, you can lie to, but I'm a human lie detector. Ask any nurse or doctor on this floor. I ask a patient if they've taken their medication, I know immediately if that patient is lying. A lot of the doctors and nurses come to me if they can't tell if a patient is telling the truth. I always can."

"Oh."

"So maybe you were a little embarrassed."

"Yeah."

"You shouldn't be."

Jenny frowned. "Look, I know you probably mean well and everything, but I'm really not ready for one of those God-loves-you speeches."

Tony's eyebrows rose over his glasses. "Wow. I guess you got a lot of those."

"Growing up, sure." Anyone who knew Jackson McGrath as he really was and who believed in God had told her that. She'd always assumed it was so she'd think at least someone loved her.

But if God really loved me, would He have given me Jackson McGrath as a father? or the mother who ran away and left me?

Those questions had plagued Jenny since she'd first started to think about God and where she was supposed to fit into the world. All these years later, she still didn't have any answers.

"I got a lot of them too," Tony said. "My mom was really into church. She tried to cram it down my throat every time I turned around. So I resisted, you know. The way kids will."

Jenny just looked at him.

"Okay, so maybe I extended my childhood a couple of decades. I still like my Xbox 360 and PS3 and maybe horror movies a little more than I should. The point is, I didn't listen to my mom. I went with her to church, but instead of listening, I was busy skulling out whatever level in the game I was currently playing that was giving me problems. I wasn't really paying attention. I stood when she stood. I bowed my head when she bowed her head. And I pretended to pray while she prayed for me."

The conversation wasn't relaxing Jenny at all. She realized in that moment that part of the reason she hadn't been back to see Megan Gander these days was because Megan had found God.

But Jenny just couldn't buy into it, though she still didn't have another explanation for all the disappearances.

"The point is," Tony went on, "my mother disappeared during the rapture."

There was that word again. When Jenny had heard it in church, she hadn't thought much about it. It was just one of those terms like *heaven, good, evil, apostle,* and others. The Bible was filled with words that didn't mean what she'd thought they meant while reading on her own. She'd gotten easily confused, and she hadn't wanted to ask anyone about anything she'd read.

"After I found out what was going on," Tony said, "I thought I knew what was happening. I called home. Got no answer. During the confusion, I slipped away and went home. When I got there, Mom was gone. Laundry was still spread out on the couch. I knew then that the rapture had happened."

Drawn into the story, Jenny couldn't help asking, "Why?"

Tony grinned. "Because God calling her home is the only thing that would have gotten my mom to stop in the middle of laundry. The woman was a factory when it came to washing, drying, and folding. The U.S. post office is a bunch of pikers compared to my mom." His dark eyes glimmered with unshed tears.

"I'm sorry," Jenny said quietly.

"Me too," Tony admitted. "Not because she's gone but because now I'm going to have to wait seven years to see her again. And mostly I'm sorry because I didn't believe in God enough to go with her."

Jenny didn't know what to say.

"Believing is important."

Jenny shook her head. "I don't think I know how to believe."

Tony smiled. "Sure you do. There are a lot of things you believe in. Just think for a minute, and you'll start to realize it. For me, it was my mom. Didn't you ever believe in your . . ." He stopped and looked at Jackson McGrath.

"No," Jenny said quietly. "Believing in my father ended way before believing in Santa Claus and the tooth fairy."

Tony looked horribly embarrassed. "Sorry. Didn't mean to bring up bad thoughts."

Just being in this room brings up bad thoughts. Jenny decided not to mention that.

"But this can't be all you've ever had," Tony persisted. "What about friends?"

"No. None that I could talk to for long. Every time I made a friend, they ended up meeting my dad. That was kind of a deal breaker."

"Oh." Tony smiled at her. "Well, I'm your friend. And I know a lot of the women here at the hospital have taken to you too. A lot of people care about you, Jenny."

For a moment Jenny thought she was going to cry. But she wouldn't allow herself to. It was almost like being back in Mrs. Wilson's class in the fifth grade, when she'd started getting her figure. She'd worked hard at school that year and had attended class most of the time. The teachers took up a collection to buy her some new clothes and a winter coat. Until that time she'd been stuck with boys' hand-me-downs that her father had wheedled from the women running the thrift stores.

For a while Jenny had actually felt good about going to school. She'd looked good and been warm. Then the other kids, jealous of the attention from the teachers Jenny was receiving, found out where she'd gotten the clothes. They started making fun of her, referring to her as a "ghetto" child. Wearing the clothes and the coat had never been the same. It wasn't until she'd gotten to junior high school and learned to make her own clothes that she started taking some pride in herself. And she'd never trusted that to anyone else.

"Thank you," Jenny said.

"You're welcome. Praying is the best thing you can do. You may not feel like you're getting anywhere at first. I gotta admit, I didn't. But praying for me was like talking to my mom. I talked to her a lot at first; then somewhere in there I started talking to God. He hasn't quite started answering back. At least, not the way you think of conversation. But I'm starting to notice things. Guideposts. A feeling of the way things are supposed to be." Tony shook his head. "I really can't explain it any better than that."

Jenny nodded, tried to think of a response, then gave up.

"What I'm telling you is, don't be afraid of prayer. I think more people should be doing it. And if you stay with it, you might be surprised at what you learn."

"Okay."

"And if you ever need anything, Jenny, I'm usually around. Just let me know."

"I will."

"Light off or on?"

"Off, please."

Tony switched the light off.

Jenny thanked him again and watched him leave. She looked back at her father. In the blue glow given off by the television mounted on the wall, Jackson McGrath looked like a specter swaddled in the hospital bedding. A feeling came over her that she was supposed to say something, but she had no idea what. Or to whom.

She glanced up at the television again. The anchor on OneWorld NewsNet was talking now. His words, printed in block letters, appeared and scrolled on the screen.

Jenny thought about calling Megan. She couldn't imagine what her friend was going through at the moment with her husband's life hanging in the balance in the middle of that conflict. Then again, when she stared at her father, she thought maybe she did know part of what Megan was going through.

At least Megan knows how she's supposed to feel, God. Why don't I?

United States 75th Army Rangers Outpost
Harran
Sanliurfa Province, Turkey
Local Time 0758 Hours

The sound of the heavy war machines tearing through the town assaulted Goose's eardrums. He concentrated on the task at hand, putting one foot in front of the other as he carried the wounded Ranger on the door even though his knee felt like it was on fire. It was an exercise of will more than strength that got him to the noisily idling van next to the wrecked APC. Flames still danced along the top of the Syrian vehicle.

"Oh, man," Gary the cameraman whispered as he stepped over one of the burned corpses. "I think I'm gonna be sick."

"You're not going to be sick," Goose said. "Not right now. Don't you drop this, man. If you want to be sick, you be sick later. Do you hear me?"

Gary swallowed hard and nodded.

"Breathe through your mouth instead of your nose," Goose said. "The smell's not as bad that way."

Gary opened his mouth and breathed. Danielle did the same.

Goose pushed the makeshift stretcher into the back of the van and turned to the others. "I'm driving. Ma'am, you and the camera jockey are going to have to hold this man as still as you can. We're going to be in a hurry, but this man can't be sliding around back here."

Danielle climbed in, followed by the cameraman. They sat on the floor of the cargo area on either side of the wounded Ranger and braced themselves.

"We'll take care of him," Danielle promised.

Goose nodded and shut the cargo door. "Corporal, you're with me."

"Yes, First Sergeant." Rainier walked up on the other side of the van. "Man, this thing looks like it's already put in its time in the trenches." He pushed the barrel of his rifle through the hole in the windshield.

"As long as it moves, it beats walking," Goose said. "Guess we're going to find out how long it beats walking."

After he slid behind the steering wheel, Goose found the seat belt and strapped in. Rainier had trouble managing the feat with one hand and Goose had to help. The fact that the interior was shot to pieces didn't raise any hopes.

"Thanks."

"No problem." Goose glanced back at Danielle. "Did this van have this much damage done to it when you found it?"

"No."

"You got lucky."

"Maybe I was just that good."

"Yeah. That was probably it." Goose couldn't believe she hadn't been killed or wasn't a nervous wreck at the moment. He rapped a hand against the wire mesh that separated the cargo area from the cab. It bounced a little but felt secure enough. "Hang on." The van snorted and backfired, then got underway. The heady aroma of the fuel-rich carburetor flooded the vehicle's interior.

"Carb's overloading," Rainier said.

"Yeah," Goose said. "I've been meaning to fix that."

Rainier hesitated a minute, then looked over at Goose. "That was a joke, right?"

"Yep. Probably not much of one, but I figured we needed it."

"It'll be funnier when I tell it later." The corporal paused. "I'll be telling it later, won't I, Sarge?"

"Yeah," Goose said with more confidence than he felt. "You'll be telling it." His eyes swept the streets constantly.

"Goose," Remington said.

"I hear you, Captain."

"We're only going to get the one chance at this, and it's going to be dicey."

"Yes, sir. I understand that. I'd also understand it if you chose not to risk a helo. One of those birds is worth a lot more than a handful of men."

"Do you believe that?"

Not for a minute, Goose thought. *But I'm not you, and you haven't been you in a long time.*

"If you were me, you'd move heaven and hell to make this happen."

Remington's sentiment surprised Goose. For a moment there, the captain sounded the way he had back when they'd come up through boot and the noncom ranks together. The feeling of friendship touched Goose deeply, though it was extremely confusing after spending the night in a basement under house arrest.

"He's being broadcast live on television," Danielle said from the cargo area.

Goose glanced at her in the rearview mirror, which sat crookedly on the broken windshield.

"I don't mean to burst your bubble," Danielle said. "I just wanted you to know what's going on." She indicated the earpiece she wore, letting him know she was still tied into OneWorld NewsNet's broadcast. "They're staying with us."

"There are the helos." Rainer pointed with his good hand.

The Black Hawks roared over the city. Outfitted with an External Stores Support System, a stubby wing protruding from each side of the aircraft designed for carrying weapons, the choppers looked a lot like mechanical birds of prey. With the weapons the ESSS carried, the helicopters were aerial dreadnoughts. Rockets and machine-gun fire strafed the Syrian armor south of Goose's position. He headed north as fast as the van was able.

The helos drew fire at once, but they ducked and wove as gracefully as dancers. Door gunners manned M240H machine guns and blasted the Syrian helicopters that flew spotter support for the tanks and APCs.

"Pedal to the metal, Goose," Remington urged.

The false note in the captain's voice rankled Goose somewhat. It wasn't like Remington to constantly use his name or provide cheerleading.

"The Hawks are loaded up with VOLCANOs," Remington said. "They'll buy you some breathing room, but not much."

"Understood, sir." Goose hauled on the wheel and cut a corner sharply. The transmission whined more than the bald tires did.

"What are VOLCANOs?" Danielle asked.

"They're designated the M139 Volcano mine system, ma'am." Goose shifted again, willing the van's engine to summon more speed. "They can be outfitted to the helos. Those Black Hawks can lay down a minefield a kilometer long—that's almost a thousand mines—in seventeen seconds. They're antitank mines, but they'll slow the Syrians down."

"They're not all antitank mines," Remington said. "I had them mixed special. Every sixth one is antipersonnel. Just like back in the old days."

"That's not normal?" Danielle asked.

Even fleeing for her life, the woman's curiosity seemed to consume her. Goose couldn't believe it. "No, ma'am. Not since the first Iraqi war. In 1993, the decision was made not to use antipersonnel mines."

"It wasn't my decision," Remington said.

"No, sir."

"I'm giving you over to Corporal Reilly, Goose. He'll feed you directions on where to make your evac."

"Affirmative, sir. Thank you, sir." From the corner of his eye, Goose saw the Black Hawks jettison their deadly cargo. The BLU-91/B AT and BLU-92/B mines were flat cylinders that tumbled for just a moment, then stabilized. A series of detonations sounded.

"Are they blowing up?" Danielle asked.

"No, ma'am." Goose took another corner. "The mines come down in aeroballistic shells. When they hit the ground, they trigger. The antipersonnel mine fires a squib that throws out eight trip wires. Like a spiderweb."

"Won't they be seen?"

"They're thin wires, ma'am, but, yes, they can be seen if they're looked for."

Fresh explosions sounded nearby.

Goose took one of the turns Corporal Reilly told him to take, again heading north. "But soldiers in a hurry—either running from a fight or running to one—won't take time to look. Those Syrian boys, they'll figure out what's what in just a little bit, and they'll ease up on the throttle."

"You got a hiccup coming up here, Sarge," Reilly said. He talked fast and sounded like an Easterner. "The Syrian line bulged ahead of you. You're going to encounter stragglers."

"No way around it?"

"Not at the rate the Syrians are coming in. That group is tracking the Black Hawk I've got coming to you."

"Or they could be headed north, operating on old intel from the jets' flyby. That's where we had our helos stashed."

"Roger that, Sarge. Either way, you're in for a rough ride."

Goose looked back over his shoulder at Danielle and the cameraman. "Get down. Flat as you can. Lie beside Private Johnson."

"Why?" Danielle asked.

"You ever watch Western movies?"

"Occasionally."

"Ever see *Tombstone*?"

"Val Kilmer. Kurt Russell."

"Yep. Just imagine we're them and headed into the O.K. Corral and the Clanton boys are already set up and waiting."

"Oh."

"You know," Rainier said, "until now I always liked that movie. I don't think I'm ever going to watch it the same way again."

At the next intersection, Goose glanced down the street to the right. Syrian troops hovered around a pair of T-62 battle tanks. One of the tanks fired its main gun. The shell wobbled through the air in front of the van, and the distinct hum filled Goose's entire world for that instant.

Rainier cursed.

Then the 115mm round struck a building on the other side of the street and blew up. Rock and mortar sprayed into the air and battered the side of the van. Windows shattered, and glass spilled all over Goose. He had his left arm up, blocking the barrage from his face, but a rock rolled under the van, got caught under the frame for a moment, and almost caused him to lose control.

"You still with me, Sarge?" Reilly asked.

"Barely," Goose answered.

"For a minute, it looked like that one had your name on it."

"You should have seen it from this angle."

"Take a left. Let me get you away from them for a moment."

"I'm all for that." Goose pulled hard on the wheel and shot down the next street.

"Take the next two rights," Reilly instructed. "Then go three blocks straight ahead; then take a left again. I got the helo touching ground just ahead of you."

Goose glanced in his rearview mirror and spotted two Syrian jeeps racing in pursuit. They skidded around the corner, fishtailing on the loose debris from the wrecked building, and barely avoided wrecking against another building.

"Tell those boys in the helo I'm coming in hot," Goose warned.

United States 75th Army Rangers Outpost
Harran
Sanliurfa Province, Turkey
Local Time 0803 Hours

Goose reached into his combat harness and took out a smoke grenade. He armed the grenade and whipped it toward the building on the corner as he prepared to make the turn. As he went around, the grenade unleashed a torrent of red smoke that partially masked the intersection.

The first Syrian jeep missed the turn and went too wide. On a direct course with the building on the other side of the street, the driver overcorrected and lost the vehicle. It skidded sideways for a moment; then the wheels caught in a pothole and on debris. The jeep flipped and went sideways.

The second jeep crossed bumpers with the first, swerved wildly for a moment, then made it through. It sped up again, quickly eating up Goose's short lead.

"Corporal," Goose said.

"I'm on it." Because of his injured arm, Rainier turned awkwardly in the seat, but he got into position. He shoved his M-4A1 through the window and aimed behind them. He fired in short bursts, just the way he'd been trained. Return fire came from the Syrians and peppered the van.

Goose heard bullets whiz by his ears as he went into serpentine evasive action that made it difficult to watch the street and control the van. Then something struck him in the back with bruising force. He struggled to get the air in his lungs again, hoping the bullet hadn't made it through his Kevlar vest. He pushed his panic aside and concentrated on his driving.

Two blocks farther on, Rainier's bullets must have hit the driver or wrecked something in the steering column. The Syrian jeep pulled sharply to the left and planted into the side of a home. The mud bricks held for a moment, then buckled, and the jeep disappeared from view.

"Better to be lucky than to be good." Rainier drew his weapon back into the van. He held the carbine between his knees and managed to feed in a fresh clip with his good hand.

"Sometimes."

"Sarge," Reilly said over the headset, "you got two hostiles coming up on your right side. We missed them in all the excitement."

"What are they?"

"Jeeps."

At the same time the corporal answered, the Syrian vehicles roared into the intersection. Both of them carried machine gunners on the rear decks.

Goose knew if he tried to brake or shift directions he'd expose everyone in the van to hostile fire that would cut them to ribbons in seconds. Instead, he kept the accelerator pinned to the floor and pulled his M-4A1 up to aim through the hole in the windshield before him.

The machine gunners took aim, but they were slower than Goose because they were still rocking to a stop. Driven by adrenaline, Goose steered the van toward the gap between the jeeps and hoped it was as wide as he thought it was. He fired the M-203.

The 40mm fragmentation grenade slammed into the windscreen of the jeep on the left. The shrapnel killed or seriously wounded the two soldiers in the front seats and swept the gunner from the rear deck.

Stunned by the explosion, the machine gunner in the second jeep hesitated. By the time he remembered to fire, he was aiming behind the van. As Goose passed between the jeeps, discovering that it was wider than he'd believed, he steered the van into the jeep, bumping it enough to knock the machine gunner from the rear deck.

"Oh, man," Rainier said, "those machine-gun barrels looked huge."

"At this end of them, yeah," Goose agreed.

"Left, Sarge," Reilly called over the headset. "There's your left."

"I see it." Goose made the turn, but he knew something had gone badly wrong with the van's front end. Either the rough road and high speed had finally gotten to it or the collision with the jeep had broken something. He barely made the turn.

The Black Hawk was just settling to ground in the large intersection two blocks down. A miniature dust storm rose around the helicopter.

"First Sergeant Gander, this is Sergeant Cooper Gordon. You'll be flying the unfriendly skies with me today."

"I remember you, Cooper."

"Then come on ahead. Black Angel Eleven has got your six."

Armed men deployed from the Black Hawk and prepared to bring the wounded man aboard.

"I got five with me counting the wounded man." Goose screeched to a halt.

"Roger that," the helo commander said. "We were on a hit-and-git mission to unload mines. We've got room to spare on the way back."

The Black Hawk crew sprinted forward with a medical gurney.

When he got out of the van, Goose's bad knee nearly went out from under him. He grabbed hold of the door and remained standing with effort.

"You okay, Sarge?" one of the Black Hawk crew asked.

"Just a little shaken up," Goose answered. "I'll be fine. Let's take care of my soldier back there."

The crew members cut Johnson free of the door and moved him to the gurney. One of them set up an IV and started a glucose pack.

"Let's go; let's go," their team leader ordered.

"Goose," Remington called over the headset, "it's time to go. The Syrians are closing in on your twenty."

"Yes, sir." Goose looked back down the street but didn't see anything. Perspiration covered him from head to toe, and dirt caked over that. His clothing stank from his having been in it for two days solid. His throat was raw and parched. He felt like he would collapse if he took another step.

"You've got Rangers coming up from the west side," Reilly said.

Goose brought his weapon up and stared in that direction. Captain Miller and three other men stumbled out of the alley.

"Have you got room for four more men?" the chaplain asked. Blood smeared his face.

"How'd you get separated from your group, sir?" Goose asked.

Miller shook his head. "I don't know. I was with them till the Syrians broke through. Then everything got confused. We took a vehicle, but they shot it out from under us."

"Sergeant Gordon," Goose called, "do you have room for four more Rangers?"

"We'll make room," Gordon responded.

"Goose," Remington said, "get out of there now. That's an order."

Quickly the Rangers loaded everyone aboard the helicopter. With Johnson sacked out in the middle of the cargo area, it was standing room only. Goose felt the wind and dust whip around him as the rotors increased speed.

"Stand ready," Gordon called from the cockpit. "We've got hostiles headed in our direction."

Through the dust-stained, bullet-cracked window, Goose saw a wave of Syrian assault vehicles speeding toward them. The door gunners opened fire, and hot brass tinkled into the catchers. A Syrian T-62 tank muscled to the forefront of the array of vehicles. The main gun lifted to fire.

Gordon fired a salvo of rockets from the ESSS that turned the Syrian line into a death zone. The tank remained functioning, though, shedding the flames easily. Before it could fire, two other Black Hawks arrived on the scene and targeted the tank. Rockets and missiles struck the tank repeatedly and left it in ruins.

Rotors roaring, the Black Hawk screamed skyward. Goose stood in the doorway and watched as Harran fell away. Most of the town was in ruins. Black smoke clouds drifted up from battle zones and burning buildings.

"It's terrible, you know." Miller stood at Goose's shoulder. Behind him, Danielle and the cameraman were at work.

"What?" Goose hoped they were out of range of small-arms fire.

"That town had such a wonderful history."

"If you say so."

"It goes all the way back to the beginning of the Bible. After Adam and Eve were driven from the Garden of Eden, many biblical scholars believe this is where they came with their family."

The Black Hawk swept away from the city. Goose held on to the door. A line of Syrians had massed below and shot at the American helicopters, but the attempts went wide. In the next moment, a trio of Black Hawks peeled away from the group and returned to wreak havoc among the Syrians.

A cheer went up from the Rangers on board the helicopter.

"Christianity, Judaism, and Islam all have important roots in this area," Miller went on. "Abraham lived here after he left Sanliurfa.

His father, Terah, died here. Ongoing archaeological digs have found evidence of several civilizations and cultures in this town. Even the name has significance. Loosely translated, it means 'the road.'"

"The road to what?" Goose asked.

"To Damascus."

"The capital city of Syria?"

Miller nodded.

Goose mulled that over. "You think there's any special significance about the Syrians trying to take it over?"

"Everybody's fought in Harran." Miller shook his head. "If you were able to open every grave that's out there, where men have been buried or where the dead were simply left after a battle, you'd find Greeks, Romans, Babylonians, Assyrians, Egyptians, Parthians, and a dozen others. These lands all throughout Turkey and Syria have been hotly contested almost since God put man in this world."

"Doesn't look likely to change, does it?"

"Sadly, no."

Goose tried to find a comfortable way to stand. His left knee continued to ache fiercely, and the pain echoed inside his skull. He knew things weren't going to get any better once they got back to Sanliurfa. The Syrians had gained a toehold in southern Turkey. They'd pull their forces together, get everyone healthy and their equipment squared away, and then mount another offensive to try to take Sanliurfa as well.

He glanced over his shoulder and saw that Danielle was continuing to report. She interviewed some of the soldiers standing around her. Given the restricted confines, the Rangers were shoulder to shoulder with her, but Danielle held her own. The cameraman struggled harder to find room to use his equipment.

"You people hold on to whatever you can," Captain Gordon called over the PA in the cargo area. "We're going to be running nap-of-the-earth on the way back to Sanliurfa. Try to stay out of the sky in case the Syrians light up some of the SCUD missiles they're packing in by truck. With the heat and the thin air, the ride's going to be a little bumpy."

As he finished talking, the Black Hawk hit a thermal, bounced up into the air a few feet, and swung side to side. Gordon leveled his craft off again, holding steady some thirty to forty feet above the ground. The landscape sped by dizzyingly.

Fingers numb from holding the doorframe, Goose reached for a new hold. When he did, he caught sight of a familiar face standing beside him.

Icarus.

27

United States 75th Army Rangers Temporary Post
Sanliurfa, Turkey
Local Time 0809 Hours

Captain Cal Remington immediately recognized the man standing next to Goose in the Black Hawk as Icarus, the rogue agent CIA Section Chief Alexander Cody was pursuing. The captain took in a calm breath and let it out.

Icarus was dark-complexioned and looked like he was in his early twenties. His dark hair was longer than in the photographs Cody had shared with Remington. A five-o'clock shadow colored his chin and cheeks. Beneath thick black eyebrows, Icarus's hazel eyes looked haunted and feverish.

Remington didn't know where Icarus had gotten the army Ranger BDUs he wore, but he'd obviously worn them so he could blend into the exfiltration effort.

According to Cody, Icarus was a covert agent they'd managed to get into one of the terrorist cells inside Turkey. He was an American, not a Turkish or Syrian that the agency had managed to flip. Remington had exhausted his resources trying to find out Icarus's real name. The captain had the distinct impression that whatever intel had existed on the young undercover operative had long since been expunged.

And now it seemed Cody had been right about Icarus trying to get in touch with Goose. But why? What made Goose Gander so important? That puzzled Remington—and irritated him—to no end.

Goose looked exhausted. Beneath the dirt and blood on his face, he appeared ready to fall over.

On the television screen, Goose and Icarus wavered into and out of the background, talking together as Danielle Vinchenzo interviewed some of the Rangers regarding their rescue as well as the effort put forth by the Black Hawk pilot and crew. There was no way of guessing what the conversation was, but neither man looked happy.

"Captain Remington," Josh Campbell said.

Remington turned to the reporter and was instantly framed in the camera. It was bad timing. The captain wished they'd stayed back.

"I'd like to congratulate you on your success in getting your people out of Harran," Campbell said. "My associate Danielle Vinchenzo is still interviewing Rangers aboard the helicopter that rescued her."

"Thank you," Remington said. "But we're not out of the woods yet." He realized that was something Goose would have said—had, in fact, said—during similar occasions. Remington hated that he was mimicking Goose, but Goose always looked good on camera—plain, soft-spoken . . . and humble. Always humble.

Officers aren't supposed to be humble, Remington told himself.

"What do you think the Syrians are going to do now?" Campbell asked.

"Regroup. Refortify. Secure those positions. Then get ready to march into Sanliurfa."

"You sound certain of their intentions."

"It's what I would do." Remington glanced around furtively. Cody was no longer at his side. The CIA section chief had stepped away and was talking on a sat-phone. And keeping an eye on him. When their gazes locked, Cody folded the phone and put it away.

"You've got a reputation for being an aggressive military leader," Campbell stated.

"I'd like to think that's well earned."

"The American military position, of late, has been particularly aggressive in the pursuit of terrorism. You've been a big proponent of acting first in several highly publicized incidents."

"Even before the disappearances," Remington said, "we were facing a new world. The United States has become a target to many terrorist factions. You don't get anywhere in this life by lying back and letting someone kick sand in your face."

"Do you think you can hold Sanliurfa against the Syrian army?"

Grimly aware that the broadcast feed was going out live, Remington kept his poker face on. "I've been ordered to hold this city against hostile incursion. Until I'm ordered to do anything else, that's what I'm going to do. The Syrians have attacked before, and we held them."

"Pardon me for pointing this out, but the Syrian forces that attacked earlier weren't as prepared as the reinforcements staging in Harran are going to be. If the Syrian army starts pulling SCUD missiles into that town and launching from there, isn't that going to be tremendously different from what you've faced in the past?"

"That depends on whether the Pentagon chooses to allow the Syrians to build up arms in that area." Remington shook his head, still wondering what Cody had been up to. The captain was certain the CIA agent had recognized Icarus as well. "I'm not in favor of allowing the enemy to strengthen its position."

"Surely you're not talking about attacking the Syrians in Harran after you've retreated from there."

"Not *retreated*," Remington said. "*Repositioned*. Soldiers are more important than hardware in a battle. I needed those men here. I didn't need them lost."

"Sir," Archer called. The lieutenant stood looking over a computer tech's shoulder at one of the monitors. A worried expression filled his face.

Remington made a mental note to discuss wearing his feelings on his sleeve in front of the media. He told Campbell, "Excuse me."

"Certainly. OneWorld NewsNet looks forward to speaking with you again." Campbell stepped back.

Remington immediately regretted losing the camera. He liked the attention focused on him. He crossed to Archer. "What is it?"

"We've got a bogey in the field, Captain," Archer said in a low voice.

Remington automatically scanned the sky but didn't see anything. Then he noticed the two Land Rovers streaking across the open terrain headed south. They were off-road, traveling too fast for the broken countryside.

"Who are they?" Remington demanded.

"We don't know, sir."

"Can you tighten the view on them?"

The computer tech rapped the keyboard with his fingertips. The view on the television monitor zoomed in on the two SUVs racing south toward Harran.

"When did you pick them up?" Remington asked.

"Just now."

"Where did they come from?"

"The road." Archer moved to another computer. "Roll back the sat-feed a couple minutes," he instructed the tech.

Remington divided his attention between the two computer monitors. He glanced at Cody, but the CIA section chief was keeping his distance. On the second monitor, Remington watched as the two SUVs sped along the road. At 0809 hours, by the time-date stamp at the bottom of the screen, the SUVs suddenly altered course and went cross-country.

What had caused them to veer off the road? Cold dread twisted through his stomach as suspicion took root in his mind. The Land Rovers hurtled along like predators with the scent of prey in their nostrils. Going top speed like that, they weren't hunting anymore. They were moving in for the kill.

Remington focused on the first monitor. "Pull back the view on those SUVs."

The computer tech started doing that. "How far, sir?"

"I want the bogeys and the Black Angel squadron on-screen at the same time."

"Yes, sir."

"Captain," Archer called. He was pointing at the monitor where the focus was on Harran. "The Syrians had SCUDs in some of the supply trucks. They're setting them up."

Curiosity fled Remington as he took in the new threat. The Syrians hadn't come prepared just to take Harran. They'd also come to unleash destruction on Sanliurfa. He knew he shouldn't have been surprised. It was something he would have done.

The UN commander standing nearby cursed. So did the Turkish commander.

"Sound the alarms in the city, Lieutenant," Remington snapped. "Put everyone on red alert."

"Yes, sir." Archer turned away, already giving orders to get it done.

The warning cry of the alarm Klaxons ripped through the morning.

Remington felt uneasy. The command post was safe enough against SCUDs armed with high explosives, but biological weapons—or nuclear, if it came to that—were a different story.

Most of the people had cleared out of the city streets once the attack began in Harran. Everyone had known that it could spill over into Sanliurfa.

"Captain," the computer tech said, "I've got the Black Angels and the bogeys on-screen."

Remington studied the monitor. He wasn't surprised to see the Land Rovers were headed straight for the helos. He turned from the computer and headed over to Cody.

The CIA section chief stood his ground.

"Are those your men?" Remington snarled.

"I don't know what you're talking about," Cody replied.

"I'm talking about those two Land Rovers on an intercept course with my helos."

"No," Cody replied flatly.

Remington knew the man was lying. There were no tells, no mannerisms, and no voice inflections to give the falsehood away. But nothing else made sense.

"What are you after?" Remington asked.

Cody hesitated. "Believe it or not, Captain, the same thing you are."

"I don't believe you."

"Captain Remington," another lieutenant called, "we've just confirmed multiple Syrian launches. We're tracking eleven SCUDs in the air. All of them are headed for us."

Remington returned to the computer tech. "Tell the Patriot missile systems to engage when they've got target lock. I don't want any of those blasted things getting through."

"Yes, sir."

Remington looked again at the helo squadron and the Land Rovers. "How far away is Black Angel squadron?"

"Almost fifty klicks, sir."

"How close are the bogeys?"

"Five-point-eight klicks." The corporal sat up straighter. "The bogeys have stopped, sir."

Remington saw that for himself. The vehicles had stopped in tandem. Doors opened and ten men deployed.

"Zoom in," Remington ordered.

The corporal did.

When the magnification was great enough, Remington saw the weapons two of the men carried were rocket launchers. The Black Hawks didn't create enough heat to draw heat-seeking ordnance, but when they were flying only thirty or forty feet off the ground, a regular rocket launcher could bring them down.

If they weren't expecting to be attacked.

"What's the ETA on the Black Angels intercepting those bogeys?"

"A minute fifty-two seconds."

"Open a channel to them."

"You're connected, sir."

"Black Angel Leader, this is Base," Remington said.

"Go, Base."

"Alter your course to the west. I repeat, alter your course to the west immediately. You've got hostiles on the ground you need to avoid."

"Roger that. Changing course."

"Redirect to the north end of the city. Use the airfield there."

"Understood, Base."

Tensely Remington watched the screen. He wasn't completely surprised when the men loaded back into the Land Rovers and took off again, headed once more on an intercept path with the helos.

They're tracking them electronically. Remington knew it had to be true, but he didn't know how it was being done.

"Black Angel Leader, this is Base. Be advised that the hostiles are tracking you. They know you've changed directions and are coming to meet you."

"That'll be their mistake, then."

Remington turned back to Cody, but the CIA section chief was already beating a hasty retreat through the front door.

For just a moment Remington considered ordering security to detain him, then realized it wouldn't help. Either the helos would survive the attack or they wouldn't.

"Incoming!" someone shouted.

Then the first of the SCUDs reached Sanliurfa and detonated.

28

"What are you doing here?" Goose growled. He dropped his hand toward the M9 on his hip.

"I came to see you." Icarus talked only loud enough that Goose could hear him. They stood chest to chest, banging into each other as the Black Hawk slid and shifted through the wind. The younger man's hazel eyes regarded Goose and never looked away.

"Why?"

"Because Corporal Baker is dead."

Goose felt suddenly chilled. "What do you know about Baker's death?"

"I know it was ordered," Icarus said.

"By Remington?" Goose couldn't believe he'd put his fear into words. After Baker was killed, Goose had wondered if the captain had had anything to do with it. He hadn't wanted to believe that, but the possibility existed.

"No." Icarus seemed so sure of himself, so calm in the middle of everything that was going on.

Goose looked at the other man and tried to figure out what to say next. He was still overwhelmed from the events in Harran and from the night before. He still didn't know why Remington had chosen to take the hard road with him.

"I need to talk to you," Icarus went on. "There's a choice that will need to be made. Soon. You must understand what's going to be asked. And why."

"Why are you talking to me?"

"Because you're in a place where your actions will affect others. You're a leader." Icarus hesitated. "Now that Baker is dead, perhaps you're the only leader who can open the eyes of the men around you and keep them from selling their souls in the service of evil."

The words caused Goose's flesh to prickle despite the heat of the day. Icarus talked about evil with a capital *E*, and his words brought to mind dark things blacker than night.

"I know you're not going to want to believe all of this, Sergeant." Icarus was too young to look as tired as he was. "I wish that I had more time to convince you of what I'm saying. But our enemy has planned too well."

Goose shook his head. "I let you go once. You should have stayed gone. When we get back to Sanliurfa, I'm going to turn you in."

"If you do that," Icarus said, "then you might as well put a bullet through my head."

✷   ✷   ✷

Outside Harran
Sanliurfa Province, Turkey
Local Time 0813 Hours

Marcus Allen rode in the passenger seat of the lead Land Rover. He held an RPG launcher across his thighs. Despite the air-conditioning, sweat beaded under his shirt because he had the door open.

He was a big man, rawboned and rugged. Three inches over six feet tall, he was the kind of man who gave other men pause. He wore his black hair cut short, the way the military had cut it for him before he'd mustered out and turned professional soldier for hire. Some countries he'd worked in had called him an assassin. He supposed, in the end, he was both. While working for corporations, he'd pulled security details. His work for the Central Intelligence Agency section chiefs, men who wanted their assignments kept off the books, generally ran more toward things of a destructive nature.

Allen scanned the sky through tinted Oakley sunglasses. "We should be coming up on those helos soon."

The driver, Weaver, nodded and tapped the GPS receiver mounted in the center of the dash. "Unless Cody's GPS signature is wrong."

"It's not wrong," Allen said. "One thing Cody does right is his toys. Man's got a fetish when it comes to tech."

Weaver—a smaller, thinner man with a mustache and brown hair that hung over the tips of his ears—grinned. "Can't say that I blame him. I've got a tech-toy fetish of my own to feed. Besides, if the signature was wrong, we wouldn't have picked up the helos' change of direction."

Kosheib leaned over the backseat and threw a thick forefinger toward the sky. The man was Sudanese but claimed Nubian blood. His black skin bore that out. Like Allen, he was big and tall, dressed in a sleeveless khaki shirt that showed the tribal tattoos that ran up his arms. If caught in Sudan or Chad, those tattoos alone would have identified him and gotten him executed.

"There," Kosheib rumbled. "They are there." His language held a British inflection, but it remained guttural.

Allen saw the helos then. He watched the GPS screen. "Drive under them. Let's see if we can identify the ping."

Weaver did as ordered.

"Owens," Allen called over the radio.

"Yeah." Owens was the second-in-command of the expedition. He rode in the second Land Rover.

"I read it as the fourth helicopter back." Allen made a circular motion with his forefinger, signaling Weaver to turn around.

"Agreed." Owens had spent half his life in one jail or another. The only way he'd maintained his freedom was by staying out of the United States and killing everyone who came after him.

Weaver brought the Land Rover around in a tight circle that threw up a large dust cloud. Then they were headed back in pursuit of the helicopters. Even the SUV's special suspension was hard-pressed to keep the ride level as Allen pushed the door open and took aim with the RPG-7.

"When I touch this off," Allen warned, "they're going to know we don't have friendly intentions. Take evasive action and let's find somewhere to hide, then pick up the pieces."

The "pieces" should be the man they'd been hired by Alexander Cody to kill.

A sudden curse came from the backseat. "The Syrians just launched a SCUD offensive against Sanliurfa."

"Cody's price tag on this piece of work just went up." Allen straddled the open door and held the RPG-7 as steady as he could. Getting caught in a cross fire between the United States and the Syrian armies hadn't been part of the deal. The CIA section chief didn't have control over that, but he wasn't getting a freebie either. Risk cost.

When he was certain he had target acquisition, Allen squeezed the trigger. The 40mm grenade ignited and whooshed away from the launcher. Allen automatically reached back inside for another grenade, and Collins slapped one into his hand.

The grenade sliced through the air and detonated against the ESSS on the helo's side. The Black Hawk heeled over and lost altitude for a moment. Three figures tumbled free of the cargo area.

Allen tried to ready another shot, but a SCUD hit the ground nearby, and the concussive wave knocked him back into the Land Rover. The blast caught the SUV off-balance, and the vehicle flew onto its side. For a moment, everything turned crazy.

The Land Rover skidded on its side through rocks and underbrush. The windshield shattered and fell into the vehicle. The sounds of the crash drowned out all other noise.

✿   ✿   ✿

Black Angels Squadron
Turkish Air Space
Sanliurfa Province, Turkey
Local Time 0813 Hours

An explosion sounded just outside the cargo door hatch, temporarily deafening Danielle as she worked on an interview with one of the Black Hawk crewmen. The live feed had ended, but she wanted more material that she could edit for human interest stories later.

The helicopter viciously swung sideways. Danielle instinctively went down and grabbed Robert Johnson's litter. It had been secured to the deck.

"What was that?" someone yelled.

"Somebody's shooting at us from below."

Danielle's first thought was that some of the Bedouin spies who had sabotaged Harran's communications link had set up an intercept point. Then she thought maybe a Syrian jet had crept up on them despite the heat-seeking missiles the Black Hawk helicopters carried.

"Where's Goose?" someone yelled.

Danielle's head swiveled toward the other cargo door. The last time she'd seen Goose, he'd been standing there talking to another soldier.

He wasn't there now.

"He fell out!" someone yelled. "When the helo tilted, he and two other guys fell!"

Not believing what she was hearing, Danielle shoved through the crowd of Rangers and made her way to the cargo door. She peered down, but she didn't see any sign of Goose. Too many trees and brush covered the ground, and they'd kept moving.

"We've got to go back," Danielle said.

"Can't," one of the soldiers said. "Just heard from Base. The Syrians have launched SCUDs and are on their way here. We're going to be lucky to make it ourselves."

Danielle gazed at the ground below. "How high are we?"

"Forty, fifty feet."

She thought about all the news stories she'd read and covered. "You can survive a fall that high. People have done it."

No one said anything, but she got the feeling no one believed her either. She stared at the trees below, then—for the first time— saw the crater left by a SCUD that had fallen short. They were still twenty or so miles from Sanliurfa. They were going to be lucky to make it.

❋   ❋   ❋

Local Time 0813 Hours

Goose didn't register what had happened until his fingers were torn from the doorframe and he was in a free fall. He toppled backward from the cargo door and saw flames clinging to the helo's skin.

Somebody shot us. That crossed his mind just before he realized two other people were in the air with him. Icarus didn't fly any better than his namesake, and David Miller screamed in terror, except that the wind and the noise of the helos washed it away.

Vaguely Goose remembered that Miller had staggered into him and Icarus when the explosion happened outside the helo. Goose had tried to maintain his hold on the doorframe, but he'd been precariously balanced after the blast and hadn't been able to. Icarus had been caught in the same situation.

Turn over. Get your feet down. Forty feet. You can tuck and roll out of that.

He managed to turn over and slide his assault rifle off his shoulder so he held it by the strap in one hand. The ground came up fast.

Trees seemed to be everywhere. He hoped Miller and Icarus missed them.

Then branches whipped into his face and eyes as he plummeted. He hit the ground and threw himself to one side, remembering all the horror stories of men who'd landed from a high jump and had their legs pushed up into their hipbones. The air rushed out of him, and he saw the tree beside his head too late to avoid it.

His forehead slammed into the tree, and everything went black.

Joey's heart hammered as he stood at the door and stared at Jenny McGrath sleeping in one of the chairs against the back wall. The room was quiet except for the low rumble of late-night television reruns. Muted lighting barely revealed the other people sitting around the room.

Jenny slept under a Windbreaker and looked like a kid. That reminded Joey of the way his little brother, Chris, would curl up and drowse whenever he was tired. Thinking about Chris hurt. There was something about having a little brother that had made him feel invincible, like not everything was all about him.

But that was gone now. So much was gone.

He hadn't intended to end up at the hospital. It had just happened. He'd started riding his bike at seven o'clock, trying not to think about the rec hall at eight and Bones and Zero looking for him. But after finding his mom at the hospital and seeing Goose on TV, it seemed as if all Joey's problems were crashing in on him at once.

He hadn't gone home, just kept riding, and now here he was.

He'd known Jenny was at the hospital with her dad, and he hadn't exactly *meant* to track her down, but somehow his bike had just sort of found its way here. And now he found he really wanted to talk to her. Goose was over in Turkey, right in the middle of the fighting, already dead for all Joey knew. His mom was focused on that and on all the kids in their house. And then there was the problem of Bones and Zero and the rest, out to kill him. That wasn't going to go away. Joey had seen enough true crime shows and detective movies to know that. He was a witness. If he had an attack of conscience, he'd name them all.

They'd never understand that all he wanted was to go free.

If there were just some way to keep the nightmares of the shop-keeper's death out of his head, Joey thought everything would be okay. It was an accident. That was all. Just a bad accident.

Only he knew it wasn't. He could fool himself for a little while, but that didn't last long.

Suddenly he felt eyes on him. When he glanced at Jenny, he saw that she was staring at him.

"Joey."

He didn't hear her. He watched his name form on her lips. He knew he should walk over to her, but he couldn't invade that room with his problems. Those people were in there trying to rest, trying to stay strong enough to support someone they cared about who was going through something threatening.

You don't belong here, he told himself. *You need to go.* He tried to leave. He honestly did. He willed everything inside him to leave.

Instead, Jenny got up from the chair and walked over to him.

"Are you okay?" she asked in a quiet voice. She pulled her hair from the corner of her mouth and studied him.

"Yeah. I'm fine."

"What are you doing here?"

Joey shrugged and hated the reflex action immediately. Shrugging was dumb and immature. But he hadn't learned what else he was supposed to do.

"Is your mom all right?"

"She's fine."

"Then what's wrong?"

"Nothing's wrong. I was in the neighborhood, that's all."

Jenny glanced at the clock on the wall. "In the neighborhood. At one in the morning?"

The way she said it, her words sounded like an accusation.

"Look," Joey said, "if this is a bad time—"

"It's not a bad time."

"Good. That's good." He stared at her, remembering how cute she'd looked out on the dance floor the night of all the weirdness. "That's really good."

She waited.

"So how's your dad?" he asked.

"The same. Nothing's changed."

"He's gonna be okay," Joey said automatically.

"How do you know?"

Joey shrugged again before he could stop himself. "I just do." He was afraid Jenny was going to be mad at him.

"Then you know more than the doctors," she said.

"Doctors don't know everything."

Jenny looked into his eyes. "You want to talk?"

"I don't know. You feel like talking?"

"Sure."

"That's good." Joey nodded in relief. He didn't know what he would have done if she'd said no.

"But we can't talk here," Jenny said. "People are trying to sleep."

"Yeah. I see. Want to grab a coffee somewhere?"

"Cafeteria's closed."

"We could go out."

She shook her head. "I don't want to leave the hospital. In case . . . something changes."

"Okay." Joey glanced up and down the hall.

"I know a place we can talk." Jenny reached out, took him by the hand, and led him down the hall.

❋   ❋   ❋

Local Time 0124 Hours

"The chapel?" Joey glanced around the room.

"It's quiet. Usually this time of morning there isn't anyone here."

No one occupied the room. Jenny pulled Joey into motion and got him seated in the back row. The light was dim. Joey sat beside her. She didn't let go of his hand. He was glad for the physical contact, but the sensation made him feel weak and vulnerable, and he hated that.

"So," Jenny said.

Joey looked at her.

"You just happened to be in the neighborhood," Jenny prompted.

"Yeah."

"Want to tell me *why* you just happened to be in the neighborhood?"

Joey thought about it for a moment. "Couldn't sleep."

"What's keeping you awake?"

He thought about his answer for a moment, then shrugged. "Stuff."

"Want to talk about that 'stuff'?"

"Not really."

Jenny leaned back in her chair and wrapped herself in the Windbreaker. She closed her eyes and breathed regularly. For a minute Joey thought she'd gone back to sleep.

"I've just got a lot on my mind," Joey whispered.

"You try talking to your mom about it?"

Joey grimaced. "I'd have to take a number. Besides that, this isn't something I can talk to my mom about. She'd freak."

"Then talk to me."

"I can't."

Jenny sighed. "Then don't talk to me."

"I'm not trying to make you mad."

"I'm not getting mad."

Joey felt even more guilt. "I'm messing this up."

"Messing what up?"

"I just came down here to spend some time with you. I just . . . wanted to be with you." Joey watched her, wondering how she was going to take that.

"I'm glad you did. It gets lonely around here. The nurses all mean well, but being here doesn't even come close to normal."

"I don't think anything is normal anymore." Joey felt the solid warmth of her hand in his. It felt good. "I'm scared that it never will be again."

"Me too."

"My mom's been talking a lot lately about the Bible. About the end times. I gotta tell you, it's freaking me out. I mean, Mom always had an interest in church. We didn't always go, and she didn't always agree with whatever the pastor was saying, but it was there. Like she knew we were supposed to go. But I didn't really get anything out of it. I don't think she did either."

"I think," Jenny said, "that if your mom is right, that's exactly why we were left behind. We didn't try harder to understand what God had planned for us. I know I didn't. If I thought about God, it was generally when my dad went on a binge or got hurt or got sick. When I couldn't take care of him, I asked God to do it for me. I don't think that's really a relationship. I mean, if you had a friend who constantly just asked you for things, and all you did was give, you wouldn't think you had a very good friendship, would you?"

"No." Guilt ate at Joey. What Jenny was describing wasn't just his relationship with God. It was a lot like the relationship he'd had lately with his mom and Goose.

"I think that's what it's about," Jenny said. "Your mom says there's going to be seven more years that we can exist on this world before God comes back. During that time, we're supposed to figure out our relationship with Him, find ways to get closer to Him."

"Yeah. But that's hard."

"What?"

"Believing God really cares. If He really cared about me, about having a relationship with me, I wouldn't be in all the trouble I'm in now." Too late, Joey realized he'd said more than he'd intended to.

"What trouble?" Jenny asked.

He tried not to tell her. He wanted to hold back and be strong. More than that, he was afraid that once he told her, Jenny would feel compelled to tell someone else. The police. Or his mother.

Instead, when he finished, while he wiped the tears from his face and felt ashamed and guilty and scared, Jenny just sat there. She didn't look at him and she didn't say a word.

Finally she asked, "What are you going to do?"

"I don't know." His voice was thin and hoarse.

"You said they came looking for you?"

"Yeah. They're at the post."

"Are they looking for you now?"

"I don't know." Joey resisted the impulse to shrug. "Maybe they came there because they heard the fort was offering shelter to kids. Maybe Bones spotting me was just bad luck. I seem to have a lot of that lately."

Jenny squeezed his hand. "You can't just ignore them. They're not going to go away. Not if they're afraid you're going to tell on them."

"I know."

"You could go to the police."

"They'd lock me up, Jenny. According to the law, I'm as guilty of murdering that man as Zero is. He made us all murderers when he pulled that trigger." Joey shook his head. "I couldn't handle being locked up. I'd rather kill myself."

"Don't talk like that."

"It's true," he whispered. "And maybe that's how this is supposed to work out."

"I don't believe that."

Jenny's words made Joey feel hopeful. For just a moment. Then reality set in again. She would tell him that. She had to. It's what he would have told her if their roles had been reversed.

"There's something else," Joey said. "I heard Mom's trying to fix it so that the families of the soldiers in Turkey can go over there."

"Why?"

"So we can be together. And so we can help them. At least until the government decides to bring them home."

"Do you think she's going to be able to make that happen?"

"Yeah, I think so. A lot of people at the fort look up to Mom these days."

"Are you going?"

"It would give me a chance to get away from all of this," Joey answered. "I could get away from Zero and the rest of those guys."

Jenny was quiet for a time. "I think," she said finally, "that might be the best thing you could do."

"I know." Joey focused on her. "Mom could arrange it so you could come with us."

Jenny shook her head.

Joey squeezed her hand. "Please. I really want you to go."

"I can't." Her voice sounded dry and husky, as if she was about to cry. "I've got to stay here. With my dad. He needs me."

Silently Joey cursed his bad luck. He leaned back against the wall and stared at the darkened ceiling. "I can't stay," he whispered. "I just wanted you to understand."

"And I can't go," she replied. "I hope you understand."

Joey nodded.

"If things were different," Jenny said, "I'd go."

"If they were, I'd stay."

"But they're not," she said.

Joey sat there and tried to think of something to say. The attraction he'd initially felt for Jenny had changed. It was no longer purely physical, but now it was stronger than anything he'd ever felt before. And he was being forced to walk away from her. It wasn't fair.

"When your mom goes," Jenny said, "you need to go with her. I don't want you to get hurt. And your mom will need you. Those soldiers can use whatever help you can give."

"I know." Joey sat there quietly and held her hand. He didn't want to think about leaving her. But he knew he couldn't stay. He felt helpless and trapped.

And alone. Even though Jenny was sitting next to him, he was pretty certain she felt the same way. It was incredibly lousy.

Pain filled Marcus Allen's world. He opened his eyes and stared up at the blinding sun. Automatically, after listening and hearing no movement around him, he felt for his Oakleys, but they weren't there. He cursed the pain and the fact that the sunglasses were probably broken. The expense didn't bother him so much as the effort it had taken to get them.

He rolled onto his side and located the Galil rifle he carried as his lead weapon. The RPG was nowhere to be seen. He dragged himself to his feet and walked over to the wrecked Land Rover, which sat upside down.

Weaver was just rousing, dangling from the seat belt that had kept him locked in. He groaned as he felt his chest.

"Anything broken?" Allen asked.

"No, but there was definitely no lack of trying."

Kosheib cut himself free of his jammed seat restraints with a combat knife. "Collins is dead." He jerked a thumb at the man on his right.

Kneeling, Allen peered through the passenger window. All the glass had broken out. Collins, in his forties and a habitual smoker, hung upside down with his arms over his head like he was involved in a bank holdup. A lit cigarette singed his dead lips.

"What happened?" Allen asked.

"Broken neck." Kosheib grabbed the dead man's hair and jerked

his head to one side. It lay almost on his shoulder, obviously discon-
nected. Without another word, the Sudanese released the dead man
and kicked the passenger door open with a screech.

"What about Heinrich?" Allen asked.

"I'm alive," the young German killer answered calmly. "Just waiting for the opportunity to get out." He was thin and had a mop
of unruly black hair. Even on his best days he reminded Allen of a
weasel.

"What do you want to do with Collins?" Kosheib asked.

"Leave him." Nobody got a burial in Allen's unit. If they survived
to the end of a contract, they got the rest of their bounty and maybe
a bonus from a happy client. No one in the group had any kind of
history that would tie them to the others.

"Is the truck going to be driveable?" Heinrich climbed out through
the door as well.

"Doesn't matter," Allen replied. "We're trapped between the devil
and the deep blue sea. We can't go forward because we'll be running
into the American forces in Sanliurfa that aren't going to be happy
with us. We try to go back, we're going to end up in the midst of the
advancing Syrian army."

Weaver dusted himself off. "You thinking we're going to get out
of Turkey on foot?"

"Or find a roundabout way into Sanliurfa. We get there, Cody will
help us get out of the country. Or at least keep us hid out."

SCUDs flew by overhead. The heavy thunder of their passing
echoed against the hard-packed earth.

"Maybe Sanliurfa isn't the best place we could be," Kosheib
observed.

"We took on the contract," Allen replied. "We haven't been pulled
off of it."

"We're not exactly going to have the element of surprise on our
side if we go into Sanliurfa." Heinrich kneeled by Collins's body
and quickly rifled the dead man's pockets. He took money from the
man's pants. When he saw the others staring at him, he looked a little
guilty. "What? I'm going to share it with you." He shoved Collins's
half pack of cigarettes into his shirt pocket.

"Where's Owens and his team?" Allen asked.

No one knew.

"Spread out and find them." Allen held his carbine across his
body and walked farther into the thick trees around them.

❊   ❊   ❊

Local Time 0826 Hours

Goose woke with blood in his eyes and a splitting headache. He lay on his back and took a breath. Keeping calm took effort.

Move slowly, he told himself. *If you're hurt bad, you don't want to make it worse.* He'd seen wounded soldiers in the field go from manageable casualties to life-and-death situations in a heartbeat. All it took was a piece of broken bone to slice an artery.

He worked his hands and feet first. Then he drew his right arm up to wipe the blood from his eyes. He'd figured out what it was from the copper taste that leaked into his mouth. Blurred vision returned to him.

He stared up at the tree canopy. The white flesh of broken branches stood out against the verdant green and dull charcoal gray bark. Those partly explained how the fall hadn't killed him.

He moved gingerly to explore his body. Sudden movements would be stupid. As he shifted more and more of himself, there was more pain.

Push through the pain. Pain just means you're still alive.

The distant thunder of the Syrian heavy armor grew closer.

And you're not outta the woods yet. Goose looked around at the trees. *Literally.*

A few minutes later, after he'd made sure he was intact and nothing was ruptured so that nothing that belonged inside his body was suddenly going to be outside, he forced himself to his feet. His M-4A1 lay nearby. He picked it up.

He spent a few minutes trying to connect with the Ranger communications but wasn't successful. Either he was in a black hole for the signal or the Syrians were jamming the frequencies.

Remembering that Miller and Icarus had fallen with him, he went in search of the other two men. The throbbing in his knee hurt terribly, and he had difficulty walking. He tracked the others through the broken branches that blazed a trail through the canopy. Thankfully none of them had been impaled on the way down.

Miller lay twenty yards away, behind a large boulder he'd missed by less than a foot. The man was out cold, and at first Goose feared that he was dead. Miller's chest rose and fell slowly, though. Relieved, Goose went over to the chaplain and did a visual inspection for injuries without moving him. There was no blood around Miller, so Goose took that as a positive. Gently Goose touched the man's shoulder.

"Captain Miller," Goose said.

Miller didn't move.

Goose shook the man a little harder. "Captain Miller, you got to get up. The Syrians are coming."

Footsteps sounded behind Goose. He spun and brought the M-4A1 up in one hand.

Icarus stepped out through the trees. He tucked his right arm behind his Kevlar vest. His features looked pale. "We've got trouble," he said.

❋ ❋ ❋

Local Time 0829 Hours

Allen found Owens's vehicle jammed between trees and brush. A broken tree limb protruded from the driver's chest. The jagged shard had pierced his heart and stopped it so suddenly that there was little blood.

Manfred Owens, a native Bostonian with a short-cropped beard and long hair, fumbled in an effort to free himself from the passenger seat. He was a broad bulldog of a man with burn scarring on the left side of his face and neck.

"Cody's target I'm going to assassinate for the fee," Owens declared as he pushed himself out and up. "I get the chance, though, I'm going to throw some of those Syrians in for free. What was that? A dud?"

"If it had been a dud, it wouldn't have blown up," Weaver said. "Must have had a fuel problem. Something. Fell way short of the target."

"No joke," Owens growled.

"Heinrich, Weaver, Kosheib," Allen said. "Set up a loose perimeter. Could be the Syrians saw us and may have someone along soon."

"Roger that." Heinrich swept the hair from his eyes and set off at once. The other two joined him in setting up a three-post guard, fanning out from the wreck site fifty yards away.

When he checked the rear of the Land Rover, Allen found Purvis disoriented and McElroy just regaining consciousness. With Owens's help, he helped both of them from the wreck. Newton was a different story. He was semiconscious and in pain. But his right leg was broken in three places.

"Can you walk?" Allen asked.

Fear tightened Newton's eyes. He was young and desperate. The United States had a murder charge waiting on him if he returned there.

"Sure," Newton answered. "I can walk."

Without a word, Allen stood by and waited.

Newton forced his way out of the Land Rover and stood on his good leg. Allen shoved a hand into the man's chest, catching him off guard. Newton tried to remain standing, but his broken leg buckled and he went down with a scream of pain. He pulled himself back up, clawing at the Land Rover like an animal.

"No! Allen, please don't!"

Allen already had his pistol in his fist. He held it only a few inches from Newton's face and pulled the trigger three times. The dead man's blood spattered Allen's fist. He wiped his weapon clean on Newton's shirt.

Allen's sat-phone rang. Only three people had the number. He answered.

"You missed your target," Alexander Cody said.

"Do you know that for a fact?"

"I'm looking at video footage of Icarus and two other men falling from the helicopter at the same time the SCUD landed near you."

Allen turned and looked north. The woods were thick and filled with brush. He suspected there was an underground spring or watershed concealed somewhere within the forest.

"Your fee isn't going to be paid until you can guarantee the kill," Cody said.

"Understood," Allen said. "Are you sure the target is alive?"

"I'm sure I don't know that he's dead. It's your job to get me proof."

"I will." Allen closed the phone, looked at his men, and explained the situation.

"More than likely," Owens said, "all we have to do is find their bodies."

"Then that's what we're going to do."

Owens glanced back to the south. The loud noise of the Syrian advancement filled the forest around them. "This is gonna be a bad place to get caught by those Syrian soldiers."

"Let's plan on not getting caught," Allen suggested.

Owens still didn't look happy.

"If you want to hump out on your own," Allen said, "I'll understand. I don't mind finding a dead guy and splitting the bounty six ways."

Owens cursed. "I'm in."

Allen called the others in, then explained the situation to Weaver, Kosheib, and Heinrich. They didn't look happy either.

"I do not like this," Kosheib said.

"Neither do I," Allen admitted. "But that missile didn't take us off the board—"

"Not all of us," Heinrich said, looking down at Newton.

"—so I figure we've got enough luck to get paid for this." Allen paused. "And no matter how you look at it, we're going to have to go north in order to keep from encountering the Syrians."

"The target may still be alive," Heinrich pointed out.

"Then he's not going to be that way for long." Allen slung his rifle over his shoulder, grabbed extra canteens from the Land Rover, and set off into the brush.

Grumbling and cursing, his pack of wolves trailed at his heels.

Goose lowered his weapon but didn't put it away. "What kind of trouble?"

"The guys who shot us down are going to come looking for us," Icarus said. "I know some of them. Their leader, for one. His name is Marcus Allen. They're all stone killers."

Reflecting on the explosion outside the helicopter, Goose knew the attack had come from the ground. There'd been no Syrian aircraft around, and they'd been far enough ahead of the enemy ground troops that he hadn't believed they'd accounted for the attack.

"How far back are they?" Goose asked.

"Six, seven hundred yards."

"You saw them?"

"Yes."

"And they're hunting us?"

"If they aren't yet, they will be soon."

"What kind of vehicles do they have?"

"Both their vehicles are disabled. They're on foot."

Goose nodded. "Gives us a chance. How do you know them?"

"They work for Alexander Cody. And for Nicolae Carpathia."

"Where did you get that information?" Goose wasn't happy with how little he knew about the situation they were all in.

Icarus shook his head. "We don't have time for a question and answer session. If they catch us, we're dead."

"If the Syrian army catches us, we're dead." Goose gazed back to the south. "We don't have anything but trouble all the way around us."

Icarus glanced at Miller. "How's he?"

"Just knocked out. I was about to wake him when you came up on me."

"We need to get him up and moving." Icarus shifted his arm and grimaced.

"How's the wing?" Goose asked.

"Broken elbow."

"You're sure?"

"Yeah. I've had a broken elbow before."

"We're all lucky we didn't get real busted up coming down through those trees."

Icarus grimaced. "Not lucky enough."

"How many men back there?"

"Seven."

"They're all the same as this Allen you mentioned?"

Icarus nodded.

"What kind of training have they had?"

"Allen and some of the others were in military and spy organizations."

Tension washed over Goose. It was a long way to Sanliurfa. "You got anything for pain?"

Icarus shook his head.

Goose rummaged in his medical pack. "I got some stuff in here that should dull it." He took pain pills from the kit and passed them to Icarus. Goose took a couple himself to ease the throbbing in his knee. He also followed up with some anti-inflammatories to help with the swelling. His knee already felt incredibly tight.

He broke an ammonia capsule beneath Miller's nose and got him up.

❈   ❈   ❈

Local Time 0839 Hours

Goose chose a course that would keep them within the trees. To the right, out in the massive open area, the Syrian armor rumbled past. As he limped through the trees, Goose watched the tanks, APCs, and field artillery roll along amid dust clouds. He felt guilty that he wasn't going to be at Sanliurfa when the Rangers there needed him most.

"Goose," Miller said, looking anguished, "it's my fault we're down here. I should have been holding on better. If I had been, maybe I wouldn't have knocked us all off the helicopter."

"If the guy who fired the rocket launcher at us had shot a little straighter," Goose said, "none of us would be here right now. You can't fault yourself, sir. This thing—it just turned out the way it did. Can't go back and change it now. Our job at this point is to get back to our unit as soon as we can and hope they're still holding their own."

Miller nodded and kept trudging along.

None of them could forget the men who combed the forest behind them.

✸ ✸ ✸

Local Time 1017 Hours

Goose called for a breather while they were on the side of a hill. They took cover between rocks and a copse of trees. Overhead, the sky had turned dark with the threat of a sudden storm. The wind had picked up, and the air had cooled slightly. Goose hoped the rain came soon and that it wasn't just a false promise as it sometimes was in Turkey. If it rained, it might slow the Syrian assault on Sanliurfa.

"Hydrate or die," Goose said and drank from the tube to his LCE. "Don't try to conserve water. Drink your fill. As hard as we're pushing ourselves, we've got to keep fluid in our systems. Isn't going to do anyone any good to drop halfway there while holding on to a full canteen."

Miller sat wearily on a rock, breathing hard. Even the constant physical conditioning the army required clearly hadn't prepared him for the long march through rough country. He made himself drink.

"The chaplain is struggling to keep up," Icarus said softly.

"I know that," Goose said.

"Allen and his men are gaining on us."

"I know that, too."

"Given our present rate of travel, they'll catch us within the next hour."

Goose nodded. "I'm going to have to do something about that."

"What?"

"I'm going to whittle the odds down a little." Goose stared through the binoculars he carried. The forest was thick, but every now and again he caught a glimpse of one of the men who pursued them so relentlessly. "How are you holding up?"

"I can make the walk," Icarus said. "I've had to do worse things."

"Then why don't you take the chaplain further on."

"What are you going to do?"

"Stay a little while. Set up a few surprises for those killers."

Icarus was silent a moment. "Don't underestimate those men, Goose. They're very dangerous, and they won't hesitate a moment to kill you."

"Then neither will I," Goose replied. "You two best get started. I'll catch up to you when I can."

"Even with that bad knee?"

Goose grinned with false confidence. "I don't know what you're seeing, buddy, but I'm genuine GI. A hard road just separates the men from the boys. I'll be with you soon enough."

Icarus offered his good hand. "I hope so, Sergeant. Truly I do. Your men need you. Otherwise, they'll be lost."

Goose wanted to ask about that cryptic statement, but he didn't. There wasn't time. And he couldn't allow any other thoughts inside his mind other than how he was going to deal with their pursuers.

As he watched Miller and Icarus get underway again, Goose divested himself of insecurities and pain. He donned the mental armor of the hunter. At this point, there could be no mercy.

✳   ✳   ✳

Local Time 1023 Hours

"I'm getting tired of all these trees and brush," Heinrich complained. He pushed and shoved his way through the dense foliage.

"That is because you are out of shape," Kosheib said. "You have become lazy from all the easy work you have been getting lately. Killing someone in their bed or out in front of a restaurant is not the same as stalking them through the bush." The Sudanese strode through the forest like a big cat.

"Yeah, well I for one am glad to work in the civilized world. It's easier to pop someone who's following a routine in the city than to try to flush them out of the brush."

Allen ignored the men's banter. Kosheib and Heinrich usually griped to and about each other. Trying to get them to stop only exacerbated the problem. Allen stayed locked on Weaver, who was walking point at the moment.

The sat-phone vibrated in Allen's pocket. He didn't look at caller ID to see who it was. He already knew. Alexander Cody had called twice so far to find out if they'd caught up with Icarus.

Allen was actually impressed the three men they pursued had covered as much ground as they had. Their prey had tried to be coy about their flight on a few occasions, changing directions and trying to conceal their trail. In the end, all they'd done was lose time. Allen, Owens, Weaver, and Kosheib were all trained trackers.

A few minutes later, Weaver signaled a stop, then waved Allen forward.

"What do you think he's found?" Owens asked.

Allen didn't look at Owens but kept his eyes constantly moving, glancing around using the periphery of his vision to track movement. "Only one way to find out. Kosheib, you're with me."

The big man stepped up beside Allen and moved soundlessly through the brush.

"They've split up." Weaver pointed at the footprints that showed on the ground.

Allen knelt and studied the tracks. Two sets of prints showed in the soft earth. He looked back the way they'd come and spotted the ridge of stone showing above the earth.

"They hid their footprints for as long as they could," Kosheib said.

"You think they had a falling-out?" Weaver asked.

"No." Allen glared along the stone ridge. "They knew we were following them."

"They could have split up to take their chances."

Allen shook his head. He stayed low and surveyed the surrounding terrain.

Kosheib hunkered down beside him. "I am thinking this could be good spot for ambush."

"Me too." Allen placed his assault rifle across his knees and tried to tell himself he wasn't vulnerable.

A flicker of movement disrupted the trees over the heads of Owens, Purvis, and McElroy as they stood and talked. Allen recognized the spherical shape immediately, but he still had to try to warn his men.

"Grenade!"

Owens ran and threw himself to one side without a wasted second. Purvis and McElroy looked at Allen, awaiting further orders. There wasn't time for any more.

The antipersonnel grenade blew up and slung their bodies backward. Allen had no illusions about either man still being among the living.

The split had just dropped to five.

Quietly Allen waved Kosheib to the other side of the stone ridge. The mercenary leader took his weapon and duckwalked through the brush, circling around to where he thought the grenade had come from. Whoever had stayed back was about to regret being born.

That would be only for a short while, though. Allen intended to put the man out of his misery quickly. He only hoped it was their prey.

"Staring at the screen isn't going to make that program go any faster."

Danielle glanced at Pete Farrier, the audio-visual tech assigned to the OneWorld NewsNet team. He was gangly and looked young despite being in his early thirties. His dark hair was cut short enough to let him pass as one of the soldiers in the Ranger unit. He wore khaki shorts and a T-shirt advertising a video game popular five years earlier.

"I know," Danielle admitted.

They sat at a table in the foyer of a small hotel. The old building had weathered the test of time and had survived the Syrian assaults over the last few weeks. The decor was Old World with Moorish influence in high arches over the doorways. The electrical lighting barely held its own against the darkness lurking by the covered windows. Original paintings adorned the walls.

A dozen men and women sat around the tables. Small children, sharing the tension felt by their parents, hunkered under the tables. None of them looked confident to be there.

No, Danielle silently amended, *none of them look* safe. They all looked pensive and ill at ease. Every time an explosion or a long string of gunfire sounded, they flinched.

On the notebook computer screen in front of Danielle, an image constantly pixilated. She'd taken a still from the video her cameraman had shot aboard the helicopter before Goose and two others had plunged from the cargo door. Danielle had recognized one of those other men as Icarus, the mysterious rogue agent CIA Section Chief Cody was hunting. There was no way that Icarus being on board the helicopter that had been shot at could be coincidence.

"You could rest," Pete suggested.

Danielle looked at him and shook her head. "In the middle of a war?"

"Hey," Pete said, "over the last few weeks I've discovered that I can sleep anywhere, anytime. You're tired enough. How about you get horizontal for about five minutes and see what happens."

Danielle shook her head. "I can't."

"You ask me, you're foolish not to." Pete sipped a little of the dark, sweet Turkish coffee at his elbow. "When this image gets cleaned up—although I'm still not certain that it will—I'll wake you."

Jets screamed by overhead, followed almost instantly by a string of explosions. The heavy bellow of antiaircraft guns chattered through it all. The ease with which she identified the military hardware and weapons surprised Danielle.

It's because you're in survival mode, she told herself.

Many of the adults joined the children under the tables. A little girl started crying. Her mother gathered her into her arms and tried to shush her.

"I feel too guilty to sleep," Danielle said.

"Why?"

She shook her head, trying to keep a lock on her emotions.

"Because Sergeant Gander was knocked out of the helicopter and you weren't?"

"Maybe. I keep thinking that I was standing right there, that I could have just reached out and grabbed hold of him."

"And maybe gotten pulled out yourself."

"Maybe."

"I don't see how any good would have come from that."

"At least Goose would know he has someone on his side." Danielle clung to the thought that Goose was alive. Some of the Rangers she'd talked to after the helicopters reached Sanliurfa had assured her Goose had the training to survive a fall like that. In her mind, she pictured Goose holed up somewhere awaiting rescue. She knew that wasn't the case, though. If Goose Gander was able to walk—or drag himself—he'd be on his way to the city. To his unit.

"No," Pete disagreed calmly. "If you'd fallen and survived, he'd have one more person to look after."

Danielle frowned at him.

"Hey." Pete spread his hands and smiled. "You're not exactly *Survivorman* out there."

Danielle took a deep breath and let it out.

"You don't even know if Goose is still alive," Pete said quietly.

"I know. But somehow I can tell he is."

"How?" Pete studied her.

She shook her head, trying to figure out how to put into words what she knew instinctively. The problem was, it didn't make sense even to her. "I just . . . I just know."

"Spider senses?"

"No."

"I haven't seen a crystal ball."

"No crystal ball."

Pete smiled. "Are you crushing on the sergeant?"

Feeling guilty, Danielle started to say no, but Pete's arched brows told her he already knew her answer before she said a word.

"Maybe a little," she replied.

"He's married."

Danielle nodded. "Very married. He talks about Megan all the time. Doesn't stop me from wishing I'd meet someone just like him. Or that he had a brother."

"I suppose not." Pete took a breath. "You're not the only one. Me? I look at him, watch him, I wish I had a friend just like him. He's just that guy, you know? That guy who, no matter how tough things get, will never let you down."

"That's why the viewers love Goose. He's got that solidness about him. Honor."

"Makes you wonder," Pete said, "if all those religious people are right and all of us who have been left behind are locked into some kind of Tribulation, what is Goose doing here?"

"I did an interview with Corporal Baker right after we got to Sanliurfa," Danielle said. "None of the television stations were interested in airing it. Corporal Baker said that some of the people were left behind because they were guilty of sin and had fallen away from God. But the majority were left behind because they weren't true believers—they hadn't brought God into their hearts and accepted salvation through Jesus."

Pete studied the computer screen. "You put any stock into that?"

Danielle thought about her answer. She didn't like talking about things like this, and she felt increasingly uneasy doing so. "I'm not sure. More so than before."

"What about Goose?"

"He's focused on getting through this war and keeping as many of his men intact as he can."

"So he's not a big believer either?"

"Not that I can see."

Pete shook his head. "I wish I knew what to believe."

"I know. Baker told me that even with everything going on around us, a lot of people still aren't going to believe this is the Tribulation. They're going to deny it and look for other reasons for what happened."

"I suppose."

"Baker also pointed out that faith is based on what you *believe* in, not what you know. If we knew the answers, we still wouldn't have faith."

"Sounds like you've been thinking about it."

Danielle wanted to deny that immediately because that was how she'd always handled discussions about religion. Like the topic was beneath her. Especially since there was no clear-cut answer in her mind. She started to deny it again, then stopped. "Maybe I have been thinking about it," she agreed. "But I still don't have any of the answers I need."

At that moment, the computer screen blinked, and the image came into clearer focus. Danielle leaned forward and studied the men in the vehicles below the helicopter. The image came from the footage shot just before Goose and the others had tumbled from the chopper. The focus was almost there.

"I got to admit," Pete said, "this software package your friend put together is impressive. He could probably sell it to motion picture studios out in Hollywood."

The software was designed to clean up images. According to Mystic, the computer hacker Danielle had struck up a relationship with a few years ago while pursuing a story, the program filled in missing details based on references gleaned from the rest of the image as well as a large data bank.

"I don't know that much about software," Danielle admitted.

"Well, take it from me—what this guy is doing is computer magic. Not impossible, and other people have probably got similar software, but I'd hate to have to pay for it."

Another SCUD hit nearby and caused the building to shake.

Ceiling tiles smashed against the floor. This time the ceiling fan that had threatened to tear loose since the beginning of the attack crashed to the floor. Jagged glass shrapnel flew in all directions.

33

Outside Harran
Sanliurfa Province, Turkey
Local Time 1036 Hours

Goose held his position next to a thick-boled tree and took deliberate aim. The M-4A1's open sights bracketed the head of the mercenary standing where the big white man and the black man had stood only moments ago. Letting out half a breath, Goose squeezed the trigger once and trusted his sharpshooting skills.

The man fell backward with a bullet hole high in his forehead.

Three down, Goose thought grimly.

As the sound of the shot echoed through the forest, the first raindrops zipped through the leafy branches of the tall trees and spattered against the backs of Goose's hands and neck.

Thunder rumbled in the distance and reminded him of the Syrian armor rolling against Sanliurfa. He forced that out of his mind. The Rangers would hold there. The rain would come in time. Things would be fine until he got back. He had to believe that.

With his back to the tree, hidden within the undergrowth, Goose listened. The thunder made it harder to hear, and the pattering of the rain confused things as well.

Then there was no mistaking the cautious sound of a man's feet sliding through the brush. The *whisk-whisk-whisk* of leaves against the man's pants grew closer.

The man stopped. Goose knew he was only a few feet away, just out of Goose's peripheral vision. If Goose turned his head to see the man, he was certain the motion would be seen. He breathed shallowly and waited.

Quietly the man shifted his feet. Goose knew then that he wasn't a trained soldier or a hunter. Nervousness chafed at the man. Silence and forced stillness were his enemies instead of bringing him security and peace.

A moment later, the man stepped into view.

With the M-4A1 already at his shoulder, Goose moved the muzzle only slightly and shot the man just under the ear. The report of the gunshot shattered the quiet of the forest.

Knowing the man was dead or dying, no longer a threat, Goose shoved back against the tree.

A fusillade of bullets chopped into the tree. Bark splinters leaped from the trunk and spun in the air.

Goose pulled out a smoke grenade and threw it in front of the tree. The grenade went off with a loud explosion and filled the immediate vicinity with red smoke.

"He's trying to escape in the smoke!" someone yelled. "Watch for him!"

Instead, Goose remained seated only a few feet from the dead man.

"Did you see him?" The voice was on the move, coming up on the right.

"No."

"He can't have gotten away."

"He didn't. He's somewhere close by."

For a moment, fear touched Goose. He thought about Megan and Joey and about how he was only one bullet away from not ever going home.

Don't do that, he told himself. *That's the weakest thing you can do as a soldier. You've got to think about living.*

But he kept thinking about Chris too. About how Chris was gone and he was never going to see his son again.

Is that how it's really going to be? Am I never going to see him again?

Goose's eyes burned as he listened for men moving in the brush. They were good. They hadn't broken cover or backed away in fear. They'd settled into their positions as well.

The talks Goose had shared with Joseph Baker before the corporal was killed trickled through his mind. Baker had promised a better end to everything than Goose could imagine. Baker's faith in God had filled the corporal's life after all those people disappeared. Goose still didn't know how that had happened, but Baker's experience had reminded Goose of Bill Townsend. Bill was among those who'd disappeared, and he'd always said he felt close to God.

How about it, God? Goose couldn't help wondering. *Am I closest to You? Or am I closest to death? Are those even separate things?*

The rain fell in sheets now, whipping through the forest. Goose thought about what it would mean for the Syrian assault. Hopefully the heavy vehicles would be mired in mud and never reach Sanliurfa. At the very least he hoped the mud had slowed the enemy advance.

Remembering all his days in Sunday school, Goose thought about how often rain and water had played a part in the Bible stories. The parting of the Red Sea. The Flood. Baptism.

Does baptism count when you don't really believe? Can you be baptized without really knowing God? Is that what I did? Sometimes in church he'd seen people get rebaptized as a testimony of renewed or restored faith. Others hadn't been certain they'd really known how to accept salvation at the time they had.

Goose held on to his rifle and listened to the world around him. There was no noise other than the rain.

God, I don't want to die out here. Not so far from my family. Not so far from my men. This can't be what You have in mind for me. I know it's not what I have in mind for me.

Goose couldn't believe his thoughts. He'd prayed before, reflexive efforts that he'd learned as a child, but he'd never really tried to talk to God. Mostly because he'd figured if there was a God, He was probably pretty busy. And he doubted that God would concern Himself with one small sergeant in a world of trouble.

A branch, still too dry, cracked behind the tree less than ten feet away. The smoke had dissipated. Goose breathed more shallowly and waited. The next events were going to happen very fast.

A minute later, while rain dripped from the brim of his helmet, Goose saw the man ease forward in a duckwalk. He carried a rifle in both hands as he stepped toward the dead man lying only a short distance from Goose.

Goose moved his rifle into position. The small flicker of movement alerted the man. He threw himself backward and tried to bring up his weapon. Knowing his life was on the line and that it was better to be outnumbered two to one than three to one, Goose fired into the center of the man's chest.

As Goose had expected, Kevlar armor blocked the bullet, but the impact drove the man backward. His boots churned at the loose mud created by the torrential rain and he couldn't find traction.

Goose rose, knowing the hiding spot no longer concealed him. He took aim and put three rounds into the man's face and neck.

Coordination left the man, and he sprawled onto the ground. Blood mixed with the running water and mud.

Throwing himself from the tree, Goose ran straight ahead. He kept the tree between himself and the place where he thought the remaining two men were. A bullet smacked into the middle of his shoulder blades and probably would have killed him if he hadn't been wearing his vest. He stumbled and nearly fell. His injured knee almost gave out on him, and pain scraped raw nerves. Agony racked the inside of his skull.

But he ran.

The large black man stepped out in front of Goose and pointed his rifle at him. In that instant, Goose realized they'd almost flanked him.

Knowing he hung suspended between life and death, Goose went down in a baseball slide only a few feet from the man. Goose's knee screeched in protest as he folded it into the familiar figure 4 beneath him.

A line of bullets sprayed over Goose's head. One of them ricocheted from his helmet. Then he slammed into the big man and took him to the ground. They rolled in a tangle of arms and legs. The man lost his weapon, and Goose struggled to bring his rifle to bear.

Shouting in a language that Goose didn't understand, the big man pulled a machete from his hip and swung at Goose's head while they were still both on the ground. Reacting instantly, Goose released the M-4A1 and grabbed the man's wrist. It took everything he had to slow the man's attack, but he couldn't stop it. The keen edge came down toward his face.

"Now you will die!" the man said.

Goose focused on keeping the knife from his head. His arm quavered from the strain of holding the man's arm back. Desperate, he bunched his fist and drove it into the man's face again and again.

The man shouted and snorted in pain and rage. His eyes reddened as capillaries swelled and broke. His nose bled profusely.

Getting his leg up between them, Goose levered the man onto his side and crawled on top. In that position, with gravity helping, it was easier to hold back the man's machete. Goose again hammered his fist into the man's face, hoping his opponent would lose consciousness soon.

With a surge, the big man backhanded Goose in the mouth. The ache in Goose's forehead from the collision with the tree reignited and pounded at his temples. Blood filled his mouth. The big man hit him again and succeeded in knocking him off.

Goose lost his grip on the man's wrist and rolled as quickly as he could. The machete missed his legs by inches. Ignoring the pain in his knee, Goose got to his feet as the big man bared his teeth in a confident, angry grin and rushed at him.

Unable to move quickly without his knee giving out on him, Goose pulled his M9 from his hip, shoved the pistol forward, and fired. The first two rounds were wide of the target, and the next one thumped into the big man's Kevlared chest. By then he was almost on top of Goose, already swinging the machete.

Goose fired four more times, and all of the rounds hit the man's unprotected head and destroyed his features. The massive arm came down anyway. Stepping forward, feeling his leg go out from under him, Goose moved inside the swinging arm, felt it bang against his side so the blade missed him. He lowered his arm immediately and trapped his opponent's limb. Then he twisted and fell, dragging the man down. On the ground now, Goose shoved the pistol into the man's neck and pulled the trigger two more times.

The man shivered and went slack as life left him.

Running footsteps splashed across the muddy ground.

Goose heaved himself from the dead man toward the M-4A1. His hands found the grips even in the mud and the rain, with pain filling his head. For seventeen years, he'd carried a weapon like this rifle. It had been his constant companion. He was more familiar with it than anything else in his life.

The last of the mercenaries ran at him and opened fire. Unable to get to his feet because his knee wouldn't hold him, Goose rolled onto his stomach with the rifle propped on his elbows before him. It was the basic position the army had taught him in boot, and it was the first position his daddy had taught him when he'd taken him deer hunting.

The man's bullets dug holes in the mud beside Goose's face. One clipped his helmet, and two others ricocheted from the body armor covering his back.

Goose sighted on the man's face and pulled the trigger. The man stopped running and stood there swaying. A look of disbelief was frozen on his face. Goose fired again and the man's head jerked back. Then he slumped forward on his knees and went face-first into the mud.

Not believing what had happened himself, Goose lay there and stared at the dead men around him. The rain came down harder, covering him in a gentle wash that cleaned him of the mud and the blood.

After he got his breath, he stood and walked, limping on his bad knee and trying to ignore the pain.

34

Downtown Sanliurfa
Sanliurfa Province, Turkey
Local Time 1039 Hours

Danielle covered her face with her hands and shoved her head down between her knees as glass from the fallen ceiling fan sprayed around her. Fragments pelted her, and she felt a few sharp stings on her forearms and the back of her neck. When the worst of it seemed over, she cautiously looked up again.

Pete had roped his arms protectively around the notebook computer on the table. He held his position for a few moments, then leaned back and studied the ceiling with some trepidation.

"You know," he said, "I'm beginning to wonder if we should take this meeting down into the wine cellar."

Shaking, Danielle studied the cuts on her bare arms. Glass fragments glittered on her clothing. She started to brush at it, then realized that she'd only cut up her hands. She took a napkin off the table and knocked the glass from her lap.

"If we go down there," she said, "we'll lose the Internet connection. We're lucky we have it now."

"Yeah, but part of me keeps wondering if the Syrians are using Internet hot spots as targets."

The thought chilled Danielle. She swept her gaze over the people around them. She didn't like thinking she was responsible for bringing death closer to them.

"That's not what's happening," Pete said. "I didn't mean to drop that on you. That wasn't fair."

Danielle nodded.

The screen pixilated again. This time the image reformed even sharper than before. She stared hard at the faces of the two men revealed in the video footage. The driver remained mostly hidden behind the glare reflecting off the windshield. The man on the passenger side of the vehicle held a rocket launcher over his shoulder. Three-quarters of his face showed.

"That rocket launcher blocks a lot of his face," Danielle said.

"We knew that when we started this. So did your friend. We all agreed that this was the best image we had."

"I know."

"If we don't get anything from this photo, it's not going to happen. And we're lucky to get this much."

Danielle glared at the image and willed it to give up its secrets. "Do those men look Syrian to you?"

Pete shook his head. "No. But that doesn't mean they weren't hired by the Syrians."

"Whoever those men were, they singled us out. They knew which helicopter Icarus evaced on."

"You're assuming that."

"It's a safe assumption. No one else on any of those helicopters would have been a target."

"What about you?"

"Me?" That thought hadn't occurred to Danielle.

"Sure. You're a reporter. OneWorld NewsNet. You've been hot-dogging screen time out here, becoming the voice of the people of the free world. At least for American television." Pete grinned sheepishly. "The Syrians might like the idea of taking out a significant member of the American press."

Danielle hadn't thought of herself in that way. It was flattering, she supposed. And maybe even a little true.

"You were doing spots from Harran," Pete pointed out. "They knew you were there."

"They wouldn't hire an assassination team to come after me."

Pete nodded at the image on the computer. "Like you said, those men don't look like Syrian military. Somebody hired them. That's why you wanted to take a closer look at them."

Danielle knew that was true. But she'd also concentrated on the men because it was all she could do. Remington had given orders that the press were to stay out of the street and out of the way of his men. The Rangers had orders to take into custody any press members they found roaming and lock them up for the duration of the attack.

Many of the reporters felt certain that being placed under such "protection" would actually turn out to be a death sentence. All of them had cleared immediately.

Abruptly a line of script ran across the bottom of the computer screen.

Mystic:>TALK TO ME, MUCKRAKER.

Danielle slid forward, placed her hands on the keyboard, and opened up a chat application. She went immediately to a private room she'd arranged with Mystic.

Muckraker:>YOU THERE?

Almost immediately a response appeared on the screen.

Mystic:>YES. GLAD TO KNOW YOU'RE STILL ALL IN ONE PIECE.

Another nearby explosion shook the hotel.

Muckraker:>SO FAR. DOESN'T APPEAR HOPEFUL.

Mystic:>I'M WATCHING THE COVERAGE ON CNN.

Danielle knew that OneWorld NewsNet and others continued carrying the story through a few automated cameras set up throughout the city.

Mystic:>I SAW A MODEL REENACTMENT OF SANTA ANNA'S ARMY TAKING THE ALAMO. LOOKS A LOT LIKE WHAT YOU GUYS ARE GOING THROUGH NOW. VASTLY OUTNUMBERED.

Muckraker:>AREN'T YOU FULL OF GOOD CHEER.

Mystic:>WELL, AT LEAST I COME BEARING GIFTS.

Danielle's heart leaped.

Muckraker:>YOU IDENTIFIED THE MEN IN THE IMAGE.

Mystic:>ONLY ONE OF THEM. BUT HE'S A BIG PIECE. I'M SENDING YOU A PACKET. LOG IN TO YOUR FTP SITE AND PICK IT UP. I SQUEEZED IT AND DRAINED IT. SHOULD DOWNLOAD FAST FOR YOU.

Danielle opened up another window and accessed the FTP client she had on the computer. Once activated, the program searched for new packages and found one immediately. She started the download.

Muckraker:>GOT IT.

Mystic:>YOU'RE GOING TO LIKE THIS.

Muckraker:>THE SHOOTER TIES BACK TO OUR CIA SECTION CHIEF.

Mystic:>IMPRESSIVE. PSYCHIC MUCH?

Muckraker:>NOT HARD TO FIGURE OUT WHO AROUND HERE

WOULD HIRE AN ASSASSINATION TEAM TO TAKE OUT THE MAN
ABOARD THAT HELICOPTER.

Mystic:>TRUE. THAT'S HOW I WAS ABLE TO TURN THIS SO
QUICKLY. I HAD MY SUSPICIONS TOO.

Muckraker:>WHO IS HE?

Mystic:>GOT THE PACKET?

Danielle watched the last of the transfer take place. She opened it
and saw thumbnail images pop up in neat rows. Some of the images
were of people. Others showed newspaper stories and official-looking
documents.

Muckraker:>LOOKING AT IT NOW. HIS NAME IS MARCUS
ALLEN? REAL OR ALIAS?

Mystic:>EVERYTHING I'VE BEEN ABLE TO DIG UP SAYS THAT
IT'S HIS TRUE NAME. GUY HAS A HISTORY. CAREER SOLDIER
GOT BOOTED FOR PLAYING HARDBALL WITH PRISONERS. HE
QUIETLY MUSTERED OUT AS THE HEAT STARTED TURNING
UP. THEN HE STARTED HITTING THE MERCENARY SCENE.
IT DIDN'T TAKE ME LONG TO FIND OUT HE'S ONE OF THE
GUYS YOUR SPY GUY HAS GONE TO IN THE PAST. USUALLY
FOR BLACK-BAG AND DIRTY-TRICKS ASSIGNMENTS. AND FOR
ASSASSINATIONS.

Beside Danielle, Pete grimaced and cursed. "You know what? I
didn't think, given the fact that we're getting bombed, that I could
feel any worse. But this?" He shook his head. "Thinking these guys
are still walking around out there gives me the willies."

Danielle silently agreed.

Muckraker:>YOU'VE GOT EVIDENCE OF THIS?

She pulled some of the news stories up.

Mystic:>NO. I DON'T HAVE SOLID EVIDENCE. WHAT I
HAVE WOULD NEVER MAKE A COURT CASE. BUT I DO HAVE
SUBSTANTIVE. CONNECTING THE DOTS IS NO PROBLEM.

Danielle's mind flew. If Goose was still alive, this man in the
image—*Marcus Allen*, she thought, putting a name to the fear she
felt—could still be alive also.

Mystic:>YOU NEED TO THINK ABOUT GETTING OUT OF
THERE. THIS GUY MIGHT NOT BE THE ONLY ONE YOUR SECTION
CHIEF HAS IN MOTION. I TRIPPED A FEW ALARMS GETTING THIS
GUY'S INFO.

Muckraker:>NOT LIKE YOU TO BE LESS THAN GRACEFUL.

Mystic:>YOU CAN HAVE STEALTH OR YOU CAN HAVE SPEED
WHEN IT COMES TO THESE THINGS. IT'S HARD TO ACHIEVE

BOTH. SINCE THERE'S A BIG CHANCE THE SYRIAN ARMY IS GOING TO INVADE THAT CITY AT ANY MOMENT . . .

Muckraker:>UNDERSTOOD. CAN YOU KEEP WORKING WITH THIS NAME? MAYBE GET ME A LIST AND PIX OF KNOWN ASSOCIATES.

Mystic:>I CAN. I WILL. BUT IF THIS THING STARTS GETTING DICEY AGAIN, I'M ALL ABOUT DISCRETION BEING THE BETTER PART OF VALOR.

Muckraker:>I KNOW.

Someone had already tried to trace Mystic through Internet connections during an earlier investigation.

Muckraker:>TAKE CARE OF YOURSELF.

Mystic:>I ALWAYS DO. WHAT ARE YOU GOING TO DO?

Muckraker:>WHAT I CAN. SEE IF I CAN FIND THE SECTION CHIEF AND STIR UP TROUBLE. IF HE'S STILL IN THE CITY. HE'S GOT A HABIT OF DISAPPEARING WHEN THINGS GET REALLY DANGEROUS.

Mystic:>ACTUALLY I CAN HELP YOU WITH THAT TOO. I'VE BEEN TRACKING SOME INTERNET TRAFFIC COMING OUT OF SANLIURFA THAT'S NOT COMING OUT OF THE ESTABLISHED MIL-NET.

Muckraker:>MIL-NET?

Mystic:>MILITARY NETWORK. I'VE BEEN WATCHING SOME OF THE TRAFFIC GOING INTO AND OUT OF THE AREA THERE. FIGURED IF I COULD GIVE YOU SOME EARLY HEADS-UP WARNING, IT MIGHT HELP.

"Wow," Pete said. "I'm even more impressed."

"He's an impressive guy."

Muckraker:>THANKS FOR THAT. I'LL BE MONITORING YOU WHEN I CAN.

Mystic:>COOL. I'VE GOT A COUPLE OTHER PEOPLE THAT I'M SHEPHERDING IN THAT PART OF THE WORLD.

Danielle's curiosity came to the forefront immediately.

Muckraker:>ANYONE I SHOULD KNOW ABOUT?

Mystic:>. . .

Mystic:>SORRY. I'M TIRED. TYPED THAT BEFORE I THOUGHT. FINGERS WORK FASTER THAN MY BRAIN SOMETIMES. I CAN'T TALK ABOUT THOSE PEOPLE.

Danielle cursed. For years, Mystic had been a ghost. He'd never asked for anything, but he'd aided her from time to time with key pieces of information. She'd have given a lot to find out more about him.

Muckraker:>YOU SAID YOU KNEW WHERE I COULD FIND MY GUY?

Mystic:>YEAH. HE'S HOLED UP AT A HOTEL THERE IN THE CITY. LET ME GIVE YOU THE ADDRESS.

Hell descended on Sanliurfa. The war, snarling and blistering hot, ravaged the city and sucked the marrow from its broken bones despite the pounding rain. A few of the SCUD missiles the Syrians were firing had gotten past the Patriot defensive systems, and Remington felt the explosions shake the earth and quiver through his boot soles.

He stood at parade rest in front of the ops board and kept the battlefield in view in his mind even when the satellite systems occasionally failed and the screens went dark. Fear came at him harder then. His dependence on technology left him crippled and floundering.

It's not me, Remington told himself, struggling for a calm, clear head. *It's war the way it's fought now. Battles these days move too fast for an unaided man to keep up with. No one could adequately track developing fronts and unit strength without computers.*

Back when war had first been invented, generals had peered over a battlefield from a cliff or a hill, or they had led their troops from the front lines. They'd been able to see everything they needed to.

Remington had studied war, from the Chinese texts to the Romans to MOUT battles staged inside cities. In the beginning, war had started in communities as one faction inside a metropolitan area— no matter how large or how small—had fought to contain or destroy another. Then war had gotten too large and was waged outside the city, partly to make sure there was still something left standing for the victor to claim. From there war had spread to the struggles between the cities, where economies and religions threatened to conquer all.

War was still waged for the same reasons. Spin doctors simply tried to put different faces on it.

The Greek city-states had battled each other. The nations comprising the German confederacy had battled each other. The North had battled the South in the United States. Remington believed it was man's nature to battle other men.

There could, in the end, be only one conqueror, one world leader.

He gazed at the ops board in disbelief. The Syrians seriously outgunned and outnumbered his troops. Sanliurfa had been under constant attack for almost three hours. The Syrian military and air force had settled into the ridges around the city and contented themselves with shelling and bombing the Turkish, American, and United Nations forces into submission. Time was on their side.

At least the rain that continued to fall slowed them. The huge tract of land in front of the city's walls had become a lake of mud that jammed the Syrian cavalry units. A few of them that tried to cross the expanse became targets for Remington's artillery squads. Those squads hadn't hesitated about blowing tanks, APCs, and field artillery to pieces.

Remington knew that several Syrian units sat out there in smoking ruins. He took pride in those small successes. What he needed was a way to turn those into more and larger successes.

What he needed—though he was loath to admit it—was Goose. Whenever circumstances had threatened to get out of hand in the past, whether in Iraq or Bosnia or in one of the African countries where they'd fought for survival in the early years, Goose had always been by Remington's side.

Don't you think about him, Remington commanded himself. *Goose is part of the problem these days. He's picked up Baker's slack and has split the attention of this army. These men need to stay worried about saving their butts, not their souls.*

"Captain," the com officer said. He was young and bright faced.

Remington looked at the man.

"I've got Doyle."

Remington nodded, then reached up and switched his headset to the frequency he used for Corporal Raymond Doyle. "Go."

"I found your bird." Doyle's voice carried the lilt of New Orleans in it. Before entering the army, he'd been a street enforcer in that city and a part-time bounty hunter for a bail bondsman. His attorney had gotten him a sweetheart deal into the army to settle a manslaughter charge the DA's office had leveled against him.

Before the army, Doyle had been a violent man conditioned to using his fists and a gun to solve problems. After Remington found out about him, he'd put the man's talents to work. He still employed his fists and gun, and he did the dark, dirty jobs behind the scenes that Goose wouldn't.

The "bird" was CIA Section Chief Alexander Cody.

"Where is he?" Remington asked.

"North end of the city."

That didn't surprise Remington. "Is he getting ready to run?"

"He's still here, but I'm willing to bet if things turn much more sour, he'll bolt like a striped ape."

Remington wasn't sure what the colloquialism meant, but he understood the sentiment. "He's probably afraid to head out of the city with the SCUDs dropping out there." The other end of Sanliurfa was easily within reach of the Syrians' missiles, and some of those who had chosen to flee late in the game lay dead on the highway now.

"That's the way I figure it too. But if he decides he likes his chances better out on the open road, what do you want me to do?"

"Prevent that. I'm not done with him."

"Yes, sir. Probably be better to bag him and bring him in."

"Can you do that?"

"Yes, sir, but it'll be bloody. He's got him a squad of hard-core boys around him."

Remington's mind flipped that around. "He's not waiting here to see if he can get out of the city. He's waiting to see how things turn out with Goose and Icarus."

"You could be right, sir. But seeing as how we haven't had any radio communication with Gander, there's every chance that—"

"Goose would keep radio silence at this point," Remington said. "He's behind enemy lines. He's not going to want to call attention to himself."

"No, sir. I reckon not. If I was in his shoes, I wouldn't want nobody to know where I was either. Out in that brush, he'll have a chance."

If he's still alive.

Even though Doyle didn't say the words, Remington knew the man was thinking them. Remington wasn't going to believe Goose was dead till he saw the sergeant's body.

"Keep a loose watch on your target," Remington said. "I don't want to lose track of him in the confusion."

Another SCUD landed nearby and shook the earth. Particleboard dropped from the ceiling and landed on soldiers as well as the floor.

A flurry of curses ran through the room, and a few of the men hit the deck and went flat. The electronics went out for a moment, then came back on.

"Are you still there?" Remington asked.

"Yes, sir."

Remington let out a tense breath. He needed the communications array to stay intact. "Did you copy my last instructions?"

"Stay on top of the target. Don't engage."

"Right. He's probably waiting around at least till nightfall. That's when Goose will most likely try to make it back into the city. If Icarus is still alive, Goose will bring him in at that time too."

"Yes, sir." Doyle's calm tone told Remington he'd already thought of that. "The target's wired into a communications array himself. He's staying on the horn to some of his people."

"He'll have spotters around the city." Remington's mind flew, working out everything Cody would probably be planning for. Remington turned and gazed around the room. "He's probably going to have someone on me."

"Yes, sir. If I was the target, that's what I'd do."

Remington hated the insecurity that fell over him. He hated having to accept that he didn't control everyone in the room. Cody, and the agency the man worked for, had enough resources to buy any one of the soldiers in the command center who wasn't convinced his future lay in Remington's hands. At the moment, there were probably a lot of soldiers like that.

"The good thing is," Doyle said, "the target doesn't appear willing to leave the city till he deals with his objective. It's easier to hunt something that has a reason to stay around. That way you don't have to worry about just one chance to get it right. Him hunting that Icarus guy, that's just a honey pot to a bear. I got a feeling this guy won't jump till he's settled his target's hash. Works out for us."

"I'm relying on you," Remington said.

"Yes, sir. You're in good hands."

For the kind of work he was doing, Remington knew that was true. Goose would have asked too many questions, insisted on knowing too many things.

Making himself breathe, Remington started to flip the headset back to the frequency carrying the main information for the army maneuvers. Doyle's next announcement stayed his hand.

"We got a problem," Doyle stated in a flat, dead voice.

"What?"

"That woman news reporter just showed up."

"What's she doing there?"

"Nothing at the moment. Looks like she's just watching him."

"How did she know where the target was?"

"Don't know, sir. You want me to—"

"Stay out of it," Remington commanded. He didn't know what Danielle Vinchenzo's game was, but he was willing to let that develop a little as well. "Let her draw the heat for a while. Maybe she'll force the target's hand."

"Yes, sir."

"If something changes—"

"I'll let you know immediately."

Remington flipped frequencies and concentrated on the board, where Archer labored to put up the latest stats relayed by the intelligence teams. Men and women talked incessantly as they brought information together to hand off.

The monitors that fed video from cameras strung through the city kept breaking down. The feeds had to restart constantly. But the blank screens gave only a short reprieve from the absolute carnage unleashed on the city.

Dead lay in the streets. Survivors fought with the United States Army and with the United Nations units, demanding to be taken to a place of safety or to have help with a loved one who was wounded or dead.

In addition to death, the heavy hand of madness lay over the city as well.

"Hey, get back!" a man's voice yelled.

Drawn by the fierce protectiveness in the words, Remington turned to face the entrance. A handful of soldiers held four civilians back. Three men and one woman, all Americans or Europeans from the sound of them, fought with the soldiers.

"Get those people out of here," Remington commanded.

The soldiers pulled at the intruders, but they weren't making much headway.

"You need to evacuate us," the oldest man said. He looked like he was in his late thirties, powerfully built and broad. "You have planes. We've seen them." He swatted one of the soldiers away with a vicious backhand that showed he was no stranger to violence. "We just want out of the city. You owe us that. We're civilians. You're supposed to save us. That's your job, and I expect you to do it."

The soldiers formed a line but gave up trying to remove the people.

They didn't have the heart to do their jobs. Most of the younger soldiers hadn't ever had to fight the people they were supposed to be rescuing. Remington understood, but he faulted them all the same.

Without another word, Remington walked over to the group. The soldiers stepped away. The big man leading them smiled and looked at Remington.

"Now this is more like it," the big man said.

Remington stopped ten feet from the man, well out of range of an easy grab. "Sir, I'm asking you one more time to vacate these premises. This is a very sensitive area."

The man scowled. "You're supposed to save us."

"You were told to leave days ago," Remington said. "Leave this room. I'm no longer asking you. This city is under martial law, and I'm the law."

"I want a plane," the big man said. "I know you can make that happen."

Rage hammered Remington's temples. He wasn't going to brook insubordination, and something like this could undermine his authority.

Smoothly, without warning, he drew his sidearm and took immediate aim at the man. The man stood his ground, jaw thrust out defiantly. Dispassionately, Remington shot the man in his left thigh, aiming for the thick meat of the outer thigh so he wouldn't accidently nick the femoral artery and kill him.

The pistol report cracked loudly inside the building. All the techs, and even the security men, stepped back as the man dropped to the floor. Shock twisted his face and pulled his mouth into a gaping O of surprise.

"You can't—," one of the civilians started to say.

Remington pointed the pistol at that man, putting an instant halt to the objection. The man threw his hands up in front of his face and turned away.

"Anybody else want to make any demands?" Remington asked calmly.

No one responded.

Remington didn't put his pistol away, but he did drop it to his side. "We're in desperate straits here. The army is doing the best that it can. You will not interfere with the command post again." He flicked his glance to the security teams. "I don't want to have to shoot another civilian to enforce something you should already be doing. If I do, you'll be in lockdown. Is that understood?"

"Yes, sir," one of the men responded. The others quickly nodded.

The wounded man wrapped both hands around his bleeding leg.

"Get this man to medical," Remington said. "Have them patch him up." He glanced at the man writhing on the floor. "Once they're done with you, if you feel like walking out of the city, be my guest." He waved to the security team.

Quickly the soldiers herded the civilians out of the building. They carried the wounded man.

Remington glanced around the room. Every eye was fixed on him. The OneWorld NewsNet team shot footage. Remington idly wondered when they'd started filming and suspected it had been from the beginning.

"We're facing a crisis," Remington stated. "I'm not going to settle for saving a handful of people. I'm going to save us all. And no one is going to prevent me from doing that."

He said that as forcefully and believably as he could, but he knew he wasn't the only one in the room who wasn't convinced he was able to deliver on that promise.

36

United States of America
Fort Benning, Georgia
Local Time 0723

"Mrs. Gander?"

Megan looked up from the yellow legal pad she worked on. A young corporal stood at Major Thomas Francher's door and regarded her expectantly.

"I'm Mrs. Gander."

The corporal looked a little bleary-eyed, but he smiled all the same. "Yes, ma'am. I figured that you were."

When Megan looked around, she discovered that she was still the only one in the waiting room. She'd wanted to get here first thing to ensure she would be able to meet with Major Francher, the base commander's right-hand man. Her time while waiting had been divided between the small television in the corner and the legal pad.

FOX News continued to carry coverage of the attack on Sanliurfa, but other breaking news stories occupied the screen as well. Paranoia over the disappearances still raged and caused riots as well as individual problems.

One of the main stories that had shocked Megan to her core involved the burning of a church in Atlanta. A crowd had objected to the pastor's delivery of a message about the Tribulation, and they'd burned the church to the ground. Thankfully no serious injuries had come of it.

Everyone remained afraid and uncertain, though many people simply tried to bury themselves in their lives as if nothing had happened. They went back to jobs and routines. Megan had seen similar instances at the post. In the end, that wasn't going to work. Denial never kept bad things from happening.

Megan stood, smoothed her dress, and shoved the legal pad into her tote. She followed the corporal into the major's office.

"Ah, Mrs. Gander." Major Francher was a big man and had put on a few extra pounds since drawing the desk assignment, but he appeared dedicated and alert. The fact that he was at his desk before seven thirty said a lot. He waved her to one of the chairs in front of his desk. "Please. Have a seat."

The office definitely belonged to a man. Pictures of past postings, of children involved in sporting activities, and of Francher fishing hung on the walls. Manuals filled the bookshelves, but there were a few paperback thrillers as well.

Megan sat and put her tote beside the chair. "You're working early today, Major."

Francher sat and smiled. "I think a lot of us are. I know from several people that you're burning the candle at both ends these days."

"And maybe in the middle as well."

Francher's smile broadened. "I'd agree with that assessment." He spread his hands. "So what brings you to me?"

"They tell me that your office is the shortest route to the base commander's ear."

Francher leaned back in his chair and looked wary. "Sometimes, I suppose," he admitted. "Depends on the subject matter."

"The subject matter," Megan said, making her voice strong and trying not to think about Goose facing down the Syrian army along with so many other men whose children and families she knew, "is the Ranger unit over in Sanliurfa."

Francher sighed, and his shoulders bowed slightly. "That's a tough situation. If you came here to ask us what we're doing to help those soldiers, we're doing everything humanly possible."

"I believe you."

"It's just that we're spread so thin over there now, and there are a lot of problem areas. I don't have to tell you that a number of countries blame the United States for the disappearances because we're the last superpower remaining and because we're known for pushing science when it comes to developing superweapons."

"No, you don't," Megan agreed. "The situation around the globe is complicated. I understand that."

A puzzled expression filled Francher's face. "Okay, you've stymied me. Maybe I'm more tired than I thought, because I have no clue what you're here to talk about."

Megan considered how to lay out what she'd come to say. Deciding how best to do that had consumed her thoughts, and she was nervous that she still didn't know. *Just put it out there. This is in God's hands. Let Him do the heavy work.*

She cleared her throat and began. "I've been in discussions with some of the other base wives, Major, and several of us are in agreement about this matter."

Francher grinned hesitantly. "Sounds potentially scary already. With everything going on, there aren't a lot of people agreeing with anybody about anything."

Megan had thought about the ways she could present what she wanted to say. Different approaches existed, but none of them seemed any less troublesome or more honest than the naked truth. "Those Rangers in Turkey need help," Megan said. *Start with the undeniable facts. Keep him in safe territory.* "They need support staff. Medical assistance."

"I couldn't agree more, but finding people to pick up those duties—"

"You don't have to find those people," Megan stated quietly. "We're already here."

The major frowned. "I'm not quite following what you're suggesting."

"Several of the wives, husbands, and families want to go over there," Megan said. "To Turkey. To Sanliurfa if possible. As close as you can get us. We want to be with our soldiers. We want to help them survive what's going on over there so we can get them home."

Francher leaned back in his chair. He took in a deep breath of air and let it out. Then he flicked his gaze to the ceiling for a moment more before looking back at Megan. "You're suggesting that the United States Army send civilians into a war zone?"

"Civilians have worked in war zones before," Megan said. "Volunteers as well as employees. The military remains one of the highest employers of civilians in this country."

"Those people work on defensible posts, bases, and camps. Not on the battlefield."

"You've got an untapped workforce here at Fort Benning," Megan said. "Some of the wives and husbands of those soldiers are medical personnel. Some of them have been in the military before. As soldiers. Others are clerks, mechanics, food-service employees, and a dozen other things that the army—and those Rangers—need."

"No one's going to just draft those people—"

"You don't have to draft anyone," Megan said. "We want to volunteer."

Francher was quiet. "What you're suggesting is impossible."

"I disagree."

"Mrs. Gander—"

Megan cut him off and made her voice harder, more crisp. "Major, right now you're talking to me. I'm one soldier's wife. If I go back to the people I've been talking to and tell them that you stonewalled me, your office is going to be flooded with people by lunchtime. Do you want that?"

"No."

"I didn't think so. They wanted to come with me. I got them to let me talk to you first. This way you can have a discussion, not an invasion."

Francher looked slightly overwhelmed. "I appreciate that."

"Please forgive me for being so blunt, but I need to take back more than your appreciation to them. They'll want something more concrete."

"Don't they realize how dangerous what you're're suggesting is?"

"Of course they do. But they believe they're potentially in as much danger here. And we want to be with our soldiers. With the way things are, no one can be certain we'll see those soldiers again." Megan's voice broke. "Especially not after everything that's been going on over there yesterday and today."

"Even if we could put this together, those soldiers . . ." Francher hesitated. "Well, to be brutally honest, they may not be anywhere we can help them."

"We're prepared to grieve, Major," Megan said. "But we're also prepared to do something to help those men. We expect the military—we expect this fort—to do something about that. About helping us help them."

Francher was silent.

"We're not going to go away," Megan said. She kept thinking about the footage she'd seen of Goose and Sanliurfa. The need to be over there with Goose and the other soldiers grew stronger with each passing minute. "For the moment, the others have agreed to let me represent them. But if no one listens to me, they're going to become louder. They'll keep getting louder until someone listens."

"But—"

Megan cut him off. "People believe the end of the world is at hand, and they want to be united as families. If it can't happen here, then they want it to happen there."

The major sat silent for a moment. "The end of the world." Those words obviously didn't come easily to him.

"Yes. It sounds silly when you say it aloud, but there's no other description that fits. I don't know what kind of faith you have, or how strong it is, but surely you can feel what's going on."

Francher nodded. "I don't doubt you, Mrs. Gander. I heard about what happened that day in court. I can guarantee you've made believers of a lot of people."

Some of the army chaplains who had opposed her had taken leaves of absence. They'd seen the video footage of Gerry Fletcher disappearing in midair. The story had been told and retold throughout the fort.

"It wasn't me, Major. God made believers out of those people."

Francher nodded. "Yes, ma'am. I suppose He did." He took in a quiet breath and let it out. "I have to be honest with you. Since I heard about that, I've been making sure I spend a little more time with my Bible. I make sure my wife and kids do too." He grimaced. "None of them disappeared. My kids are all older. I don't know whether to feel relieved that we didn't lose anyone or scared because we might not all be together . . . later."

"If you're thinking like that, if you turn to God, you won't have anything to worry about." Megan knew how much her own perspectives had changed since she'd asked God to come into her life.

"I'm working on believing that. As far as your request goes—"

"We're being polite," Megan insisted. "If we wanted to, we could simply book a flight over there. Several of the people I'm talking to want to do that now. I've asked them to wait."

"Why?"

"Because if we're going to help those soldiers, this needs to be an organized movement. We need supplies and equipment. We need to help them, not become additional worries for them."

Francher rubbed his stubbled jaw, and his rough palm made a rasping sound. "Mrs. Gander, I appreciate what you—and these other people—are offering, but I don't think you see the danger you're suggesting the U.S. Army help bring you into."

"I do see. So do they. We believe in what we want to do, Major. Very much. Like I said, either the army can help coordinate our arrival

over there—and provide us meaningful ways to help our soldiers—or
we're going over there on our own. Either way, we're not going to stay
here when they need us there."

"The fort also needs many of those people here," Francher pointed
out. "Those support positions you're wanting to fill over there? Many
of them exist here. Stripping this fort of valuable personnel isn't the
answer."

"We'll go over in waves," Megan said. "We'll train our replace-
ments. The economy's restructuring. There are people who have lost
jobs and now need work."

"The work you're doing with the kids on this base is invaluable.
If that stopped—"

"It's not going to stop," Megan interrupted. "We're going to
transition. Like I said, we've talked among ourselves. We know our
responsibilities there—and here. We're not willing to walk away from
either." She paused. "But mark my words, Major. We're going to go.
One way or another, we're going to go."

Francher eyed Megan levelly. "I believe you will, Mrs. Gander. I
believe you will."

37

Downtown Sanliurfa
Sanliurfa Province, Turkey
Local Time 1408 Hours

Alexander Cody sat in the bar of the American Hotel and drank while he watched the television intermittently flash on and off as the signal was interrupted. A few other people sat somberly at the tables and booths, surrounded by pictures of sports and entertainment stars that seemed a lifetime removed from the world they all currently inhabited.

Danielle felt strange spying on Cody, knowing that he was watching a news story that covered their current situation. It was all surreal.

She thought she recognized one of the patrons as a soldier who usually hovered around Remington, but she couldn't be sure because he was in street clothes. The haircut fit, though. And he watched her as she approached Cody.

She put the other man out of her mind for the moment and focused on the CIA section chief.

"Excuse me," Danielle said.

Cody didn't move, but his gaze cut to the big mirror behind the bar. "Miss Vinchenzo." His voice came out flat and uninviting.

An explosion sounded outside. Danielle grabbed the bar and prepared to hurl herself behind it. When she glanced back at Cody, the man grinned at her.

"Somewhat apprehensive, aren't you?" he taunted. He tipped his drink and sipped casually. "You'll never hear the one that gets you. Those missiles travel faster than the speed of sound."

Danielle ignored the comment. "I'd like to talk to you."

"As a reporter? Or as a woman?"

"A reporter."

"Too bad." Cody sipped his drink and set the glass on the bar. "I'm not currently interested in talking with the press."

"You're a CIA section chief."

Some of the spirit went out of Cody's smile, but he kept it in place. "Quite an imagination you have there."

"It's not my imagination."

"If you air something like that, you'd better have proof to back it up."

"When I air it," Danielle said, "I'll have proof."

"Bully for you." Cody drained his glass and gestured to the bartender to bring another. "Did you just come down here to share conspiracy theories, Miss Vinchenzo? Or did you have something you really wanted to get around to?"

Danielle slid onto the stool next to Cody. She looked at him in the mirror. The bartender approached and asked her if she wanted a drink; she politely refused.

"Marcus Allen," Danielle stated. "Your guy that shot down the helicopter I was on?"

Cody didn't miss a beat. "Don't know what you're talking about. I don't know anyone named Marcus Allen, and I don't know about any helicopter."

"Allen is a mercenary. An ex-soldier. You've worked with him before."

"I'd like to see you try to prove that."

"I will."

Cody frowned. "As amusing as this conversation is, and as grateful as I am to have a diversion while bombs are flying through the air around us, Miss Vinchenzo, I really don't have the inclination to sit and listen to it."

"Goose is still alive, and so is Icarus," Danielle said. "Whatever you're hiding is going to come out."

"I," Cody declared, "am not hiding a thing." He drained his fresh drink and stood. Then he asked the bartender for a bottle and a glass. "I'm headed up to my room. If you want to continue this discussion, you're welcome to come up. I can get another glass, and there's a big whirlpool tub in the room."

Danielle's face burned.

"I didn't think so," Cody stated. He laughed, and the sound

was thin and brittle. "A word to the wise," he said quietly. "If a CIA section chief *were* trying to hide something like you suspect, I'd be really careful if I were you. Maybe he'd start thinking that Icarus and Sergeant Gander aren't the only people who need killing, that maybe I've stuck my head up just a little too far and gotten noticed." He turned and walked away.

Helplessly, feeling a little frightened despite her resolve not to be intimidated, Danielle watched him go.

❂   ❂   ❂

United States 75th Army Rangers Temporary Post
Sanliurfa, Turkey
Local Time 1623 Hours

Remington scanned the battlefield through the satellite feeds. The Syrian cavalry crept closer, braving the mud now that they'd knocked in the fortifications fronting the city. Inside, Remington cursed. His position was rapidly becoming untenable.

They were going to have to concede part of the city to the Syrians. The idea of doing that filled him with rage and helplessness.

He didn't care for either feeling.

"Captain?" the corporal at the com called.

"Yes?"

"I've got a caller here who says he's Nicolae Carpathia."

"Is he?"

The corporal looked embarrassed. "I don't know, sir, but he sounds sincere."

"*Sincere.*"

"Yes, sir." The corporal broke eye contact.

Remington took a deep breath and let it out. "Put him through."

"Yes, sir."

Remington flicked his headset over to receive the incoming call. There was a brief burst of static; then Nicolae Carpathia's melodic baritone filled Remington's ear.

"Captain Remington," Carpathia greeted.

"Mr. Secretary-General," Remington said, "please forgive my tactlessness, but I'm somewhat pressed for time at the moment."

"So I see."

"What can I do for you, Mr. Secretary-General?"

"Please, Cal. We are practically old friends, you and I. And I am hoping we get to know each other much better in the future. Call me Nicolae."

"All right." A vague feeling of well-being spread throughout Remington, but part of him insisted on remaining wary.

"And actually I was calling in regard to something I may be able to do for you."

"Me?"

"Yes. That is what I was calling about. As secretary-general, I have been given unlimited control over troop movements and recruitment. The general consensus seems to be that I will know best what to do."

In spite of the tension that filled Remington as he watched medical corpsmen carry three litters of wounded back to a Hummer, the captain smiled.

"The reason for my call is that I have directed several UN troop contingents to join you there," Carpathia said.

"Troops?" Remington couldn't believe he'd heard right.

"Yes. Reinforcements, actually."

Remington felt certain he hadn't heard correctly.

"I have asked some of the European countries to supplement the United Nations forces I have ordered to help you," Carpathia went on. "They were unusually responsive in appropriating men and weapons. In fact, if you take a look at your radar, you should see some of the new arrivals now."

"Sir," one of the radar techs called excitedly, "UN forces have just informed us about troop ships they've got entering our airspace."

"Did you confirm that?"

"I'm in the process, sir."

"Those are my men," Carpathia said. "Soon they will be yours. Since you know the terrain and the situation there in Sanliurfa better than anyone else, I have placed you in charge of them."

Excitement flared through Remington. He'd seized control of the Rangers after his superior officers had disappeared or been killed in the opening confrontation with the Syrians, and he'd been dreading the time the U.S. Army flew someone in with more seniority.

"Do you see the airplanes?" Carpathia asked.

"I'm confirming them," Remington said. As he watched, several dots separated from the plane above the city.

"I have given the fighter jets among them the freedom to engage Syrian aggressors in your airspace," Carpathia said. "But you can request they follow your direction."

"No," Remington said, watching the radar screen and the satellite monitor. "We need some breathing room."

"I thought you might."

Several jets screamed by overhead, racing toward the Syrians instead of away from them.

As Remington watched, the satellite feeds strengthened and became more certain. The United Nations jets swooped into the area and slagged several of the Syrian tanks before they retreated. Gratification filled Remington as he watched the onslaught.

"I hope this will help you out there," Carpathia said.

"It will. We'll make the most of it."

"I am glad. I would hate to lose you, Cal."

The warmth and well-being spread throughout Remington, overcoming the trepidation.

Like wildfire, the command post staff discovered that the new forces belonged to the United Nations. Not only that, but the new arrivals systematically mopped the floor with the Syrian units staggered out across the muddy no-man's-land in front of the city.

That knowledge quickly transmuted into a ragged cheer that echoed through the building.

Remington felt an immediate pang of jealousy as he watched the celebration. That should have been his. He should have been reveling in his glory. He should have solved their problems.

Given time and resources, I could have brought them a victory too, Remington thought.

"I see that everyone there has figured out what is going on," Carpathia said.

"Yes," Remington replied.

"I am convinced that you would have done well on your own, but I thought maybe quick action on my part might save a few lives."

"It will."

"Then I am pleased I was able to be of assistance. Your people are still in dire straits, and those lands—as well as the Middle East—are going to be hotly contested in the coming days."

"They always have been."

"And there will be no change in that," Carpathia said. "That is why I want to start recruiting."

"Recruiting?"

"Yes. To the army I am going to build. I want to make some positive changes in the world, and to do that, I need a force that will be able to respond quickly and decisively to threats. I need a win in Turkey, and I think you are just the man to give it to me. I had planned to ask you at a later time, but since the subject has come up . . ."

Remington found himself hanging on Carpathia's every word.

"I would like you to be part of this new world force," Carpathia said.

"I've already got a career with the army," Remington said.

"I want you as a colonel. I am prepared to offer you a full commission whenever you are ready."

Remington's mind spun. If that happened, he'd be a very young colonel. He'd also, his thoughts assured him, be a very powerful colonel in a position to make a name and a career for himself in Turkey.

"I want young men in this endeavor," Carpathia said as if reading his mind. "And I want them in positions of authority. In short, I want you."

Remington stared at the smoldering battlefield visible on the computer screens. "Let me figure out what I'm doing here first, and I'll be happy to talk with you about it sometime soon."

"Good," Carpathia responded. "We shall talk soon. In the meantime, see to your men."

"Yes, sir. Thank you." Remington ended the connection and gazed out at the battlefield as it changed once again. He couldn't help thinking about Carpathia's offer.

Colonel Remington.

He liked the sound of that. And all he had to do was survive to claim it.

Goose knelt under a copse of young trees atop a hill that overlooked the big plain just outside Sanliurfa. The journey on foot back to the city had been arduous. The pain in his knee was constant now. But at last they had made it to the city. Now all they had to do was wait for their chance to get inside.

He tracked the action with his binoculars. Things had looked bad, but it seemed Cal Remington had turned the tables on the Syrians with a surprise aerial attack that had orphaned part of the invading army. Goose didn't know where the additional planes had come from, but now if the Syrians wanted to press on, they had to do so with increased risk and over the bodies of their own people and the remains of their destroyed vehicles.

"What's going on?" Chaplain Miller asked. It was hard to carry on a conversation with all the explosions and gunfire, but he leaned over Goose's shoulder and spoke into his ear.

"We're holding our own," Goose replied. "Don't know where the captain got the additional munitions, but he's putting them to good use."

Miller squinted. "Are those United Nations insignias on the new planes?"

"Maybe so. The Syrians seem as surprised as we are."

Icarus hunkered down only a short distance away. Dried blood covered the side of his face and one ear. He frowned. "Aren't you a little curious about where the help came from, Sergeant?"

"Not at this particular moment," Goose replied. "I'm just glad they found their way here. Otherwise the city might have been overrun."

"At some point," Icarus said, "you should ask where the planes came from."

"What are we going to do?" Miller asked.

Goose lowered his binoculars and put them away. "We're going to lie low, sir. Dig in where we can, hope the Syrians don't stumble across us, and wait for night to cover us over. Then we're going to try to return to Sanliurfa. Without getting killed."

All of that was easy to say. Accomplishing it was going to be a different matter entirely. Goose stretched his bad knee out and sat next to a tree behind a wall of brush. Rain soaked his clothing, and he felt miserable. He kept his rifle next to him.

He turned his face up into the rain and slowly drank to preserve the water he had in the LCE. Then he looked at the line of destruction Remington had wrought. Glancing at Icarus, Goose knew that getting back didn't necessarily mean they would be safe.

Someone had sent those men to ambush them, and Goose didn't think that was the only team assigned the task of killing Icarus. With the primary team out of play, a secondary team should have been put into the field.

It was what he would have done if the roles had been reversed.

He settled in and tried to find a new position for his knee but failed. He waited for the sun to set and wondered if he'd live to see the morning.

❖ ❖ ❖

Southern District
Sanliurfa, Turkey
Local Time 1647 Hours

"Colonel Remington. Major Rebreanu at your service." The man saluted smartly.

The title sounded like music in Remington's ears as he gazed at the sharply dressed United Nations major standing in front of him. He didn't bother to point out that he hadn't yet accepted Carpathia's offered commission.

"Major." Remington returned the man's salute.

"I've been instructed by Secretary-General Carpathia to put myself and my men at your disposal."

"Acknowledged, Major. Glad to have you."

The man stood at rigid attention. He was medium height but broad shouldered. His uniform blouse stretched across his chest, and his muscles rolled beneath his skin. His square jaw thrust out prominently.

"At ease," Remington said.

Rebreanu fell into parade rest and stood beside the jeep that had brought him to meet Remington. Three other soldiers stood with him. All of them wore the bright blue helmets of the United Nations Peacekeeping Forces.

"I'll depend on you to keep me up-to-date with your staff, Major," Remington said. "When I get more time, I'll know them all."

"Yes, sir. I'd be happy to help."

Remington wondered if that was true. Getting ordered into a potentially highly lethal losing situation wasn't something any soldier would wish for. He wouldn't have wanted to be Rebreanu.

"We need to shore up the south end of the city," Remington said. "Create some space between ourselves and the Syrians. I don't want them inside the metro area if I can help it."

"Yes, sir. Permission to speak freely, sir?"

That, Remington knew, was dangerous given that he didn't know the man. But Remington nodded anyway.

"Holding the city in its entirety might be impossible." Rebreanu's words held only a hint of an accent.

"That's not the kind of thinking I need out here," Remington said. "If we give up any part of this city, we're going to have to give it all up. So we're not going to give the Syrians anything."

Rebreanu nodded stiffly. "Yes, sir."

Underneath the major's calm words, though, Remington knew that the man didn't believe it could be done. "We're going to make this happen," Remington said.

"Yes, sir. The secretary-general said that you would be a man of conviction and that you'd have high expectations."

"I do. Allowing the Syrians to entrench themselves in this city means they don't have to depend on supply lines as much as they currently do. I'm not going to allow that. If they have supply lines, they're exposed. We're going to concentrate on holding our position and make them pay the cost for being in an indefensible posture." Remington stared at the battlefield, across the smoking ruin of the Syrian armored and downed planes. "Put simply, we're going to outbleed them."

"Yes, sir." Rebreanu frowned a little.

"I'm aware that this isn't the kind of action your team is used to seeing," Remington went on. "They'll adjust. The same way we've adjusted."

"That's what the secretary-general said too, Colonel."

Remington smiled. "He's a smart man."

"He has absolute faith in you, sir."

"That just means he's more intelligent than I realized." Remington saluted. "Now let's get out there and put a boot to some Syrian butts."

✵ ✵ ✵

Local Time 1743 Hours

"Incoming!"

Remington dropped down behind a barricade of sandbags and tucked his face into the crook of his elbow. A tank round struck a building behind him. A storm of cracked stone and mortar peppered his helmet and body armor. A few chunks ricocheted from exposed and unprotected flesh. He'd have bruises on his forearms, thighs, and calves later.

The explosion left Remington partially deafened. The hoarse yelling and screams of the wounded sounded like they were a million miles away from him. He straightened and peered over the sandbag wall.

"They're massing," Sergeant Whitaker said. Young but experienced, the sergeant held the line beside Remington.

"I see them." Remington stared through his protective eye gear. On the other side of the bare ground, the Syrian army prepared to launch an offensive. "We should have mined that area."

Remington had ordered his men to use the local earthmoving equipment to clear all trees and rock in a two-hundred-yard band on all sides of the city. That task still wasn't finished, but all the areas along the thoroughfares had been plucked clean.

"Yeah," Whitaker agreed. He grinned a little. "When we give 'em the fall line, they're going to be in for a nasty surprise."

Under Remington's direction, a line of claymore antipersonnel mines lay beyond the first defensive barrier outside the city. Holding that position long enough to convince the Syrians they were determined to keep it was risky and would undoubtedly prove costly.

The Rangers and the United Nations troops held solid, but Remington recognized fear in those mud-streaked faces. The rain continued unabated and washed out gullies across the barren land the earthmovers had left.

"Sparrow Leader," Remington called over the com.

"Sparrow Leader reads you."

"Ready?"

"We were born ready."

"On my go," Remington stated quietly.

"Sparrow Unit is standing by."

Remington watched the line taking shape. Despite the torrential downpour and the quagmire of mud pits that had formed in front of them, the cavalry of the Syrian army advanced. Tires and tank treads churned through the loose soil. Men marched beside them. The grinding roar of machinery came closer.

Someone opened fire. Remington didn't know if it came from the defenders or the Syrians, but the shot escalated the approach into a full-fledged firefight. He remained behind cover and took aim with his M-4A1. He snapped off tri-bursts at the human targets. They fell, tumbled, and twisted away.

Bullets ripped across the heap of sandbags and through the air only inches from his ear. One slammed into his helmet and startled him. Controlling the fear that writhed within him, he shook the rain from his eyes and took aim again.

Syrian soldiers trailed the tanks, APCs, and mobile artillery pieces. They were exposed and knew it. Handfuls of them fell at a time; lifeless bodies and wounded were left behind. The advance was inexorable. Without the reinforcements, Remington knew his soldiers wouldn't have been able to hold the city from the invaders.

Timing, he reminded himself. *It's all about the timing.* He fired again and again. One of the soldiers he aimed at went down.

The trick, Remington knew, was to reshape the front line. Then he had to attack before the second wave followed. Once the Syrians had their full momentum up, the city could still be overrun.

"Sparrow Leader," Remington called.

"Ready."

"Hit 'em. Hit 'em hard."

Immediately a dozen attack helos lifted up from the streets back in the middle of the city. They thundered by overhead and divided into two groups of six, then launched rockets and 20mm cannon rounds at the ends of the advancing line.

Devastated by the withering fire, giving in to their instincts for self-preservation, the units on the ends of the Syrian line pushed in toward each other, and the front lost a third of its width. The helos came under fierce attack. One of them exploded in midair, struck by a surface-to-air missile that rained down debris. Another lost its main rotor and went down, smashing against an APC before exploding and taking out the tank and several infantrymen.

Remington cursed. Even with Carpathia's promise of still more machines and troops, losing hardware like the attack helos chafed him.

The second wave of Syrians formed but held their positions.

"Sparrow," Remington called, "get out of there."

The remaining helicopters swooped around and streaked back toward the city.

"Keep firing till I call for the retreat," Remington ordered his men.

The first wave of Syrians kept coming. They smelled victory even though they took steady losses. All they had to do was secure an anchoring position. Then they'd be inside the city.

The second wave started forward.

"Fall back," Remington ordered. "Fall back now."

As one, the city's defenders retreated from the forward line and ran into the city. Syrian bullets followed them. Some of the soldiers didn't make it. Remington stumbled twice as rounds hammered his body armor. He went down after a third round struck, his face digging into the mud, then got back to his feet and ran harder.

Less than a minute later, the advancing line of Syrians reached the sandbags. The antipersonnel claymores opened up as the invaders reached them. Solid steel shot chopped into human flesh and tore it to pieces. Tankbuster bomblets blew apart the treads on some of the Syrian vehicles. The ones still capable of moving rolled into the sights of artillery teams.

Destruction opened up along the forward line. At the second line of defense, taking cover behind a section of a building wall that remained standing, Remington watched as his enemies died. Savage glee filled him. This was why he'd been born: to be a warrior, a winner, a survivor against all odds.

His talent for bringing death and mayhem to his enemies stood him in good stead. He loved his calling, and he embraced it wholly as he watched his counterattack take shape.

"Hound Leader," Remington called.

"Hound Leader standing by."

"You're up."

"Roger that. We'll clean and set the table, sir. Count on us."

"Artillery," Remington went on, "light 'em up." He ducked around the wall and shot a Syrian who burst into view. The enemy soldier took two more steps, then went down and didn't get back up.

Across the front of the second line of defenders, laser target designators painted the enemy vehicles that milled around in confusion at the line of sandbags. TOW and Hawk missiles launched, taking out the targets in quick succession.

The Syrian survivors tried to pull back. The second wave had frozen in its tracks.

Then the Hound units swept by from the outskirts of the city, flying toward each other at speed. The six cargo helicopters crossed over the empty land behind the first-line Syrians and the empty space that separated them from the other troops hidden within the treeline. The Hound helos spewed bomblets, spreading hundreds of them over the space in less than a minute.

The bomblets were tankbusters and antipersonnel pressure mines. Remington had found a storehouse of Turkish military equipment and had put it to good use.

Syrian men and machines tried to retreat from the brutal attack that faced them. When they rolled back over or stepped on the mines, the vehicles blew their tires or their treads. Men died in bloody ruin, tattered by the shrapnel.

When they realized they were trapped, the Syrians tried to make use of the sandbags. Remington gave the order to detonate the plastic explosives they'd planted within some of the piles. The barrier vanished, and more of the enemy died.

"Not exactly playing by the Geneva Convention, are we?" Rebreanu asked over the com.

"I didn't come out here to get my butt kicked," Remington responded. "I came out here to win." He stood and surveyed the battleground, watching as the Syrians died.

"Not going to ask if they want to surrender?"

"No," Remington said. "I don't want a mass of prisoners inside the city. We can't look after them anyway." He paused. "When those people have had enough, they can take their chances fleeing back to the main forces."

The Syrian tanks and artillery located within the treeline continued firing, but they made fine targets for the laser painters as well. Three Syrian soldiers tried to dash back across the open land. Unfortunately for them, the mud had swallowed some of the bomblets. Two of the men blew up almost instantly. The third one made it almost halfway when his luck ran out.

All right, Remington thought, *we've earned some distance and respect. What are you people going to do now?*

Goose waited in the darkness. After the sun had set and the moon slid
behind the cloud bank, he'd crept toward the city. Miller and Icarus
trailed after him. The rain, which had been a blessing earlier because
it had reduced visibility, turned the terrain treacherous. Thick mud
sucked at his boots and added several pounds to his feet. The extra
weight also made traveling silently even harder.

Hostilities had come to a stop between the U.S. and UN forces
within Sanliurfa and the Syrian forces outside the city. Fighting at
night in the rain was risky. However, it perfectly masked efforts to
get into the city. None of the forces on either side of the deadly no-
man's-land chose to keep lights on. Those only made men targets for
snipers.

The problem was that Goose and the two men with him weren't
the only ones attempting to get into Sanliurfa. Instead of advancing toward the city in a straight line across the dangerous stretch of
corpses and ragged earth, Goose had decided to circle around farther
to the west. He noticed the shadows east of their position before they
left the treeline.

Goose held a hand up and waved Icarus and Miller to ground.

"What's wrong?" Miller whispered.

"Quiet," Goose ordered. He used his peripheral vision to track
the shadows he'd spotted through the falling rain. His M-4A1 slid
easily into his hands. But using the rifle would immediately draw the
attention of every Syrian soldier camped nearby.

Miller lay belly-down in the mud and didn't move.

Icarus held up one hand and showed three fingers.

Goose waited a moment, checking the movement of the shadows. Then he nodded and held up three fingers. *Three Syrian soldiers.*

Almost effortlessly, Icarus pushed up into a crouch and slid a knife from his boot. The dulled matte finish didn't gleam.

Goose passed his rifle back to Miller. "Hold that," he told the chaplain. "Me and Icarus will be back in a minute."

"What if you're not?"

"Trust me. You'll know about it. If this goes bust, hightail it to somewhere safe." Goose pulled the knife from his harness and made certain his sidearm was secured in its holster. Then he stayed low and went forward, toward the three Syrians.

❋   ❋   ❋

Local Time 2108 Hours

Goose moved slowly. In the dark, he knew he could remain almost invisible as long as he stayed low and didn't move quickly. He took a fresh grip on the knife in his hand. The rain turned the handle slick.

Almost twenty feet away, moving parallel to him, Icarus remained hunkered down. Goose thought about how easily the man had taken on the role of assassin. There hadn't been any time to think about it. Icarus had just shifted into killer mode without a second thought.

That was enough to give Goose pause. Then again, he realized he'd done the same thing. When it came to survival, people made choices quickly about living and dying.

The three Syrians carried backpacks. Goose figured they were loaded with plastic explosives. Something to provide a quick punch back at their enemies. The three men concentrated on watching in front of them, obviously expecting any trouble they might experience to come from the direction of the city.

Icarus waved his free hand to get Goose's attention. Goose nodded at him. Icarus pointed to the man at the end of the Syrians, then at himself. The meaning was clear. Goose nodded again.

Without another gesture or word, Icarus rushed toward the Syrians. Goose did the same. When he reached the man he'd set his sights on, Icarus wrapped a hand around the man's mouth to stifle any outcry, then slipped his knife between the man's ribs. The Syrian soldier shuddered and died.

By then Goose had reached the man he had chosen. He clapped a hand over the man's mouth as well, then drove the knife point into the back of the man's neck at the base of the skull. It was a clean, immediate kill when the blade separated the spinal cord. The body sprawled in the mud.

After yanking his knife free, Goose moved forward with long strides. His knee quaked and throbbed, pain hammering at the inside of his head. He came up behind the third man, then saw the man's head jerk backward.

Something warm and wet splashed across Goose's face. As the Syrian suddenly went limp and fell, Goose knew the man had been shot.

"Down!" Goose told Icarus.

The younger man went to ground at once, barely beating Goose. Something zipped through the air over his head, and another bullet pocked the mud only inches from his hand.

None of the shots made a sound.

"Sniper," Goose whispered to Icarus. "He's using a silenced weapon. Move."

Together, they headed back the way they'd come.

✵ ✵ ✵

Local Time 2113 Hours

Miller was still in position where they'd left him. He gazed at them anxiously.

The pain in Goose's knee felt like shark's teeth grinding into his flesh and bone.

"Why aren't we going on?" Miller whispered. "We're practically to the city."

"Because there are men hunting us out there," Icarus said. Both men locked their gaze on Goose.

"That's the way it is," Goose said. He quickly recounted what had happened.

"Syrians?" Miller asked.

"Not with silenced rifles cycling subsonic rounds. They're more like those men hunting us earlier," Goose replied.

Miller sat down with his back to a tree. The fifteen-mile trek that had taken place throughout the day had almost done him in. He stayed active, but it was different when adrenaline spiked in a man's system all day from being surrounded by enemies.

"Who's sending those men?" Miller asked.

Goose didn't answer. He didn't want to lie, and he didn't want Miller to know everything he knew.

"It doesn't matter," Icarus said. "We have to get around them if we're going to survive." He glanced at Goose. "And waiting isn't going to make it any easier."

Goose nodded. He took a sip of water, tasted the earthy flavor that came from refilling the LCE bladder in pools of rain, and got into motion. "We gotta get help if we're going to get inside," Goose said.

"How do you plan on doing that?" Icarus demanded.

"By letting Captain Remington know we're out here."

Icarus shook his head. "You're a fool, Goose. Remington's as much a part of this as those men out there hunting us."

"I don't believe that." Goose knew he was being stubborn, and he knew that Cal Remington was following his own goals at the moment. Those goals, Goose was painfully aware, were different from his own. "The captain wouldn't leave us out here to die."

"He's been sending you to the hot spots," Icarus said. "He's been expecting you to die. He had you under lockdown only a few hours ago. I'd say that Remington isn't your greatest fan."

Goose knew that was true. But he knew something else too. "Those men inside that city, they're Rangers. We don't leave a man behind. If they know we're here, they'll tell the captain. The captain won't have any choice but to try to save us."

Rain dappled Icarus's tight features. "You put a lot of stock in this captain of yours."

"Yes, sir. I do. I've worked with him for a long time." Goose knew that if pressed, he wouldn't have been able to say exactly when his and Remington's paths had started to diverge. "It's not just the captain I'm putting my faith in. It's those Rangers inside as well."

Icarus shook his head. Jagged lightning traced a white-hot vein across the sky.

"If you see another way of doing this," Goose said, "I'm all ears."

Miller looked from Goose to Icarus a few times. "Staying out here isn't an answer. When morning comes, the Syrians are going to start moving again."

"Once they do that," Goose said, "they'll flush us out of hiding. Come dawn, we're not going to have a chance at all."

Icarus gazed at the city.

Goose knew how the man felt. Safety was so close, but it was still a world away.

"How do you propose to signal them without giving away our position to the Syrians or to the men out there hunting us?" Icarus asked finally.

"I'm working on that," Goose replied.

"We shouldn't be up here," Gary said softly.

Danielle ignored the cameraman as she swept the building on the other side of the street with a pair of night-vision binoculars she'd gotten from a black market dealer.

"They said being in the upper floors was dangerous." Fear tightened Gary's voice. "If a missile hits up here, or below, there's a good chance we'll get buried in the rubble."

"I know. But we're this close to a story. I can feel it."

"That CIA guy isn't the story OneWorld NewsNet wants. They want footage of the arrival of the UN troops."

"We got that." Danielle increased the magnification, trying desperately to find Cody within the room. She'd spotted him for a short time earlier. He'd been fearlessly—though she was more prone to think of him as *drunkenly*—staring out the window at the battlefield in front of the city. Cody made no effort to involve himself in the rescue of the city.

That's because his agenda is somewhere else, Danielle told herself.

"They want more footage," Gary said.

"We'll get it." Danielle started to wonder about the pressure her producer was putting on her. To her, adding footage to what they'd already gotten was just busywork. The world already knew that Nicolae Carpathia had been voted in as secretary-general and that he'd sent reinforcements to Sanliurfa.

As innocently as she could, Danielle had tried to send a question through channels as to why Carpathia had ordered that when so much of the rest of the world was just as chaotic. No answer had been forthcoming. None of the other news agencies speculated about that move either.

On the surface, Carpathia was doing a humane act by shoring up the defenses.

That's on the surface, Danielle reminded herself. But she couldn't help thinking of Lizuca Carutasu and the way she'd been murdered in Romania for digging into the relationship between Carpathia and Alexander Cody. *The surface isn't the story. It never is.* She studied the darkened window. *So what are you protecting here, Carpathia?*

"Look," Gary said, "maybe you don't care about your job, but I do. I think we should—"

Danielle cut him off. "Do you care more about your job than you do about getting back home in one piece?"

"No."

"Then pay attention."

"To what?"

"What's going on around you."

"We're rescued," Gary said belligerently. "All we gotta do is shoot some footage of the UN troops, and we're home free."

"Then OneWorld is sending you home?"

"I've asked to be sent back home."

"Did they say yes?"

"No. Not yet."

"Then they're not going to send you home yet. They need a cameraman over here."

"I told them I've had enough."

"Have you stopped and wondered what this is about?" Danielle asked.

"What what's about? The war? The Syrians have always—"

"No. The reinforcements. Why now?"

"Maybe this was as soon as Carpathia could make it happen."

"Doesn't reinforcing Sanliurfa seem like a lost cause to you? What do we need to hold here? There are no oil fields, no natural resources. Most of the civilians have cleared away, and the ones who have stayed can't be viewed as our responsibility."

Gary remained silent.

"And if reinforcing this city *was* a good idea, don't you think the previous secretary-general would have thought of that?"

"I don't know."

"I think he would have," Danielle said.

"Maybe he had trouble selling it?"

"Then how was Carpathia able to sell it to the rest of the United Nations?"

"Don't know. I've listened to the guy talk. He's awfully convincing."

Danielle silently agreed. "What if Carpathia wants Icarus?"

"Now you're scaring me."

"Why?"

"Conspiracy theories aren't my thing."

"They're not mine either."

"Then we should be out there on the street interviewing some of those UN soldiers."

"I can't do that."

Gary sighed.

At that moment, across the street, Alexander Cody stepped back into the wan moonlight pouring down from the darkened sky.

"Bring your camera over here," Danielle ordered.

✸   ✸   ✸

Outside Sanliurfa
Local Time 2116 Hours

Goose inched across the muddy ground. In his mind, he was just another layer of mud. And he moved slow as molasses, oozing across the slippery ground rather than sliding. Mud caked his face. Half the time when he breathed, he sucked in dirty water from the ground.

His first objective lay eighty yards away. He felt certain the burned and blasted remnants of the tank provided sufficient cover.

Unless those guys gunning for you have moved around. Goose tried to keep from thinking about that. Likewise, he tried to keep from thinking that the unknown gunners were even now creeping up on Miller and Icarus. *There was no way you could bring them with you. They're not trained for this.*

Goose dug his boot toes into the ground and started oozing forward again. A sharp stone dug into his face. He didn't say anything, and he didn't make an adjustment. He just slid over the stone and kept going.

Long minutes later, he reached the tank. Smoke, diesel, and the distinct odor of burned flesh clung to the broken metal. Goose remained low and got his bearings. The muted moonlight splashed across bodies of the dead. The rain had washed the blood from the corpses, and the thirsty ground had drunk it in. But the horrible wounds remained visible. Torn flesh, limbs that had been ripped away, incomplete heads—all of them lay before him.

Goose steeled himself against the sight. He'd seen worse, but there in the darkness, with only the whisper-soft voice of the rain all around him, he couldn't remember the last time death had affected him so deeply.

He thought of Chris and the way his son had vanished. He thought of the young Rangers he'd seen die. They were just boys. Not much older than Joey.

This wasn't how it was supposed to be. They weren't supposed to be abandoned behind enemy lines. They weren't supposed to be left here to die.

My son was not supposed to be taken from me. The anger that had nourished Goose since the beginning of the Syrian attack simmered inside him. His hurt and uncertainty dwindled, but he knew it would be back. As soon as his thoughts turned back to living past the moment, he'd regard the future with as much fear and hate as he had since he'd learned of Chris's disappearance.

"*God took your son,*" Joseph Baker had said. "*He took that little boy on up to heaven to watch over him till you get there.*"

There aren't any guarantees that I'm headed there, Goose thought. *I got left behind.*

"*I'm going to heaven,*" Baker had told him. "*When I die, when my time comes, even if I last through these next seven years, I'm going to heaven.*"

Did you? Goose thought. *Is that where you ended up, Baker?* He moved toward one of the bodies and searched the man's assault rifle. It was an AK-47, standard issue. The rifles of the next three corpses were the same.

Lord, You're gonna have to cut me some slack, Goose thought. *Reason dictates that at least some of the men accompanying these tanks as they moved forward would be snipers. Gotta be a range-finding laser here somewhere.*

He searched three more mutilated bodies before he found a Russian sniper weapon equipped with a range-finding laser.

Cautiously Goose used his Swiss Army knife to remove the range finder from the weapon. Then he started the laborious trip back to Miller and Icarus.

❋   ❋   ❋

Downtown Sanliurfa
Local Time 2120 Hours

Excitement flowed through Danielle as she studied the CIA section chief. Her heart thudded.

Cody was barely visible in profile against the doorframe leading to the balcony. Moonlight made the man's face look bone white. He smoked a cigar and drank straight from a bottle as he stared out through the rain.

For a moment Danielle thought he was staring at her; then she realized he was still focused on the battlefield. His lips moved. She increased the magnification.

She wasn't an expert lip-reader, but the skill wasn't as hard as many people believed, and she'd starting picking it up as a girl while spying on her older brothers. It just required concentration, visibility, and some experience. Most people could pick it up easily, which was one of the problems sports networks faced when they stayed in close on an upset player.

Cody's lips moved again.

"Gary?" Danielle said.

"Yeah."

"The camera?"

"I'm on him."

"Tight on his face. I want to see what he's saying."

"'Kay."

Danielle hoped the night lenses could filter in enough light to illuminate the scene.

Cody wasn't alone. Another man, one Danielle hadn't seen in the bar downstairs, stood beside Cody. She concentrated on the men's lips.

"—*out there,*" the man said.

"*You're positive?*" Cody asked.

"*Yes, sir.*"

"*All of them?*"

"*Yes, sir.*"

Cody said something else, but he turned his face away from Danielle.

"*We haven't given up, sir. We'll find them.*"

Cody nodded. *"I want Hander"*—no, that had to be *Gander*—*"dead. I do not want him back in this city."*

"Yes, sir."

Excitement rose in Danielle again. Goose was alive. The thought thrilled her. Tears burned her eyes. Then she concentrated on Cody again, mentally cursing him. There was no guarantee that Goose would stay that way for long.

Across the street, Cody took another drink from the neck of the bottle. *"Tell them to get to it."*

"Yes, sir." The other man faded out of sight.

Danielle turned to Gary. "Did you get that?"

"Yeah, but without audio, all you got is one guy talking to another guy in a dark room."

"Didn't you read his lips?" Danielle opened her notebook computer on the room's table.

"No. I'm not a lip-reader."

"Hook the video feed into my computer. Download that piece." Danielle stepped back and let the cameraman work. She tried to ignore the infrequent small-arms fire and missiles. The Syrians evidently used them as reminders, ensuring that no one in the city would get a good night's sleep.

When Gary had the video uploaded to her computer, she played it back. This time she made notes of what she'd read.

Danielle was relieved to know Goose was still alive. She'd felt guilty ever since she saw him fall from the helicopter. She kept playing it back through her mind, realizing how she could have simply grabbed him and halted his fall.

"I want Gander dead." That reverberated in Danielle's head in Alexander Cody's voice.

Danielle copied the video file to her flash drive and headed for the door. "C'mon. We've got to find Remington."

Goose felt gun sights on him. He froze immediately. Even though he couldn't see the weapon, he knew someone had a bead on him. He resisted the immediate impulse to move and forced himself to wait to see what happened. He had to trust in the body armor.

"Sergeant," Icarus called softly, "come ahead."

Goose let out a long breath, then slid forward again.

Icarus lowered the assault rifle he carried. Miller sat nearby.

"See anything?" Icarus asked.

"Syrians," Goose replied. "But not the men stalking us."

"They're out there."

"I know."

Icarus glanced grimly at the expanse of ground separating them from the city. "They don't have to risk crossing that area."

"I know," Goose said as he rose to a sitting position. His back and knee ached terribly. "All they gotta do is hold us here. In the morning, the Syrians can do their jobs for them. They can watch."

"That's what they'll do," Icarus said. "Carpathia won't let Alexander Cody rest until he brings me down."

Goose cleaned the range finder. The power supply was good, but one of the lenses had been knocked out of alignment. "The information you have is really that dangerous?"

"I've got documents that link Carpathia's companies with some of the terrorist groups working with the Syrians," Icarus said.

Miller looked at the two of them. "What? What are you talking about?"

"The reason those men are lying out there right now to kill us," Goose said.

"Carpathia? You've got to be kidding." Miller's face showed disbelief. "That man has done more to unify the countries since the disappearances than anyone else in the world."

"That's just cover," Icarus said. "What he's really after is something else."

"What do you think he's after?"

"All these people left behind in the balance of God's judgment."

"That's insane."

Icarus smiled wearily. "Is it? A third of the world vanished a few short weeks ago. Is that insane too?"

Miller didn't say anything.

"If I'd tried to tell anyone before those disappearances took place that they were going to happen, they would have locked me up. Don't you agree?"

Reluctantly Miller nodded. "But what you're saying about Carpathia . . . what does that . . . "

"What does that make him?" Icarus shook his head. "If you ask me, I think the man is the devil himself. If not, then he's part of the blackest evil you've ever seen."

"But he's working to pull everyone together. To help us see through everything."

"You're familiar with the Bible, right?"

"Of course."

"What is the Antichrist supposed to do in the end times?"

Miller didn't speak. Goose saw the fear on the man's face.

Icarus continued. "The Antichrist is supposed to bring the people of the world, those whom God left behind during the time of the Tribulation, together. And in doing so, he will lead them away from God. That's what Carpathia is doing."

Goose studied Miller's face. Although the chaplain clearly wanted to repudiate Icarus's claims, Goose knew the man was taking them in.

Miller looked at Goose. "Do you believe this?"

"I don't know what to believe," Goose said. "I'm not here to believe. At the moment, I'm working on getting us out of this mess alive. I reckon after that moment, the next moment will take care of itself." But the truth was, he didn't have enough room in his head to think about everything he needed to think about.

"You got what you went after?" Icarus asked.

"I did." Goose showed him the range finder.

"What is that?"

The question told Goose that Icarus wasn't a military man. "It's a laser range finder. Snipers mount it on a rifle to get an accurate measurement of how far away a target is."

Icarus frowned. "Knowing how far we are from the city walls isn't going to help us."

Goose grinned grimly. "No, sir, I have to agree with you on that."

"And unless it can help you see those men in the dark, I don't see that it's going to be a lot of help."

"It can't do that either. But what I *can* do is use it to let our boys know we're out here. The trick is going to be doing that while at the same time not alerting those snipers out there to our position."

❋   ❋   ❋

Downtown Sanliurfa
Local Time 2156 Hours

"Captain Remington, Danielle Vinchenzo of OneWorld NewsNet is here."

Remington looked at the corporal. The man stood beside him as if awaiting execution. For a long moment, Remington listened to the rain drum against the tarpaulin roof above his head. He ran the scenarios through his mind, wondering what had sparked the woman's interest.

In the end, he decided it didn't matter. He wasn't going to be afraid of her or her interest. After all, he'd just shot a civilian a short time ago. At this point, with everything so unsettled around them, *accidents* could happen to anyone.

"Bring her," Remington said.

"Yes, sir." The corporal walked away, then quickly returned with the woman and her cameraman in tow.

"Miss Vinchenzo," Remington said. "Make this snappy. As you can see, I've got pressing business here."

"I understand that, Captain, but I think you'll want to see this." Danielle started to open her computer.

Remington caught the computer with one hand and kept it shut. Recognizing the fear in her eyes, he grinned a little. Having other

people afraid of him was a good thing. It put them off their game. Fear
motivated people to move more quickly when he gave an order.

"Why don't you paint a target on our heads instead?" Remington
asked. "Opening that computer out here will reveal us to any Syrian
snipers who might be waiting for a clear target."

Danielle frowned. She didn't like making mistakes.

"I've got something to show you," she said.

"I can catch it in reruns in the morning."

She looked at him. "Goose is alive. He survived the fall from the
helicopter."

Relief and distaste warred within Remington. If Goose had died,
Remington would have lost a good right hand when he needed it
most. Bringing the UN forces and the Rangers together would be a
struggle. Having Goose help him would make things a lot easier.

However, Goose wasn't exactly running on the correct rails these
days. And Remington felt jealous of the interest the woman had in
Goose's survival. He knew a lot of the Rangers felt the same way
about Goose that she did.

"How do you know this?" Remington demanded.

"Alexander Cody gave orders to kill him."

Remington frowned. "You heard Cody give those orders?"

"No. I saw him do it."

"You . . . *saw* . . . Cody give orders to kill Goose."

"Yes." Danielle didn't hesitate a second. "Look, if I could just
show you what I've got on this computer, you'll see for yourself."

"All right, Miss Vinchenzo. I'll grant you that you've made me
curious." Remington guided her toward a set of stairs that led down
into the earth.

✼ ✼ ✼

Outside Sanliurfa
Local Time 2204 Hours

Goose lay prone in the mud under a bush and aimed the laser range
finder at the top of the wall surrounding the city.

"Wait," Icarus said. "You're going to shine that around?"

"Nope," Goose said. "I'm going to direct it at one of the places
I suspect our artillery people will have positioned a LADAR."

"What's a LADAR?" At Goose's instruction, Icarus lay a few feet away. In case they were spotted, they need not both be taken out in one burst.

"It's an acronym for laser detection and radar. Artillery grunts use it to paint targets. I'm betting they're tagging targets out here despite the rain. Just to keep everyone honest."

"What good does that do us?"

"If everything works right, I'm going to get the attention of the LADAR ops crews. Then I'm going to tell them who we are." He aimed the range finder at the top of the wall and slowly moved it along. He watched the readout through the ocular. When it suddenly changed, he knew he'd caught the attention of an alert ops tech. Calmly he switched the range finder off and on in a series of long and short bursts.

❁ ❁ ❁

Downtown Sanliurfa
Local Time 2208 Hours

The bunker held food and water. There was no electricity.

Danielle placed the computer on a stack of metal ammo crates and opened it. The battery power was low, but she knew there was enough to show the video to Remington. She brought the file up and let it run.

"There's no audio," Danielle said. "But if you look closely, you can read Cody's lips." She enhanced the image and centered on Cody's mouth.

The blue tint of the computer screen played over Remington's face. His expression never changed, never offered her a clue as to what he was thinking.

"Play it again," he ordered.

Danielle did. Then she played it twice more after that. The low-battery warning flashed.

"There's not enough power to run the video again," Danielle said.

Remington didn't say anything.

"Did you see Cody give the orders?" Danielle demanded.

Remington fixed her with his gaze. "I don't know why this man would want Goose dead."

"It's not Cody. It's Carpathia. Cody works for Carpathia."

At that, Remington grinned. "You're accusing the newly elected secretary-general of the United Nations of trying to kill a U.S. Army staff sergeant?" He shook his head in disbelief. "How much attention do you think this little conspiracy theory of yours is going to net you?"

Anger filled Danielle. She wanted to lash out at Remington. He was the only one in the city who had the power to act, and he wasn't making a move to do anything.

"It's not a theory," Danielle said. "It's the truth."

"Cody didn't say anything about Carpathia."

"I've got proof that Cody works for Carpathia."

Remington drew in a breath and let it out. Like he had all the time in the world. "Do you like your job, Miss Vinchenzo?"

Danielle hadn't expected the question and didn't know how to react to it.

"The reason I ask," Remington stated calmly, "is because you're about to commit career suicide if you try to go on the air with this."

"Goose is out there," Danielle said. "Doesn't that matter?"

"Even if I believed your story, which I'm not entirely convinced of, there's a lot of territory out there. Where would you suggest I start looking for him? And how do you suppose I keep the Syrians from killing him outright when I do?"

"Make Cody tell you."

"Maybe you're in a rush to throw away your career, but I'm not. I've worked long and hard to get where I am. I'm not going to jeopardize that."

"I thought Goose was your friend."

"That," Remington said, "makes two of us."

A soldier entered the bunker and drew an immediate scathing look from Remington.

"Pardon me, sir," the soldier said. "I was ordered to bring you a message."

"Then do it," Remington snapped.

"It's Goose." The man smiled. "I mean, it's First Sergeant Gander, sir. He's alive."

Danielle let go the tense breath she'd been holding.

"How do you know that?" Remington demanded.

"Because we've been in contact with him, sir. Sergeant Gander managed to signal one of the LADAR operators. They've been communicating through Morse code. He says he needs help to get back inside the city."

Like a bad penny, Remington couldn't help thinking as he stood at the wall and surveyed the night-darkened ground through the gentle rain that persisted. He stood beside the LADAR operator and wondered where he'd be out there if he were Goose.

The night-vision binoculars picked the Syrian forces—the living and the dead—from the night. But where was Goose?

More than that, though, where were the killers Cody had sent? Remington knew they'd have no hesitation about killing anyone in the field they felt was affiliated with Goose.

Although Remington had ordered the news kept quiet, word of Goose's survival and presence outside the wall quickly passed through the Rangers. Remington felt the pressure to act growing within him. Most of the men were aware of Goose. Some of them owed him their lives.

It was more than that, though. Corporal Joseph Baker had enthralled several of the soldiers with the promise of salvation. Those men—those weak-minded soldiers—had followed Baker blindly, and Remington felt that Goose was capable of furthering that kind of foolish devotion.

Remington didn't intend to have to deal with that situation again. The men's desperation had to be shored up in order to keep them thinking like soldiers.

But Goose was out there, and every Ranger around Remington was busy thinking the first sergeant was going to turn into John Wayne, Bruce Willis, or Arnold Schwarzenegger.

"Show me the communication," Remington told the corporal manning the LADAR.

The device looked like a small version of a television camera on telescoping legs. The low profile made it hard for the enemy to spot.

"It's the readout, sir," the corporal answered. "Unless I move it around, we get a pretty constant readout. But a few minutes ago, Goose—Sergeant Gander—was able to ping the LADAR."

"With what?"

"A laser range finder from an enemy gun, sir."

Remington chuckled at that. That was Goose—inventive and ingenious under pressure. Remington realized again why he needed Goose alive at the moment and why having Goose around was going to be dangerous.

"He's been using Morse code?" Remington asked.

"Yes, sir."

"And you know Morse code?"

"Yes, sir."

"How?" Other than a cursory introduction, most soldiers were no longer taught the antiquated skill. Everything on the battlefield these days moved in hyperbursts of encrypted transmissions.

"I was an Eagle Scout, sir."

Remington looked at the young man and saw the innocence in his features. "Of course you were." He had to give it to Goose. There probably weren't many Eagle Scouts spread throughout the Rangers, and Goose had managed to find one who was operating a LADAR tonight. The sergeant's luck was nothing short of incredible.

"Of course you were," Remington said again.

The corporal clearly didn't know how to react to that.

"Can you signal the sergeant?"

"Yes, sir. Unless something's happened to him. But we haven't heard anything."

That didn't mean that Cody's mercenaries hadn't slipped through the brush and slit Goose's throat. Remington realized he hoped that hadn't happened. He needed Goose if he was going to turn the battle at Sanliurfa into a victory.

And he fully intended to do that.

"Contact him," Remington ordered.

"Yes, sir." The corporal turned to the task. "You going to send a team after him, sir?"

Aware of all the eyes on him, from Danielle Vinchenzo's to the other Rangers', Remington knew there could be only one answer. He hated feeling the pressure, but he also knew that with one word he'd be painted a hero.

"Yes."

"Thank God," Danielle whispered. Several of the soldiers echoed the sentiment.

"You'll need a team to go get Goose," the corporal said. "I'm volunteering."

"Noted, Corporal." Remington looked out into the darkness. "But this is one mission I'm going to lead myself."

❈   ❈   ❈

Outside Sanliurfa
Local Time 2235 Hours

Goose watched the range finder's digital readout increase and decrease as the LADAR painted it. He translated the Morse code in his head.

Remington here.

Yes, sir, Goose signaled back. There was a lot more he could have written. Confusion warred within him. He hadn't expected to talk to Remington.

U R in a fix.

Yes, sir.

I'm coming.

Just like that, Goose felt a huge weight lifted from his shoulders. He wouldn't have put money on that outcome. The smart thing for Remington to do would be to provide a distraction and cover fire while Goose and his companions beat it for the city walls.

U OK? Remington asked.

Yes, sir.

Mobile?

Yes, sir.

All of U?

Yes, sir. All three.

There was a pause. *How many hostiles looking for U?*

Unknown.

Sit tight.

Yes, sir. Wearily Goose let out a tense breath.

"Are they coming?" Miller asked.

"Yeah," Goose replied. "I talked to Captain Remington. We're to sit tight until he signals."

"Do you trust him?" Icarus asked. His gaze was flat and uncompromising.

The question brought Goose's own inner turmoil to a head. "Yes." In this, with so many Rangers watching, Goose did.

But if the circumstances were different? He didn't know. That bothered him. He shoved the question from his mind. *Concentrate on staying alive and getting back to your unit. That's your job right now.*

"Get ready," Goose advised them. "When we start moving, there's gonna be no looking back." He turned to face the darkness again.

✽   ✽   ✽

Local Time 2304 Hours

The rain slackened off. Water still ran on the muddy ground, but it didn't have the same volume as before. Rain dropped steadily from the trees and brush where Goose lay concealed. With the night covering them, the water was cold and felt like it seeped into his bones. He shoved his injured knee into the mud and hoped the chill would numb some of the gnawing pain.

Evidently one of the more enterprising Syrian officers had decided to take advantage of the lull in the rain. Scout teams moved over the terrain, probably looking for new areas to dig in against the attacks they felt certain would come in the morning.

Or to prepare for the attacks they would launch themselves.

Things were going to continue to be bloody. Goose knew that and tried not to think of the lives yet to be sacrificed.

At 2308 hours, the laser range finder registered an incoming message.

In position. Have your six. Remington.

Goose took a deep breath and pushed himself up into a squatting position. His left knee screamed in pain. It had swelled so badly he had trouble getting it to fold properly under him.

"Get up," Goose said. He readied his M-4A1.

Miller prayed aloud as he got to his feet.

Icarus stood without comment. His face was solemn, streaked with mud.

"We go slow," Goose said, "until we have a reason not to."

"Is there going to be some kind of signal?" Miller asked.

"When the bullets start flying, if you live long enough to see them or hear them," Icarus said, "that'll be your signal."

Goose didn't think he could have put the situation any more succinctly. "All right, let's go." He led the way, staying with the brush line as much as he could, not taking a direct path toward the city.

The enemy—all of them—would be watching for that.

※ ※ ※

Local Time 2310 Hours

Remington waited in the territory where he knew Goose was headed. Satellite recon had picked up Goose and the other two men coming through the trees on the southwest side of the city. There wasn't much cover there, but it was enough. The Syrian scout forces kept trying to encroach from the southeast, where the trees were thicker. Snipers kept those efforts thinned out.

In a prone position, Remington lay with a sniper rifle resting on a bipod and took aim 517 yards away. He was good with the weapon, better than many of the men in his unit. And there wasn't anyone he trusted more to make the shots he needed to make.

He swept the crosshairs across Goose, thought momentarily how easy it would be to erase that threat, then struck the thought from his mind. He could still use Goose.

Instead, Remington tracked the two men who crept up on Goose's position. The captain slid his finger over the trigger and let out half a breath. Then he squeezed.

※ ※ ※

Local Time 2310 Hours

A warning tingle ran through Goose and let him know he was in someone's sights. The warning was more instinct than physical, one of those skills that tended to vanish as men got more civilized about their killing. But he'd honed it on dozens of battlefields and trusted it completely.

Someone was ahead of them in the darkness, lying in wait in the scrub brush. And he had his sights on the three of them.

"Down!" Goose whispered hoarsely, twisting and reaching for the chaplain behind him. He caught Miller's Kevlar vest and yanked him down just as someone ahead fired. The muzzle flashes were almost invisible in the darkness, letting Goose know the shooter was using a flash hider, and the sound was barely audible, signaling the use of a silencer. The bullet smacked against the Kevlar covering Goose's back. If the armor hadn't been there, the round would have cored through his heart.

Icarus cursed as he took cover behind a tree.

Goose placed his free hand on the back of Miller's helmet and forced the man's face into the mud. The chaplain's first response was to try to look up, but Goose held him down. Goose lay still and held his assault weapon in one hand. He kept his head pressed against the earth and scanned the skyline.

In the next moment, a body pitched out of the darkness. A second passed, and another ambusher sprawled to the ground only a few feet away from the first. Goose didn't know who the sniper was that had saved them, but he was grateful to be watched over.

Then the sound of both shots echoed over the immediate area.

Syrian soldiers yelled to each other not far away. Someone swung a spotlight in Goose's direction. The light missed him by inches, but already Syrian troops massed to investigate.

"Time to go." Goose grabbed Miller's harness and yanked him to his feet. "Stay up with me. You slow down, we're both going to die." He ran, keeping his rifle forward.

He checked the first body he came to, wanting to make sure he wasn't leaving a wounded enemy behind. He didn't recognize what was left of the man's face, but he knew he wasn't Syrian. The battle-dress was black, and there were no markings. Goose took the extra magazines and moved on to the second man, all too aware of the Syrian troops dogging their trail.

The second man had been shot through the throat and lay drowning in his own blood. He tried to raise a pistol when Goose came up on him. Goose knocked the pistol away and it flew from the dying man's hand. The man gasped once; then his gaze dulled.

Miller whispered something unintelligible behind him, but Goose ignored the chaplain.

The Syrian voices continued, and the spotlight pierced the night, swinging closer and closer. The bright yellow beam splashed across Goose once, and then gunfire erupted.

Almost immediately the yellow light winked out as the sniper scored again. Goose stayed focused on the intervening distance between him and the city. If they could close the gap, get inside the city, they'd be safe. His knee felt like it was shredding, coming completely apart. Everything the surgeons had done to it in the past was coming undone.

He pushed himself through the pain and kept running. He dragged Miller after him, and that put an even greater strain on his knee.

Bullets thudded into the ground around him. Icarus cursed as he ran. Miller prayed, reciting the Twenty-third Psalm in a jerky voice.

A trio of Syrian soldiers formed out of the darkness, stepping into Goose's vision like ghosts out of the night. They swung their weapons toward Goose.

Aiming the M-4A1 one-handed while he dragged Miller with the other, Goose started a line of bullets at the knees of the man on the left and brought the rifle in a line across the men as he fired on full-auto. The first two men crumpled, but the assault weapon cycled dry before he could shoot the third.

Goose yelled inarticulately, anything to scare the man facing him. He never broke stride, not even with the trembling rattling through his knee. The joint felt spongy and loose, and he feared it was going to fail under him.

He lowered a shoulder and ran headlong into the man. They went down in a tangle of arms and legs. Miller joined them in the mud.

Then everything was madness. Goose scrambled for his life, unable to get to his pistol because the Syrian soldier grappled him and rolled him onto that hip. Abandoning the pistol, Goose went for his knife. He ripped the blade free, rolled his opponent over, held the man flat with his own body weight, and drove the knife home between the man's third and fourth ribs.

Miller lay nearby, watching in stunned horror. "God help us."

"You start out by helping yourself," Goose said. "God takes over from there."

Bullets tore at the earth. Icarus had dropped to a knee nearby and fired controlled three-round bursts at targets. A nearby Syrian tank lurched into motion. The turret spun around.

"C'mon." Goose pulled Miller to his feet. "You stay here, that tank will mash what's left of you into the mud."

Miller started running.

With his knee throbbing painfully, it was all Goose could do to stay up.

"Goose!"

Remington's voice came out of the darkness. Immediately Goose steered straight for it. His body hurt from exertion, and he was operating purely on autopilot, but his trust in Remington was there. In times like this, that had been one thing he'd always been able to count on.

But a small fear quavered through him, causing him to wonder if he was running into a bullet this time.

The tank got off a round that exploded several yards away. The concussion nearly knocked Goose from his feet. He steadied, put a hand on Miller's shoulder to steady him as well, and ran harder.

The tank turret swiveled again as the gunner adjusted. A pair of Syrian jeeps streaked for the rendezvous point. In the next few seconds, all of the vehicles turned into whirling fireballs as the artillery lining Sanliurfa's walls opened up.

Only a few yards short of his goal, surrounded by the heat of the explosions, Goose's knee finally gave out. He felt it snap, felt the burning pain explode so fiercely that it almost swept his senses away. He went down at once, releasing Miller so the chaplain could keep running toward safety.

Instinctively Goose pulled his rifle up and looked around. Icarus was at his side, grabbing him by the arm and trying to haul him to his feet.

Shadows came at them out of the night. Goose recognized Remington at once.

"I've got to go," Icarus said. "Maybe you trust your friends, but I don't."

Stunned and in more pain than he could ever remember, Goose heard Icarus's words, but they sounded strangely distorted. Like he was speaking through water.

Goose wanted to tell the man to stay, but before he could speak, Icarus had vanished. Evidently he'd chosen to go his own way rather than risk capture by Remington. Goose leaned onto the rifle and tried to force himself up. It was no use. The leg was gone. The knee wouldn't hold him.

Footsteps slapped through the mud toward Goose. When he looked up, he saw Remington's face tiger-striped by combat cosmetics. Before he knew it, Goose had his weapon loosely pointed at Remington. Remington had his weapon centered on Goose's chest.

Then Remington offered his hand. "Need help?"

"Yeah." Goose got to his feet with Remington's help. Together, they limped back to Sanliurfa as the other Rangers around them provided covering fire.

Remington strode up to the hotel door and kicked it open. The hinges shrieked as they ripped free of the wood.

Cody lay on the king-size bed smoking a cigar. He had a glass of liquor in one hand and a pistol in the other.

Remington looked at the man. "Put that away or I'm going to make you eat it."

Cody didn't look convinced at first; then Remington stepped toward him. The CIA agent laid the pistol aside.

"What are you doing here?" Cody demanded.

"I came to let you know I killed two more of your playmates outside the city. They were planning on ambushing Goose. I couldn't let that happen."

"You could have."

"I didn't want it to."

"Where's Icarus?"

"Gone. Disappeared while we were swapping lead with the Syrians."

Cody cursed.

"I wanted to clear up the situation between us regarding Goose," Remington said, venting some of the rage he felt roaring around inside him. "So I thought I'd come here and deliver the message in person."

Cody stared at him without saying a word.

"Goose is mine," Remington said. "He lives or dies by my decision.

On my time. In my way. If you try to touch a hair on his head before I say otherwise, I'm going to kill you. Do you read me?"

"You're making a mistake."

With blinding speed, Remington drew the pistol from his hip and pointed it at Cody. He fired. Cody closed his eyes as the sound filled the room. Then he opened them, obviously surprised to find that he wasn't dead. Instead, the pillow next to his head bore a smoking hole.

"I'm not going to tell you again," Remington said. "This is your one pass. Do you read me?"

Cody nodded.

Barely able to restrain himself from killing the man anyway, Remington backed out of the room, then turned and walked down the hall. Letting Cody live was a mistake. He felt it in his bones. But he didn't know how much Carpathia cared about the CIA section chief. Yet. Once Remington had a better idea, once he knew Cody could disappear without Carpathia becoming too upset, he was going to make that happen.

In the meantime, he needed to speak with Goose as soon as the first sergeant was up and around.

※　※　※

Local Time 0643 Hours

When Goose woke, he was exactly where he thought he would be: in a hospital bed. His leg was elevated on blankets in front of him. Pain, wrapped in cotton by painkillers, nevertheless throbbed at his temples.

He pulled his leg from the supports, tried to get up, and couldn't. His knee lacked the strength. The pain was so unbearable that he was on the verge of losing consciousness again.

"You need to get back into that bed."

Goose looked up at the nurse who entered his room. "I got men I need to be looking after."

The nurse shook her head. "You're going to need to spend all your time looking after yourself for a while, First Sergeant." She paused. "I would wait until the doctor got here, but he's dealing with so many wounded right now that I don't know when he'll be in here to tell you."

"Tell me what?"

"That your knee is gone. You're going to be lucky if you can walk with a cane after you heal up. They might be able to outfit you with an artificial knee at some point, but we can't do it here. And with the extent of the damage, you're not going to be able to stay in the military." Her voice softened. "I'm sorry."

Goose nodded. "Thank you, ma'am." He lay back on the bed and tried to think about what he was going to do, then realized there was nothing he could do, so he tried desperately not to think about anything at all.

The painkillers helped. He let them drag him down into the darkness.

❋   ❋   ❋

Local Time 1612 Hours

Goose dozed, surprised at how tired he was. Despite the erratic artillery fire, with the narcotic in his veins, sleep came a lot more easily than he'd thought it would.

One of the nurses walked into the room carrying a cell phone. She looked tired and disheveled, but she flashed him a warm smile. "First Sergeant Gander?"

"Yes, ma'am."

The woman's smile grew bigger. "I didn't know if you'd be awake."

"You caught me napping, but I'm awake now."

"If you weren't awake, I was going to wake you. The woman on the other end of this line sounds like she needs a reassuring word."

Goose said thanks and took the handset. "Hello."

"Goose," Megan said, "it's me."

"Hey," Goose said, feeling his voice suddenly get so thick that he couldn't force any more words through his mouth.

"Cal called and let me know you were still alive. He told me you were wounded."

"Not wounded. A few scratches and bruises, maybe. But my knee went out on me. I'm glad the captain gave you the update. I'll have to thank him." Goose stared at his immobilized knee. He wanted to talk things over with Megan, but he didn't. From everything he'd heard, she'd been staying busy as well. She didn't need to worry about him on top of everything else she was handling. And there was nothing she could do.

"How are you?" she asked.

"I'm fine."

"You sound tired."

"I am tired."

"But you're going to be all right?"

"Yes, ma'am. I'm fit as a fiddle."

"Goose . . ."

He waited. After all those years of marriage, he knew not to hurry her. She'd say what she wanted to when she got good and ready.

"I've asked for permission to bring civilians over there in support positions. Families here are going crazy with the need to do something for the soldiers stationed there. After reviewing the offer from those civilians, the general has agreed."

"There's no call to involve civilians in this situation. A lot of people have already gotten hurt. A lot more are gonna be. This isn't a good place for civilians to be, Megan."

"It's not a good place for you, either."

"No, it's not." Goose gazed unhappily at his injured leg. He'd never before felt so helpless. *You're going to be lucky if you can walk with a cane.* The words had cycled endlessly through his head and haunted his dreams.

"I'm coming too, Goose," Megan told him. "Over there. As soon as we can set up a schedule."

Fierce pride filled Goose as he heard her. From the time he'd known her, Megan had never backed down from a challenge. She'd never cut and run.

"Nothing to say?" she asked.

"I know when to steer clear of trouble," Goose replied. "But I don't like the thought of you being in this mess."

"I don't like the thought of you being over there. I guess we're at a stalemate, First Sergeant. So if you can't come to me, I guess I'm going to come to you."

"Yes, ma'am." But Goose hoped it wouldn't be anytime soon or that the commanding officers would reconsider. He understood the sense of what Megan was proposing, and God knew they needed the help, but he didn't want families on the firing line.

Megan interrupted his thoughts. "They're telling me I have to keep this call short."

"I understand." Goose squeezed the phone more tightly than he'd intended. He didn't want to surrender the contact he had with her. He wanted to feel her close to him. He wanted her to understand that he was going to walk again. More than that, he was going to soldier again. The doctor was wrong. He *had* to be wrong.

"I love you, Goose," Megan said.

"I love you too."

"God willing, I'll see you soon."

The broken connection clicked in Goose's ear. He swallowed hard and struggled to keep his emotions in check. Then he folded the cell phone and handed it back to the waiting nurse.

"Sounds like you've got yourself a good woman, First Sergeant."

"Yes, ma'am. One of the finest women I've ever met."

"Excluding present company."

Despite the fear that gripped him from the debilitating effects of his knee injury and the thought of Megan being anywhere on the ground in Turkey, Goose summoned a smile. "Of course, ma'am. Excluding present company."

"You see if you can get some more rest, First Sergeant. If you need anything, just let me know."

"Yes, ma'am." Goose lay back and closed his eyes. Even though he felt certain sleep wouldn't come, it took him under its wing so softly and suddenly he wasn't even aware of it.

Goose came awake feeling someone staring at him. He blinked against the thick darkness. For a moment, with the drugs coursing through his system, he was lost and thought he was in the field somewhere. He wasn't sure if it was the Middle East or Africa or even one of the wilderness jaunts he'd been on in Eastern Europe.

Then he felt the bed beneath him and remembered he was in the medical facility in Sanliurfa. That realization wasn't any more restful. For all he knew, one of the CIA's assassins lurked in the room.

Out of years of habit, he reached for a weapon, but one wasn't close to hand.

"At ease, First Sergeant," Remington spoke out of the darkness.

"Yes, sir." Goose started to get up but his leg remained in traction. "I can't get up, sir."

"I knew that. You ready for the light?"

Goose squinted against the coming brightness. "Yes, sir."

Remington turned the light on. The illumination stabbed into Goose's eyes. Thankfully the dimmer muted the full strength, but the sudden brightness still gave him an instant headache.

"How are things out there, sir?"

Remington approached the bed. Despite the fatigue that clung to him, he appeared unstoppable. "We've held the enemy in abeyance. They're still there, but we've convinced them that taking this city isn't going to be as easy as they'd first thought."

"That's good, sir."

"It's good, but it's not enough. The Syrians are still convinced they can get the job done." Remington took in a breath and let it out. "Even with the UN reinforcements, our situation hasn't improved enough to promise that we can hold the line here."

"At least we're not being run out of town on a rail in full rout, sir."

A tight, humorless smile curved Remington's lips. "That's true. But I don't like looking for how things could be worse. I want to concentrate on making them better."

"Yes, sir."

Remington studied Goose for a moment. "Your friend Icarus managed to disappear again."

Goose heard and felt the bald accusation in Remington's words. "That man's not my friend, sir."

"Yet the two of you seem to end up spending an inordinate amount of time together," Remington countered.

"Not through any effort on my part, sir."

Slowly Remington nodded. "I'd like to believe that."

"It's the truth, sir." Goose had a feeling that whatever was going to happen with Icarus, the mysterious agent had disappeared from his life for good. He was in God's hands now.

"Moving on," Remington said. "You've noticed that we have reinforcements."

"Couldn't help but notice that on the way in, sir."

"The secretary-general of the United Nations routed them to us."

"Carpathia did that, sir?"

"Yes." Remington studied Goose's face. "Do you have a problem with that, First Sergeant?"

"No, sir."

"That's good, because without those men we wouldn't have been here waiting when you finished your little trek through hostile territory."

"Roger that, sir."

"There's been an interesting twist to come out of their arrival."

Goose waited.

"Secretary-General Carpathia wants to reorganize the world's military forces. In light of everything that's gone on, the secretary-general recognizes the need to combine those armies into one unit. Put all our toys in one box. With everything facing the world today, the confusion and chaos, I think it would be a good idea."

Maybe under other circumstances, Goose would have thought

so too. Instead, as he thought about the situation, Icarus's warnings about Carpathia kept coming to mind.

"Even more interesting, Carpathia offered me a new position: he wants to make me a full colonel."

"You're thinking of leaving the army?" Goose was so surprised he forgot to address Remington as sir. He hastily amended that.

"I don't think of it as leaving the army. I took this position to serve my country. At the moment, I believe the best way to serve my country is by joining Carpathia's efforts. The man has done a lot of good in the world in just a short time. He's made a believer out of me."

At those words, a chill ghosted through Goose, leaving him unsettled. "I guess congratulations are in order, sir," Goose said.

"Thanks." Remington paused. "But something else brought me here. In this new position, I'm going to need good people. Men I can count on. You and I haven't been totally in sync for a while, but I think that's because of the situation, not because of any fundamental differences. We still soldier the same."

Goose chose not to say anything, thinking that was the wisest course.

"I'd like you to think about coming along with me," Remington said.

"Thank you, sir, but I don't see how I can do something like that. In case you hadn't heard, my knee—"

"Is totally blown," Remington interrupted. "I talked to the doctor. The plain fact of the matter is, if you stay with the army, Goose, your career is over."

The words hit Goose like physical blows. It was one thing to deal with the facts by himself in the quiet of the room. But it was another for Remington to give voice to them.

"Yes, sir. I know that's what the doc says, but that's not necessarily—"

"Sergeant, unless you can pull a miracle out of your butt, that's how it's going to be."

Goose struggled to find his voice. "Yes, sir."

"I've got you scheduled to depart on the first medevac we can put together. I don't know when that's going to be. We're still in the planning stages."

Goose accepted that without comment, but everything in him wanted to fight, to resist.

"That's how the army wants to do it," Remington said. "But I've got something else I can offer. In my new capacity as colonel."

Even though he tried, Goose couldn't speak.

"You're a soldier, Goose," Remington declared. "That's all you're ever going to be."

"That's all I ever wanted to be, sir."

"I know. That's why you passed on Officer Candidates School. But I can use soldiers in this new army. Maybe you'll never be field-ready again, but you've got a lot of knowledge locked away in that thick skull of yours. A lot of spit and polish. I need that. If you want, I can offer you a position with me. As my aide. Once you get back on your feet."

"That's considerate of you, sir."

Remington frowned. "It's not just considerate, Sergeant. It's downright generous."

"Yes, sir. I'm still just a little fogged from the pain meds. Thank you, sir."

"When you get out of that bed, report to me, and we'll get squared away on the paperwork."

"Yes, sir." Goose answered automatically, but he knew he wanted time to think about the offer. Everything was coming down on him too fast.

"I also heard that Megan and some of the civvies from Fort Benning are going to be joining us here," Remington said.

"Yes, sir. She said that was in the works."

"I convinced Secretary-General Carpathia to assist in making that happen."

Goose couldn't believe it. "But, sir, those are civilians. This is a war zone."

"We also need support staff, Sergeant, as I'm sure you're well aware."

"Yes, sir."

"I was just thinking that it would be a pity if you shipped out from here on a medical discharge at the same time Megan arrived."

That thought filled Goose with a deep, visceral fear. "I wouldn't want to do that, sir." *Megan's not experienced enough to handle something like this. And we're barely holding our own here.* In the end, Goose knew he didn't have a choice.

Remington knew it too. He nodded. "When you're able, come by my office. Let's make that paperwork official."

"Yes, sir."

"As you were, First Sergeant."

"Yes, sir." Goose saluted from the bed. Silently he watched

Remington leave the room. Then he tried to relax and let the meds claim him again. His mind whirled, trying to figure out what he was supposed to do.

✹ ✹ ✹

Local Time 0441 Hours

Goose swayed awkwardly on the crutches as he stood in front of the hospital. He hadn't been able to sleep. The meds were no longer having an effect, and he felt restless for no reason that he could name. He just knew he couldn't stay in the hospital any longer. So he'd hobbled from his room and out of the hospital without the duty nurse catching him.

Now that he was out, he didn't know where to go.

The throbbing pain in his knee increased, and he wondered if he could make it back to his room without falling on his face. Needing help to get back to his bed would be embarrassing.

The early morning light was just beginning to lift the shadows night had draped over the beleaguered city. Several of the sandbags stacked against the building to reinforce the walls had been blown open by explosions. Deep craters scarred the street. Hummers and other military vehicles whizzed past, resupplying men and ammo.

Watching them, Goose felt guilty and useless. *Lord*, he thought, *I never thought I'd finish my career up like this. I signed on to be a soldier, to be a man who made changes in the world.*

As he thought that, he wondered if that very desire had been the thing keeping him from having a closer relationship with God.

He'd never considered that before. But he remembered the talks with Bill Townsend when they'd discussed church and faith. Bill had been a consummate soldier, but that wasn't all he'd wanted to be, wasn't all he'd worked at. There wasn't a day that went by that Bill hadn't ministered to someone, even if it was for five minutes over a cup of coffee at a diner. He'd carried his message to every country they'd ever served in together.

Goose had listened to it all, but he'd never really taken it in. Bill had seemed able to serve God and the military at the same time. But Goose knew that he'd given God short shrift over the years.

Was his commitment to the army the reason he was still here in this world when Chris was in the next? Thoughts of his son nearly overwhelmed him.

Is my boy alone, God? Is he scared? Please, I don't care what You do to me, but please take care of that boy.

Goose's eyes burned with unshed tears. When Megan had started talking so hopefully about what was taking place and that they would soon be reunited with Chris, Goose had felt angry toward her. That surprised him. In all the years he'd been married to her, he seldom felt that way.

Somehow, though, for the first time in their marriage, Goose knew Megan had moved on without him. He resented her for that. And he resented the fact that she could so quickly adjust to Chris being gone.

Even more, he resented the fact that she would soon be in Sanliurfa while he was going to be shipped out.

You're being unfair, Goose told himself. But he couldn't help it. The feelings were strong within him.

He kept thinking about the offer Remington had made to bring him along into the new army Nicolae Carpathia was putting together. Even with his physical disability, Remington would keep him close to hand. He could be there with Megan.

Except it would—to Goose's way of thinking, at least—compromise the oath and promise he'd made to his country and to the Rangers. Stepping away from that wasn't as easy for him as it had obviously been for Remington.

Goose checked himself, wondering if he was being unfair to the captain. He'd known the man a long time. Down deep inside, Goose refused to believe that Remington was anything less than a good man. The captain was just confused these days. With everything that had gone on, that was understandable.

And if that one-world army was coming, as Remington seemed to believe so fervently and the news channels were only now starting to talk up, then Goose was going to end up among their ranks anyway. Wasn't he?

Even trying to think it through logically didn't help. Goose knew it still felt wrong. He just didn't know why.

Icarus's stories about Carpathia kept cycling through Goose's head.

A tank passed by on the street. The vibrations of its passage were almost enough to make Goose fall off the crutches. He repositioned himself and leaned against the sandbags.

So where are you going to go, Sergeant? Goose asked himself. *Just what exactly is it you're doing out here?*

A jeep passed him, then braked to a halt and reversed to pull up in front of him. Danielle Vinchenzo sat behind the steering wheel. Her cameraman sat in the passenger seat.

Danielle looked at Goose. "Aren't you supposed to be in bed?"

"Got tired of lying around," Goose replied. "Thought I'd get a breath of fresh air."

Concern tightened the lines of her face. Her eyes were red-rimmed, and Goose would have bet his last dollar she hadn't slept all night. "You look like you're ready to fall over," she said.

"Ma'am," Goose said with a smile, "I'd say that's a case of the pot calling the kettle black."

Danielle grinned in return. "I guess neither one of us was meant for the life of a spectator, First Sergeant."

"No, ma'am."

"Want to go anywhere?"

Goose thought about it. "I don't know. I just knew I couldn't stay laid up in that bed anymore."

"Gary and I were heading out to breakfast. If we can find a place. If I eat another MRE, I'm going to barf."

Goose grinned. "Yes, ma'am. But like my first sergeant told me back in the day, if you find yourself turning your nose up at an MRE, you just ain't gone hungry long enough."

Danielle laughed. "I think it's more likely an acquired taste. But the offer stands. If you stand out here much longer, one of those nurses is going to find you."

"Yes, ma'am. You're probably right about that."

"Then get in."

"You don't mind?"

"First Sergeant, I insist."

"Yes, ma'am." As Goose hobbled over, the cameraman abandoned the passenger seat and sat on the rear deck. With difficulty and considerable pain, Goose managed to lever his bad leg into the jeep. A fine sheen of perspiration covered him by the time he was in.

"Are you sure you're up to this?" Danielle asked.

"Yes, ma'am."

"These streets aren't smooth anymore."

"No, ma'am. I can see that. It'll be all right. But thank you for asking."

Danielle put the jeep in gear and pulled out onto the street behind a convoy of United Nations vehicles. "I suppose you're aware of what Carpathia is doing with the military?"

"Yes, ma'am."

"I've heard that Captain Remington is accepting a position with them."

"You'd have to talk to the captain about that, ma'am."

"I don't think I'm one of the captain's favorite people these days. Not only that, but I've heard a lot of Rangers aren't happy about it either. Several of them plan to stay with the army."

Goose didn't say anything. He'd heard the same thing, and it weighed on his mind.

"Many of those Rangers," Danielle added, "are the same men who were following Corporal Baker's church. Before he was murdered."

That statement gave Goose unpleasant thoughts about Alexander Cody. "Have you done any more follow-up on Cody?"

"Enough to get myself in trouble with the network."

"They tell you to stay away from him?"

"Not in so many words."

"It appears to me, ma'am, that you're working for the man you're wanting to declare as an enemy."

Danielle smiled. "For the moment, yes. But Nicolae Carpathia, and especially OneWorld NewsNet, can't control me."

Seeing the fiery independence in the woman, Goose nodded. "I reckon not, ma'am."

"I'm going to stay until they force me out. And I'm going to use my position to ferret out everything I can."

"Given what you've found, ma'am, that might not be the smartest thing you could do."

"You're out here wandering around on crutches when you can't even stand up, First Sergeant. I don't think I'd be talking about smart things to do."

"No, ma'am. I suppose not."

"What about you, Goose?" she asked.

"Ma'am?"

"Are you going to join Carpathia's army?"

Goose chose his words carefully. "The docs tell me I'll be doing good to walk again after this. I get back stateside, I'll talk to a few specialists. But I don't think their diagnosis is gonna be much different. Me and this knee, we been through a lot. Got a lot of miles on us. A lot of pain." But Goose couldn't stop thinking about Megan and how she was coming to Sanliurfa.

"And if your knee wasn't hurt?"

"I try not to deal in guesswork like that, ma'am. I'm a U.S. Army Ranger. I was trained to deal in realistic situations."

"I think we left behind the kind of realistic situations you were trained for weeks ago," Danielle said.

"Maybe so, ma'am." Goose shifted and tried in vain to find a comfortable position. Even if he managed that, the bumpy street guaranteed a lot of pain. Some of his discomfort must have shown on his face.

"Sorry," Danielle said. "If I go much slower, the engine stalls out."

"I'll be okay, ma'am." Goose stared at the blocks lined with bombed-out and wrecked shops. Only a few days ago, many of them had still been open.

"Do you think Remington, as a captain or a colonel, is going to be able to hold this city?"

"If it can be done, I'm sure he's just the man to do it."

"You put a lot of faith in him."

"He's been a friend for a long time, ma'am."

"He hasn't seemed like much of a friend lately."

Goose didn't answer for a moment. "The captain's got a lot on his mind lately, ma'am, but when push comes to shove, I've never known him not to do the right thing." He tried not to pay attention to the doubts he felt as soon as he spoke.

Silence stretched out between them for a time. Goose shoved the pain to the back of his mind, but he didn't know how much longer he could stand the drive.

Danielle said, "Maybe you've still got faith in your boss, but I'm losing faith in mine."

Goose wondered at the word choice. *Faith* seemed like an awfully big word to throw around these days. Especially when you weren't sure what you were supposed to have faith in.

"*Goose.*"

The voice echoed in Goose's head and it was so familiar that he started and stared over his shoulder.

"Something wrong?" Danielle asked.

"No," Goose answered automatically. "Thought I heard something."

"I don't see how you could hear anything over the noise this jeep makes."

"I must not have." But Goose was sure that he did.

"Street's blocked," the cameraman said. "You can't go that way."

Goose looked forward and saw that the statement was true. One of the cargo trucks had broken down in the intersection. A ruined tank occupied one of the side streets. Danielle turned left and crept by the sawhorses the military had put out.

"*Goose.*"

The voice sounded so uncannily like Bill Townsend's that Goose's nape prickled. *Gotta be more out of it than I thought. Shoulda stayed in bed.*

Only a couple of blocks later, Danielle approached a bridge stretching across the river that ran through the city.

"*Stop.*"

"Stop here." Goose spoke before he knew he was going to.

Danielle braked the jeep to the side of the street and looked over at him. "Is something wrong?"

"I don't know." Goose searched the thinning darkness that clung to the riverbanks and couldn't find anything that stood out. A few boats sailed sedately across the smooth surface. Judging from the amount of boxes and people aboard, a lot more of the citizens had finally decided to throw in the towel and abandon the city.

Goose stared at the river, following it with his gaze as it wound through Sanliurfa. Then, only a short distance off the road, down the gentle hillside, he spotted a group of Rangers lining the riverbank.

At first Goose thought they were part of a scouting expedition. But there were simply too many of them. Dozens of men sat along the riverbank with their weapons. One of them stood in the water and called out to another. The man walked down the hill and into the slow-moving river. When he reached the waiting man, they talked briefly; then the first man held the other, lowered him into the water, and brought him back up.

"They're baptizing," Danielle said. "Gary, get the camera on them."

"No, ma'am," Goose said, turning to her. "This is a private ceremony."

Danielle's gaze met his without flinching. "This is important."

"If Captain Remington finds out this is going on, he'll likely put a stop to it." Goose didn't have any doubts about that.

"Are you planning on not reporting them?"

Goose didn't speak.

"Isn't that a declaration of some sort about your loyalties?" Danielle pressed.

The question troubled Goose. He tried to find an answer.

"Goose."

The nape of Goose's neck prickled again. "My loyalties are to those men."

"Even if what they're doing flies in the face of what Remington wants?"

Goose watched the men. He was torn over the issue, but there was something greater at stake. He was certain of that now.

"If you'll excuse me, ma'am, there's something I gotta go do." Goose swung his legs out of the jeep and set the crutches on the ground. His knee throbbed painfully, and his other leg almost buckled underneath him on the uneven ground.

"Goose." Danielle ran up to him. "Let me help."

"No, ma'am. I appreciate it, but this is something I gotta do on my own." Slowly, with great difficulty, Goose made his way down the hillside to the gentle river.

The men caught sight of him and stopped what they were doing. Fear showed on their faces.

"First Sergeant," one of the young men said.

Goose looked around at them. "You boys on your own time?"

"Supposed to take our downtime as we can, First Sergeant."

"Well then, carry on." Goose waited, not knowing for certain what had drawn him down the hillside. Looking up it, he felt stupid. There was no way he was going up that hillside under his own power. Coming down had all but exhausted him. *You're gonna feel mighty foolish having to ask for help getting back up there.*

"Have faith."

That was Bill Townsend's voice again. Goose was sure of it. He looked at the river and thought about Chris. *Heaven has to exist,* Goose told himself. *There's no other place my boy would be.* Before he knew it, tears ran down his cheeks. *Chris, I'm sorry I didn't go with you. But I just didn't know where I was going wrong then. I didn't know that faith had to be that strong in you.*

"You do now," that familiar voice whispered. *"So what are you going to do about it, Sarge?"*

Carefully Goose let the crutches fall from his hands. He was conscious of everyone's eyes on him as he limped through the mud. The pain rushed at him, stronger than ever, and he didn't know if he was going to give in to it or pass out from it first.

Instead, he did just what the military trained him to do. He kept putting one foot after another into the water. He walked until the river closed over his head, filled his ears, and drowned out all other noise. The river took his weight and buoyed him up, lifting some of the pain from him.

For a time, Goose hung there, afraid at any minute that one of the Rangers would come after him because they thought he might be trying to drown himself. Instead, Goose drank in the peace that he felt. It was like nothing he'd ever before experienced.

"It can be better."

Goose believed that voice. More than that, he believed for certain that he knew where Chris was.

And most of all—he believed.

He let that belief wash over him, buoying him up even more. The pain receded, and he wasn't at all surprised. He reached for the warmth and security that he knew would be there.

God, I'm at that point where there's nothing left. The tears came then and he felt them slide hotly from his eyes despite the river's embrace. *I'm away from Megan and Joey. Chris is gone, though I guess he's with You now. Please take care of him. Tell him I love him.* He paused, trying to assemble his thoughts. *I can't walk, God. My knee is shot. Whatever was there, it's gone now. I'm not even a soldier.*

Bill always said You have a plan for everybody. He said You see every sparrow that falls. Well, God, I've fallen. I'm here, and I can't even stand on my own two feet. The helplessness that filled Goose was almost overwhelming. *If Bill was right, if I couldn't come to You until there was nowhere else to go, then I'm here.*

I'm just an old, broken-down soldier, God. Not much use to anybody. But I love my family, and I love my unit. It hurts me to think that I'm not going to be there for them.

But I'm not ready to give in, God. I'm not ready to stop fighting for them. I'll crawl to the front line if I have to. Just give me the strength to do it. Please. Goose paused again. *I don't know if You can find a use for me, but if there's something I can do for You, help me do it. Please. I pray in Jesus' blessed name.*

Exhausted, Goose couldn't feel anything but the pain throbbing through him and the sickness twisting in his belly. The cold water pressed against him. He searched for God, then just dialed himself down and concentrated on the emptiness inside him.

I'm here, God. Take me as I am. This is as good as I'll ever be.

Then Goose felt his pain ease. Floating there in the river, he didn't feel alone anymore. A quiet, confident joy boiled away the fear and the uncertainty, filling him up and warming his heart.

In that instant, his tears turned from sadness to happiness.

He looked up at the brightening sky through the water, blinking understanding that he'd never before felt, laughing out loud despite the fact that he was submerged. Silvery bubbles exploded from his lips.

The need to be up and moving filled him too. Then, not believing what he was doing, he turned and swam back toward the riverbank. Gradually his feet found purchase in the thick mud, and he stood. His knee felt as strong and stable as it ever had.

"Sarge," one of the men said, "are you doing okay? We thought..." Whatever he'd thought, he chose to keep it to himself.

They gathered around Goose. Danielle pressed in among them.

In amazement, feeling the difference and needing to see it, Goose clawed at the bandages covering his knee. They were reluctant to come free. One of the Rangers handed over a knife, and the job went much easier. In another minute, white bandages littered the river mud.

All of the swelling in Goose's knee was gone, as was all the pain. He took experimental steps and found he could easily walk.

Healed, he thought. And for the first time in his life, he didn't doubt that such a thing could happen. He believed and was thankful.

"Problem," someone said.

Following the men's attention, Goose looked up and saw Cal Remington standing on the bridge beside his Hummer. Even at the distance, Goose saw the anger and disapproval in the captain's eyes.

"Looks like you made your decision, Goose," Remington called down.

Goose didn't respond for a moment, not knowing what to say. Finally he said, "Yes, sir."

"You disappoint me, First Sergeant." Before Goose could respond, Remington clambered back into his Hummer and drove away. Rubber shrieked.

"He's not a happy man," Danielle observed.

"No, ma'am. I reckon not." Goose looked around at the Rangers. "You men carry on. When you get done here, we got work to do."

"Yes, First Sergeant."

Goose walked away, feeling the strength he had in his knee. It felt brand-new. Maybe even better than brand-new.

"Looks like your choice got made for you," Danielle said.

Goose looked back at the river. "No, ma'am. That choice was mine. I walked into that water of my own free will. Standing on the legs I had left."

"Remington's not going to let this go."

"No, ma'am. But with my knee healed, I won't be off on medical discharge. I'll be here to do my job."

"That doesn't mean you're safe."

Goose nodded. "I think we left safe back with realistic weeks ago, ma'am. Now, if you're still up for that breakfast, I'm buying. I suddenly feel a powerful appetite."

Danielle smiled. "All right." She led the way up the riverbank.

Goose followed her effortlessly. *Thank You, God. I'll find a way to get those Rangers to You. What Baker started, I intend to finish. And I'm trusting You to bring Megan and the others here safely, if that's Your will, and then keep them out of harm's way. In the meantime, I got a war to get back to, Lord. Just guide me in whatever You want me to do. I'm Yours.*

There were no doubts or illusions about what lay before him. With the devil loose in the world and the immortal souls of so many in the balance, Goose knew he was going to do his best to see through whatever missions God chose to assign him.

He was ready.

Roger that.

THE END

GO MILITARY.

NAVAL CRIMINAL INVESTIGATIVE SERVICE

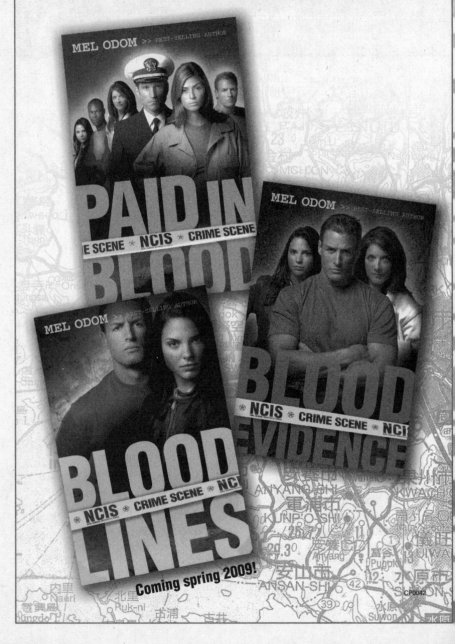